THE SCI-FI CHANNEL

TRIVIA BOOK

THE SCI-FI CHANNEL
TRIVIA BOOK

EDITED BY

JOHN GREGORY BETANCOURT

Byron Preiss Multimedia Company, Inc.
New York

BOULEVARD BOOKS, NEW YORK

Check out the Byron Preiss Multimedia Co., Inc. site on the
World Wide Web:
http://www.byronpreiss.com

Make sure to check out *PB Plug*, the science fiction/fantasy
newsletter, at
http://www.pbplug.com

Visit the Sci-Fi Channel site on the World Wide Web at
http://www.scifi.com

THE SCI-FI CHANNEL TRIVIA BOOK

A Byron Preiss Multimedia Company, Inc. Book

A Boulevard Book / published by arrangement with
Byron Preiss Visual Publications, Inc.

Cover design by Claude Goodwin
Interior design by Design 2000
Photo conversions by David Hutchison

PRINTING HISTORY
Boulevard edition / November 1996

The Putnam Berkley World Wide Web site address is
http://www.berkley.com/berkley

ISBN: 1-57297-110-X

BOULEVARD
Boulevard Books are published by The Berkley Publishing Group,
200 Madison Avenue, New York, New York 10016.
BOULEVARD and its logo are trademarks
belonging to Berkley Publishing Corporation.

PRINTED IN THE UNITED STATES OF AMERICA

10 9 8 7 6 5 4 3 2 1

CONTENTS

INTRODUCTION

What has three eyes, four arms, and shoots death-rays from its fingers? I don't know, but it's standing behind you—an old joke, but entirely appropriate here. *The Sci-Fi Channel Trivia Book* is designed to be fun. From goofy old movies starring current top stars to best-forgotten TV series, from ancient Greek mythology to current mythmakers in the comics industry, everything fantastic under the sun has become fair game for this book, with only one criterion: it must be fun.

Most trivia books are nothing new. What you're holding in your hands is, I think, an exception to that rule . . . precisely because it *wasn't* conceived as a book.

Let me give you a quick history. The Sci-Fi Channel Trivia Project originally began as a science-fiction trivia game designed to be played on computers, thanks to the miracle technology of CD-ROM.

If you're not familiar with CD-ROM disks, they look like compact discs, but they hold information for computers: sound, live-action video, text, and interactive elements. Imagine being on a TV game show like *Jeopardy!*, where all the questions are based on science fiction, fantasy, and horror in movies, television, books, comics, and other related media, and you'll have an idea of the effect we were striving for: something fast, fun, and interactive.

For a CD-ROM game to have any depth of playability, you need a large database of questions. We decided on 5,000 different questions covering five categories: books, television, movies, comics, and "miscellaneous," which we called "wormhole." (If you figure you'll run into 100 questions in a typical game, 5,000 questions will allow you to play 50 games with no duplication.) Plus some bonus questions would use sound and video clips for clues.

That CD-ROM is currently in stores.

This book is another product of the Trivia Project: the questions have been winnowed down to only the best, and they are presented here for your reading and amusement pleasure (and perhaps as a way to get some hints as you play the CD-ROM game!).

The book doesn't stop at trivia questions, however. There are some other fun elements that readers will appreciate: the "Marooned off Vesta" section, a kind of "Desert Island Books" where famous and upcoming science-fiction writers say which titles they'd like to have along if they were marooned in space. Plus there's recommended reading lists and more . . . enough material that you won't get bored right away. I think that's important. For as long as I can remember, I've been seeing (usually very slender) books of science-fiction trivia. They're fun for an hour or two, but by their very nature are limited in appeal. Once you've read it, you're done. You can't very well go back and try to figure out questions whose answers you already know. But this book has enough depth that you'll be checking it out for weeks (and possibly years) to come.

I also wish to take a moment to thank all the people involved with this project from the start: Byron Preiss, Chris Colborn, Howard Zimmerman, and Keith R. A. DeCandido at Byron Preiss Multimedia and Byron Preiss Visual Publications; Susan Allison and Lou Aronica at the Berkley Publishing Group; the entire staff at the Sci-Fi Channel; the membership of the Science-Fiction Writers of America, who responded so well to my trivia survey; and the following people who helped write trivia questions: Richard Gilliam (who went above and beyond the call of duty, contributing nearly a thousand ter-rific movie questions), Edo Van Belkom, Michael Betancourt, Jon Cohen, Keith R. A. DeCandido, Lois H. Gresh, F. Gwynplaine MacIntyre, Stephen Mark Rainey, Marty Soderstrom, Clark Perry, and Lawrence Watt-Evans; and most especially to Leigh Grossman and Lesley McBain, whose help in putting together the "Marooned off Vesta" section and tabulating the survey results proved invaluable.

—John Gregory Betancourt

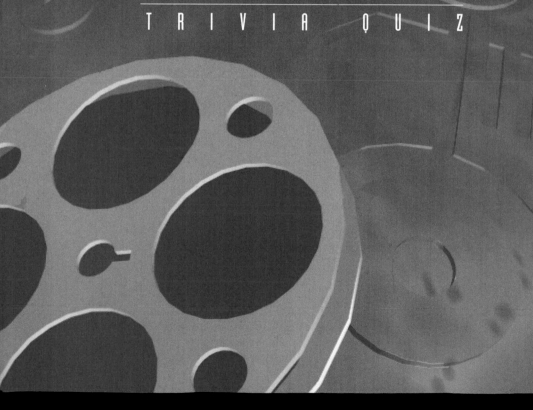

SCIENCE FICTION
Movies
TRIVIA QUIZ

10-POINT QUESTIONS

1   Molly Ringwald appeared in which of these films?

- ☐ 1. SPACEHUNTER: ADVENTURES IN THE FORBIDDEN ZONE
- ☐ 2. SPACE RAGE
- ☐ 3. THE TEXAS CHAINSAW MASSACRE
- ☐ 4. THE VAMPIRE LOVERS
- ☐ 5. ZOMBIE HIGH

2   Name the director of both ANDY WARHOL'S DRACULA and ANDY WARHOL'S FRANKENSTEIN.

- ☐ 1. Andy Warhol
- ☐ 2. Joe Dallesandro
- ☐ 3. Paul Morrissey
- ☐ 4. Roman Polanski
- ☐ 5. Udo Kier

3   There are only two films in which Bela Lugosi plays Dracula. The first, of course, is DRACULA. Name the other.

- ☐ 1. ABBOTT AND COSTELLO MEET FRANKENSTEIN
- ☐ 2. DRACULA HAS RISEN FROM THE GRAVE
- ☐ 3. HOUSE OF FRANKENSTEIN
- ☐ 4. THE VAMPIRE LOVERS
- ☐ 5. THE WOLF MAN

4   Who won a Best Supporting Actress Oscar for the movie GHOST?

- ☐ 1. Diana Ross
- ☐ 2. Demi Moore
- ☐ 3. Isabella Rossellini
- ☐ 4. Michelle Johnson
- ☐ 5. Whoopi Goldberg

5   In GROUNDHOG DAY, what is the profession of the character played by Bill Murray?

- ☐ 1. Major league baseball player
- ☐ 2. Used-car salesman
- ☐ 3. Unemployed homeless person
- ☐ 4. Small-town doctor
- ☐ 5. Television weatherman

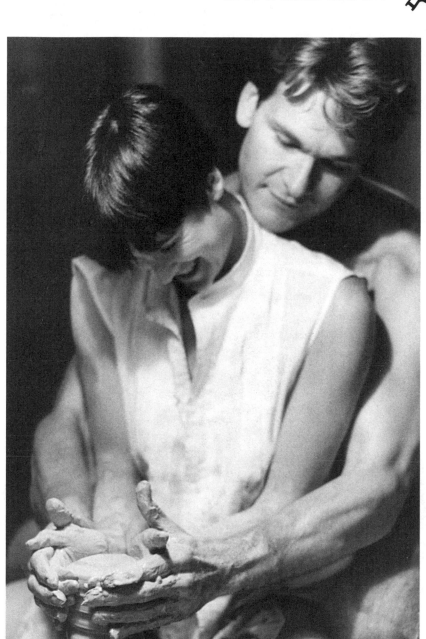

6

Who narrates PLAN 9 FROM OUTER SPACE?

- ☐ 1. Bela Lugosi
- ☐ 2. Criswell
- ☐ 3. Edward D. Wood, Jr.
- ☐ 4. Tom Keene
- ☐ 5. Vampira

7

All of the following are a part of the cast of THE LAST STARFIGHTER, except . . .

- ☐ 1. Barbara Bosson
- ☐ 2. Catherine Mary Stewart
- ☐ 3. Danny De Vito
- ☐ 4. Robert Preston
- ☐ 5. Wil Wheaton

8

Who directed the classic 1931 FRANKENSTEIN?

- ☐ 1. Anthony Asquith
- ☐ 2. Frank McDonald
- ☐ 3. James Whale
- ☐ 4. Roy Del Ruth
- ☐ 5. William A. Seiter

9

Who wrote the novel on which ROSEMARY'S BABY is based?

- ☐ 1. Harper Lee
- ☐ 2. Ira Levin
- ☐ 3. Norman Mailer
- ☐ 4. Truman Capote
- ☐ 5. William Peter Blatty

10

All of the following movies involve time travel, except . . .

- ☐ 1. SLAUGHTERHOUSE 5
- ☐ 2. THE LAND THAT TIME FORGOT
- ☐ 3. THE PHILADELPHIA EXPERIMENT
- ☐ 4. THE TERMINATOR
- ☐ 5. TIME AFTER TIME

11 In which of the following films does a retarded man gain genius-level mental powers through an experimental medical procedure?

- ☐ 1. BEING THERE
- ☐ 2. CHARLY
- ☐ 3. DONOVAN'S BRAIN
- ☐ 4. FORREST GUMP
- ☐ 5. OF MICE AND MEN

12 In what city does THE DAY THE EARTH STOOD STILL take place?

- ☐ 1. Moscow
- ☐ 2. New York City
- ☐ 3. Paris
- ☐ 4. Tokyo
- ☐ 5. Washington, DC

13 In THE DAY THE EARTH STOOD STILL, who plays the visitor from space?

- ☐ 1. Charlton Heston
- ☐ 2. Gary Cooper
- ☐ 3. Kirk Douglas
- ☐ 4. Michael Rennie
- ☐ 5. Rod Taylor

14 Which of the following costarred with Arnold Schwarzenegger in both CONAN THE BARBARIAN and CONAN THE DESTROYER?

- ☐ 1. Ben Davidson
- ☐ 2. Grace Jones
- ☐ 3. Mako
- ☐ 4. Sandahl Bergman
- ☐ 5. Tracey Walter

15 In the 1994 movie THE MASK, how many characters wear the mask?

- ☐ 1. One
- ☐ 2. Two
- ☐ 3. Three
- ☐ 4. Four
- ☐ 5. Five

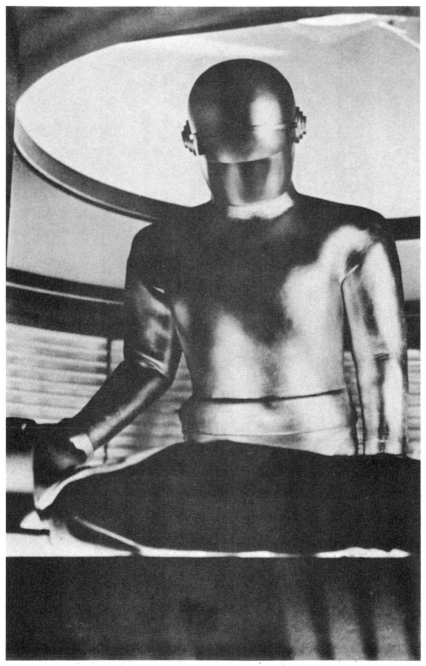

16

What sort of monsters will you find in the 1989 film
DAUGHTER OF DARKNESS?

- ☐ 1. Androids
- ☐ 2. Dinosaurs
- ☐ 3. Vampires
- ☐ 4. Werewolves
- ☐ 5. Zombies

17

In 2001: A SPACE ODYSSEY, what Richard Strauss music
is played at the ending when the star child appears?

- ☐ 1. "Ariadne auf Naxos"
- ☐ 2. "Death and Transfiguration"
- ☐ 3. "Till Eulenspiegel's Merry Pranks"
- ☐ 4. "The Blue Danube"
- ☐ 5. "Thus Spake Zarathustra"

18

In STARGATE, why is the character played by James
Spader included in the exploration team?

- ☐ 1. He figures out how to work the Stargate.
- ☐ 2. He finances the project.
- ☐ 3. He's a demolition expert.
- ☐ 4. He's a telepath.
- ☐ 5. He sneaks through the Stargate.

19

In BACK TO THE FUTURE, what early rock 'n' roll classic
does Marty McFly play at his parents' high school dance?

- ☐ 1. "At the Hop"
- ☐ 2. "Don't Be Cruel"
- ☐ 3. "Good Golly Miss Molly"
- ☐ 4. "Johnny B. Goode"
- ☐ 5. "Time Is on My Side"

20

In which one of the following films are people terrorized by
giant rabbits?

- ☐ 1. NIGHT OF MYSTERY
- ☐ 2. NIGHT OF THE JUGGLER
- ☐ 3. NIGHT OF THE LEPUS
- ☐ 4. NIGHT OF THE LIVING DEAD
- ☐ 5. NIGHT OF THE QUARTER MOON

21 Who plays the title role in the 1931 version of FRANKENSTEIN?

☐ 1. Boris Karloff
☐ 2. Colin Clive
☐ 3. Dwight Frye
☐ 4. Edward Van Sloan
☐ 5. John Boles

22 Who played the role of the pain-loving dental patient in the 1960 low-budget classic THE LITTLE SHOP OF HORRORS?

☐ 1. Dick Miller
☐ 2. Jack Nicholson
☐ 3. Jonathan Haze
☐ 4. Mel Welles
☐ 5. Myrtle Vail

23 What is the only film produced by Walt Disney to have been nominated for a Best Picture Oscar?

☐ 1. FANTASIA
☐ 2. MARY POPPINS
☐ 3. SLEEPING BEAUTY
☐ 4. SNOW WHITE AND THE SEVEN DWARFS
☐ 5. 20,000 LEAGUES UNDER THE SEA

24 What satirical comedy stars John Ritter and Pam Dawber as a couple trying to find their way out of television hell?

☐ 1. BROADCAST NEWS
☐ 2. MURDER BY TELEVISION
☐ 3. NETWORK
☐ 4. STAY TUNED
☐ 5. SWITCHING CHANNELS

25 What former regular on television's SATURDAY NIGHT LIVE plays Emperor Tod Spengo in MOM AND DAD SAVE THE WORLD?

☐ 1. Dan Aykroyd
☐ 2. Chevy Chase
☐ 3. Eddie Murphy
☐ 4. Jon Lovitz
☐ 5. Phil Hartman

12

26 What was Dino de Laurentiis' 1986 sequel to his 1976 film KING KONG?

☐ 1. KING KONG ESCAPES
☐ 2. KING KONG LIVES
☐ 3. KING KONG VS. GODZILLA
☐ 4. RETURN TO SKULL ISLAND
☐ 5. SON OF KONG

27 What was the first film to feature a werewolf as the central character?

☐ 1. AN AMERICAN WEREWOLF IN LONDON
☐ 2. CRY OF THE WEREWOLF
☐ 3. FRANKENSTEIN MEETS THE WOLF MAN
☐ 4. THE WOLF MAN
☐ 5. WEREWOLF OF LONDON

28 What prolific adventure storyteller wrote the novel on which THE LAND THAT TIME FORGOT is based?

☐ 1. Arthur Conan Doyle
☐ 2. Edgar Rice Burroughs
☐ 3. Edgar Wallace
☐ 4. H. Rider Haggard
☐ 5. Robert E. Howard

29 Which of the following Arnold Schwarzenegger films is set in a South American jungle?

☐ 1. CONAN THE BARBARIAN
☐ 2. LAST ACTION HERO
☐ 3. PREDATOR
☐ 4. THE RUNNING MAN
☐ 5. TOTAL RECALL

30 The dinosaur adventure classic THE LOST WORLD was first filmed in 1925, and remade in 1960 and 1993. Who wrote the novel on which these films are based?

☐ 1. Arthur Conan Doyle
☐ 2. Edgar Rice Burroughs
☐ 3. H. G. Wells
☐ 4. Jules Verne
☐ 5. Robert E. Howard

31 What STAR TREK cast member starred in the 1978 version of INVASION OF THE BODY SNATCHERS?

- ☐ 1. DeForest Kelly
- ☐ 2. James Doohan
- ☐ 3. Leonard Nimoy
- ☐ 4. Nichelle Nichols
- ☐ 5. William Shatner

32 One of the best-remembered moments in science fiction is the scene in ALIEN when the creature bursts out of John Hurt's chest. What is the name of the character played by Hurt?

- ☐ 1. Ash
- ☐ 2. Brett
- ☐ 3. Kane
- ☐ 4. Lambert
- ☐ 5. Parker

33 In what country was Bela Lugosi born?

- ☐ 1. Albania
- ☐ 2. Germany
- ☐ 3. Hungary
- ☐ 4. Russia
- ☐ 5. Egypt

34 Name the 1992 film starring Anthony Hopkins that's loosely based on Robert Sheckley's novel IMMORTALITY, INC.

- ☐ 1. BRAM STOKER'S DRACULA
- ☐ 2. DESPERATE HOURS
- ☐ 3. FREEJACK
- ☐ 4. SHADOWLANDS
- ☐ 5. THE SILENCE OF THE LAMBS

35 In which of the following adaptations of one of his novels does Stephen King have a cameo performance as a minister?

- ☐ 1. CARRIE
- ☐ 2. CUJO
- ☐ 3. DOLORES CLAIBORNE
- ☐ 4. PET SEMATARY
- ☐ 5. THE SHAWSHANK REDEMPTION

36 Her performance in CLOSE ENCOUNTERS OF THE THIRD KIND as Jillian Guiler earned an Oscar nomination for Best Supporting Actress.

- ☐ 1. Dee Wallace Stone
- ☐ 2. Jessica Lange
- ☐ 3. Karen Allen
- ☐ 4. Melinda Dillon
- ☐ 5. Teri Garr

37 William Shatner stars in each of the following movies. In which one does he play a veterinarian?

- ☐ 1. IMPULSE
- ☐ 2. KINGDOM OF THE SPIDERS
- ☐ 3. THE DEVIL'S RAIN
- ☐ 4. THE LAND OF NO RETURN
- ☐ 5. VISITING HOURS

38 In which of the following films will you find Snake Plissken?

- ☐ 1. BIG TROUBLE IN LITTLE CHINA
- ☐ 2. DARK STAR
- ☐ 3. ESCAPE FROM NEW YORK
- ☐ 4. HALLOWEEN
- ☐ 5. THEY LIVE

39 What classic comic played Humpty Dumpty in the 1933 version of ALICE IN WONDERLAND?

- ☐ 1. Bob Hope
- ☐ 2. Buster Keaton
- ☐ 3. Jack Benny
- ☐ 4. Oliver Hardy
- ☐ 5. W. C. Fields

40 What is the name of the ice planet on which the opening scenes of THE EMPIRE STRIKES BACK are set?

- ☐ 1. Dagobah
- ☐ 2. Endor
- ☐ 3. Hoth
- ☐ 4. Tatooine
- ☐ 5. Ugnaught

41 What best-selling author had his first big hit with the novel on which the 1971 film THE ANDROMEDA STRAIN is based?

☐ 1. Dean Koontz
☐ 2. John Updike
☐ 3. Michael Crichton
☐ 4. Stephen King
☐ 5. Tom Clancy

42 Which of the following describes the 1971 film THE OMEGA MAN?

☐ 1. A professor builds a computer to predict lottery results.
☐ 2. A plague transforms people into vampirelike albinos.
☐ 3. Due to atomic war, there is only one fertile male left on Earth.
☐ 4. Planet Omega holds a contest to find the strongest warrior.
☐ 5. UFOs deposit breeding stock on prehistoric Earth.

43 Name the 1974 futuristic classic with Sean Connery as a hunter whose curiosity takes him inside a giant floating stone head and to the society that built it.

☐ 1. DARK STAR
☐ 2. PHASE IV
☐ 3. SOLARIS
☐ 4. THE MAN WHO FELL TO EARTH
☐ 5. ZARDOZ

44 Name the satiric 1974 cult favorite about a space crew on a mission to explode unstable suns.

☐ 1. ALPHAVILLE
☐ 2. DARK STAR
☐ 3. PHASE IV
☐ 4. QUINTET
☐ 5. ZARDOZ

45 Which of the following contains a protagonist named Frankenstein, though the character is neither a part of the family of Dr. Frankenstein nor the monster?

☐ 1. ALIEN
☐ 2. DEATH RACE 2000
☐ 3. IT'S ALIVE
☐ 4. NEAR DARK
☐ 5. QUINTET

46 In what film are visitors to the castle invited to "Come up to the lab, and see what's on the slab"?

☐ 1. HOUSE OF DARK SHADOWS
☐ 2. I WAS A TEENAGE FRANKENSTEIN
☐ 3. THE HOUSE OF FRANKENSTEIN
☐ 4. THE ROCKY HORROR PICTURE SHOW
☐ 5. YOUNG FRANKENSTEIN

47 Name the 1993 satirical action film about a politically correct future that finds itself unable to deal with a violent criminal who escapes from cryogenic imprisonment.

☐ 1. A PERFECT WORLD
☐ 2. DEMOLITION MAN
☐ 3. ESCAPE 2000
☐ 4. SHADOWZONE
☐ 5. ZENTROPA

48 Name the 1977 film based on a Roger Zelazny novel about a postatomic war future, and a group of survivors trying to reach the safety of civilization.

☐ 1. A BOY AND HIS DOG
☐ 2. DAMNATION ALLEY
☐ 3. NIGHT CROSSING
☐ 4. RAVAGERS
☐ 5. THE SWARM

49 What football star was the other head in the 1972 Ray Milland film THE THING WITH TWO HEADS?

☐ 1. Ben Davidson
☐ 2. Jim Brown
☐ 3. Joe Namath
☐ 4. O. J. Simpson
☐ 5. Rosie Grier

50 In CLOSE ENCOUNTERS OF THE THIRD KIND, where do the UFOs land to meet the Earth scientists?

☐ 1. Alabama
☐ 2. Alaska
☐ 3. California
☐ 4. Vermont
☐ 5. Wyoming

20-POINT QUESTIONS

1

After its initial theatrical release, this subtitle and the legend "Episode IV" were added to STAR WARS.

- ☐ 1. "A Battle Beyond the Galaxy"
- ☐ 2. "New Hope"
- ☐ 3. "May the Force Be with You"
- ☐ 4. "Starring Mark Hamill and Carrie Fisher"
- ☐ 5. "Vader's Revenge"

2

Who wrote the script for AN AMERICAN WEREWOLF IN LONDON?

- ☐ 1. Joe Dante
- ☐ 2. John Landis
- ☐ 3. Steven Spielberg
- ☐ 4. Tobe Hooper
- ☐ 5. Wes Craven

3

In THE ANGRY RED PLANET, what are the Earthmen doing on Mars?

- ☐ 1. Establishing a colony
- ☐ 2. Exploring, as a part of the first human landing on Mars
- ☐ 3. Capturing creatures for zoos on Earth
- ☐ 4. Selling land stolen from Martian natives
- ☐ 5. None of the above

4

Who is the only actor to play both the Frankenstein monster and a character who was either Doctor Frankenstein or one of his descendants?

- ☐ 1. Bela Lugosi
- ☐ 2. Boris Karloff
- ☐ 3. Jack Palance
- ☐ 4. Kenneth Branagh
- ☐ 5. Robert De Niro

5

This 1953 film features a screenplay cowritten by Robert Heinlein.

- ☐ 1. EARTH VS. THE FLYING SAUCERS
- ☐ 2. INVASION OF THE BODY SNATCHERS
- ☐ 3. NIGHT OF THE COMET
- ☐ 4. PROJECT MOONBASE
- ☐ 5. ROCKETSHIP X-M

6 Which actress provides the voice of the brain in the jar that Steve Martin's character falls in love with in THE MAN WITH TWO BRAINS?

- ☐ 1. Amy Irving
- ☐ 2. Glenn Close
- ☐ 3. Kathleen Turner
- ☐ 4. Sean Young
- ☐ 5. Sissy Spacek

7 Which CLOSE ENCOUNTERS OF THE THIRD KIND cast member performed with the Second City comedy troupe while still in high school?

- ☐ 1. Bob Balaban
- ☐ 2. Francois Truffaut
- ☐ 3. Melinda Dillon
- ☐ 4. Richard Dreyfuss
- ☐ 5. Teri Garr

8 What was the first film with predominant and identifiable science fiction or fantasy elements to be nominated for a Best Picture Oscar?

- ☐ 1. A MIDSUMMER NIGHT'S DREAM
- ☐ 2. BABES IN TOYLAND
- ☐ 3. DR. JEKYLL AND MR. HYDE
- ☐ 4. JUST IMAGINE
- ☐ 5. KING KONG

9 Which author is a prominent character in TIME AFTER TIME?

- ☐ 1. Edgar Rice Burroughs
- ☐ 2. H. G. Wells
- ☐ 3. Jules Verne
- ☐ 4. Rudyard Kipling
- ☐ 5. William Shakespeare

10 Who was the makeup artist who created the distinctive look for such 1930s creature films as FRANKENSTEIN, DRACULA, and WHITE ZOMBIE?

- ☐ 1. Carl Laemelle
- ☐ 2. Cedric Gibbons
- ☐ 3. Jack Pierce
- ☐ 4. John Balderston
- ☐ 5. William Cameron Menzies

11 In RED SONJA, what is the name of the character played by Arnold Schwarzenegger?

- ☐ 1. Bombaata
- ☐ 2. Conan
- ☐ 3. Kalidor
- ☐ 4. Malak
- ☐ 5. Thongor

12 Which of the following describes the cameo appearance of author Arthur C. Clarke in 2010?

- ☐ 1. He is buying a ticket at a movie house.
- ☐ 2. He is eating a hot dog at a baseball game.
- ☐ 3. He is jogging along a mountain road.
- ☐ 4. He is signing autographs at a science-fiction convention.
- ☐ 5. He is sitting on a park bench in Washington, D.C.

13 What sort of beast is central to the 1974 film THE BEAST MUST DIE?

- ☐ 1. An escaped serial killer
- ☐ 2. A rabid dog
- ☐ 3. A vampire
- ☐ 4. A werewolf
- ☐ 5. A zombie

14 In what film does Tor Johnson play Bela Lugosi's laboratory assistant?

- ☐ 1. BLACK FRIDAY
- ☐ 2. BRIDE OF THE MONSTER
- ☐ 3. PLAN 9 FROM OUTER SPACE
- ☐ 4. THE BLACK CAT (1934)
- ☐ 5. THE BLACK CAT (1941)

15 Who directed all three Mad Max films?

- ☐ 1. George Lucas
- ☐ 2. George Miller
- ☐ 3. Mel Gibson
- ☐ 4. Ridley Scott
- ☐ 5. Walter Hill

MOVIES   20-POINT QUESTIONS

16 In what film are the Beatles menaced by people seeking a sacred ring worn by Ringo?

- ☐ 1. A HARD DAY'S NIGHT
- ☐ 2. HELP!
- ☐ 3. LET IT BE
- ☐ 4. MAGICAL MYSTERY TOUR
- ☐ 5. WOODSTOCK

17 What happens to the title character in FIRST MAN INTO SPACE?

- ☐ 1. He becomes a blood-drinking monster.
- ☐ 2. He dies in space from a lack of oxygen.
- ☐ 3. He returns safely to Earth.
- ☐ 4. His funding runs out, and he never makes it into space.
- ☐ 5. He is watched by a flying saucer.

18 Who stars in the 1932 horror classic WHITE ZOMBIE?

- ☐ 1. Basil Rathbone
- ☐ 2. Bela Lugosi
- ☐ 3. Boris Karloff
- ☐ 4. Fredric March
- ☐ 5. Humphrey Bogart

19 How many Oscars did ED WOOD win?

- ☐ 1. One
- ☐ 2. Two
- ☐ 3. Three
- ☐ 4. Four
- ☐ 5. None

20 This Canadian actor has often played villains, particularly in such films as SCANNERS and BLACK ICE.

- ☐ 1. Christopher Plummer
- ☐ 2. Dan Aykroyd
- ☐ 3. Michael Ironside
- ☐ 4. Neil Young
- ☐ 5. William Shatner

21   Although this actor has starred in several films, including THE SEVENTH SIGN, he's best known for his supporting performances in such films as THE TERMINATOR, ALIENS, and THE ABYSS.

☐ 1. Bill Paxson
☐ 2. Dick Miller
☐ 3. Lance Henriksen
☐ 4. Michael Biehn
☐ 5. Todd Graff

22   Who wrote the classic short story on which the 1988 film NIGHTFALL is based?

☐ 1. Harlan Ellison
☐ 2. Isaac Asimov
☐ 3. Leigh Brackett
☐ 4. Ray Bradbury
☐ 5. Robert Bloch

23   Although this prolific actor often played mad scientists, he is perhaps best remembered as the police inspector with the artificial arm in SON OF FRANKENSTEIN.

☐ 1. John Carradine
☐ 2. Bela Lugosi
☐ 3. Boris Karloff
☐ 4. Kenneth Mars
☐ 5. Lionel Atwill

24   He directed Arnold Schwarzenegger to great success in PREDATOR, and to much less success in LAST ACTION HERO.

☐ 1. Fred Olen Ray
☐ 2. James Cameron
☐ 3. John McTiernan
☐ 4. Roger Corman
☐ 5. Paul Schrader

25   Each of the following appears in the 1981 film EXCALIBUR. Who plays Merlin?

☐ 1. Gabriel Byrne
☐ 2. Liam Neeson
☐ 3. Nicol Williamson
☐ 4. Nigel Terry
☐ 5. Patrick Stewart

26 The films of this actress include the 1953 classic HOUSE OF WAX and the 1956 version of INVASION OF THE BODY SNATCHERS.

☐ 1. Brooke Adams
☐ 2. Carolyn Jones
☐ 3. Dana Wynter
☐ 4. Marilyn Burns
☐ 5. Veronica Cartwright

27 What real-life game show host plays a sleazy game show host in the 1987 futuristic action-thriller THE RUNNING MAN?

☐ 1. Bob Barker
☐ 2. Dick Clark
☐ 3. Monty Hall
☐ 4. Pat Sajak
☐ 5. Richard Dawson

28 In FREEJACK, what's the profession of Alex Furlong, the character played by Emilio Estevez?

☐ 1. Banker
☐ 2. Computer programmer
☐ 3. Genetic researcher
☐ 4. Race-car driver
☐ 5. Surgeon

29 Which actor plays the male lead in the 1975 film A BOY AND HIS DOG?

☐ 1. Arnold Schwarzenegger
☐ 2. Don Johnson
☐ 3. Harrison Ford
☐ 4. Mark Hamill
☐ 5. William Shatner

30 Who played the title role in the 1976 film THE MAN WHO FELL TO EARTH?

☐ 1. Bernie Casey
☐ 2. Buck Henry
☐ 3. David Bowie
☐ 4. Nicolas Roeg
☐ 5. Rip Torn

MOVIES   20-POINT QUESTIONS

31 What is the name of the character played by Max von Sydow in CONAN THE BARBARIAN?

- ☐ 1. King Osric
- ☐ 2. Malak
- ☐ 3. Rexor
- ☐ 4. Subotai
- ☐ 5. Thulsa Doom

32 What former child actor played Perry White in the 1978 film SUPERMAN?

- ☐ 1. Carl Switzer
- ☐ 2. Jackie Coogan
- ☐ 3. Jackie Cooper
- ☐ 4. Scotty Beckett
- ☐ 5. Spanky McFarland

33 Who wrote the novel on which the 1994 film THE PUPPET MASTERS is based?

- ☐ 1. Alan Dean Foster
- ☐ 2. Arthur C. Clarke
- ☐ 3. H. G. Wells
- ☐ 4. Ray Bradbury
- ☐ 5. Robert A. Heinlein

34 In THE ANDROMEDA STRAIN, what is the name of the supersecret research facility where scientists try to control the deadly microbe?

- ☐ 1. Project Alpha
- ☐ 2. Project Microbe
- ☐ 3. Project Scoop
- ☐ 4. Project Seal
- ☐ 5. Project Wildfire

35 In what futuristic film will you find society divided into three groups: the Brutals, the Exterminators, and the Eternals?

- ☐ 1. A BOY AND HIS DOG
- ☐ 2. A CLOCKWORK ORANGE
- ☐ 3. OUTLAND
- ☐ 4. SOYLENT GREEN
- ☐ 5. ZARDOZ

36 Name John Carpenter's first feature film, which began as a student project at the University of Southern California.

- ☐ 1. DARK STAR
- ☐ 2. DEMON
- ☐ 3. SOLARIS
- ☐ 4. STAR KNIGHT
- ☐ 5. THX-1138

37 In which of the following films will you find the classic scene of the blind hermit making friends with the monster, a scene well parodied in YOUNG FRANKENSTEIN?

- ☐ 1. BRIDE OF FRANKENSTEIN
- ☐ 2. FRANKENSTEIN'S DAUGHTER
- ☐ 3. GHOST OF FRANKENSTEIN
- ☐ 4. HOUSE OF FRANKENSTEIN
- ☐ 5. SON OF FRANKENSTEIN

38 Who plays Machine Gun Joe Viterbo in the 1975 film DEATH RACE 2000?

- ☐ 1. David Carradine
- ☐ 2. James Caan
- ☐ 3. John Beck
- ☐ 4. Peter Fonda
- ☐ 5. Sylvester Stallone

39 In LOGAN'S RUN, what is the name for the policemen who track and kill people trying to escape the totalitarian government?

- ☐ 1. Community Relations Officers
- ☐ 2. Exterminators
- ☐ 3. Ghost Catchers
- ☐ 4. Sandmen
- ☐ 5. Watchers

40 What film contains animation voice-overs from STAR TREK television stars Patrick Stewart, Whoopi Goldberg, and Leonard Nimoy?

- ☐ 1. ALADDIN
- ☐ 2. BEAUTY AND THE BEAST
- ☐ 3. THE LION KING
- ☐ 4. THE PAGEMASTER
- ☐ 5. THE SECRET OF NIMH

41

In THE ROCKY HORROR PICTURE SHOW, why do Brad and Janet go to the castle?

- ☐ 1. Their car breaks down, and it's the only building nearby.
- ☐ 2. They're door-to-door salespeople.
- ☐ 3. They're hired to appraise the real estate.
- ☐ 4. They're hired to repair the castle's moat.
- ☐ 5. They've been invited to a party.

42

In what year is the futuristic action comedy DEMOLITION MAN set?

- ☐ 1. 1996
- ☐ 2. 2036
- ☐ 3. 2093
- ☐ 4. 2102
- ☐ 5. 2419

43

Which of the following David Cronenberg films is based on the life and works of William S. Burroughs?

- ☐ 1. DEAD RINGERS
- ☐ 2. NAKED LUNCH
- ☐ 3. RABID
- ☐ 4. THE BROOD
- ☐ 5. THE FLY

44

What role was played by Bela Lugosi in ISLAND OF LOST SOULS and by Richard Basehart in THE ISLAND OF DR. MOREAU?

- ☐ 1. Bearman
- ☐ 2. Braddock
- ☐ 3. Dr. Moreau
- ☐ 4. M'Ling
- ☐ 5. Sayer of the Law

45

Name the 1971 four-part horror film written by Robert Bloch and starring Peter Cushing, Christopher Lee, and Denholm Elliott.

- ☐ 1. COUNT DRACULA
- ☐ 2. NOTHING BUT THE NIGHT
- ☐ 3. PSYCHO
- ☐ 4. THE HOUSE THAT DRIPPED BLOOD
- ☐ 5. THE SKULL

46 What is the name of the character played by Drew Barrymore in E.T.—THE EXTRATERRESTRIAL?

- ☐ 1. Angie
- ☐ 2. Gertie
- ☐ 3. Molly
- ☐ 4. Susan
- ☐ 5. Tracy

47 Who directed the 1983 film RETURN OF THE JEDI?

- ☐ 1. George Lucas
- ☐ 2. Irvin Kershner
- ☐ 3. James Cameron
- ☐ 4. Richard Marquand
- ☐ 5. Steven Spielberg

48 Who plays rougish hero Madmartigan in the 1988 film WILLOW?

- ☐ 1. Cary Elwes
- ☐ 2. Harrison Ford
- ☐ 3. Rob Lowe
- ☐ 4. Tom Cruise
- ☐ 5. Val Kilmer

49 Who plays Aunty Entity in the 1985 film MAD MAX: BEYOND THUNDERDOME?

- ☐ 1. Angela Bassett
- ☐ 2. Cicely Tyson
- ☐ 3. Diana Ross
- ☐ 4. Tina Turner
- ☐ 5. Whoopi Goldberg

50 Who plays Dr. Mengele in the 1978 thriller THE BOYS FROM BRAZIL?

- ☐ 1. Chuck Conners
- ☐ 2. Gregory Peck
- ☐ 3. James Brolin
- ☐ 4. Sam Waterston
- ☐ 5. Telly Savalas

30-POINT QUESTIONS

1 The team that made RE-ANIMATOR also made which one of the following?

☐ 1. BRIDE OF RE-ANIMATOR
☐ 2. FROM BEYOND
☐ 3. RETURN FROM THE PAST
☐ 4. REVIVIFIER
☐ 5. THE TOMB OF DRACULA

2 Steven Spielberg's movie ALWAYS is a reworking of which of the following?

☐ 1. A GUY NAMED JOE
☐ 2. FOREVER YOUNG
☐ 3. HEAVEN CAN WAIT
☐ 4. HERE COMES MR. JORDAN
☐ 5. SOMEBODY UP THERE LIKES ME

3 In BLADE RUNNER, who played the replicant Leon?

☐ 1. Brion James
☐ 2. Edward James Olmos
☐ 3. Joe Turkel
☐ 4. M. Emmet Walsh
☐ 5. Sean Young

4 Who wrote both the novel and the screenplay for THE PRINCESS BRIDE?

☐ 1. Bruce Joel Rubin
☐ 2. Harlan Ellison
☐ 3. Michael Crichton
☐ 4. Ray Bradbury
☐ 5. William Goldman

5 Which film is not a part of the Quatermass film series?

☐ 1. ENEMY FROM SPACE
☐ 2. FIVE MILLION MILES TO EARTH
☐ 3. THE CREEPING UNKNOWN
☐ 4. THE QUATERMASS CONCLUSION
☐ 5. X—THE UNKNOWN

6 Who directed the 1946 French version of BEAUTY AND THE BEAST?

☐ 1. Abel Gance
☐ 2. Francois Truffaut
☐ 3. Jean Cocteau
☐ 4. Louis Malle
☐ 5. Jean Renoir

7 In what city does the interview portion of INTERVIEW WITH THE VAMPIRE take place?

☐ 1. London
☐ 2. New Orleans
☐ 3. Paris
☐ 4. Rome
☐ 5. San Francisco

8 What film is based on the Daniel Keyes story "Flowers for Algernon"?

☐ 1. ALPHAVILLE
☐ 2. CHARLY
☐ 3. SLEEPER
☐ 4. THE INCREDIBLE SHRINKING MAN
☐ 5. WORLD WITHOUT END

9 Who played the title role in 4-D MAN?

☐ 1. Dana Andrews
☐ 2. Jeff Morrow
☐ 3. Ray Milland
☐ 4. Richard Carlson
☐ 5. Robert Lansing

10 This author of the novel on which THE BEASTMASTER is based had her name removed from the movie's credits.

☐ 1. Andre Norton
☐ 2. Anne Rice
☐ 3. Carrie Fisher
☐ 4. Edna Ferber
☐ 5. Jackie Collins

42

11

In the 1994 movie THE MASK, who plays Peggy?

- ☐ 1. Amy Yasbeck
- ☐ 2. Cameron Diaz
- ☐ 3. Geena Davis
- ☐ 4. Helen Hunt
- ☐ 5. Julie Brown

12

In the movie PROJECT: METALBEAST, what sort of beast is the metalbeast?

- ☐ 1. Android
- ☐ 2. Dinosaur
- ☐ 3. Dolphin
- ☐ 4. Vampire
- ☐ 5. Werewolf

13

Who provides the voice of the computer HAL in both 2001: A SPACE ODYSSEY and 2010?

- ☐ 1. Bob Balaban
- ☐ 2. Douglas Rain
- ☐ 3. Gary Lockwood
- ☐ 4. Keir Dullea
- ☐ 5. Stanley Kubrick

14

In JURASSIC PARK, where is the amber mine that is visited by the corporate attorney?

- ☐ 1. Afghanistan
- ☐ 2. Argentina
- ☐ 3. Dominican Republic
- ☐ 4. Ethiopia
- ☐ 5. Korea

15

Who directed the 1972 sequel to the 1958 film THE BLOB?

- ☐ 1. Chuck Russell
- ☐ 2. Irvin S. Yeaworth, Jr.
- ☐ 3. Larry Hagman
- ☐ 4. Leonard Nimoy
- ☐ 5. Roger Corman

16 Which comedy team costarred in the haunted house movie GHOST CATCHERS?

- ☐ 1. Bob and Ray
- ☐ 2. Laurel and Hardy
- ☐ 3. Olsen and Johnson
- ☐ 4. The Blues Brothers
- ☐ 5. The Bowery Boys

17 What sort of monsters are THEM!?

- ☐ 1. Giant ants
- ☐ 2. Flying monkeys
- ☐ 3. Telepathic vultures
- ☐ 4. Vampire kangaroos
- ☐ 5. Werewolves

18 In which one of the following films will you find Darth Vader from the planet Vulcan?

- ☐ 1. AMERICAN GRAFFITI
- ☐ 2. BACK TO THE FUTURE
- ☐ 3. RETURN OF THE JEDI
- ☐ 4. STAR TREK: THE MOTION PICTURE
- ☐ 5. ZARDOZ

19 What was the first film to feature both Bela Lugosi and Boris Karloff?

- ☐ 1. THE BLACK CAT
- ☐ 2. BLACK FRIDAY
- ☐ 3. SON OF FRANKENSTEIN
- ☐ 4. THE INVISIBLE RAY
- ☐ 5. THE RAVEN

20 Which of the following animated films is a retelling of the Snow White story?

- ☐ 1. ALL DOGS GO TO HEAVEN
- ☐ 2. AN AMERICAN TAIL
- ☐ 3. HAPPILY EVER AFTER
- ☐ 4. ROCK-A-DOODLE
- ☐ 5. THE SECRET OF NIMH

21 Who played the evil Overdog in SPACEHUNTER: ADVENTURES IN THE FORBIDDEN ZONE?

- ☐ 1. Andrea Marcovicci
- ☐ 2. Ernie Hudson
- ☐ 3. Michael Ironside
- ☐ 4. Molly Ringwald
- ☐ 5. Peter Strauss

22 What is the setting for the 1966 film CHAMBER OF HORRORS?

- ☐ 1. A haunted castle
- ☐ 2. An abandoned resort hotel
- ☐ 3. An amusement park
- ☐ 4. A motion picture studio
- ☐ 5. A wax museum

23 Who plays the cryptkeeper in the 1972 film TALES FROM THE CRYPT?

- ☐ 1. Alec Guinness
- ☐ 2. Bernard Hepton
- ☐ 3. Derek Jacobi
- ☐ 4. Ian Holm
- ☐ 5. Ralph Richardson

24 Who played the title role in the 1925 silent film version of THE PHANTOM OF THE OPERA?

- ☐ 1. Conrad Veidt
- ☐ 2. Francis X. Bushman
- ☐ 3. John Barrymore
- ☐ 4. Lon Chaney
- ☐ 5. Warner Baxter

25 What city is the primary setting for the 1982 version of CAT PEOPLE?

- ☐ 1. Boston
- ☐ 2. Chicago
- ☐ 3. Los Angeles
- ☐ 4. Miami
- ☐ 5. New Orleans

26 This actress gained a cult following for her performance in the 1967 Hammer epic, PREHISTORIC WOMEN. Her later films include DR. JEKYLL AND SISTER HYDE.

- ☐ 1. Cassandra Peterson
- ☐ 2. Heather Thomas
- ☐ 3. Martine Beswick
- ☐ 4. Mary Woronov
- ☐ 5. Susan Kellerman

27 In which of the following films does Paul Reubens play a vampire?

- ☐ 1. BEVERLY HILLS VAMP
- ☐ 2. BUFFY THE VAMPIRE SLAYER
- ☐ 3. DANCE OF THE VAMPIRES
- ☐ 4. MY BEST FRIEND IS A VAMPIRE
- ☐ 5. VAMPIRE'S KISS

28 This veteran screen performer appeared in well over 100 films, but is most often remembered for his chilling portrayal of the sinister Roman Castevet in the 1968 classic ROSEMARY'S BABY.

- ☐ 1. Elisha Cook, Jr.
- ☐ 2. Maurice Evans
- ☐ 3. Ralph Bellamy
- ☐ 4. Sidney Blackmer
- ☐ 5. William Castle

29 This Russian-born actor's screen credits include FROM THE EARTH TO THE MOON and VILLAGE OF THE DAMNED.

- ☐ 1. Cornel Wilde
- ☐ 2. Dean Jagger
- ☐ 3. George Sanders
- ☐ 4. Leo G. Carroll
- ☐ 5. Richard Boone

30 Name the 1958 low-budget thriller over which science-fiction author Robert Heinlein successfully sued and received an out-of-court settlement for plagiarism of his novel THE PUPPET MASTERS.

- ☐ 1. THE BRAIN EATERS
- ☐ 2. THE BRAIN FROM THE PLANET AROUS
- ☐ 3. I MARRIED A MONSTER FROM OUTER SPACE
- ☐ 4. TERROR FROM THE YEAR 5000
- ☐ 5. WAR OF THE SATELLITES

MOVIES   30-POINT QUESTIONS

31
Which member of the Monkees was one of the producers of the 1984 cult comedy REPO MAN?

☐ 1. Davey Jones
☐ 2. Michael Nesmith
☐ 3. Mickey Dolenz
☐ 4. Peter Tork
☐ 5. None of the above

32
This actor gained popularity on television's STAR TREK: THE NEXT GENERATION. His films include THE FISHER KING and THE HAND THAT ROCKS THE CRADLE.

☐ 1. John de Lancie
☐ 2. Lawrence Tierney
☐ 3. LeVar Burton
☐ 4. Michael Dorn
☐ 5. Ronny Cox

33
Name the 1954 film, cowritten by comedian Lenny Bruce, in which a space gun turns crooked people into honest people.

☐ 1. DONOVAN'S BRAIN
☐ 2. GOG
☐ 3. TARGET EARTH!
☐ 4. THE ATOMIC KID
☐ 5. THE ROCKET MAN

34
This well-regarded 1976 film featured the screen debuts of Amy Irving and P. J. Soles.

☐ 1. CARRIE
☐ 2. DEATH RACE 2000
☐ 3. LOGAN'S RUN
☐ 4. THE BIG BUS
☐ 5. THE MAN WHO FELL TO EARTH

35
According to STAR TREK IV: THE VOYAGE HOME, in what century did humpback whales become extinct?

☐ 1. 20th century
☐ 2. 21st century
☐ 3. 22nd century
☐ 4. 23rd century
☐ 5. 24th century

36

In which of the following films did Darryl Hannah make her screen debut?

☐ 1. BLADE RUNNER
☐ 2. CARRIE
☐ 3. SPLASH
☐ 4. THE FINAL TERROR
☐ 5. THE FURY

37

In THE ANDROMEDA STRAIN, what happens to the deadly microbe that's brought to Earth by a space probe?

☐ 1. An antidote to the microbe is found.
☐ 2. The microbe is exterminated through genetic engineering.
☐ 3. The microbe mutates into a nonharmful form.
☐ 4. The microbe wipes out all life on Earth.
☐ 5. The research facility self-destructs, destroying the microbe.

38

In the movie SILENT RUNNING, what's the name of the spaceship that contains the last of Earth's forests?

☐ 1. Amazon Ranger
☐ 2. Biosphere II
☐ 3. Forestship Omega
☐ 4. Reunion
☐ 5. Valley Forge

39

Who directed the disturbing 1974 horror film IT'S ALIVE, about a mutant baby that kills to survive?

☐ 1. Brian de Palma
☐ 2. George Romero
☐ 3. Larry Cohen
☐ 4. L. Q. Jones
☐ 5. Peter Hyams

40

In the 1969 film THE ILLUSTRATED MAN, who plays the title role?

☐ 1. Andy Warhol
☐ 2. David Bowie
☐ 3. James Caan
☐ 4. Rod Steiger
☐ 5. Rod Taylor

41 In YOUNG FRANKENSTEIN, what song do Dr. Frankenstein and the monster perform as part of their stage show?

☐ 1. "Lullaby of Broadway"
☐ 2. "Puttin' on the Ritz"
☐ 3. "Singing in the Rain"
☐ 4. "Swinging on a Star"
☐ 5. "The Continental"

42 In LOGAN'S RUN, what is the name of the ceremony at which the domed city kills off its older population?

☐ 1. Termination
☐ 2. Carousel
☐ 3. Horizon
☐ 4. Renewal
☐ 5. Transition

43 What sort of restaurants will you find in the future society of DEMOLITION MAN?

☐ 1. Boston Chicken
☐ 2. Burger King
☐ 3. McDonald's
☐ 4. Taco Bell
☐ 5. Wendy's

44 Which character narrates the movie DUNE?

☐ 1. De Vries
☐ 2. Feyd-Rautha
☐ 3. Lady Jessica
☐ 4. Paul Atreides
☐ 5. Princess Irulian

45 In DUNE, what is the name of the planet where the sandworms live?

☐ 1. Arrakis
☐ 2. Atreides
☐ 3. Rautha
☐ 4. Solaris
☐ 5. Zardoz

46 In which of the following films does Christopher Lee costar with Bette Davis?

☐ 1. BURNT OFFERINGS
☐ 2. DEATH ON THE NILE
☐ 3. RETURN FROM WITCH MOUNTAIN
☐ 4. THE WATCHER IN THE WOODS
☐ 5. WICKED STEPMOTHER

47 Name the 1980 comic horror film about people in a desert valley battling wormlike predators.

☐ 1. OFF LIMITS
☐ 2. TILT
☐ 3. TIMERIDER
☐ 4. TREMORS
☐ 5. UFORIA

48 Of the several versions of A CHRISTMAS CAROL, the 1951 film directed by Brian Desmond-Hurst is considered by many to be the best. Who played Scrooge?

☐ 1. Alastair Sim
☐ 2. Ernest Thesiger
☐ 3. Michael Horden
☐ 4. Patrick Macnee
☐ 5. Peter Bull

49 In the 1954 thriller GOG, what is Gog?

☐ 1. A bear
☐ 2. A building
☐ 3. A robot
☐ 4. A vampire
☐ 5. A zoo

50 Who directed INNERSPACE, the 1987 Oscar winner for Best Visual Effects?

☐ 1. Joe Dante
☐ 2. Robert Zemeckis
☐ 3. Steven Spielberg
☐ 4. Tobe Hooper
☐ 5. Wes Craven

40-POINT QUESTIONS

1 What was the first science-fiction film to win an Oscar in the Best Actor category?

- [ ] 1. Bela Lugosi for DRACULA
- [ ] 2. Boris Karloff for FRANKENSTEIN
- [ ] 3. Fredric March for DR. JEKYLL AND MR. HYDE
- [ ] 4. Lionel Barrymore for THE DEVIL DOLL
- [ ] 5. Ralph Richardson for THINGS TO COME

2 Who starred in the movie ALIEN NATION?

- [ ] 1. James Caan
- [ ] 2. Kevin Major Howard
- [ ] 3. Mandy Patinkin
- [ ] 4. Terence Stamp
- [ ] 5. All of the above

3 What was the gimmick in the original showing of ANDY WARHOL'S FRANKENSTEIN?

- [ ] 1. It had a scratch-and-sniff card for key scenes.
- [ ] 2. It was shown in 3-D.
- [ ] 3. Theaters offered "blood" popcorn with red food coloring.
- [ ] 4. Warhol appeared in an animated cartoon that preceded the film.
- [ ] 5. All of the above.

4 What 1943 low-budget effort from Monogram featured Bela Lugosi and Ava Gardner?

- [ ] 1. BLACK DRAGONS
- [ ] 2. BOWERY AT MIDNIGHT
- [ ] 3. GHOSTS ON THE LOOSE
- [ ] 4. REVENGE OF THE ZOMBIES
- [ ] 5. VOODOO MAN

5 All of the following were directed by Kurt Neumann, except . . .

- [ ] 1. BRIDE OF THE GORILLA
- [ ] 2. ISLAND OF LOST MEN
- [ ] 3. ROCKETSHIP X-M
- [ ] 4. TARZAN AND THE LEOPARD WOMAN
- [ ] 5. THE UNKNOWN GUEST

6

Which of the following features Vincent Price?

☐ 1. SON OF ALI BABA
☐ 2. SON OF FLUBBER
☐ 3. SON OF FRANKENSTEIN
☐ 4. SON OF GODZILLA
☐ 5. SON OF SINBAD

7

The dreamlike continuity of this surrealistic 1979 horror film presaged the use of similar themes in the successful NIGHTMARE ON ELM STREET series.

☐ 1. HALLOWEEN
☐ 2. PHANTASM
☐ 3. PROPHECY
☐ 4. WOLFEN
☐ 5. ZOMBIE

8

In THE DAY THE EARTH STOOD STILL, what name does the visitor from space take while living in the guise of an ordinary human?

☐ 1. Bobby
☐ 2. Gort
☐ 3. Klaatu
☐ 4. Mr. Carpenter
☐ 5. Professor Barnhard

9

What director/producer was nicknamed "Drella"—a combination of Cinderella and Dracula?

☐ 1. Andy Warhol
☐ 2. Edward D. Wood, Jr.
☐ 3. James Whale
☐ 4. Stanley Kubrick
☐ 5. Tod Browning

10

Who composed the music score for the 1978 film HALLOWEEN?

☐ 1. Howard Shore
☐ 2. James Horner
☐ 3. Jerry Goldsmith
☐ 4. John Carpenter
☐ 5. John Williams

11 In WHO FRAMED ROGER RABBIT, who dubbed the singing voice of Jessica Rabbit?

- ☐ 1. Amy Irving
- ☐ 2. Janet Jackson
- ☐ 3. Kathleen Turner
- ☐ 4. Madonna
- ☐ 5. Marni Nixon

12 In JURASSIC PARK, where is the excavation site that Alan Grant and Ellie Sattler are working when they are invited to examine Jurassic Park?

- ☐ 1. Alaska
- ☐ 2. Brazil
- ☐ 3. Japan
- ☐ 4. Montana
- ☐ 5. Uganda

13 Who directed the 1988 remake of THE BLOB?

- ☐ 1. Chuck Russell
- ☐ 2. Fred Olen Ray
- ☐ 3. Larry Hagman
- ☐ 4. Ron Howard
- ☐ 5. Roger Corman

14 Which of the following 1950s science-fiction films includes a brief appearance by Leonard Nimoy?

- ☐ 1. DESTINATION MOON
- ☐ 2. FORBIDDEN PLANET
- ☐ 3. SPACE MASTER X-7
- ☐ 4. THEM!
- ☐ 5. WAR OF THE WORLDS

15 Who wrote the story "There Shall Be No Darkness," on which the film THE BEAST MUST DIE is based?

- ☐ 1. Alan Dean Foster
- ☐ 2. Andre Norton
- ☐ 3. H. P. Lovecraft
- ☐ 4. James Blish
- ☐ 5. Robert Heinlein

56

16 FORBIDDEN PLANET is loosely based on what play by William Shakespeare?

- ☐ 1. A MIDSUMMER NIGHT'S DREAM
- ☐ 2. HAMLET
- ☐ 3. KING LEAR
- ☐ 4. THE TEMPEST
- ☐ 5. THE TAMING OF THE SHREW

17 Who directed the 1930s undead classics WHITE ZOMBIE and REVOLT OF THE ZOMBIES?

- ☐ 1. Howard Hawks
- ☐ 2. James Whale
- ☐ 3. Michael Curtiz
- ☐ 4. Tod Browning
- ☐ 5. Victor Halperin

18 Early in his career he directed Boris Karloff in THE MAN WHO LIVED AGAIN, and Paul Robeson in KING SOLOMON'S MINES. His later films include MARY POPPINS.

- ☐ 1. James Whale
- ☐ 2. Karl Freund
- ☐ 3. Michael Curtiz
- ☐ 4. Robert Stevenson
- ☐ 5. Victor Fleming

19 He directed Boris Karloff in THE INVISIBLE MENACE and WEST OF SHANGHAI. Later he won an Oscar for the screenplay for AROUND THE WORLD IN EIGHTY DAYS.

- ☐ 1. Felix Feist
- ☐ 2. John Cromwell
- ☐ 3. John Farrow
- ☐ 4. King Vidor
- ☐ 5. Michael Curtiz

20 Who directed the 1983 film SPACEHUNTER: ADVENTURES IN THE FORBIDDEN ZONE?

- ☐ 1. Edward Zwick
- ☐ 2. Joe Dante
- ☐ 3. Lamont Johnson
- ☐ 4. Stephen Frears
- ☐ 5. Terry Morse

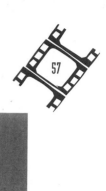

21

What Oscar-winning actor wrote and directed the 1948 comedy VICE VERSA, in which a father and son change places after wishing on a magic stone?

- ☐ 1. Alec Guinness
- ☐ 2. Dean Jagger
- ☐ 3. George Sanders
- ☐ 4. Peter Ustinov
- ☐ 5. Walter Huston

22

What is the sequel to the 1969 low-budget shocker MAD DOCTOR OF BLOOD ISLAND?

- ☐ 1. ATTACK OF THE CRAB MONSTERS
- ☐ 2. BEAST OF THE DEAD
- ☐ 3. BEYOND ATLANTIS
- ☐ 4. THE CAMP ON BLOOD ISLAND
- ☐ 5. THE SECRET OF BLOOD ISLAND

23

As an actor, his film credits include BLACK SABBATH, HOUSE OF USHER, and the 1963 version of BEAUTY AND THE BEAST. As a producer, he has worked on such favorites as THE LOST BOYS and SHORT CIRCUIT.

- ☐ 1. Antony Carbone
- ☐ 2. Carl Switzer
- ☐ 3. John Kerr
- ☐ 4. L. Q. Jones
- ☐ 5. Mark Damon

24

In which of the following low-budget science-fiction thrillers did Clint Eastwood make his screen debut?

- ☐ 1. MONSTER ON THE CAMPUS
- ☐ 2. REVENGE OF THE CREATURE
- ☐ 3. TARANTULA
- ☐ 4. THE MONOLITH MONSTERS
- ☐ 5. THE SPACE CHILDREN

25

What was the first Stephen King screenplay written directly for the screen?

- ☐ 1. CARRIE
- ☐ 2. CREEPSHOW
- ☐ 3. MISERY
- ☐ 4. PET SEMATARY
- ☐ 5. SLEEPWALKERS

26 This actor starred in ERASERHEAD, and later had roles in other David Lynch films, such as DUNE, BLUE VELVET, and WILD AT HEART.

☐ 1. Dean Stockwell
☐ 2. Dennis Hopper
☐ 3. Jack Nance
☐ 4. Kyle MacLachlan
☐ 5. Patrick Stewart

27 In which of the following films is the primary character named H. George Wells?

☐ 1. EMPIRE OF THE ANTS
☐ 2. FIRST MEN IN THE MOON
☐ 3. FOOD OF THE GODS
☐ 4. THE TIME MACHINE
☐ 5. THINGS TO COME

28 What was the name of ROSEMARY'S BABY?

☐ 1. Adrian
☐ 2. Guy, Jr.
☐ 3. Hutch
☐ 4. Roman
☐ 5. The child is never referred to by name.

29 Name the 1990 science-fiction thriller that stars Tim Matheson, Charlton Heston, Jack Palance, and Peter Boyle.

☐ 1. ALIEN PREDATOR
☐ 2. ANIMAL BEHAVIOR
☐ 3. CYBORG
☐ 4. SOLAR CRISIS
☐ 5. SURVIVING THE GAME

30 What Oscar-winning actor made his screen debut as a reincarnated superhero in Philip Kaufman's low-budget 1967 comedy FEARLESS FRANK?

☐ 1. Cliff Robertson
☐ 2. Dustin Hoffman
☐ 3. Gene Hackman
☐ 4. John Voight
☐ 5. Robert De Niro

31 What 1950s sci-fi thriller has significant plot elements similar to the story of ALIEN?

☐   1.   FIRST MAN INTO SPACE
☐   2.   IT! THE TERROR FROM BEYOND SPACE
☐   3.   TERROR FROM THE YEAR 5000
☐   4.   THE COSMIC MAN
☐   5.   THE MYSTERIANS

32 This popular veteran actor can be found in such films as ROCKETSHIP X-M, AIRPLANE II: THE SEQUEL, and HONEY, I BLEW UP THE KIDS.

☐   1.   Chuck Conners
☐   2.   Lloyd Bridges
☐   3.   Peter Graves
☐   4.   Raymond Burr
☐   5.   William Shatner

33 Name the low-budget 1986 film in which Nichelle Nichols plays a drill sergeant who accidentally leads her troops into conflict with ghosts from the Civil War.

☐   1.   A SPECIAL FRIENDSHIP
☐   2.   LIBERTY
☐   3.   THE ACORN PEOPLE
☐   4.   THE MIDNIGHT HOUR
☐   5.   THE SUPERNATURALS

34 Which STAR TREK film has the longest running time, either 132 minutes or 143 minutes, depending on which version you are watching?

☐   1.   STAR TREK—THE MOTION PICTURE
☐   2.   STAR TREK II: THE WRATH OF KHAN
☐   3.   STAR TREK V: THE FINAL FRONTIER
☐   4.   STAR TREK VI: THE UNDISCOVERED COUNTRY
☐   5.   STAR TREK: GENERATIONS

35 Who wrote the story "We Can Remember It for You Wholesale," on which the 1990 film TOTAL RECALL is based?

☐   1.   Alan Dean Foster
☐   2.   Harlan Ellison
☐   3.   Philip K. Dick
☐   4.   William Gibson
☐   5.   William S. Burroughs

36 What film is based on the short story "Farewell to the Master," by Harry Bates?

☐ 1. ATTACK OF THE PUPPET PEOPLE
☐ 2. FIRST SPACESHIP ON VENUS
☐ 3. THE DAY THE EARTH STOOD STILL
☐ 4. THEM!
☐ 5. ZARDOZ

37 This character actor appeared in several of the best science-fiction films of the 1950s, including THE DAY THE EARTH STOOD STILL, EARTH VS. THE FLYING SAUCERS, and WORLD WITHOUT END.

☐ 1. Barton MacLane
☐ 2. Fritz Feld
☐ 3. Herbert Lom
☐ 4. Hugh Marlowe
☐ 5. Mike Mazurki

38 Which of the following magazines first published the story on which the 1994 movie THE PUPPET MASTERS is based?

☐ 1. ASTOUNDING SCIENCE FICTION
☐ 2. COLLIER'S
☐ 3. GALAXY
☐ 4. THE MAGAZINE OF FANTASY AND SCIENCE FICTION
☐ 5. WEIRD TALES

39 Which of the following describes the ending of COLOSSUS: THE FORBIN PROJECT?

☐ 1. The creators dismantle the computer's brain.
☐ 2. The creators' descendants travel back in time to disable the computer.
☐ 3. The computer decides to restore power to the creators.
☐ 4. The computer remains in control.
☐ 5. The computer sets off atomic warfare between the U.S. and Russia.

40 Richard Matheson's classic novel I AM LEGEND was the basis for the 1971 movie THE OMEGA MAN. What 1964 film starring Vincent Price is also based on the same novel?

☐ 1. DR. BLOOD'S COFFIN
☐ 2. I AM LEGEND
☐ 3. PANIC IN YEAR ZERO!
☐ 4. THE DAY THE WORLD ENDED
☐ 5. THE LAST MAN ON EARTH

41 This actor's death scene in SOYLENT GREEN is one of the film's few highlights—a poignant farewell from a popular performer, who knew that in real life he was dying.

- ☐ 1. Chuck Conners
- ☐ 2. Edward G. Robinson
- ☐ 3. Joseph Cotten
- ☐ 4. Pat O'Brien
- ☐ 5. Whit Bissell

42 Peter Graves stars in this 1952 anticommunist propaganda film that includes fugitive Nazis, stock-footage disasters, and an ending that claims to be the beginning.

- ☐ 1. ENEMY FROM SPACE
- ☐ 2. IMMEDIATE DISASTER
- ☐ 3. INVASION U.S.A.
- ☐ 4. RED PLANET MARS
- ☐ 5. THE NEXT VOICE YOU HEAR

43 In A BOY AND HIS DOG, what is the name of the underground city where Vic is captured and held as breeding stock?

- ☐ 1. Alphaville
- ☐ 2. Berlin
- ☐ 3. New Colony Six
- ☐ 4. Philadelphia
- ☐ 5. Topeka

44 Which character in the 1964 comedy classic DR. STRANGELOVE also played the role of the President of the United States?

- ☐ 1. Bat Guano
- ☐ 2. Buck Turgidson
- ☐ 3. Jack D. Ripper
- ☐ 4. Merkin Muffley
- ☐ 5. T. J. "King" Kong

45 Who wrote the novel on which the film SOLARIS is based?

- ☐ 1. Anthony Burgess
- ☐ 2. Ed Earl Repp
- ☐ 3. John Varley
- ☐ 4. Stanislaw Lem
- ☐ 5. Tom Clancy

46 What is the name of the computer that kidnaps its creator's wife and impregnates her in the 1977 film DEMON SEED?

- ☐ 1. Chip
- ☐ 2. Jonas
- ☐ 3. Marvin
- ☐ 4. Proteus
- ☐ 5. Robbie

47 Who wrote the novel on which the 1977 film DEMON SEED is based?

- ☐ 1. Algis Budrys
- ☐ 2. Bruce Sterling
- ☐ 3. Clive Barker
- ☐ 4. Dean Koontz
- ☐ 5. William Gibson

48 Who played the title role in 1981 Cold War comedy CONDORMAN, in which a cartoonist is transformed into a superhero?

- ☐ 1. Michael Crawford
- ☐ 2. Michael Landon
- ☐ 3. Michael Murphy
- ☐ 4. Michael Redgrave
- ☐ 5. Michael York

49 In what film will you find Master and Blaster?

- ☐ 1. ALIENS
- ☐ 2. BATMAN RETURNS
- ☐ 3. HOOK
- ☐ 4. MAD MAX: BEYOND THUNDERDOME
- ☐ 5. WHO FRAMED ROGER RABBIT

50 Which Oscar-winning cinematographer worked with Roger Corman on such films as THE PIT AND THE PENDULUM and THE FALL OF THE HOUSE OF USHER?

- ☐ 1. Floyd Crosby
- ☐ 2. Haskell Wexler
- ☐ 3. James Wong Howe
- ☐ 4. Karl Freund
- ☐ 5. Robert Surtees

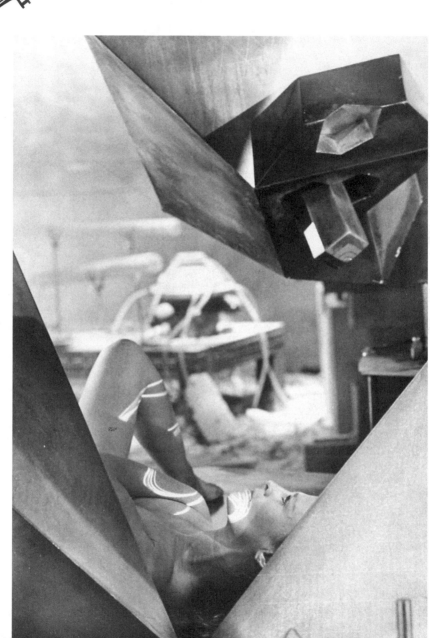

50-POINT QUESTIONS

1

What caused THE INCREDIBLE SHRINKING MAN to shrink?

- ☐ 1. A meteor shower
- ☐ 2. A mysterious fog
- ☐ 3. An atomic explosion
- ☐ 4. An experimental drug
- ☐ 5. Food stolen from a spaceship

2

In ANDY WARHOL'S DRACULA, what type of blood is Dracula searching for?

- ☐ 1. The blood of avant-garde artists
- ☐ 2. The blood of soldiers killed in battle
- ☐ 3. The blood of virgin women
- ☐ 4. The blood of young boys
- ☐ 5. Type AB-positive

3

Every live-action, full-length Tim Burton film contains which of the following features?

- ☐ 1. A black-and-white dream sequence
- ☐ 2. A voice-over narration in the opening sequence
- ☐ 3. At least one actor in white-face makeup
- ☐ 4. Bill Murray as a part of the cast
- ☐ 5. All of the above

4

Who starred in the 1933 classic, ISLAND OF LOST SOULS?

- ☐ 1. Charles Laughton
- ☐ 2. Fredric March
- ☐ 3. Lionel Barrymore
- ☐ 4. Lon Chaney
- ☐ 5. Ralph Richardson

5

Counting the 1931 version of FRANKENSTEIN as the start of the Universal cycle of Frankenstein films, what number in the series is SON OF FRANKENSTEIN?

- ☐ 1. Two
- ☐ 2. Three
- ☐ 3. Four
- ☐ 4. Five
- ☐ 5. Six

6

The cast for which of the following includes Dennis Hopper?

☐ 1. MY BEST FRIEND IS A VAMPIRE
☐ 2. MY BROTHER TALKS TO HORSES
☐ 3. MY FAVORITE SPY
☐ 4. MY SCIENCE PROJECT
☐ 5. MY STEPMOTHER IS AN ALIEN

7

Who won an Oscar for Best Costume Design for STAR WARS?

☐ 1. Bob Mackie
☐ 2. Edith Head
☐ 3. Jean Louis
☐ 4. John Mollo
☐ 5. Margaret Furse

8

In THE DAY THE EARTH STOOD STILL, what distance does the visitor from space state that he has traveled?

☐ 1. 8 light-years
☐ 2. "Not far. Only the distance between Earth and the planet you call Venus."
☐ 3. 10 parsecs
☐ 4. The visitor refuses to reveal this information.
☐ 5. 250 million miles

9

Who is the credited director for OUTLAW OF GOR?

☐ 1. Dario Argento
☐ 2. Don Coscarelli
☐ 3. Fritz Kiersch
☐ 4. John "Bud" Cardos
☐ 5. Sylvio Tabet

10

In THE BEASTMASTER, who plays the evil priest?

☐ 1. Jack Palance
☐ 2. James Earl Jones
☐ 3. Max von Sydow
☐ 4. Oliver Reed
☐ 5. Rip Torn

11 In the 1988 film BEETLEJUICE, who plays Juno, the caseworker in the social services bureau of the dead?

☐ 1. Annie McEnroe
☐ 2. Catherine O'Hara
☐ 3. Geena Davis
☐ 4. Sylvia Sidney
☐ 5. Winona Ryder

12 Who costarred with Bela Lugosi in GHOSTS ON THE LOOSE and with Martin Landau in CYCLONE?

☐ 1. Ava Gardner
☐ 2. Heather Thomas
☐ 3. Huntz Hall
☐ 4. Russ Tamblyn
☐ 5. Troy Donahue

13 How many Oscars did STAR WARS win?

☐ 1. One
☐ 2. Three
☐ 3. Five
☐ 4. Seven
☐ 5. Nine

14 What movie poster is advertised outside the movie theater where the teenagers gather in the 1958 film THE BLOB?

☐ 1. ATTACK OF THE SPACE ZOMBIES
☐ 2. JUNGLE KILLER
☐ 3. LOST ON MARS
☐ 4. WEREWOLF OF KANSAS
☐ 5. THE VAMPIRE AND THE ROBOT

15 Into what 1951 film was John W. Campbell's short story "Who Goes There?" adapted?

☐ 1. DESTINATION MOON
☐ 2. EARTH VS. THE FLYING SAUCERS
☐ 3. THE DAY THE EARTH STOOD STILL
☐ 4. THE THING (FROM ANOTHER WORLD)
☐ 5. WHO GOES THERE?

16 In BACK TO THE FUTURE, which of the following Ronald Reagan movies was playing at the local theater during the 1955 portion of the film?

- ☐ 1. BEDTIME FOR BONZO
- ☐ 2. CATTLE QUEEN OF MONTANA
- ☐ 3. HELLCATS OF THE NAVY
- ☐ 4. STORM WARNING
- ☐ 5. THE WINNING TEAM

17 What star of the 1936 low-budget horror film REVOLT OF THE ZOMBIES would later receive a Best Supporting Actor Oscar?

- ☐ 1. Dean Jagger
- ☐ 2. George Sanders
- ☐ 3. Thomas Mitchell
- ☐ 4. Walter Brennan
- ☐ 5. Walter Huston

18 Who was originally cast in the Michael J. Fox role of Marty McFly in BACK TO THE FUTURE, only to be replaced several weeks and around $4 million into the production?

- ☐ 1. Andrew McCarthy
- ☐ 2. Eric Stoltz
- ☐ 3. James Spader
- ☐ 4. Kyle MacLachlan
- ☐ 5. Rob Lowe

19 In FIELD OF DREAMS, Kevin Costner's character hears a voice that says, "If you build it, he will come." Whose arrival does the voice foretell?

- ☐ 1. Archibald Graham
- ☐ 2. Eddie Cicotte
- ☐ 3. Joe Jackson
- ☐ 4. John Kinsella
- ☐ 5. Terrence Mann

20 Who provided the voice of Jiminy Cricket in the 1940 Disney animated classic PINOCCHIO?

- ☐ 1. Charles Judels
- ☐ 2. Christian Rub
- ☐ 3. Cliff Edwards
- ☐ 4. Dickie Jones
- ☐ 5. Frankie Darro

21 This ROLLERBALL cast member later played The Supreme Being in TIME BANDITS.

☐ 1. James Caan
☐ 2. John Beck
☐ 3. John Houseman
☐ 4. Moses Gunn
☐ 5. Ralph Richardson

22 Which of these actors from GHOSTBUSTERS also appears in SPACEHUNTER: ADVENTURES IN THE FORBIDDEN ZONE?

☐ 1. Bill Murray
☐ 2. Dan Aykroyd
☐ 3. Ernie Hudson
☐ 4. Harold Ramis
☐ 5. Rick Moranis

23 Who directed the 1959 film FIRST MAN INTO SPACE?

☐ 1. Alan Dwan
☐ 2. Edward D. Wood, Jr.
☐ 3. Fred F. Sears
☐ 4. Robert Day
☐ 5. Robert Wise

24 This actor's career consists mostly of low-budget shockers, such as FRANKENSTEIN'S DAUGHTER, HOW TO MAKE A MONSTER, and BEAST OF THE DEAD. Later, he became a successful television producer.

☐ 1. Donald Murphy
☐ 2. Eddie Garcia
☐ 3. John Ashley
☐ 4. Robert Harris
☐ 5. Ronald Peary

25 Who played the title role in the 1973 comedy-fantasy MISTER SUPERINVISIBLE?

☐ 1. Dean Jones
☐ 2. Lee Majors
☐ 3. Martin Landau
☐ 4. Peter Falk
☐ 5. Tony Roberts

26 Name the Oscar-winning cinematographer who worked on such science-fiction films as SPACE CHILDREN, FANTASTIC VOYAGE, and LOGAN'S RUN.

- [ ] 1. Ernest Laszlo
- [ ] 2. Floyd Crosby
- [ ] 3. Haskell Wexler
- [ ] 4. James Wong Howe
- [ ] 5. Vilmos Zsigmond

27 This noted art director and set designer also directed several low-budget monster movies, including GORGO and THE BEAST FROM 20,000 FATHOMS.

- [ ] 1. Cedric Gibbons
- [ ] 2. Eugene Lourie
- [ ] 3. Hans Dreier
- [ ] 4. John Box
- [ ] 5. William Cameron Menzies

28 The screenplay for BLADE RUNNER was written by Hampton Fancher and David Peoples. For which Oscar-winning Best Picture did Peoples receive a screenplay credit?

- [ ] 1. AMADEUS
- [ ] 2. AROUND THE WORLD IN 80 DAYS
- [ ] 3. CHARIOTS OF FIRE
- [ ] 4. THE SILENCE OF THE LAMBS
- [ ] 5. UNFORGIVEN

29 Which of the following was the first film produced by Roger Corman?

- [ ] 1. ATTACK OF THE CRAB MONSTERS
- [ ] 2. IT CONQUERED THE WORLD
- [ ] 3. NOT OF THIS EARTH
- [ ] 4. THE LITTLE SHOP OF HORRORS
- [ ] 5. THE MONSTER FROM THE OCEAN FLOOR

30 Who directed the 1953 science-fiction classic WAR OF THE WORLDS?

- [ ] 1. Byron Haskin
- [ ] 2. George Pal
- [ ] 3. Lindsay Anderson
- [ ] 4. Roger Corman
- [ ] 5. William Cameron Menzies

31

In ROSEMARY'S BABY this stage actor played a witch hunter, and in the television series BEWITCHED he played a warlock.

☐ 1. Dick York
☐ 2. John Cassavetes
☐ 3. Maurice Evans
☐ 4. Roddy McDowall
☐ 5. Sidney Blackmer

32

Name the strongly anticommunist 1957 film about an alien who gives capsules capable of destroying life on Earth to five strangers.

☐ 1. BEGINNING OF THE END
☐ 2. ENEMY FROM SPACE
☐ 3. NOT OF THIS EARTH
☐ 4. THE NIGHT THE WORLD EXPLODED
☐ 5. THE 27TH DAY

33

Name the distinctive British actor who gave a much-acclaimed performance as Winston Smith in the 1984 version of 1984.

☐ 1. Derek Jacobi
☐ 2. Ian Holm
☐ 3. Jeremy Irons
☐ 4. John Hurt
☐ 5. Richard Burton

34

Which of the following sci-fi and/or creature features is closely associated with director Inoshiro Honda?

☐ 1. GHIDRAH, THE THREE-HEADED MONSTER
☐ 2. GODZILLA, KING OF THE MONSTERS
☐ 3. MOTHRA
☐ 4. THE MYSTERIANS
☐ 5. All of the above

35

Which author, later to become a major best-seller, wrote the screenplay for the 1958 version of THE FLY?

☐ 1. Gore Vidal
☐ 2. Harold Robbins
☐ 3. James Clavell
☐ 4. Raymond Chandler
☐ 5. William F. Buckley, Jr.

36 Name the 1962 British horror-comedy that's a remake of the 1933 Boris Karloff classic THE GHOUL.

- [ ] 1. CREATURE FROM THE HAUNTED SEA
- [ ] 2. EEGAH!
- [ ] 3. MAD MONSTER PARTY?
- [ ] 4. NO PLACE LIKE HOMICIDE
- [ ] 5. THIS IS NOT A TEST

37 Who was the first TV horror-movie host?

- [ ] 1. Dr. Morgus
- [ ] 2. Seymour
- [ ] 3. Tarantula Ghoul
- [ ] 4. Vampira
- [ ] 5. Zacherley

38 Bette Davis' final film performance was as a witch in this 1989 motion picture directed by low-budget auteur Larry Cohen.

- [ ] 1. BUNNY O'HARE
- [ ] 2. BURNT OFFERINGS
- [ ] 3. RETURN TO WITCH MOUNTAIN
- [ ] 4. THE WATCHER IN THE WOODS
- [ ] 5. WICKED STEPMOTHER

39 Name the 1958 Japanese film classic acknowledged by George Lucas as a primary inspiration for STAR WARS.

- [ ] 1. RASHOMON
- [ ] 2. THE HIDDEN FORTRESS
- [ ] 3. THE SEVEN SAMURAI
- [ ] 4. THRONE OF BLOOD
- [ ] 5. YOJIMBO

40 Who played scientist Charles Dutton, a key member of the research team fighting the deadly microbe, in THE ANDROMEDA STRAIN?

- [ ] 1. Charles Dutton
- [ ] 2. David Wayne
- [ ] 3. James Olson
- [ ] 4. Richard O'Brien
- [ ] 5. Robert Duvall

41 Name the 1971 film that examines the possible survival of insects over people, and which received a surprise Oscar win for Best Documentary.

- [ ] 1. JOURNEY TO THE OUTER LIMITS
- [ ] 2. PHASE IV
- [ ] 3. THE HELLSTROM CHRONICLE
- [ ] 4. THE SILENT REVOLUTION
- [ ] 5. WORLD WITHOUT SUN

42 Who is the only cast member of the 1958 film THE FLY to appear in the 1959 sequel THE RETURN OF THE FLY?

- [ ] 1. Al (David) Heddison
- [ ] 2. Herbert Marshall
- [ ] 3. Kathleen Freeman
- [ ] 4. Patricia Owens
- [ ] 5. Vincent Price

43 Name the 1961 film in which producer/director William Castle gave audiences the option of voting thumbs up or thumbs down as to which ending they wanted. (Only one ending was filmed, however.)

- [ ] 1. MACABRE
- [ ] 2. MR. SARDONICUS
- [ ] 3. THE NIGHT WALKER
- [ ] 4. THE TINGLER
- [ ] 5. ZOTZ!

44 Name the 1989 British-made futuristic adventure film with Bill Paxton, Bob Peck, Mark Hamill, F. Murray Abraham, and Ben Kingsley in its cast.

- [ ] 1. FOR ALL MANKIND
- [ ] 2. NIGHT WALK
- [ ] 3. PRIME TARGET
- [ ] 4. SLIPSTREAM
- [ ] 5. THE CHILLING

45 Name the influential, nonlinear 1961 French-language film from director Alan Resnais about a man ("X") and a woman ("A") who may or may not have had an affair that may or may not take place in the future.

- [ ] 1. ALPHAVILLE
- [ ] 2. BREATHLESS
- [ ] 3. HIROSHIMA, MON AMOUR
- [ ] 4. LAST YEAR AT MARIENBAD
- [ ] 5. LOLA

MOVIES   50-POINT QUESTIONS

46 Name the odd 1968 fantasy film in which Candice Bergen, Michael Caine, and Anthony Quinn gather on a Greek island for various ambiguous activities.

- ☐ 1. CORRUPTION
- ☐ 2. DARING GAME
- ☐ 3. SPIRITS OF THE DEAD
- ☐ 4. THE MAGUS
- ☐ 5. THE SAVAGE SEVEN

47 Name the film based on an H. P. Lovecraft story whose cast includes Dean Stockwell, Sandra Dee, Ed Begley, and Talia Coppola.

- ☐ 1. DIE, MONSTER, DIE!
- ☐ 2. THE CURSE
- ☐ 3. THE DUNWICH HORROR
- ☐ 4. THE HAUNTED PALACE
- ☐ 5. THE SHUTTERED ROOM

48 In what film, whose cast includes Jack Nicholson, does the captain of a U.S. Navy ship repeatedly screen YOUNG DR. JEKYLL MEETS FRANKENSTEIN for his crew?

- ☐ 1. ANCHORS AWEIGH
- ☐ 2. DON'T GIVE UP THE SHIP
- ☐ 3. ENSIGN PULVER
- ☐ 4. THE GALLANT HOURS
- ☐ 5. THE SAND PEBBLES

49 In the 1945 fantasy comedy THE HORN BLOWS AT MIDNIGHT, who plays the angel sent to destroy Earth with a blast from the horn?

- ☐ 1. Bob Hope
- ☐ 2. Bing Crosby
- ☐ 3. George Murphy
- ☐ 4. Jack Benny
- ☐ 5. Ronald Reagan

50 What cameo role does screenwriter John Sayles play in the often humorous 1981 horror film THE HOWLING?

- ☐ 1. A bookstore owner
- ☐ 2. A gas station attendant
- ☐ 3. A morgue attendant
- ☐ 4. A policeman
- ☐ 5. A tree surgeon

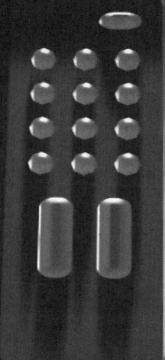

TELEVISION

TRIVIA QUIZ

10-POINT QUESTIONS

1 What did THE X-FILES' Fox Mulder study to be at Oxford University?

- ☐ 1. Doctor
- ☐ 2. Psychiatrist
- ☐ 3. Sociologist
- ☐ 4. Mathematician
- ☐ 5. Psychologist

2 Why was Agent Dana Scully teamed up with Mulder?

- ☐ 1. The X-Files needed a medical perspective.
- ☐ 2. Mulder was lonely.
- ☐ 3. To close down the X-Files.
- ☐ 4. To verify Mulder's expenses.
- ☐ 5. So Mulder would have backup.

3 Name the glass-nosed atomic submarine on VOYAGE TO THE BOTTOM OF THE SEA.

- ☐ 1. The *Seaquest*
- ☐ 2. The *Seahunt*
- ☐ 3. The *Seaweed*
- ☐ 4. The *Searcher*
- ☐ 5. The *Seaview*

4 Name the evil organization that opposed THE MAN FROM U.N.C.L.E.

- ☐ 1. Kaos
- ☐ 2. Thrush
- ☐ 3. U.O.E.
- ☐ 4. A.U.N.T.
- ☐ 5. None of these

5 What successful film director was responsible for producing the series AMAZING STORIES?

- ☐ 1. Ron Howard
- ☐ 2. Steven Spielberg
- ☐ 3. George Lucas
- ☐ 4. Brian DePalma
- ☐ 5. None of these

6

Name the first commander of BABYLON 5.

- ☐ 1. Jonathan Harris
- ☐ 2. Michael Garibaldi
- ☐ 3. Jeffrey Sinclair
- ☐ 4. Steven Franklin
- ☐ 5. None of these

7

What does "ALF" stand for?

- ☐ 1. Alfred
- ☐ 2. Alien Life Form
- ☐ 3. Annoying Little Furball
- ☐ 4. Another Lifeless Football
- ☐ 5. None of these

8

On BUCK ROGERS IN THE 25th CENTURY, what enemies of Earth woke Buck up?

- ☐ 1. Draconians
- ☐ 2. Killer Kane
- ☐ 3. Jacote
- ☐ 4. Blood Runners
- ☐ 5. None of these

9

What show dealt with "extraordinary crimes against the people and the State"?

- ☐ 1. THE PRISONER
- ☐ 2. THE AVENGERS
- ☐ 3. I SPY
- ☐ 4. THE MAN FROM U.N.C.L.E.
- ☐ 5. SECRET AGENT

10

In what country did MAX HEADROOM premiere?

- ☐ 1. USA
- ☐ 2. New Zealand
- ☐ 3. UK
- ☐ 4. France
- ☐ 5. Australia

11

For what brand of soda did MAX HEADROOM act as "spokeshead"?

☐ 1. Pepsi
☐ 2. RC
☐ 3. Coca-Cola
☐ 4. Dr. Pepper
☐ 5. He didn't advertise for any of them.

12

On THE TOMORROW PEOPLE, what did they call developing psychic abilities?

☐ 1. "Coming of age"
☐ 2. "Breaking out"
☐ 3. "Breaking in"
☐ 4. "Turning on"
☐ 5. "Waking up"

13

What was MR. BEAN?

☐ 1. An idiot
☐ 2. An alien
☐ 3. An idiot alien
☐ 4. A talking worm
☐ 5. None of these

14

In what year was a SUPERBOY pilot starring Johnny Rockwell filmed?

☐ 1. 1988
☐ 2. 1961
☐ 3. 1975
☐ 4. 1962
☐ 5. 1995

15

Mandy Patinkin played the role of George Francisco in the movie ALIEN NATION. Who played him in the TV series?

☐ 1. Eric Pierpoint
☐ 2. James Caan
☐ 3. Andrew Schneider
☐ 4. Charlie Brill
☐ 5. Jonathan Frakes

16 Who played the role of Jake Cardigan in the USA Network series TEK WAR?

☐ 1. William Shatner
☐ 2. Brent Spiner
☐ 3. David Hasselhoff
☐ 4. Greg Evigan
☐ 5. None of the above

17 Which actor took over as captain on SEAQUEST DSV in its third season, replacing Roy Scheider, who was relegated to a semiregular role?

☐ 1. Jonathan Brandis
☐ 2. Greg Evigan
☐ 3. Eric Pierpoint
☐ 4. Michael Ironside
☐ 5. Stephanie Beacham

18 Which superhero was brought to television by producer William Dozier?

☐ 1. Batman
☐ 2. The Green Hornet
☐ 3. Wonder Woman
☐ 4. Superman
☐ 5. Batman and the Green Hornet

19 LOIS AND CLARK: THE NEW ADVENTURES OF SUPERMAN star Dean Cain played football for which university?

☐ 1. Harvard
☐ 2. MIT
☐ 3. Princeton
☐ 4. Notre Dame
☐ 5. Penn State

20 Which cast member of LOST IN SPACE is now a regular on BABYLON 5?

☐ 1. Angela Cartwright
☐ 2. Guy Williams
☐ 3. Mark Goddard
☐ 4. Bill Mumy
☐ 5. June Lockhart

TELEVISION   10 - POINT QUESTIONS

21 Whose name and form did the title character of STARMAN take?

☐ 1. Ford Prefect
☐ 2. Paul Forrester
☐ 3. Scott Hayden, Jr.
☐ 4. Sam Francisco
☐ 5. George Fox

22 What rank did Ed Straker hold on UFO?

☐ 1. Colonel
☐ 2. Captain
☐ 3. Commander
☐ 4. Lieutenant
☐ 5. General

23 What was THUNDERBIRDS mavens Gerry and Sylvia Anderson's first live-action show?

☐ 1. CAPTAIN SCARLET & THE MYSTERONS
☐ 2. CAPTAIN VIDEO
☐ 3. UFO
☐ 4. FIREBALL XL-5
☐ 5. STINGRAY

24 She has played two different Romulan commanders on STAR TREK: THE NEXT GENERATION, the supervisor of the "evil Leaper" on QUANTUM LEAP, and a dissident crew member on SPACE: 1999.

☐ 1. Diana Rigg
☐ 2. Kate O'Meara
☐ 3. Martha Hackett
☐ 4. Carolyn Seymour
☐ 5. Joanna Lumley

25 The first showing of the pilot episode of BABYLON 5, "The Gathering," was not aired in New York due to what crisis?

☐ 1. The Gulf War
☐ 2. The World Trade Center bombing
☐ 3. The Oklahoma City bombing
☐ 4. The Los Angeles earthquake
☐ 5. The San Francisco earthquake

26 Former STAR TREK: THE NEXT GENERATION star Michael Dorn appeared on an episode of the new OUTER LIMITS series. Which stars of the original STAR TREK appeared in the original OUTER LIMITS episodes "Cold Hands, Warm Heart" and "I, Robot"?

☐ 1. William Shatner and DeForrest Kelley
☐ 2. Nichelle Nichols and Walter Koenig
☐ 3. George Takei and Leonard Nimoy
☐ 4. William Shatner and James Doohan
☐ 5. William Shatner and Leonard Nimoy

27 How many seasons of THE ADVENTURES OF SUPERMAN were filmed in black and white?

☐ 1. One
☐ 2. Two
☐ 3. Three
☐ 4. Four
☐ 5. None

28 Which actor from the HIGHLANDER films guest-starred in the pilot for the HIGHLANDER TV series?

☐ 1. Mario Van Peebles
☐ 2. Clancy Brown
☐ 3. Sean Connery
☐ 4. Christopher Lambert
☐ 5. Adrian Paul

29 Which former WKRP IN CINCINNATI star had a recurring role in the first season of HIGHLANDER?

☐ 1. Howard Hessman
☐ 2. Gordon Jump
☐ 3. Tim Reid
☐ 4. Loni Anderson
☐ 5. Tawny Kitaen

30 This star of the films THE YEAR OF LIVING DANGEROUSLY and SILVERADO was a regular on the short-lived series SPACE RANGERS.

☐ 1. Kevin Kline
☐ 2. Mel Gibson
☐ 3. Sigourney Weaver
☐ 4. Linda Hunt
☐ 5. Danny Glover

31 In TIME TRAX, what was the device Darian used to send criminals back to the future disguised as?

- ☐ 1. Stopwatch
- ☐ 2. Car-alarm activator
- ☐ 3. Key chain
- ☐ 4. Credit card
- ☐ 5. Wallet

32 He was the executive producer for THE SIX MILLION DOLLAR MAN, THE BIONIC WOMAN, and TIME TRAX.

- ☐ 1. Harve Bennett
- ☐ 2. Kenneth Johnson
- ☐ 3. Irwin Allen
- ☐ 4. Rod Serling
- ☐ 5. Gene Roddenberry

33 She changed careers from model to actress as one of the stars of BUCK ROGERS.

- ☐ 1. Morgan Fairchild
- ☐ 2. Erin Moran
- ☐ 3. Erin Gray
- ☐ 4. Pamela Hensley
- ☐ 5. Maren Jensen

34 Before his starring roles in PREDATOR and HARRY AND THE HENDERSONS, this actor stretched his acting muscles on the short-lived MISFITS OF SCIENCE.

- ☐ 1. Kevin Peter Hall
- ☐ 2. Anthony Michael Hall
- ☐ 3. Tom Skerritt
- ☐ 4. John Lithgow
- ☐ 5. Yaphet Kotto

35 Known for her portrayal of Dale Arden in the 1980 movie FLASH GORDON, this actress costarred in the 1983 series MANIMAL.

- ☐ 1. Jean Rogers
- ☐ 2. Melody Anderson
- ☐ 3. Pamela Anderson
- ☐ 4. JoAnna Cameron
- ☐ 5. Deborah Watling

36 This soap-opera actress once fought crime as ElectraWoman on THE KROFFT SUPER SHOW.

- ☐ 1. Deidre Hall
- ☐ 2. Jill Larson
- ☐ 3. Patsy Bruder
- ☐ 4. Marcy Walker
- ☐ 5. Maggie Reed

37 The plot of this series' pilot centered on the creation of a homemade rocket to travel to the moon to recover NASA equipment left by Apollo missions.

- ☐ 1. CAPRICORN ONE
- ☐ 2. QUARK
- ☐ 3. SALVAGE-1
- ☐ 4. MOONBASE 3
- ☐ 5. WAY OUT

38 What is the most identifiable way of spotting one of THE INVADERS?

- ☐ 1. Clawlike hands
- ☐ 2. Oddly angled pinkies
- ☐ 3. Slight limp
- ☐ 4. Catlike eyes
- ☐ 5. Poor taste in clothes

39 The 1972 NBC pilot POOR DEVIL teamed Sammy Davis, Jr.—as a denizen of Hell out to steal Jack Klugman's soul—with this Hammer Films horror star.

- ☐ 1. Peter Cushing
- ☐ 2. Caroline Munro
- ☐ 3. Christopher Lee
- ☐ 4. David Prowse
- ☐ 5. Vincent Price

40 The Robinson family was threatened by a carrot monster in this LOST IN SPACE episode.

- ☐ 1. "The Great Vegetable Rebellion"
- ☐ 2. "The Flaming Planet"
- ☐ 3. "A Day at the Zoo"
- ☐ 4. "The Space Creature"
- ☐ 5. "Deadliest of the Species"

41 A spin-off pilot seen only in syndication, this featured the end of Ralph Hinkley's superhero career and the proposed start of his replacement's adventures.

- [ ] 1. THE GREATEST AMERICAN HERO
- [ ] 2. THE GREATEST AMERICAN HEROINE
- [ ] 3. LILACS, MR. MAXWELL
- [ ] 4. OPERATION: SPOILSPORT
- [ ] 5. THE BEAST IN THE BLACK

42 After saving the galaxy from the Dark Side, this "force"-ful actor used his powers for evil as the Trickster in THE FLASH and the Joker in BATMAN: THE ANIMATED SERIES.

- [ ] 1. Harrison Ford
- [ ] 2. Billy Dee Williams
- [ ] 3. Anthony Daniels
- [ ] 4. Mark Hamill
- [ ] 5. Kenny Baker

43 This syndicated series features Immortals battling one another with large swords.

- [ ] 1. BAYWATCH
- [ ] 2. HIGHLANDER
- [ ] 3. BABYLON 5
- [ ] 4. RENEGADE
- [ ] 5. TEKWAR

44 Comedians Charlie Callas and Jeff Altman played Sinestro and the Weather Wizard, respectively, in this 1979 NBC special that featured a campy battle between DC Comics' heroes and villains.

- [ ] 1. SUPERFRIENDS
- [ ] 2. THE CHAMPIONS
- [ ] 3. THE AVENGERS
- [ ] 4. CHALLENGE OF THE SUPERHEROES
- [ ] 5. BATTLE OF THE NETWORK STARS

45 Before signing up for duty aboard SEAQUEST DSV, this actress faced different perils as Lana Lang on the syndicated SUPERBOY series.

- [ ] 1. Lauren Holly
- [ ] 2. Stephanie Beacham
- [ ] 3. Rosalind Allen
- [ ] 4. Stacy Haiduk
- [ ] 5. Yvonne Suhor

46 What 1989 telefilm introduced Marvel Comics' Daredevil and the Kingpin?

- ☐ 1. DAREDEVIL
- ☐ 2. THE INCREDIBLE HULK RETURNS
- ☐ 3. THE TRIAL OF THE INCREDIBLE HULK
- ☐ 4. THE DEATH OF THE INCREDIBLE HULK
- ☐ 5. THE HAND-PAINTED THAI

47 Which comic book artist was responsible for designing SPACE GHOST and THE MIGHTY HERCULOIDS?

- ☐ 1. Jack Kirby
- ☐ 2. Alex Toth
- ☐ 3. Alex Nino
- ☐ 4. Curt Swan
- ☐ 5. Steve Ditko

48 Before playing ace reporter Lois Lane on LOIS AND CLARK: THE NEW ADVENTURES OF SUPERMAN, this actress caused constant trouble for MACGYVER.

- ☐ 1. Margot Kidder
- ☐ 2. Teri Weigel
- ☐ 3. Teri Hatcher
- ☐ 4. Noel Neill
- ☐ 5. Tracy Scoggins

49 This 1972 ABC telefilm dealt with construction workers stalked by a murderous machine.

- ☐ 1. FEAR NO EVIL
- ☐ 2. A COLD NIGHT'S DEATH
- ☐ 3. BAFFLED
- ☐ 4. KILLDOZER
- ☐ 5. SOLE SURVIVOR

50 In DOCTOR WHO, what is the Doctor's time-and-space machine called?

- ☐ 1. TARDIS
- ☐ 2. ROOK
- ☐ 3. SIDRAT
- ☐ 4. AZTEC ACE
- ☐ 5. SOLE SURVIVOR

20-POINT QUESTIONS

1 Which of the following did NOT write for THE TWILIGHT ZONE?

☐ 1. Rod Serling
☐ 2. Richard Matheson
☐ 3. Charles Beaumont
☐ 4. George C. Johnson
☐ 5. Robert Bloch

2 What year did THE TWILIGHT ZONE first air?

☐ 1. 1958
☐ 2. 1959
☐ 3. 1960
☐ 4. 1961
☐ 5. 1974

3 Who was the woman in THE TWILIGHT ZONE episode "The After Hours"?

☐ 1. Anne Frank
☐ 2. Anne Francis
☐ 3. Frankie Avalon
☐ 4. Buster Keaton
☐ 5. Anne Frost

4 In STAR TREK: THE NEXT GENERATION, what is the name of Data's daughter?

☐ 1. Hal
☐ 2. Zen
☐ 3. Orac
☐ 4. Lal
☐ 5. Robbie

5 In which STAR TREK: THE NEXT GENERATION episode does Data create a daughter?

☐ 1. "I Sing the Body Electric"
☐ 2. "The Offspring"
☐ 3. "Father and Child"
☐ 4. "Data Builds a Daughter"
☐ 5. "A New Action-Figure is Born"

6

This warrior, who vanished in the time period between
BATTLESTAR GALACTICA and its successor, GALACTICA
1980, finally reappears in a flashback/dream episode,
where we learn his fate.

☐ 1. Apollo
☐ 2. Zeus
☐ 3. Baltar
☐ 4. Starbuck
☐ 5. Biggs

7

He plays Assistant Director Skinner on THE X-FILES.

☐ 1. David Duchovny
☐ 2. Mitch Pileggi
☐ 3. Jerry Hardin
☐ 4. Rowan Atkinson
☐ 5. William Shatner

8

In the classic TWILIGHT ZONE episode "The Invaders,"
Agnes Moorhead is plagued by little aliens. Who are they?

☐ 1. Bug-eyed monsters
☐ 2. Earthmen
☐ 3. Martians
☐ 4. Little green men
☐ 5. Venusians

9

In the TWILIGHT ZONE episode "The Shelter," what has
been announced?

☐ 1. An invasion
☐ 2. A nuclear attack
☐ 3. A thunderstorm
☐ 4. The end of the world
☐ 5. The Second Coming

10

In THE PRISONER episode "The Chimes of Big Ben," what
does Number 6 learn from the great clock?

☐ 1. That he escaped
☐ 2. That he didn't escape
☐ 3. The time of day
☐ 4. That he's in London
☐ 5. That the clock is slow

11 What was the title of the two-hour movie that resolved the cliff-hanger left after the final episode of the ALIEN NATION TV series?

- ☐ 1. *Body and Soul*
- ☐ 2. *Dark Horizon*
- ☐ 3. *Devil with the Blue Dress On*
- ☐ 4. *The Inner Light*
- ☐ 5. *Turnabout Intruder*

12 Who played the British scientist who helped create the armor in the TV series M.A.N.T.I.S.—a role that did not exist in the two-hour movie that inspired the series?

- ☐ 1. Patrick Stewart
- ☐ 2. Peter Davison
- ☐ 3. Roger Moore
- ☐ 4. David Warner
- ☐ 5. Roger Rees

13 Which of the following directors has helmed episodes of STAR TREK: THE NEXT GENERATION, ALIEN NATION, and THE X-FILES?

- ☐ 1. David Carson
- ☐ 2. D. C. Fontana
- ☐ 3. Alexander Singer
- ☐ 4. Rob Bowman
- ☐ 5. Adam Nimoy

14 Which STAR TREK: DEEP SPACE NINE star was a regular on the BEAUTY AND THE BEAST TV series?

- ☐ 1. Siddig el Fadil
- ☐ 2. Armin Shimerman
- ☐ 3. Avery Brooks
- ☐ 4. Terry Farrell
- ☐ 5. Nana Visitor

15 The sons of which comic actor became regulars on SEAQUEST DSV in its second season?

- ☐ 1. Mel Brooks
- ☐ 2. Dom DeLuise
- ☐ 3. Carl Reiner
- ☐ 4. Jerry Seinfeld
- ☐ 5. Rip Taylor

16 RED DWARF's computer, Holly, projects a disembodied head image. What gender is that head in the show's sixth season?

☐ 1. Male
☐ 2. Female
☐ 3. Both
☐ 4. Neither
☐ 5. Holly doesn't appear in the sixth season.

17 Which former STAR TREK: THE NEXT GENERATION star had a recurring role in LOIS AND CLARK's second season?

☐ 1. John DeLancie
☐ 2. Wil Wheaton
☐ 3. Denise Crosby
☐ 4. Majel Barrett
☐ 5. Diana Muldaur

18 Which episode of LOST IN SPACE listed its only guest star as "Robby the Robot"?

☐ 1. "The Derelict"
☐ 2. "The War of the Robots"
☐ 3. "The Magic Mirror"
☐ 4. "The Android Machine"
☐ 5. Robby the Robot never guest-starred on LOST IN SPACE.

19 In which of the following did Academy-Award-winning actor Martin Landau appear?

☐ 1. THE OUTER LIMITS
☐ 2. MISSION: IMPOSSIBLE
☐ 3. SPACE: 1999
☐ 4. ED WOOD
☐ 5. All of the above

20 Which future Batman was in the OUTER LIMITS episode "The Invisible Enemy"?

☐ 1. Val Kilmer
☐ 2. Michael Keaton
☐ 3. Adam West
☐ 4. Kevin Conroy
☐ 5. Robert Lowery

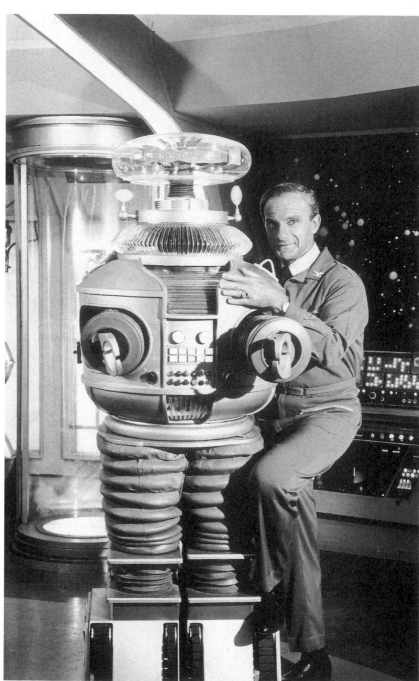

21 Better known these days for playing an antiques dealer, he played a technician who endangers anything he touches in the SPACE: 1999 episode "Force of Life."

☐ 1. Dudley Sutton
☐ 2. Ian McShane
☐ 3. Brian Blessed
☐ 4. Guy Hamilton
☐ 5. Martin Landau

22 This future cast member of SEAQUEST DSV guest-starred in the UFO episode "Destruction."

☐ 1. Roy Scheider
☐ 2. Michael Ironside
☐ 3. Jonathan Brandis
☐ 4. Richard Herd
☐ 5. Stephanie Beacham

23 The cocreator of STAR TREK: DEEP SPACE NINE, STAR TREK: VOYAGER, and LEGEND, Michael Piller, served as a producer on which short-lived genre TV series?

☐ 1. QUARK
☐ 2. SPACE: 1999
☐ 3. UFO
☐ 4. PROBE
☐ 5. SPACE RANGERS

24 Which science-fiction author cocreated PROBE with veteran TV writer Michael Wagner?

☐ 1. Isaac Asimov
☐ 2. Ray Bradbury
☐ 3. Arthur C. Clarke
☐ 4. Robert A. Heinlein
☐ 5. Harlan Ellison

25 What role did future TRANCERS film star Tim Thomerson play on the short-lived comedy QUARK?

☐ 1. Jean/Gene
☐ 2. Ficus
☐ 3. Quark
☐ 4. The robot
☐ 5. None of the above

26

This Irwin Allen-produced TV movie costarred CITIZEN KANE's Joseph Cotten.

☐ 1. LOST IN SPACE
☐ 2. CITY BENEATH THE SEA
☐ 3. LIFEPOD
☐ 4. THE LAST DINOSAUR
☐ 5. GENESIS II

27

TOM CORBETT, SPACE CADET debuted on NBC in what year?

☐ 1. 1950
☐ 2. 1951
☐ 3. 1944
☐ 4. 1960
☐ 5. 1955

28

This writer of the STAR TREK animated series episode "The Pirates of Orion" would go on to write several STAR TREK novels and comic books.

☐ 1. D. C. Fontana
☐ 2. Larry Niven
☐ 3. Howard Weinstein
☐ 4. Paul Schneider
☐ 5. Ronald D. Moore

29

Which of the following was not a Gerry and Sylvia Anderson show featuring marionettes?

☐ 1. THUNDERBIRDS
☐ 2. SPACE PATROL
☐ 3. STINGRAY
☐ 4. SUPERCAR
☐ 5. FIREBALL XL-5

30

This late actor played the villain in the two-part BATMAN episode "A Piece of the Action/Batman's Satisfaction," which guest-starred Van Williams and Bruce Lee as the Green Hornet and Kato.

☐ 1. Roger C. Carmel
☐ 2. Cesar Romero
☐ 3. Otto Preminger
☐ 4. Julie Newmar
☐ 5. Van Williams

TELEVISION   20-POINT QUESTIONS

31 How many TV movies were made of THE INCREDIBLE HULK before the show went to series?

- ☐ 1. One
- ☐ 2. Two
- ☐ 3. None
- ☐ 4. Six
- ☐ 5. Three

32 The ONE STEP BEYOND episode "Night of April 14th" featured this future AVENGERS star.

- ☐ 1. Diana Rigg
- ☐ 2. Patrick MacNee
- ☐ 3. Joanna Lumley
- ☐ 4. Linda Thorson
- ☐ 5. Honor Blackman

33 Zak, Apollo's younger brother on BATTLESTAR GALACTICA, was played by this soap opera heartthrob-turned-rock-star.

- ☐ 1. Anthony Geary
- ☐ 2. Rick Springfield
- ☐ 3. Jack Wagner
- ☐ 4. John Wesley Shipp
- ☐ 5. David Hasselhoff

34 Before he became Oscar Goldman on THE SIX MILLION DOLLAR MAN, he terrorized Seattle residents in the 1973 telefilm THE NIGHT STRANGLER.

- ☐ 1. Monte Markham
- ☐ 2. Martin Caidin
- ☐ 3. Alex Cord
- ☐ 4. Richard Anderson
- ☐ 5. Richard Dean Anderson

35 This actor played villainous characters who had their plans ruined by Batman and the Man from Atlantis.

- ☐ 1. William Conrad
- ☐ 2. Vincent Price
- ☐ 3. Cliff Robertson
- ☐ 4. Laurette Spang
- ☐ 5. Victor Buono

36

Before starting her successful film career, she played Drusilla, WONDER WOMAN's younger sister.

- ☐ 1. Darryl Hannah
- ☐ 2. Demi Moore
- ☐ 3. Kirstie Alley
- ☐ 4. Debra Winger
- ☐ 5. Pamela Sue Martin

37

Before her role as Ursa in the first two SUPERMAN films, she guest-starred in the SPACE:1999 episode "The Chrysalis A-B-C."

- ☐ 1. Caroline Munro
- ☐ 2. Martine Beswick
- ☐ 3. Pamela Stephenson
- ☐ 4. Sarah Douglas
- ☐ 5. Carolyn Seymour

38

This 1950s comedic star appeared in the KOLCHAK: THE NIGHT STALKER episode "Horror in the Heights."

- ☐ 1. Sid Caesar
- ☐ 2. Soupy Sales
- ☐ 3. Milton Berle
- ☐ 4. Lenny Bruce
- ☐ 5. Phil Silvers

39

A one-time ambassador on the original STAR TREK, this actor was anything but diplomatic on PLANET OF THE APES.

- ☐ 1. Michael Ansara
- ☐ 2. Mark Lenard
- ☐ 3. William O'Connell
- ☐ 4. Arnold Moss
- ☐ 5. Michael J. Pollard

40

The 1974 telefilm TRILOGY OF TERROR was based on this author's stories.

- ☐ 1. William F. Nolan
- ☐ 2. Robert Bloch
- ☐ 3. Jeff Rice
- ☐ 4. Richard Matheson
- ☐ 5. Stephen J. Cannell

41

This 1973 pilot, created by STAR TREK's Gene
Roddenberry, is notable for the appearance of Mariette
Hartley as a woman with two belly buttons.

☐ 1. PLANET EARTH
☐ 2. SPECTRE
☐ 3. THE QUESTOR TAPES
☐ 4. GENESIS II
☐ 5. EARTH 2

42

This educational sci-fi series starred Jon-Erik Hexum as not-
too-bright time traveler Phineas Bogg.

☐ 1. TIME TUNNEL
☐ 2. WAY OUT
☐ 3. VOYAGERS
☐ 4. IT'S ABOUT TIME
☐ 5. COSMOS

43

After battling Ming the Merciless in 1980, this actor
donned the mask and trademark blue suit of Will Eisner's
THE SPIRIT in the 1987 ABC pilot.

☐ 1. Buster Crabbe
☐ 2. Gil Gerard
☐ 3. Brian Blessed
☐ 4. Sam Jones
☐ 5. Reb Brown

44

In which 1966 comedy series do two astronauts travel
back to the Stone Age?

☐ 1. FAR-OUT SPACE NUTS
☐ 2. THE LOST SAUCER
☐ 3. GOOD HEAVENS!
☐ 4. FANTASTIC JOURNEY
☐ 5. IT'S ABOUT TIME

45

Which SPACE: 1999 episode introduced Maya, the shape-
shifting crew member?

☐ 1. "Guardian of Piri"
☐ 2. "The Mark of Archanon"
☐ 3. "War Games"
☐ 4. "Dragon's Domain"
☐ 5. "The Metamorph"

46 McCLOUD's Dennis Weaver is chased across the desert by a crazed truck driver in this 1971 telefilm, directed by Steven Spielberg.

- ☐ 1. SHE WAITS
- ☐ 2. DUEL
- ☐ 3. DON'T BE AFRAID OF THE DARK
- ☐ 4. BLACK NOON
- ☐ 5. THE DEAD DON'T DIE

47 This well-known American historical battle was the basis for episodes of THE TIME TUNNEL and THE TWILIGHT ZONE.

- ☐ 1. Custer's last stand
- ☐ 2. American Revolution
- ☐ 3. Wounded Knee
- ☐ 4. Bull Run
- ☐ 5. Gettysburg

48 The composer of music for such films as BATMAN and EDWARD SCISSORHANDS, he also provided the themes for THE FLASH and TALES FROM THE CRYPT.

- ☐ 1. Danny Elfman
- ☐ 2. John Williams
- ☐ 3. James Horner
- ☐ 4. Jerry Goldsmith
- ☐ 5. John Barry

49 In the syndicated series HERCULES: THE LEGENDARY JOURNEYS, this actor, playing the title character, constantly foils the plans of Hera and Ares.

- ☐ 1. Lou Ferrigno
- ☐ 2. Steve Reeves
- ☐ 3. Kevin Sorbo
- ☐ 4. Kevin Spacey
- ☐ 5. Jaleel White

50 This miniseries, created by horror novelist Stephen King, concerned a 70-year-old janitor who becomes younger after an explosion at a government research facility.

- ☐ 1. THE LANGOLIERS
- ☐ 2. GOLDEN YEARS
- ☐ 3. THE STAND
- ☐ 4. IT
- ☐ 5. THE TOMMYKNOCKERS

30-POINT QUESTIONS

1

In which STAR TREK: THE NEXT GENERATION episode were the Borg first encountered?

- ☐ 1. "The Borg"
- ☐ 2. "Q Who"
- ☐ 3. "Invasion Earth"
- ☐ 4. "Booby Trap"
- ☐ 5. "The Machine Men"

2

He provided the voice of Orac on BLAKE'S 7.

- ☐ 1. Paul Darrow
- ☐ 2. William Shatner
- ☐ 3. Peter Tuddenham
- ☐ 4. Terry Nation
- ☐ 5. Tony Attwood

3

In BLAKE'S 7, the alien invasion fleet that threatened the galaxy came from where?

- ☐ 1. The Magellanic Cloud
- ☐ 2. Cygnus X-1
- ☐ 3. Andromeda
- ☐ 4. The far side of the galaxy
- ☐ 5. Mars

4

On THE X-FILES, what human body organ did Tooms need to eat in order to rejuvenate himself?

- ☐ 1. Heart
- ☐ 2. Kidney
- ☐ 3. Liver
- ☐ 4. Brain
- ☐ 5. None of these

5

What is found in the X-FILES episode "Ice?"

- ☐ 1. An alien parasite
- ☐ 2. A UFO
- ☐ 3. A frozen man
- ☐ 4. A frozen alien
- ☐ 5. Scully

TELEVISION   30-POINT QUESTIONS

6

This STAR TREK episode won the 1967 Dramatic Presentation Hugo Award.

☐ 1. "City on the Edge of Forever"
☐ 2. "The Doomsday Machine"
☐ 3. "Where No Man Has Gone Before"
☐ 4. "The Trouble with Tribbles"
☐ 5. "Devil in the Dark"

7

What happens to the astronauts in the TWILIGHT ZONE episode "And When the Sky Was Opened" after they return from their groundbreaking spaceflight?

☐ 1. They die.
☐ 2. They are lost in space.
☐ 3. They are eaten.
☐ 4. They disappear.
☐ 5. Nothing happens to them.

8

What DARK SHADOWS actor later became a regular on MACGYVER?

☐ 1. Richard Dean Anderson
☐ 2. Dana Elcar
☐ 3. Anthony George
☐ 4. Robert Gerringer
☐ 5. David Ford

9

On SLIDERS, what is the name of Quinn Mallory's cat?

☐ 1. Einstein
☐ 2. Robin
☐ 3. Newton
☐ 4. Schrodinger
☐ 5. Tabby

10

What do THE INCREDIBLE HULK TV series, the first V miniseries, the ALIEN NATION TV series, and THE BIONIC WOMAN have in common?

☐ 1. They all featured Lindsay Wagner.
☐ 2. They all had themes by Mike Post.
☐ 3. Kenneth Johnson developed all four of them.
☐ 4. They all aired on CBS.
☐ 5. Diane Frolov wrote the teleplays for the first episodes of all four.

11 Which costar of THE ADVENTURES OF BUCKEROO BANZAI IN THE 8TH DIMENSION would later star on EARTH 2?

- ☐ 1. Clancy Brown
- ☐ 2. Tim Curry
- ☐ 3. Jeff Goldblum
- ☐ 4. Vincent Schiavelli
- ☐ 5. Joey Zimmerman

12 This actor has played Superman's father, a seeker of the Holy Grail, and a Cardassian interrogator on three separate TV shows.

- ☐ 1. John Shea
- ☐ 2. David Warner
- ☐ 3. Marc Alaimo
- ☐ 4. Sean Connery
- ☐ 5. None of the above

13 Which character designed the voder that allows Darwin the dolphin on SEAQUEST DSV to communicate with the crew?

- ☐ 1. Lucas
- ☐ 2. Captain Bridger
- ☐ 3. Commander Ford
- ☐ 4. Lieutenant Commander Data
- ☐ 5. Dagwood

14 Who played the Mirror Master on THE FLASH?

- ☐ 1. John Wesley Shipp
- ☐ 2. Mark Hamill
- ☐ 3. Michael Nader
- ☐ 4. David Cassidy
- ☐ 5. Danny Elfman

15 Who played the title role in the 1978 TV movie DR. STRANGE?

- ☐ 1. Clyde Kusatsu
- ☐ 2. Peter Sellers
- ☐ 3. Peter Hooten
- ☐ 4. William Hootkins
- ☐ 5. John Mills

16

Which STAR TREK II: THE WRATH OF KHAN supporting actor had the title role in the short-lived series THE PHOENIX?

- ☐ 1. Laura Banks
- ☐ 2. Judson Scott
- ☐ 3. Paul Winfield
- ☐ 4. Kirstie Alley
- ☐ 5. Nichelle Nichols

17

Which star of BEAUTY AND THE BEAST cowrote the episode "Ashes, Ashes"?

- ☐ 1. Armin Shimerman
- ☐ 2. Linda Hamilton
- ☐ 3. John Amos
- ☐ 4. Roy Dotrice
- ☐ 5. Alex Gansa

18

Which future HILL STREET BLUES star guest-starred in the LOST IN SPACE episode "Collision of the Planets"?

- ☐ 1. Daniel J. Travanti
- ☐ 2. Megan Gallagher
- ☐ 3. Veronica Hamel
- ☐ 4. Charles Haid
- ☐ 5. Bruce Weitz

19

Which of the following episodes of THE OUTER LIMITS was shown in two parts?

- ☐ 1. "The Demon with a Glass Hand"
- ☐ 2. "Soldier"
- ☐ 3. "The Probe"
- ☐ 4. "The Inheritors"
- ☐ 5. THE OUTER LIMITS never aired a two-part episode.

20

The pilot episode of the 1995 revival of THE OUTER LIMITS, titled "Sandkings," was based on a novella by what author?

- ☐ 1. Melinda M. Snodgrass
- ☐ 2. Harlan Ellison
- ☐ 3. George R. R. Martin
- ☐ 4. Michael Cassut
- ☐ 5. Isaac Asimov

21 This man, famous for playing Dracula, guest-starred in the SPACE: 1999 episode "Earthbound."

☐ 1. Christopher Lee
☐ 2. Gary Oldman
☐ 3. Bela Lugosi
☐ 4. Boris Karloff
☐ 5. William Marshall

22 He wrote 11 of the 26 episodes of UFO.

☐ 1. Gerry Anderson
☐ 2. David Tomblin
☐ 3. Tony Barwick
☐ 4. Terence Feely
☐ 5. Michael Piller

23 This person was a regular on two genre TV comedies, QUARK and MORK AND MINDY.

☐ 1. Pam Dawber
☐ 2. Robin Williams
☐ 3. Richard Benjamin
☐ 4. Tim Thomerson
☐ 5. Konrad Janis

24 What science-fiction author and screenwriter was the story editor for LAND OF THE LOST?

☐ 1. Harlan Ellison
☐ 2. Larry Niven
☐ 3. David Gerrold
☐ 4. Isaac Asimov
☐ 5. Ben Bova

25 How many new episodes of RED DWARF were aired on the BBC in 1990?

☐ 1. Six
☐ 2. Three
☐ 3. One
☐ 4. Two
☐ 5. None

26 She was originally considered for the part of Batgirl on BATMAN, but the role went instead to Yvonne Craig.

- ☐ 1. Julie Newmar
- ☐ 2. Lee Meriwether
- ☐ 3. Joan Collins
- ☐ 4. Mary Ann Mobley
- ☐ 5. Teri Garr

27 He wrote many episodes of BATMAN, including the final one, as well as the pilot for the Lynda Carter WONDER WOMAN series.

- ☐ 1. Lorenzo Semple, Jr.
- ☐ 2. Stanley Ralph Ross
- ☐ 3. William Dozier
- ☐ 4. Sam Hamm
- ☐ 5. Peter David

28 This BUCK ROGERS regular guest-starred in the WONDER WOMAN episode "Judgment from Outer Space."

- ☐ 1. Gil Gerard
- ☐ 2. Erin Gray
- ☐ 3. Mel Blanc
- ☐ 4. Tim O'Connor
- ☐ 5. Michael Ansara

29 In the RED DWARF episode "Balance of Power," what exam does Lister take in order to become an officer?

- ☐ 1. The Astronavigation exam
- ☐ 2. The Engineering exam
- ☐ 3. The Cooking exam
- ☐ 4. The Security & Tactics exam
- ☐ 5. None of the above

30 A future member of John Carpenter's acting "troupe," he starred as a prosecutor in the ONE STEP BEYOND episode "The Confession."

- ☐ 1. Donald Pleasence
- ☐ 2. Ernest Borgnine
- ☐ 3. Kurt Russell
- ☐ 4. Lee Van Cleef
- ☐ 5. Harry Dean Stanton

31 This short-lived 1973 series was so bad that it was disowned by its creator, science-fiction writer Harlan Ellison.

- ☐ 1. HOLMES AND YO-YO
- ☐ 2. THE NEW PEOPLE
- ☐ 3. THE GIRL WITH SOMETHING EXTRA
- ☐ 4. GEMINI MAN
- ☐ 5. THE STARLOST

32 This future Catwoman was the robotic star of the 1964 series MY LIVING DOLL.

- ☐ 1. Eartha Kitt
- ☐ 2. Lee Meriwether
- ☐ 3. Julie Newmar
- ☐ 4. Michelle Pfeiffer
- ☐ 5. Adrienne Barbeau

33 This NIGHT GALLERY episode, based on a story by H. P. Lovecraft, involves a doctor and his rather odd method of staying alive.

- ☐ 1. "The Painted Mirror"
- ☐ 2. "Something in the Woodwork"
- ☐ 3. "Cool Air"
- ☐ 4. "The House"
- ☐ 5. "The Black Bag"

34 James Earl Jones and Estelle Parsons portrayed real-life UFO-abductees Barney and Betty Hill in this 1975 telefilm.

- ☐ 1. INTERRUPTED JOURNEY
- ☐ 2. COMMUNION
- ☐ 3. SOMETHING IS OUT THERE
- ☐ 4. PROJECT: UFO
- ☐ 5. THE UFO INCIDENT

35 ISIS was a live-action, Saturday morning CBS series that starred this actress as a schoolteacher-turned-goddess.

- ☐ 1. Lynda Carter
- ☐ 2. Cathy Lee Crosby
- ☐ 3. JoAnna Cameron
- ☐ 4. Deidre Hall
- ☐ 5. Jody Benson

36 The NIGHT GALLERY episode "Return of the Sorcerer" featured this classic horror actor.

☐ 1. John Carradine
☐ 2. Peter Cushing
☐ 3. Vincent Price
☐ 4. Boris Karloff
☐ 5. Dwight Frye

37 An oversized Portuguese man-of-war attacks the *Seaview* in this VOYAGE TO THE BOTTOM OF THE SEA episode.

☐ 1. "The Lobster Man"
☐ 2. "Secret of the Deep"
☐ 3. "Journey with Fear"
☐ 4. "No Escape from Death"
☐ 5. "Destroy Seaview!"

38 Currently the title of an Image Comics series, this was also the title of an unfinished 1988 pilot about four people with special abilities, written by Danny Bilson and Paul DeMeo of THE FLASH.

☐ 1. CYBERFORCE
☐ 2. WILDC.A.T.S.
☐ 3. WETWORKS
☐ 4. BRIGADE
☐ 5. SPAWN

39 This 1986 pilot starred future QUANTUM LEAPer Scott Bakula as a man who gains extraordinary powers by accidentally inhaling a strange gas.

☐ 1. INFILTRATOR
☐ 2. GEMINI MAN
☐ 3. THE INVISIBLE MAN
☐ 4. EXOMAN
☐ 5. I-MAN

40 This character in the STAR WARS universe made his first appearance in THE STAR WARS HOLIDAY SPECIAL.

☐ 1. Lando Calrissian
☐ 2. Yoda
☐ 3. Boba Fett
☐ 4. Jabba the Hutt
☐ 5. The Emperor

41 Better known as Uncle Tonoose on MAKE ROOM FOR DADDY, this actor guest-starred in the KOLCHAK: THE NIGHT STALKER episode "The Knightly Murders."

☐ 1. Hans Conried
☐ 2. Wally Cox
☐ 3. Danny Thomas
☐ 4. Telly Savalas
☐ 5. Carl Reiner

42 In an episode of the series THRILLER, Sir Guy pursues this notorious killer in the adaptation of a famous Robert Bloch story.

☐ 1. Genghis Khan
☐ 2. John Wilkes Booth
☐ 3. Bluebeard
☐ 4. Jack the Ripper
☐ 5. Dracula

43 He was the host of ONE STEP BEYOND.

☐ 1. Boris Karloff
☐ 2. Rod Serling
☐ 3. Leslie Stevens
☐ 4. Irwin Allen
☐ 5. John Newland

44 Remote-controlled by Jimmy Sparks, this robot was the star of a popular 1960s Japanese cartoon.

☐ 1. SPEED RACER
☐ 2. JOE 90
☐ 3. GIGANTOR
☐ 4. ASTRO BOY
☐ 5. MARINE BOY

45 Although it suffered from limited animation, this was the first cartoon series known for its disturbing use of superimposed human mouths on its characters' faces.

☐ 1. JOHNNY QUEST
☐ 2. LAND OF THE LOST
☐ 3. SPACE ANGEL
☐ 4. CLUTCH CARGO
☐ 5. ULTRA MAN

46 He was the campy BATMAN writer who later penned the equally campy 1980 movie FLASH GORDON.

- ☐ 1. Stanley Ralph Ross
- ☐ 2. Howie Horwitz
- ☐ 3. Stanford Sherman
- ☐ 4. Lorenzo Semple, Jr.
- ☐ 5. Charles Hoffman

47 As the White Ranger, this actor fights evil on THE MIGHTY MORPHIN POWER RANGERS.

- ☐ 1. Paul Freeman
- ☐ 2. Jason David Frank
- ☐ 3. David Yost
- ☐ 4. Johnny Yong Bosch
- ☐ 5. Steve Cardenas

48 Before his run-in with a deadly ALIEN, this actor sold his soul to the Devil in the KOLCHAK: THE NIGHT STALKER episode "The Devil's Platform."

- ☐ 1. Yaphet Kotto
- ☐ 2. Harry Dean Stanton
- ☐ 3. John Hurt
- ☐ 4. Tom Skerritt
- ☐ 5. Sigourney Weaver

49 This was the name of the robot that replaced the Human Torch in the 1978 FANTASTIC FOUR cartoon series.

- ☐ 1. Robby
- ☐ 2. Herbie
- ☐ 3. Kirby
- ☐ 4. Frankenstein, Jr.
- ☐ 5. Stanley

50 On STAR TREK: THE NEXT GENERATION, who played Q2, the Q-being responsible for Q's loss of powers and expulsion onto the *Enterprise* as a human?

- ☐ 1. John deLancie
- ☐ 2. Michael Keating
- ☐ 3. Corbin Bernsen
- ☐ 4. William Shatner
- ☐ 5. Paul Darrow

40-POINT QUESTIONS

1 Who led Kirk's trial board in the STAR TREK episode "Court-Martial"?

- ☐ 1. Commander Percy
- ☐ 2. Commander Pike
- ☐ 3. Commodore Williams
- ☐ 4. Commodore Stone
- ☐ 5. Admiral Kirk

2 In THE X-FILES, what was in "The Erlenmeyer Flask"?

- ☐ 1. An explosive
- ☐ 2. A virus
- ☐ 3. Alien DNA
- ☐ 4. An alien parasite
- ☐ 5. Nothing

3 In the STAR TREK episode "The Changeling," what alien probe did Nomad combine itself with to form a new entity?

- ☐ 1. Goliath
- ☐ 2. Tan Ru
- ☐ 3. Imipak
- ☐ 4. Fon Tor
- ☐ 5. Tek

4 In the STAR TREK episode "For the World Is Hollow and I Have Touched the Sky," what was the spaceship world called?

- ☐ 1. Daron
- ☐ 2. Yonada
- ☐ 3. Earth
- ☐ 4. Fro'nath
- ☐ 5. Dabo

5 This British series was derived from the title POLICE SURGEON.

- ☐ 1. DOCTOR WHO
- ☐ 2. THE AVENGERS
- ☐ 3. BLAKE'S 7
- ☐ 4. SAPPHIRE AND STEEL
- ☐ 5. SPACE PRECINCT

6 In THE INVADERS episode "The Miracle," Barbara Hershey played a girl who received a gift from the aliens. Who played her barkeeper father?

☐ 1. Ed Asner
☐ 2. Tony Curtis
☐ 3. Robert Vaughn
☐ 4. Jack Klugman
☐ 5. Roy Scheider

7 This Bajoran character was originally intended to be a regular STAR TREK: DEEP SPACE 9 cast member, but the actress playing her chose to decline.

☐ 1. Ro
☐ 2. Kira
☐ 3. Kai Opaka
☐ 4. Troi
☐ 5. Keiko

8 In the STAR TREK cartoon episode "The Lorelei Signal," this normally secondary character comes to the fore and takes control of the *Enterprise*.

☐ 1. Sulu
☐ 2. Chekov
☐ 3. Scotty
☐ 4. Uhura
☐ 5. McCoy

9 In the STAR TREK episode "The Alternative Factor," these would be destroyed if both halves of Lazarus actually met.

☐ 1. Both halves of Lazarus
☐ 2. Both universes that the two are from
☐ 3. Both halves of Lazarus and the universes
☐ 4. Neither Lazarus nor the universes
☐ 5. Nothing would be destroyed.

10 In a series of DARK SHADOWS episodes based on the works of H. P. Lovecraft, a race of superhuman extraterrestrials schemes to take over the world. What were they called?

☐ 1. The Titans
☐ 2. The Colossi
☐ 3. The Great Old Ones
☐ 4. The Deep Ones
☐ 5. The Leviathans

11

On DARK SHADOWS, what was the name of Satan's emissary on Earth who turned Angelique into a vampire?

- ☐ 1. Nicholas Blair
- ☐ 2. Aristede
- ☐ 3. Count Petofi
- ☐ 4. Judah Zachary
- ☐ 5. Jeb Hawkes

12

When Jeb Hawkes, one of the Leviathans, turns against his masters, what is sent to torment him until he dies?

- ☐ 1. A giant spider
- ☐ 2. A screaming ghost
- ☐ 3. An unseen creature whose presence is made known by its heavy breathing
- ☐ 4. A fire demon
- ☐ 5. A shadow demon

13

On SLIDERS, when activated, the wormhole stays open for one minute. How long would the travelers have to wait for the next wormhole if they missed one?

- ☐ 1. 24 hours
- ☐ 2. 72 hours
- ☐ 3. 6 days
- ☐ 4. 30 years
- ☐ 5. There will never be another one.

14

Aside from Mulder, what role is David Duchovny best known for?

- ☐ 1. Talk show host
- ☐ 2. Willie Lomax
- ☐ 3. Transvestite detective
- ☐ 4. Ghost psychologist
- ☐ 5. Batman

15

This 3-in-1 series of movie-serial-type programs included "The Curse of Dracula," "The Secret Empire," and "Stop Susan Williams" in its brief time on NBC; only "The Curse of Dracula" managed to reach its end before the series was canceled, however.

- ☐ 1. THRILLERS
- ☐ 2. THRILLOGY
- ☐ 3. CLIFF HANGERS
- ☐ 4. EDGE
- ☐ 5. MATINEE

16

This staff writer for THE SIX MILLION DOLLAR MAN would later go on to cowrite a Hugo Award-winning episode of STAR TREK: THE NEXT GENERATION, and serve as a story editor for STAR TREK: DEEP SPACE NINE in that show's second season.

☐ 1. Ira Steven Behr
☐ 2. Michael Piller
☐ 3. Peter Allan Fields
☐ 4. Ronald D. Moore
☐ 5. Gene Roddenberry

17

What was the name of the rabbi, played by Theodore Bikel, who sat *shiva* with Commander Ivanova for her father in the BABYLON 5 episode "TKO"?

☐ 1. Ivanov
☐ 2. Frants
☐ 3. Koslov
☐ 4. Romanov
☐ 5. Irinov

18

Which actor played the android Kryten on RED DWARF?

☐ 1. Brent Spiner
☐ 2. David Ross
☐ 3. Robert Llewellyn
☐ 4. All of the above
☐ 5. Ross and Llewellyn

19

What are the names of the twin sons that Dave Lister gives birth to between the second and third seasons of RED DWARF?

☐ 1. Mutt and Jeff
☐ 2. Romulus and Remus
☐ 3. Frick and Frack
☐ 4. Jim and Bexley
☐ 5. David and Goliath

20

Who wrote the theme music that ran over the closing credits to TEK WAR?

☐ 1. Marc Cohn
☐ 2. Warren Zevon
☐ 3. Sting
☐ 4. Mike Post
☐ 5. Dennis McCarthy

21 Which of the following is one of the small transport ships used on RED DWARF?

- ☐ 1. Starbug
- ☐ 2. White Midget
- ☐ 3. Blue Midget
- ☐ 4. All of the above
- ☐ 5. None of the above

22 What company was the primary sponsor of the CAPTAIN MIDNIGHT TV series?

- ☐ 1. Kellogg's Rice Krispies
- ☐ 2. Wheaties
- ☐ 3. Ovaltine
- ☐ 4. Metamucil
- ☐ 5. Blue Coal

23 Two former cast members of THE ADVENTURES OF BRISCO COUNTY JR. appeared on LOIS AND CLARK: THE NEW ADVENTURES OF SUPERMAN during its second season. One was star Bruce "Brisco" Campbell. Who was the other?

- ☐ 1. Julius Carry
- ☐ 2. Christian Clemenson
- ☐ 3. Comet
- ☐ 4. Bronson Pinchot
- ☐ 5. None of the above

24 He directed the last episode of STAR TREK: THE NEXT GENERATION and the first episode of STAR TREK: VOYAGER.

- ☐ 1. Rob Bowman
- ☐ 2. William Shatner
- ☐ 3. Winrich Kolbe
- ☐ 4. David Livingston
- ☐ 5. David Carson

25 This former DARK SHADOWS star guest-starred on an episode of PROBE as a doctor working with an intelligent ape.

- ☐ 1. Kathryn Leigh Scott
- ☐ 2. Ben Cross
- ☐ 3. Jonathan Frid
- ☐ 4. Marie Wallace
- ☐ 5. None of the above

26 What important piece of Immortal "etiquette" was established in the HIGHLANDER episode "Road Not Taken"?

☐ 1. Immortals may not bathe.
☐ 2. Immortals may fight on holy ground.
☐ 3. Immortals may not sell drugs.
☐ 4. Immortals may use guns.
☐ 5. Immortals may not kill innocents.

27 This regular BEAUTY AND THE BEAST writing team would go on to serve as coproducers on THE X-FILES.

☐ 1. Glen Morgan and James Wong
☐ 2. Howard Gordon and Alex Gansa
☐ 3. George R. R. Martin and Melinda M. Snodgrass
☐ 4. Ronald D. Moore and Brannon Braga
☐ 5. David Duchovny and Chris Carter

28 What Oscar winner directed the 1970 TV movie L.A. 2017?

☐ 1. Kevin Costner
☐ 2. Jonathan Demme
☐ 3. Steven Spielberg
☐ 4. Sydney Pollack
☐ 5. Francis Ford Coppola

29 This famous author was one of the writers for TOM CORBETT, SPACE CADET.

☐ 1. Robert A. Heinlein
☐ 2. Alfred Bester
☐ 3. Isaac Asimov
☐ 4. Harlan Ellison
☐ 5. Ben Bova

30 Who directed the last three episodes of THE ADVENTURES OF SUPERMAN in 1957?

☐ 1. Whitney Ellsworth
☐ 2. Lee Sholem
☐ 3. Robert Maxwell
☐ 4. George Reeves
☐ 5. Bernard Luber

31

In THE ADVENTURES OF SUPERMAN, this actor portrayed Uncle Oscar—a well-intentioned but misguided scientist—when he wasn't providing voices for Disney cartoons.

- ☐ 1. Clarence Nash
- ☐ 2. Gary Owens
- ☐ 3. Sterling Halloway
- ☐ 4. Charles Fleischer
- ☐ 5. Bud Collyer

32

In the 1950 series BUCK ROGERS, this was the location of the base from which Buck and Wilma Deering traveled.

- ☐ 1. New York City
- ☐ 2. Pittsburgh, PA
- ☐ 3. Niagara Falls, NY
- ☐ 4. Newark, NJ
- ☐ 5. Washington, DC

33

CAPTAIN VIDEO used this device to see through solid objects.

- ☐ 1. Cosmic vibrator
- ☐ 2. Opticon scillometer
- ☐ 3. X-ray specs
- ☐ 4. Kirlian bombarder
- ☐ 5. Vibrational agitator

34

In what year was TOM CORBETT, SPACE CADET set?

- ☐ 1. 2495
- ☐ 2. 1995
- ☐ 3. 2315
- ☐ 4. 2525
- ☐ 5. 2335

35

Before making the beaches a frightening place for moviegoers, Steven Spielberg scared home viewers with this 1970 telefilm about a possessed child.

- ☐ 1. SOMETHING EVIL
- ☐ 2. SWEET, SWEET RACHEL
- ☐ 3. DUEL
- ☐ 4. SANDCASTLES
- ☐ 5. THE STRANGER WITHIN

36 Before FRITZ THE CAT and COOL WORLD, this 1967 ABC cartoon series featured some of the earliest work of animation director Ralph Bakshi.

☐ 1. SPACE GHOST
☐ 2. MARVEL SUPER HEROES
☐ 3. THE HERCULOIDS
☐ 4. JOE 90
☐ 5. SPIDER-MAN

37 This VOYAGE TO THE BOTTOM OF THE SEA episode, written by Harlan Ellison, pitted the crew of the *Seaview* against a deadly plankton specimen.

☐ 1. "Doomsday"
☐ 2. "No Way Out"
☐ 3. "Submarine Sunk Here"
☐ 4. "Deadly Waters"
☐ 5. "The Price of Doom"

38 The star of the syndicated SUPERBOY series, he was replaced after the first season.

☐ 1. Gerard Christopher
☐ 2. Michael Callan
☐ 3. Ilan Michael-Smith
☐ 4. John Haymes Newton
☐ 5. John Rockwell

39 In a somewhat typecast role, this veteran horror actor appeared in the LAND OF THE GIANTS episode "Comeback."

☐ 1. Vincent Price
☐ 2. Boris Karloff
☐ 3. Peter Cushing
☐ 4. Glenn Strange
☐ 5. John Carradine

40 THE INVADERS' Roy Thinnes played a Carl Kolchak wannabe in this 1973 telefilm, written by LOGAN'S RUN creator William F. Nolan.

☐ 1. THE ROCKFORD FILES
☐ 2. THE NORLISS TAPES
☐ 3. THE QUESTOR TAPES
☐ 4. SEARCH FOR THE GODS
☐ 5. JOURNEY TO THE UNKNOWN

41 This future actor on STAR TREK: DEEP SPACE 9 appeared in "Spaced Out," an episode of THE NEW ADVENTURES OF WONDER WOMAN.

- ☐ 1. Marc Alaimo
- ☐ 2. Andrew Robinson
- ☐ 3. Siddig El Fadil
- ☐ 4. Terry Farrell
- ☐ 5. Rene Auberjonois

42 In this 1976–1977 Saturday morning series, Dracula, Wolfman, and the Frankenstein Monster united to battle crime.

- ☐ 1. DRAK PACK
- ☐ 2. MISFITS OF SCIENCE
- ☐ 3. MONSTER SQUAD
- ☐ 4. LITTLE MONSTERS
- ☐ 5. THE CHAMPIONS

43 Although he starred in the pilot for FOREVER KNIGHT— originally titled NICK KNIGHT—this actor was replaced before the syndicated series started production.

- ☐ 1. Lorenzo Lamas
- ☐ 2. Richard Hatch
- ☐ 3. Dirk Benedict
- ☐ 4. Geraint Wyn Davies
- ☐ 5. Rick Springfield

44 Syndicated in the U.S. in 1963, this popular Japanese cartoon was originally called MIGHTY ATOM.

- ☐ 1. ASTRO BOY
- ☐ 2. MARINE BOY
- ☐ 3. THUNDERBIRDS
- ☐ 4. JOE 90
- ☐ 5. ROBOTECH

45 Known for his "countdown" radio shows, this D.J. was the voice of Robin in both THE BATMAN/SUPERMAN HOUR and THE ADVENTURES OF BATMAN cartoon series.

- ☐ 1. Shadow Stevens
- ☐ 2. Wolfman Jack
- ☐ 3. Howard Stern
- ☐ 4. Cousin Bruce Morrow
- ☐ 5. Casey Kasem

46 What was the title of the pilot episode of THE MAN FROM ATLANTIS?

☐ 1. "The Siren"
☐ 2. "Scavenger Hunt"
☐ 3. "The Death Scouts"
☐ 4. "The Killer Spores"
☐ 5. "The Disappearance"

47 No longer tormenting BATMAN, this actor menaced the amazing Amazon in THE NEW ADVENTURES OF WONDER WOMAN episode "The Deadly Toys."

☐ 1. Frank Gorshin
☐ 2. Burgess Meredith
☐ 3. Cesar Romero
☐ 4. Otto Preminger
☐ 5. Art Carney

48 On which LAND OF THE GIANTS episode do *Spindrift* crew members travel back in time, to just before their disastrous spaceflight?

☐ 1. "A Place Called Earth"
☐ 2. "Comeback"
☐ 3. "Home Sweet Home"
☐ 4. "Six Hours to Live"
☐ 5. "Wild Journey"

49 What 1974 telefilm, about a woman giving birth to an extraterrestrial child, was written by Richard Matheson?

☐ 1. WHEN MICHAEL CALLS
☐ 2. THE STRANGER WITHIN
☐ 3. SHE WAITS
☐ 4. THE PEOPLE
☐ 5. LOOK WHAT'S HAPPENED TO ROSEMARY'S BABY

50 A succubus preys on college students in this KOLCHAK: THE NIGHT STALKER episode.

☐ 1. "Demon in Lace"
☐ 2. "The Youth Killer"
☐ 3. "The Energy Eater"
☐ 4. "Legacy of Terror"
☐ 5. "Bad Medicine"

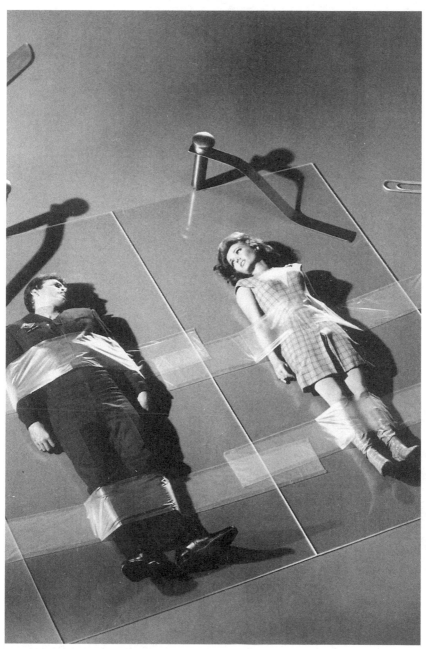

50-POINT QUESTIONS

1 Who was the captain of the *Enterprise* in the STAR TREK: THE NEXT GENERATION episode "Tapestry"?

- ☐ 1. Picard
- ☐ 2. Riker
- ☐ 3. Jameson
- ☐ 4. Halloway
- ☐ 5. Kirk

2 Where are the billion-year-old ruins in the STAR TREK: THE NEXT GENERATION episode "Qpid"?

- ☐ 1. Gamma Tauri
- ☐ 2. Gauda Prime
- ☐ 3. Tagus III
- ☐ 4. Bejor
- ☐ 5. Helix IV

3 In what STAR TREK: THE NEXT GENERATION episode was BUCKAROO BANZAI mentioned?

- ☐ 1. "Gateway"
- ☐ 2. "Tapestry"
- ☐ 3. "Timescape"
- ☐ 4. "Up the Long Ladder"
- ☐ 5. "Counter-Clock Incident"

4 In DOCTOR WHO, what was the end of the E-Space trilogy called?

- ☐ 1. "Full Circle"
- ☐ 2. "State of Decay"
- ☐ 3. "Warrior's Gate"
- ☐ 4. "The Zero Point"
- ☐ 5. "Logopolis"

5 What was the longest single DOCTOR WHO adventure?

- ☐ 1. "The Key to Time"
- ☐ 2. "The Invasion of Time"
- ☐ 3. "Genesis of the Daleks"
- ☐ 4. "The Dalek Masterplan"
- ☐ 5. "The War Games"

6 What well-known Hollywood makeup man provided the grotesque "old man" vampire makeup for Jonathan Frid in HOUSE OF DARK SHADOWS?

☐ 1. Dick Smith
☐ 2. Rob Bottin
☐ 3. Rick Baker
☐ 4. Jack Pierce
☐ 5. John Chambers

7 What famous writer visited the DARK SHADOWS set on the day of the taping of the final episode of the original series?

☐ 1. August Derleth
☐ 2. Neil Simon
☐ 3. William Peter Blatty
☐ 4. Joyce Carol Oates
☐ 5. Peter Benchley

8 In the "Asteroid Endangering Earth" episode of SLIDERS, what was Quinn's doppelganger working on instead of Sliding?

☐ 1. Teleportation
☐ 2. Anti-gravity
☐ 3. Faster-than-light travel
☐ 4. Cancer cure
☐ 5. Time travel

9 Where did the X-FILES production company get the name Ten Thirteen Productions?

☐ 1. The time the show was created
☐ 2. The date the show was created
☐ 3. FBI code for an X-file
☐ 4. The show's creator's birthday
☐ 5. CB code for "on the air"

10 What is the password on Mulder's home computer?

☐ 1. SAMANTHA
☐ 2. NOTALONE
☐ 3. SCULLY
☐ 4. TRUSTNO1
☐ 5. UNKNOWN

11 On LAND OF THE GIANTS, he played heroic Capt. Steve Burton, pilot of the lost craft that strayed into another dimension—where all the people were much, much bigger than Earthmen (though, oddly enough, they spoke English).

- ☐ 1. Don Matheson
- ☐ 2. Stefen Arngrim
- ☐ 3. Don Marshall
- ☐ 4. Gary Conway
- ☐ 5. Kurt Kaznar

12 On THE AVENGERS, who played "Mother," John Steed's boss?

- ☐ 1. Diana Rigg
- ☐ 2. Honor Blackman
- ☐ 3. Jon Rollason
- ☐ 4. Patrick Newell
- ☐ 5. Linda Thorson

13 When Rimmer on RED DWARF signs his name, what title does he add after his name?

- ☐ 1. Ph.D.
- ☐ 2. B.Sc., S.Sc.
- ☐ 3. D.D.S.
- ☐ 4. One Helluva Guy
- ☐ 5. M.B.A.

14 How many times has an actress played Marilyn Monroe (or a reasonable facsimile thereof) on RED DWARF?

- ☐ 1. Once
- ☐ 2. Twice
- ☐ 3. Thrice
- ☐ 4. Four times
- ☐ 5. Never

15 In which episode of THE TOMORROW PEOPLE did Peter Davison, best known as the fifth Doctor on DOCTOR WHO, guest-star?

- ☐ 1. "Worlds Away"
- ☐ 2. "The Medusa Strain"
- ☐ 3. "The Doomsday Men"
- ☐ 4. "The Secret Weapon"
- ☐ 5. "A Man for Emily"

16 Besides being one of the stable of STAR TREK directors, having directed episodes of THE NEXT GENERATION and DEEP SPACE NINE, veteran Alexander Singer also directed the second episode of what 1960s series?

☐ 1. STAR TREK
☐ 2. TIME TUNNEL
☐ 3. LOST IN SPACE
☐ 4. THE SIX MILLION DOLLAR MAN
☐ 5. THE TWILIGHT ZONE

17 The final episode of the short-lived British series MOON BASE 3 guest-starred what actor best known for playing BATMAN's butler Alfred?

☐ 1. Michael Gough
☐ 2. Alan Napier
☐ 3. Efrem Zimbalist, Jr.
☐ 4. Clive Revill
☐ 5. Nathan Lane

18 Who played the sexy Vena Ray on ROCKY JONES?

☐ 1. Erin Gray
☐ 2. Lynda Carter
☐ 3. Sally Mansfield
☐ 4. Jayne Mansfield
☐ 5. Catherine Schell

19 Who was the first kid sidekick on genre TV?

☐ 1. Robin
☐ 2. The Video Ranger
☐ 3. Kato
☐ 4. Kid Flash
☐ 5. None of the above

20 Which comic strip was the inspiration for a 1951 Dumont network TV series?

☐ 1. BUCK ROGERS
☐ 2. LI'L ABNER
☐ 3. TARZAN
☐ 4. PRINCE VALIANT
☐ 5. FLASH GORDON

21 BLAKE'S 7 star Gareth Thomas was also in which British genre TV production?

- ☐ 1. STAR MAIDENS
- ☐ 2. STAR COPS
- ☐ 3. MOON BASE 3
- ☐ 4. K9 AND COMPANY
- ☐ 5. PROBE

22 In the HIGHLANDER episode "For Evil's Sake," we learn that drinking absinthe over time does what to Immortals?

- ☐ 1. Makes them insane
- ☐ 2. Kills them
- ☐ 3. Eats holes in their livers
- ☐ 4. Causes leprosy
- ☐ 5. Has no effect whatsoever

23 A gesture used in which TV show was used by the Bester character played by Walter Koenig in the BABYLON 5 episode "Mind War"?

- ☐ 1. STAR TREK
- ☐ 2. THE PRISONER
- ☐ 3. MORK AND MINDY
- ☐ 4. BLAKE'S 7
- ☐ 5. THE OUTER LIMITS

24 What was the name of the Ranger played by Jack Weston in ROD BROWN?

- ☐ 1. Rod Brown
- ☐ 2. Frank Boyle
- ☐ 3. Cliff Robertson
- ☐ 4. Dudley Doright
- ☐ 5. Wilbur Wormsley

25 On what day of the week did SPACE ACADEMY run during the 1977–1978 season?

- ☐ 1. Monday
- ☐ 2. Tuesday
- ☐ 3. Thursday
- ☐ 4. Saturday
- ☐ 5. Sunday

26 In what TV season did the CBS series MEN IN SPACE air?

- ☐ 1. 1949–1950
- ☐ 2. 1951–1952
- ☐ 3. 1955–1956
- ☐ 4. 1957–1958
- ☐ 5. 1959–1960

27 Which STAR TREK producer wrote the screenplay for the 1970 TV movie CITY BENEATH THE SEA?

- ☐ 1. Gene L. Coon
- ☐ 2. Gene Roddenberry
- ☐ 3. D. C. Fontana
- ☐ 4. John Meredyth Lucas
- ☐ 5. Rick Berman

28 In the ROBOCOP episode "Provision 22," what does the acronym "the M.A.U.D. Squad" stand for?

- ☐ 1. Manpower Authority Utilization Department
- ☐ 2. Mothers Against Unsafe Driving
- ☐ 3. Men Against Uppity Dimwits
- ☐ 4. Machine-gun Armed Urban Devils
- ☐ 5. Merchants Against Underwriting Delta

29 Who starred with Richard Boone in the 1977 TV movie THE LAST DINOSAUR?

- ☐ 1. Catherine Schell
- ☐ 2. Heather Young
- ☐ 3. Joan Collins
- ☐ 4. Barbara Bain
- ☐ 5. Joan Van Ark

30 This producer of TOM CORBETT, SPACE CADET would move on to produce the anthology series TALES OF TOMORROW.

- ☐ 1. Mort Abrams
- ☐ 2. Rod Serling
- ☐ 3. Irwin Allen
- ☐ 4. Muriel Buckridge
- ☐ 5. Gerry Anderson

31 Who wrote the teleplay for the 1977 TV movie THE AMAZING SPIDER-MAN?

- ☐ 1. Stan Lee
- ☐ 2. Alvin Boretz
- ☐ 3. Nicholas Hammond
- ☐ 4. Ted Newsom
- ☐ 5. John Brancato

32 Who starred in the 1959 TV series WORLD OF GIANTS?

- ☐ 1. Marshall Thompson
- ☐ 2. Jack Palance
- ☐ 3. Lee Majors
- ☐ 4. Jack Klugman
- ☐ 5. Martin Landau

33 This recurring character actor on THE ADVENTURES OF SUPERMAN played such memorable hoodlums as Lefty, Carni, and Leftover Louie.

- ☐ 1. Herb Vigran
- ☐ 2. Paul Burke
- ☐ 3. Ben Welden
- ☐ 4. Tommy Carr
- ☐ 5. James Craven

34 In THE TIME TUNNEL episode "The Night of the Long Knives," what famous author is met by the time travelers?

- ☐ 1. Arthur Conan Doyle
- ☐ 2. Robert E. Howard
- ☐ 3. Oscar Wilde
- ☐ 4. Joseph Conrad
- ☐ 5. Rudyard Kipling

35 The 1955 syndicated series JET JACKSON, FLYING COMMANDO was also known by this title.

- ☐ 1. CAPTAIN VIDEO
- ☐ 2. COMMANDO CODY
- ☐ 3. CAPTAIN MIDNIGHT
- ☐ 4. CAPTAIN Z-RO
- ☐ 5. SPACE PATROL

36 In 1967, Monte Markham starred in this short-lived NBC series about an Alaskan gold prospector trapped in a glacier in 1900 and thawed out in 1967.

☐ 1. THE SIXTH SENSE
☐ 2. THE SECOND HUNDRED YEARS
☐ 3. STRANGE PARADISE
☐ 4. THE NEW PEOPLE
☐ 5. MY WORLD AND WELCOME TO IT

37 Richard Crane, wearing a baseball cap, T-shirt, and striped pants played the title character of this 1953 syndicated SF series.

☐ 1. ROD BROWN OF THE ROCKET RANGERS
☐ 2. SPACE PATROL
☐ 3. MR. TERRIFIC
☐ 4. THE MAN AND THE CHALLENGE
☐ 5. ROCKY JONES, SPACE RANGER

38 Widely known for his acting on THE MARY TYLER MOORE SHOW, this actor, from 1967–1969, was the voice of the cartoon AQUAMAN.

☐ 1. Ed Asner
☐ 2. Gavin MacLeod
☐ 3. John Amos
☐ 4. Ted Knight
☐ 5. David Groh

39 In this OUTER LIMITS episode, a couple is pursued by tumbleweeds controlled by an alien intelligence.

☐ 1. "The Probe"
☐ 2. "Fun and Games"
☐ 3. "The Invisible Energy"
☐ 4. "Cry of Silence"
☐ 5. "Tourist Attraction"

40 This actor starred in the 1975 telefilm adaptation of DRACULA, which was produced by Dan Curtis, producer of DARK SHADOWS and THE NIGHT STALKER.

☐ 1. Louis Jourdan
☐ 2. Jack Palance
☐ 3. Alex Cord
☐ 4. Fritz Weaver
☐ 5. Jonathan Frid

41 Which OUTER LIMITS episode deals with a device that can "tilt time" and bring the dead back to life?

☐ 1. "Keeper of the Purple Twilight"
☐ 2. "The Special One"
☐ 3. "Controlled Experiment"
☐ 4. "The Forms of Things Unknown"
☐ 5. "It Crawled out of the Woodwork"

42 Which THRILLER episode deals with a woman who unknowingly carries a bomb in her handbag, placed there by a psychopath?

☐ 1. "Choose a Victim"
☐ 2. "The Fingers of Fear"
☐ 3. "Girl with a Secret"
☐ 4. "The Fatal Impulse"
☐ 5. "The Innocent Bystanders"

43 In THE INVADERS episode "The Mutation," this actress played a nightclub stripper who doesn't know that she is actually one of the aliens.

☐ 1. Diane Baker
☐ 2. Joanne Linville
☐ 3. Lynn Loring
☐ 4. Diana Hyland
☐ 5. Suzanne Pleshette

44 Which short-lived 1960s animated series, created by Ralph Bakshi, was a send-up of superhero teams?

☐ 1. FRANKENSTEIN JR. AND THE IMPOSSIBLES
☐ 2. THE MIGHTY HEROES
☐ 3. BIRDMAN AND THE GALAXY TRIO
☐ 4. THE HERCULOIDS
☐ 5. THE WAY-OUTS

45 Which SPACE: 1999 episode was written by DOCTOR WHO scripter Terence Dicks?

☐ 1. "Space Warp"
☐ 2. "New Adam, New Eve"
☐ 3. "Breakaway"
☐ 4. "Voyager's Return"
☐ 5. "The Lambda Factor"

46 Comedian George Carlin appears as a vampire hunter in this NIGHT GALLERY episode.

- ☐ 1. "A Feast of Blood"
- ☐ 2. "The Devil Is Not Mocked"
- ☐ 3. "Clean Kills and Other Trophies"
- ☐ 4. "How to Cure the Common Vampire"
- ☐ 5. "Midnight Never Ends"

47 This term was used by OUTER LIMITS producer Joseph Stefano to describe the monsters used in each episode.

- ☐ 1. Monsters
- ☐ 2. Bears
- ☐ 3. Creatures
- ☐ 4. Predators
- ☐ 5. Rube Goldbergs

48 A pilot for a never-launched series, this 1975 telefilm dealt with scientists going back in time to prevent the legendary Great Chicago Fire.

- ☐ 1. THE NIGHT THAT PANICKED AMERICA
- ☐ 2. HAUSER'S MEMORY
- ☐ 3. ATOM SQUAD
- ☐ 4. THE TIME TRAVELERS
- ☐ 5. FANTASTIC JOURNEY

49 A talented character actor, he played editor in chief Tony Vincenzo in THE NIGHT STALKER, THE NIGHT STRANGLER, and KOLCHAK: THE NIGHT STALKER.

- ☐ 1. Eric Braeden
- ☐ 2. Jack Grinnage
- ☐ 3. John Fiedler
- ☐ 4. Darren McGavin
- ☐ 5. Simon Oakland

50 Host John Newland and producer Collier Young appear in this ONE STEP BEYOND episode, in which they experiment with a catalyst that affects an individual's ESP powers.

- ☐ 1. "The Peter Hurkos Story"
- ☐ 2. "The Forests of the Night"
- ☐ 3. "The Secret"
- ☐ 4. "Premonition"
- ☐ 5. "The Sacred Mushroom"

SCIENCE FICTION

Comics

TRIVIA QUIZ

10-POINT QUESTIONS

1

After the 1993 "Death of Superman" storyline, four people briefly took on the mantle of Superman before the genuine article was resurrected. Which one of them was in truth the Eradicator, a Kryptonian villain?

- ☐ 1. The "Last Son of Krypton"
- ☐ 2. Steel
- ☐ 3. Superboy
- ☐ 4. The cyborg Superman
- ☐ 5. None of the above

2

Before becoming Robin, the Boy Wonder, Dick Grayson was which of the following?

- ☐ 1. A circus acrobat
- ☐ 2. A clown
- ☐ 3. A child movie star
- ☐ 4. A crippled newsboy
- ☐ 5. Mascot of an armored regiment

3

Besides her own title, Wonder Woman was the lead feature in what Golden Age title?

- ☐ 1. NATIONAL COMICS
- ☐ 2. SENSATION COMICS
- ☐ 3. ALL-AMERICAN COMICS
- ☐ 4. ADVENTURE COMICS
- ☐ 5. BLUE RIBBON COMICS

4

Cloak and Dagger's powers were triggered by _____ .

- ☐ 1. Radiation
- ☐ 2. Darkness
- ☐ 3. Doctor Doom
- ☐ 4. Drugs
- ☐ 5. Mail order

5

Due to what ailment did Tony Stark turn over the Iron Man armor to his friend Jim Rhodes (now known as War Machine) in IRON MAN #167?

- ☐ 1. Chronic Fatigue Syndrome
- ☐ 2. Alcoholism
- ☐ 3. Epstein-Barr Syndrome
- ☐ 4. Heart failure
- ☐ 5. Overeating

6

E.C.'s science-fiction titles, WEIRD SCIENCE and WEIRD FANTASY, were never very profitable; they were eventually combined into a single title to save money. What was the ultimate name of that title?

☐ 1. INCREDIBLE SCIENCE FICTION
☐ 2. SPACE ADVENTURES
☐ 3. SHOCK SUSPENSTORIES
☐ 4. WEIRD TALES OF THE FUTURE
☐ 5. WEIRD SCIENCE-FANTASY

7

Frank Thorne gained prominence providing the illustrations for a comic based on which Robert E. Howard character?

☐ 1. Conan the Barbarian
☐ 2. Red Sonja
☐ 3. Kull the Conqueror
☐ 4. Ghita of Alizarr
☐ 5. Batman

8

In 1954, a psychiatrist named Dr. Frederic Wertham published a best-selling book that denounced "crime comics" as a major cause of juvenile delinquency. What was the title?

☐ 1. LOVE AND DEATH
☐ 2. SHOW OF VIOLENCE
☐ 3. PARADE OF PLEASURE
☐ 4. SEDUCTION OF THE INNOCENT
☐ 5. BEHIND THE MASK

9

What does "E.C." stand for?

☐ 1. Exciting Comics
☐ 2. Educational Comics
☐ 3. Entertaining Comics
☐ 4. Both "Exciting Comics" and "Educational Comics"
☐ 5. Both "Entertaining Comics" and "Educational Comics"

10

His comic strips spoofed technology and added a phrase to the English language.

☐ 1. Rube Goldberg
☐ 2. Charles Schulz
☐ 3. Jack Kerouac
☐ 4. Matt Groening
☐ 5. Alfred E. Newman

11 In how many parts was THE DARK KNIGHT RETURNS series?

☐ 1. One
☐ 2. Two
☐ 3. Three
☐ 4. Four
☐ 5. Five

12 In England, MIRACLEMAN was published under a different name. What was it?

☐ 1. Captain Marvel
☐ 2. Shazam
☐ 3. Marvelman
☐ 4. Captain Britain
☐ 5. Big Ben

13 In what comic book did ELFQUEST make its first appearance?

☐ 1. ELFQUEST
☐ 2. CEREBUS
☐ 3. DESTROYER DUCK
☐ 4. EPIC MAGAZINE
☐ 5. FANTASY QUARTERLY

14 What was Jim Lee's Image comic book?

☐ 1. YOUNGBLOOD
☐ 2. WILDC.A.T.S.
☐ 3. SPAWN
☐ 4. THE X-MEN
☐ 5. CYBERFORCE

15 Little Lulu entertained her friends with stories about an evil witch by the name of Witch Hazel, and a little-girl witch. What was the young witch's name?

☐ 1. Wendy
☐ 2. Witchypoo
☐ 3. Little Eva
☐ 4. Iodine
☐ 5. Little Itch

16   Ms. Marvel lost her powers to whom?

☐ 1. Mystique
☐ 2. Rogue
☐ 3. Doctor Doom
☐ 4. Silver Surfer
☐ 5. Namorita

17   Stan Lee collaborated with which artist on Spider-Man's first appearance in AMAZING FANTASY #15 in 1962?

☐ 1. Jack Kirby
☐ 2. Steve Ditko
☐ 3. Todd MacFarlane
☐ 4. Don Heck
☐ 5. Joe Sinnott

18   Who was the artist who roughed out the cover for AMAZING FANTASY #15?

☐ 1. Steve Ditko
☐ 2. Dick Ayers
☐ 3. Jack Kirby
☐ 4. Dan Adkins
☐ 5. Don Heck

19   TEENAGE MUTANT NINJA TURTLES cocreator Kevin Eastman founded this comic book company to support and publish new comics.

☐ 1. Mirage
☐ 2. Valiant
☐ 3. Kitchen Sink
☐ 4. Metal Mammoth
☐ 5. Tundra

20   The original run of this comic had scripts by science-fiction writers like Alfred Bester and Henry Kuttner.

☐ 1. SUPERMAN
☐ 2. BATMAN
☐ 3. THE AMAZING SPIDER-MAN
☐ 4. GREEN LANTERN
☐ 5. THE SHADOW

21

The slogan "Humor in a jugular vein" is associated with which comic magazine?

☐ 1. CRACK'D
☐ 2. MAD
☐ 3. SPY
☐ 4. THE SAVAGE SWORD OF CONAN
☐ 5. SPIDER-MAN MAGAZINE

22

Who brought The Spectre back from the dead and gave him his powers?

☐ 1. The god Apollo
☐ 2. The ghosts of a hundred murdered innocents
☐ 3. A mysterious voice
☐ 4. A scientist named Dr. Horton
☐ 5. Tibetan monks

23

This ancient barbarian hero got his start in a series of fantasy stories by Robert E. Howard.

☐ 1. Conan
☐ 2. Asterix
☐ 3. Tarzan
☐ 4. Beavis
☐ 5. Howard the Duck

24

Tony Stark was a veteran of what war?

☐ 1. WWI
☐ 2. WWII
☐ 3. Korea
☐ 4. Vietnam
☐ 5. Afghanistan

25

What Batman classic tale featured a female Robin?

☐ 1. VENOM
☐ 2. THE DARK KNIGHT RETURNS
☐ 3. BATMAN RETURNS
☐ 4. BATMAN FOREVER
☐ 5. GOTHAM BY GASLIGHT

26 What comic book barbarian was Cerebus originally based upon?

- ☐ 1. Kull
- ☐ 2. Conan
- ☐ 3. Tarzan
- ☐ 4. Korak
- ☐ 5. John Carter

27 Which DC character has never been made into a live-action TV series?

- ☐ 1. Batman
- ☐ 2. Superman
- ☐ 3. Superboy
- ☐ 4. The Flash
- ☐ 5. The Green Lantern

28 What famous comedian is Lord Julius, from the pages of CEREBUS, based on?

- ☐ 1. Jerry Lewis
- ☐ 2. Charlie Chaplin
- ☐ 3. Red Skelton
- ☐ 4. George Burns
- ☐ 5. Groucho Marx

29 What was the name of Captain America's first partner?

- ☐ 1. Bucky
- ☐ 2. Star-Spangled Kid
- ☐ 3. Namor, the Sub-Mariner
- ☐ 4. Toro
- ☐ 5. The Human Torch

30 What planet did J'onn J'onzz come from?

- ☐ 1. Earth
- ☐ 2. Uranus
- ☐ 3. Mercury
- ☐ 4. Mars
- ☐ 5. Jupiter

31 What unique weapon did Phantom Lady use?

☐ 1. The Cosmic Rod
☐ 2. A gas gun
☐ 3. An invisible boomerang
☐ 4. A magic lasso
☐ 5. A blackout ray

32 What word is on Stan Lee's calling card?

☐ 1. Excellent
☐ 2. Tremendous
☐ 3. Tubular
☐ 4. Excelsior
☐ 5. Spectacular

33 Where did Wonder Woman come from?

☐ 1. The planet Amazonia
☐ 2. A lost world deep inside Earth
☐ 3. Blackhawk Island
☐ 4. The distant past, by way of suspended animation
☐ 5. Paradise Island

34 Which of the following companies has published a comic book based on one of the STAR TREK TV series?

☐ 1. DC Comics
☐ 2. Marvel Comics
☐ 3. Gold Key
☐ 4. Malibu Comics
☐ 5. All of the above

35 Who is Elongated Man's wife?

☐ 1. Mary
☐ 2. Jane
☐ 3. Sue
☐ 4. Cheryl
☐ 5. Ann

36 Who was Denny Colt?

☐ 1. The Spirit
☐ 2. The Spook
☐ 3. Deadman
☐ 4. The Destroyer
☐ 5. The Avenger

37 Who was the comics' first female superhero?

☐ 1. Power Girl
☐ 2. Supergirl
☐ 3. Mary Marvel
☐ 4. Miss America
☐ 5. Wonder Woman

38 Who was the first god to join the Marvel pantheon?

☐ 1. Hercules
☐ 2. Odin
☐ 3. Zeus
☐ 4. Thor
☐ 5. Loki

39 Who was the pioneering cartoonist responsible for LITTLE NEMO IN SLUMBERLAND?

☐ 1. Garry Trudeau
☐ 2. Milton Caniff
☐ 3. Al Capp
☐ 4. Winsor McCay
☐ 5. E. C. Segar

40 Who was Vance Astro?

☐ 1. A butler
☐ 2. A hero from an alternate timeline
☐ 3. A villain from the past
☐ 4. An alien
☐ 5. A taxi driver

41

_____ began as a radio show.

☐ 1. The Green Lantern
☐ 2. The Green Hornet
☐ 3. The Jolly Green Giant
☐ 4. Green Arrow
☐ 5. Green Bean

42

_____ was the first comic to spoof TV, films, and even other comics.

☐ 1. PLOP!
☐ 2. CRACKED
☐ 3. CRAZED
☐ 4. MAD
☐ 5. NUTS

43

This Disney artist, known as "the good Duck artist," influenced many comics artists and writers, including Stan Lee.

☐ 1. Carl Barks
☐ 2. Chuck Jones
☐ 3. Walt Disney
☐ 4. Ron Disney
☐ 5. Walter Lantz

44

The underground comic movement began with his work on ZAP and SNATCH. More recently he's been the subject of a movie, and his characters have been used in computer programs.

☐ 1. Robert Crumb
☐ 2. Joe Eisenberg
☐ 3. Barry Blair
☐ 4. Howard Williams
☐ 5. None of these

45

This artist worked on LITTLE ANNIE FANNY for PLAYBOY; his work for EC included such memorable pieces as "Outer Sanctum" for MAD.

☐ 1. William Elder
☐ 2. Gil Kane
☐ 3. Jim Lee
☐ 4. Frank Kelly Freas
☐ 5. None of these

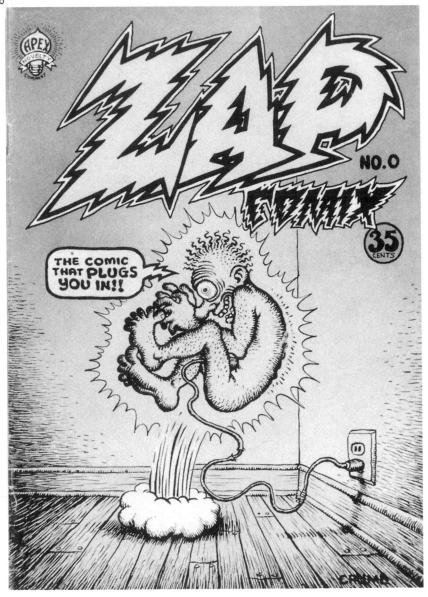

46   Name the artist who drew the definitive TARZAN strip in the 1930s. (His attention to detail has influenced several generations of comic book artists and illustrators.)

☐ 1. Hal Foster
☐ 2. Gil Kane
☐ 3. Burne Hogarth
☐ 4. Wally Wood
☐ 5. Frank Frazetta

47   This artist, also known as Paul Earrol, created the Golden Age heroes Arrow, Black Panther, A-Man, and The Jester. He was known for his ability to produce lots of good art, fast.

☐ 1. Carl Barks
☐ 2. Paul Gustavson
☐ 3. Mark Rimple
☐ 4. Paul Simon
☐ 5. Lou Fine

48   Many of the important Golden Age artists got their start in his and Will Eisner's "shop."

☐ 1. Jerry Iger
☐ 2. Burne Hogarth
☐ 3. Mike Grell
☐ 4. Carl Barks
☐ 5. Walter Fox

49   Of all the comic artists to appear during the 1980s, he has had the most varied career: a Levi's 501 commercial, coplotting X-FORCE #1, and appearing on THE DENNIS MILLER SHOW.

☐ 1. Erik Larsen
☐ 2. Rob Liefeld
☐ 3. Frank Miller
☐ 4. Klaus R. Janson
☐ 5. Todd MacFarlane

50   This innovative French artist cofounded METAL HURLANT, a comic that ran groundbreaking SF and fantasy stories like "Arzach" and "The Airtight Garage."

☐ 1. Ghastly
☐ 2. Moebius
☐ 3. Gil Kane
☐ 4. Arturo
☐ 5. M. DeMille

20-POINT QUESTIONS

1

An aviator, shot down in combat, crashed into a Polish swamp and emerged as a misshapen monster known as _____ .

- ☐ 1. Blackhawk
- ☐ 2. Red Dragon
- ☐ 3. The Heap
- ☐ 4. The Thing
- ☐ 5. The Crypt Keeper

2

An issue of which title from DC Comics' Vertigo imprint won a World Fantasy Award for Best Short Story?

- ☐ 1. SANDMAN MYSTERY THEATRE
- ☐ 2. HELLBLAZER
- ☐ 3. SWAMP THING
- ☐ 4. ANIMAL MAN
- ☐ 5. THE SANDMAN

3

Blastaar was a native of _____ .

- ☐ 1. The Negative Zone
- ☐ 2. The Dark Planet
- ☐ 3. The fourth dimension
- ☐ 4. Jupiter
- ☐ 5. Andromeda

4

Who is Bob Burden's esoteric superhero who encounters everything from Martians to mail-order brides?

- ☐ 1. Madman
- ☐ 2. Flaming Carrot
- ☐ 3. Gnatrat
- ☐ 4. The Tick
- ☐ 5. Roachmill

5

Captain Marvel spent several issues battling an evil genius known as Mr. Mind. What did Mr. Mind turn out to be?

- ☐ 1. A computer
- ☐ 2. A little kid
- ☐ 3. A talking tiger
- ☐ 4. A worm
- ☐ 5. A dwarf

6 Casper the Friendly Ghost has a ghost horse for a friend; what is her name?

- [ ] 1. Wendy
- [ ] 2. Susie
- [ ] 3. Silver
- [ ] 4. Buttercup
- [ ] 5. Nightmare

7 Comic book publishers of the late Golden Age were always looking for new genres to try, and experimented with several peculiar hybrids. Which of the following is NOT a real title?

- [ ] 1. MONSTER CRIME (combining crime and horror)
- [ ] 2. SPACE WESTERN (combining Western and sci-fi)
- [ ] 3. SADDLE ROMANCES (combining romance and Western)
- [ ] 4. TERRORS OF THE JUNGLE (combining horror and jungle stories)
- [ ] 5. FUTURE LOVE (combining sci-fi and romance)

8 Who was the creator of the first nonunderground hardcore XXX comic book, BLACK KISS?

- [ ] 1. Robert Crumb
- [ ] 2. Frank Miller
- [ ] 3. Barry Blair
- [ ] 4. Reed Waller
- [ ] 5. Howard Chaykin

9 Eel O'Brien, a petty crook, eventually wound up as which superhero?

- [ ] 1. Bulletman
- [ ] 2. The Hangman
- [ ] 3. The Shadow
- [ ] 4. Captain Aero
- [ ] 5. Plastic Man

10 Lev Gleason created an entire new genre of comics when he transformed SILVER STREAK COMICS into this 1942 hit title.

- [ ] 1. CRIME DOES NOT PAY
- [ ] 2. CRIME AND PUNISHMENT
- [ ] 3. TALES FROM THE CRYPT
- [ ] 4. WESTERN ADVENTURES
- [ ] 5. BLACK DIAMOND WESTERN

11   In comics, Asterix is best known as one of these.

☐ 1. A punctuation mark
☐ 2. A Gaul
☐ 3. A ghost
☐ 4. A dog
☐ 5. A Druid

12   In the 1980s, why did Superman leave Earth for outer space?

☐ 1. Exploration
☐ 2. A goodwill tour
☐ 3. To save an alien planet from a destruction similar to that of Krypton
☐ 4. He feared for his sanity.
☐ 5. To find Mon-El

13   In the 1970s, who actually raced each other?

☐ 1. Aquaman and Aqualad
☐ 2. Green Lantern and Superman
☐ 3. Wonder Woman and Batman (in their airplanes)
☐ 4. Superman and The Flash
☐ 5. Green Lantern and The Flash

14   In the 1970s, who gave the JIMMY OLSEN comic a whole new feel?

☐ 1. Julius Schwartz
☐ 2. Bob Kane
☐ 3. Jim Shooter
☐ 4. Jack Kirby
☐ 5. Mort Weisinger

15   In what comic book did Grendel, by Matt Wagner, first appear?

☐ 1. MEGATON
☐ 2. DESTROYER DUCK
☐ 3. NEW TALENT SHOWCASE
☐ 4. COMICO PRIMER
☐ 5. SOLSTON'S TALENT SEARCH

16 Jack Tenrec of XENOZOIC TALES is the last practitioner of what occupation?

- ☐ 1. Surgeon
- ☐ 2. Dentist
- ☐ 3. Mechanic
- ☐ 4. Gunsmith
- ☐ 5. Painter

17 Jamie and Gilbert Hernandez spawned a new genre of comic books with their LOVE AND ROCKETS. What is it?

- ☐ 1. Adult XXX
- ☐ 2. Splatterpunk
- ☐ 3. Slice of life
- ☐ 4. Hispanic
- ☐ 5. Euro sci-fi

18 Which artist created Marvel's first superhero character, the Sub-Mariner, who debuted in 1939?

- ☐ 1. Will Eisner
- ☐ 2. Jack Kirby
- ☐ 3. Joe Simon
- ☐ 4. Alex Schomburg
- ☐ 5. Bill Everett

19 Scott McCloud's ZOT is derivitive of what country's artistic influence and quick descriptive style?

- ☐ 1. France
- ☐ 2. Greece
- ☐ 3. Japan
- ☐ 4. Hungary
- ☐ 5. Argentina

20 Batman's 1995 sidekick, Robin, is a teenager named Tim Drake, the third boy to be Batman's sidekick. What was the name of the second?

- ☐ 1. Bruce Wayne
- ☐ 2. Dick Grayson
- ☐ 3. Burt Ward
- ☐ 4. Jack Monroe
- ☐ 5. Jason Todd

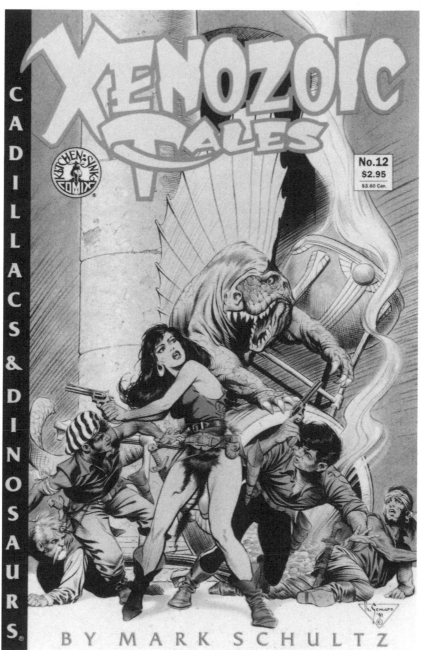

21 The earliest comic books included stories of many kinds. What genre was the first specialized comic devoted to?

☐ 1. Westerns
☐ 2. Superheroes
☐ 3. Romance
☐ 4. Detective stories
☐ 5. Science fiction

22 The founding members of the AVENGERS included Ant-Man, the Wasp, Iron Man, Thor, and _____.

☐ 1. The Hulk
☐ 2. Captain America
☐ 3. Wonder Man
☐ 4. Superman
☐ 5. Captain Marvel

23 The Vision was married to whom?

☐ 1. Scarlet Witch
☐ 2. Black Widow
☐ 3. Sheena
☐ 4. Jocasta
☐ 5. Wasp

24 This underground artist often signed his name as "Gore."

☐ 1. Richard Corben
☐ 2. Grass Green
☐ 3. Lee Marrs
☐ 4. Robert Williams
☐ 5. Tom Veitch

25 To avoid confusion with the Marvel comic, Eclipse's 1990s comic based on THE AVENGERS TV series was called what?

☐ 1. STEED AND MRS. PEEL
☐ 2. STEED AND KING
☐ 3. BOWLER HATS AND UMBRELLAS
☐ 4. THE REVENGERS
☐ 5. SECRET AGENTS

AVENGERS © 1968 Marvel Comics Group

26 What comics artist most influenced the early work of Dave Sim in CEREBUS?

☐ 1. Barry Smith
☐ 2. Jack Kirby
☐ 3. Neal Adams
☐ 4. John Buscema
☐ 5. Irv Novick

27 What group of villains destroyed the Avengers' mansion?

☐ 1. The Fearsome Four
☐ 2. The Masters of Evil
☐ 3. The Wrecking Crew
☐ 4. The Black Widowers
☐ 5. The Suicide Squad

28 What is the former occupation of Concrete?

☐ 1. Journalist
☐ 2. Firefighter
☐ 3. Police officer
☐ 4. Speechwriter
☐ 5. Building foundation

29 What is the real name of the Milestone superhero Static?

☐ 1. Arnus
☐ 2. Augustus Freeman IV
☐ 3. Curtis Metcalfe
☐ 4. Virgil Ovid Hawkins
☐ 5. Clark Kent

30 What is the Tick's battle cry?

☐ 1. "Charge!"
☐ 2. "Spoon!"
☐ 3. "Gott in Himmel!"
☐ 4. "Yee-Ha!"
☐ 5. "Acha-cha-cha!"

31 What is the weapon of choice used by the early incarnations of Grendel?

- ☐ 1. Spear
- ☐ 2. Sword
- ☐ 3. Pistol
- ☐ 4. Chainsaw
- ☐ 5. Fork

32 What is Wolverine's real name?

- ☐ 1. Joe Mundane
- ☐ 2. Fred
- ☐ 3. Kitty
- ☐ 4. Otto
- ☐ 5. Logan

33 What makes the Silver Age Atom so powerful?

- ☐ 1. Spinach
- ☐ 2. He only picks on villains his own size.
- ☐ 3. He has an atomic punch.
- ☐ 4. He can control his weight as well as his mass.
- ☐ 5. He can control gravity.

34 What organization pitted itself against the Doom Patrol?

- ☐ 1. Thrush
- ☐ 2. The Brotherhood of Evil
- ☐ 3. The Revenge Squad
- ☐ 4. The Suicide Squad
- ☐ 5. The Boy Scouts

35 What renders the Silver Age Green Lantern's power ring useless?

- ☐ 1. Wooden objects
- ☐ 2. Iron objects
- ☐ 3. Glad Wrap
- ☐ 4. Objects colored red
- ☐ 5. Objects colored yellow

36 What substance affected Mon-El like Kryptonite?

☐ 1. Gold
☐ 2. Silver
☐ 3. Double Bubble
☐ 4. Lead
☐ 5. Mercury

37 What was Adam Strange's profession?

☐ 1. A magician
☐ 2. A biologist
☐ 3. A construction worker
☐ 4. An archaeologist
☐ 5. A math teacher

38 What was the amorphous force in SECRET WARS called?

☐ 1. Galactus
☐ 2. Beyonder
☐ 3. God
☐ 4. Zeus
☐ 5. Ouranos

39 What was the first science-fiction comic strip?

☐ 1. FLASH GORDON
☐ 2. BUCK ROGERS
☐ 3. BATMAN
☐ 4. SUPERMAN
☐ 5. STAR TREK

40 Which team of superheroes has the most members?

☐ 1. The Justice League of America
☐ 2. The Doom Patrol
☐ 3. The Justice Society of America
☐ 4. The Titans
☐ 5. The Legion of Superheroes

41 What was the name of the Silver Age Green Lantern's sidekick?

☐ 1. Pieface
☐ 2. Cake-face
☐ 3. Derby
☐ 4. Pete Ross
☐ 5. Ace

42 Which comic adapted novels into comic form?

☐ 1. DC PRESENTS
☐ 2. DC SHOWCASE
☐ 3. MARVEL CLASSIC
☐ 4. MARVEL PRESENTS
☐ 5. MARVEL SPECIAL EDITION

43 Which company originally published TUROK, SON OF STONE?

☐ 1. Fawcett
☐ 2. Quality
☐ 3. E.C.
☐ 4. Dell
☐ 5. Avon

44 Which longtime supporting character died in THE AMAZING SPIDER-MAN #400?

☐ 1. Gwen Stacey
☐ 2. Mary Jane Watson-Parker
☐ 3. Harry Osborne
☐ 4. Aunt May
☐ 5. Peter Parker

45 Which of the following comics has won a Hugo Award?

☐ 1. THE SANDMAN
☐ 2. MAUS: A SURVIVOR'S TALE
☐ 3. TEAM AMERICA
☐ 4. WATCHMEN
☐ 5. DAVID CHELSEA IN LOVE

46 Which of the following science-fiction hybrids is NOT an actual comic book of the 1950s?

☐ 1. SPACE ROMANCE
☐ 2. SPACE DETECTIVE
☐ 3. SPACE MOUSE
☐ 4. SPACE WESTERN
☐ 5. SPACE WAR

47 Which of the following words was still allowed in comic book titles under the Comics Code?

☐ 1. Weird
☐ 2. Horror
☐ 3. Terror
☐ 4. Crime
☐ 5. Suspense

48 Which published work is considered the first "graphic novel"?

☐ 1. SABRE
☐ 2. X-MEN: GOD LOVES, MAN KILLS
☐ 3. CONTRACT WITH GOD
☐ 4. STEWART THE RAT
☐ 5. MAUS

49 Which underground cartoonist did the cover to the famous ZAP COMIX #0?

☐ 1. Gilbert Shelton
☐ 2. Spain
☐ 3. R. Crumb
☐ 4. Jack Kirby
☐ 5. Bill Watterson

50 From 1966 to 1972, this innovative artist was one of the most popular ever to work on DAREDEVIL.

☐ 1. Wally Wood
☐ 2. Gene Colan
☐ 3. Joe Orlando
☐ 4. Jack Kirby
☐ 5. John Buscema

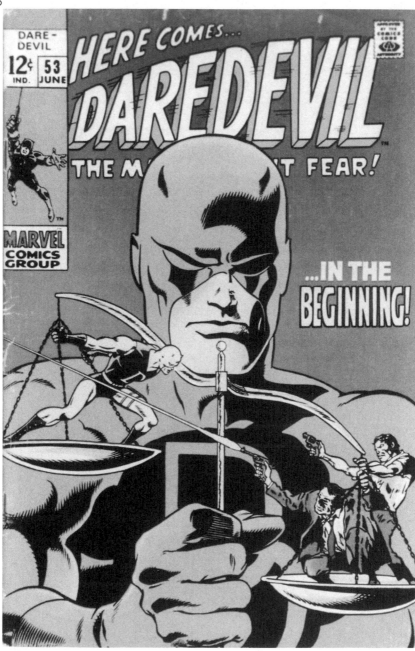

30-POINT QUESTIONS

1

Alan Moore and Eddie Campbell's Jack the Ripper narrative FROM HELL began life as a serial in what now-defunct anthology comic?

☐ 1. 2001 A.D.
☐ 2. TABOO
☐ 3. A-1
☐ 4. MARVEL COMICS PRESENTS
☐ 5. RAW

2

Ben Dunn created this *manga*-style comic, published and created in the United States.

☐ 1. DRUNKEN FIST
☐ 2. RANMA 1/2
☐ 3. APPLESEED
☐ 4. ORION
☐ 5. NINJA HIGH SCHOOL

3

DESTINATION MOON was adapted in the first issue of what comic?

☐ 1. MARVEL SUPER SPECIAL
☐ 2. MARVEL PRESENTS
☐ 3. STRANGE ADVENTURES
☐ 4. SPACE ADVENTURES
☐ 5. MYSTERY IN SPACE

4

To which magazine did Harlan Ellison make his first professional comics sale?

☐ 1. WEIRD TALES
☐ 2. PLANET COMICS
☐ 3. WEIRD SCIENCE-FANTASY
☐ 4. SPACE MYSTERIES
☐ 5. SPACE COWBOY

5

How many STAR TREK comics series have been based on the original 1960s TV show?

☐ 1. One
☐ 2. Two
☐ 3. Three
☐ 4. Four
☐ 5. Five

6

In the 1970s, some issues of THE AMAZING SPIDER-MAN ran without the Comics Code Authority seal of approval. Why was the seal removed?

- ☐ 1. A story involving explicit sex
- ☐ 2. A story involving drug use
- ☐ 3. The artist rendering blood in a panel
- ☐ 4. Marvel forgot to submit the issues for approval
- ☐ 5. The death of a major cast member

7

Jon Sable had two occupations. Besides being a freelance mercenary, what else was he?

- ☐ 1. A rock singer
- ☐ 2. A newspaper reporter
- ☐ 3. A children's book author
- ☐ 4. A video store clerk
- ☐ 5. A bank teller

8

Mysta of the Moon was just one of the lovely stars in which classic Golden Age science-fiction comic?

- ☐ 1. WONDER WOMAN
- ☐ 2. STARTLING COMICS
- ☐ 3. SPACE ADVENTURES
- ☐ 4. PLANET COMICS
- ☐ 5. LOST WORLDS

9

THE CROW, by James O'Barr, was first published by which comic book company?

- ☐ 1. Caliber
- ☐ 2. Fantagraphics
- ☐ 3. Kitchen Sink
- ☐ 4. Slave Labor
- ☐ 5. Tundra

10

The first ongoing monthly comic book, FAMOUS FUNNIES, frequently cover-featured which famous science-fiction hero?

- ☐ 1. Flash Gordon
- ☐ 2. Buck Rogers
- ☐ 3. Major Matt Mason
- ☐ 4. Captain Comet
- ☐ 5. Captain Future

11 To which supervillain organization did Emma Frost, the White Queen, belong?

- ☐ 1. The Masters of Evil
- ☐ 2. The Wrecking Crew
- ☐ 3. The Four Horsemen
- ☐ 4. The White Chessmen
- ☐ 5. The Hellfire Club

12 Two comics using the same title came out at the same time. What were they both called?

- ☐ 1. BATTLESTAR GALACTICA
- ☐ 2. STAR TREK
- ☐ 3. STAR WARS
- ☐ 4. SPACE: 1999
- ☐ 5. ROCKETMAN

13 WEIRD SCIENCE-FANTASY became this magazine.

- ☐ 1. WEIRD TALES
- ☐ 2. WEIRD STORIES
- ☐ 3. INCREDIBLE STORIES
- ☐ 4. INCREDIBLE SCIENCE FICTION
- ☐ 5. SCIENCE FICTION TALES

14 What comic had its creator's photo on every cover?

- ☐ 1. STAR TREK
- ☐ 2. STAR WARS
- ☐ 3. THE TWILIGHT ZONE
- ☐ 4. LOST IN SPACE
- ☐ 5. BUCK ROGERS

15 What comic took a pilot from World War I to 500 years in the future?

- ☐ 1. FLASH GORDON
- ☐ 2. BUCK ROGERS
- ☐ 3. DUCK DODGERS
- ☐ 4. MIGHTY SAMPSON
- ☐ 5. STAR WARS

16

What fictional comic became a film, and only later became an actual comic?

- ☐ 1. BLADE RUNNER
- ☐ 2. BUCKAROO BANZAI
- ☐ 3. HOWARD THE DUCK
- ☐ 4. THE SUB-MARINER
- ☐ 5. SUPERMAN

17

In the French comic ASTERIX, what made the Gauls invincible?

- ☐ 1. Their hair
- ☐ 2. Their unity
- ☐ 3. Their magic potion
- ☐ 4. Their powerful gods
- ☐ 5. It's not clear

18

This science-fiction author, whose novel THE DEMOLISHED MAN became a groundbreaking fiction classic, also wrote comics in the early 1940s.

- ☐ 1. Isaac Asimov
- ☐ 2. Harry Harrison
- ☐ 3. Alfred Bester
- ☐ 4. Joe Orlando
- ☐ 5. Robert A. Heinlein

19

This science-fiction author spent some time in the 1940s and 1950s editing, writing, and drawing comics.

- ☐ 1. Isaac Asimov
- ☐ 2. Robert Silverberg
- ☐ 3. Harry Harrison
- ☐ 4. Robert A. Heinlein
- ☐ 5. Harlan Ellison

20

What was DC Comics' first science-fiction comic?

- ☐ 1. STRANGE ADVENTURES
- ☐ 2. WEIRD SCIENCE-FANTASY
- ☐ 3. TOM CORBETT, SPACE CADET
- ☐ 4. INCREDIBLE SCIENCE FICTION
- ☐ 5. WEIRD TALES

21 What was the first 1950s taboo tackled by EC in WEIRD SCIENCE?

- ☐ 1. Race relations
- ☐ 2. Sex
- ☐ 3. Economics
- ☐ 4. Politics
- ☐ 5. Religion

22 What was the first exclusively science-fiction comic book?

- ☐ 1. WEIRD TALES
- ☐ 2. PLANET STORIES
- ☐ 3. PLANET COMICS
- ☐ 4. WEIRD COMICS
- ☐ 5. AMAZING COMICS

23 What was the Phoenix Force?

- ☐ 1. An alien entity
- ☐ 2. A paramilitary group
- ☐ 3. A superhero group
- ☐ 4. A great drink
- ☐ 5. A small spaceship

24 What is the Silver Surfer's real name?

- ☐ 1. Norrin Radd
- ☐ 2. Rom
- ☐ 3. Johnny Storm
- ☐ 4. Matt Murdock
- ☐ 5. Wilson Fisk

25 What were the names of the children in SPACE FAMILY ROBINSON?

- ☐ 1. Will and Penny
- ☐ 2. Tim and Tam
- ☐ 3. John and Jenny
- ☐ 4. Mary and Mark
- ☐ 5. There were no children.

26 Where did the "Zeta-Beam" that Adam Strange discovered come from?

- ☐ 1. Mars
- ☐ 2. The Moon
- ☐ 3. Alpha Centauri
- ☐ 4. Cygnus Alpha
- ☐ 5. Cygnus Centauri

27 Which of the following actors have written or cowritten a STAR TREK comic book?

- ☐ 1. Walter Koenig
- ☐ 2. John deLancie
- ☐ 3. George Takei
- ☐ 4. All of the above
- ☐ 5. None of the above

28 Which of the following comics began as a radio show?

- ☐ 1. CAPTAIN ROCKET
- ☐ 2. STAR TREK
- ☐ 3. SPACE RANGERS
- ☐ 4. SPACE PATROL
- ☐ 5. SPACE SQUADRON

29 Which popular comics writer wrote a nonfiction book, called DON'T PANIC, about THE HITCHHIKER'S GUIDE TO THE GALAXY series?

- ☐ 1. John Carnell
- ☐ 2. Neil Gaiman
- ☐ 3. Chris Claremont
- ☐ 4. Peter David
- ☐ 5. Stan Lee

30 Who created the Next Men?

- ☐ 1. Jack Kirby
- ☐ 2. Jim Mooney
- ☐ 3. Stan Lee
- ☐ 4. Harry Harrison
- ☐ 5. John Byrne

31 Who published the first STAR TREK comics?

☐ 1. E.C.
☐ 2. DC
☐ 3. AC
☐ 4. Dell
☐ 5. Gold Key

32 Who was Plastic Man?

☐ 1. Eel O'Brien
☐ 2. Stretch Cunningham
☐ 3. Ralph Relaxing
☐ 4. Peter Plyman
☐ 5. Ralph Digby

33 Who was responsible for the death of Barry Allen, the Silver Age Flash?

☐ 1. The Trickster
☐ 2. Harbinger
☐ 3. The Anti-Monitor
☐ 4. Grodd the Super Gorilla
☐ 5. The Psycho Pirate

34 Who was the editor for every issue of the comic book version of MAD?

☐ 1. William M. Gaines
☐ 2. Max C. Gaines
☐ 3. Al Feldstein
☐ 4. Harvey Kurtzman
☐ 5. Sheldon Mayer

35 Who was the first X-Man to die?

☐ 1. Professor X
☐ 2. Cyclops
☐ 3. Wolverine
☐ 4. Thunderbird
☐ 5. Phoenix

36   Who was the only superhero at E.C. to have her own title?

☐   1. Miss America
☐   2. Sun Girl
☐   3. Moon Girl
☐   4. Star Girl
☐   5. Venus

37   Who is Vril Dox?

☐   1. A real stud
☐   2. Leader of L.E.G.I.O.N.
☐   3. Leader of Warworld
☐   4. A Guardian of the Universe
☐   5. Leader of the Darkstars

38   Which science-fiction author worked on the LIGHTYEARS comic?

☐   1. Robert A. Heinlein
☐   2. Isaac Asimov
☐   3. Arthur C. Clarke
☐   4. Harry Harrison
☐   5. Robert Silverberg

39   Which artist produced the acclaimed comics adaptation of THE STARS MY DESTINATION, a classic science-fiction novel?

☐   1. John Byrne
☐   2. Howard Chaykin
☐   3. Bill Sienkiewicz
☐   4. P. Craig Russell
☐   5. Al Williamson

40   Both CAPTAIN VIDEO and WHEN WORLDS COLLIDE were drawn by the same artist, who didn't always get credit for his work.

☐   1. Steve Ditko
☐   2. Wayne Boring
☐   3. George Evans
☐   4. Neal Adams
☐   5. Joe Orlando

41 The original IRON MAN comics were created by Stan Lee, written by Larry Lieber, and drawn by _____ .

- ☐ 1. Art Simek
- ☐ 2. Steve Ditko
- ☐ 3. Don Heck
- ☐ 4. Dick Giordano
- ☐ 5. Jack Kirby

42 His work in horror comics in the 1950s helped to define what the genre looked like; his work was so horrific, he adopted an appropriate pen name: "Ghastly."

- ☐ 1. Wally Wood
- ☐ 2. Johnny Craig
- ☐ 3. Barry Blair
- ☐ 4. Graham Ingels
- ☐ 5. Jack Davis

43 This artist cocreated PLASM for Defiant and H.A.R.D. CORPS for Valiant, but his first work appeared in the science-fiction comic MAGNUS: ROBOT FIGHTER.

- ☐ 1. Don Perlin
- ☐ 2. Jim Shooter
- ☐ 3. David Lapham
- ☐ 4. Frank Miller
- ☐ 5. None of these

44 This artist is best known for his batty stuff at DC, but his first published work was uncredited in Gold Key's TWILIGHT ZONE.

- ☐ 1. Bob McLeod
- ☐ 2. Todd MacFarlane
- ☐ 3. Frank Miller
- ☐ 4. Gil Kane
- ☐ 5. Simon Bisley

45 He created FLASH GORDON, SECRET AGENT X-9, and JUNGLE JIM.

- ☐ 1. Alex Raymond
- ☐ 2. Mac Raboy
- ☐ 3. Joe Orlando
- ☐ 4. Don Heck
- ☐ 5. Al Williamson

46 He drew the Frank Miller-scripted ROBOCOP VS. TERMINATOR miniseries, and wrote as well as drew the HAVOK/WOLVERINE: MELTDOWN miniseries for Dark Horse.

- ☐ 1. Marc Silvestri
- ☐ 2. Walt Simonson
- ☐ 3. Graham Nolan
- ☐ 4. Gill Fox
- ☐ 5. Bill Everett

47 This creation, which became so popular that it was filmed in the 1980s, was originally a backup feature to STARSLAYER.

- ☐ 1. STARHAWKS
- ☐ 2. THE ROCKETEER
- ☐ 3. GRIMJACK
- ☐ 4. CEREBUS
- ☐ 5. MAGNUS: ROBOT FIGHTER

48 This artist, whose style was heavily influenced by EC's science-fiction and horror titles, cocreated SWAMP THING.

- ☐ 1. Kelly Jones
- ☐ 2. Bernie Wrightson
- ☐ 3. Hal Foster
- ☐ 4. Neal Adams
- ☐ 5. Joe Orlando

49 The Golden Age Vigilante in ACTION COMICS was the creation of Mort Weisinger and this Eisner-Iger Shop artist.

- ☐ 1. Lou Fine
- ☐ 2. Mort Meskin
- ☐ 3. Reed Crandall
- ☐ 4. Al Feldstein
- ☐ 5. Jack Kirby

50 In 1941, Captain Marvel received his own book, CAPTAIN MARVEL ADVENTURES, after appearing for several issues in this comic.

- ☐ 1. MARVEL COMICS
- ☐ 2. ALL-STAR COMICS
- ☐ 3. ALL-ADVENTURE COMICS
- ☐ 4. WHIZ COMICS
- ☐ 5. None of these

40-POINT QUESTIONS

1 Who edited the Superman titles during the 1950s and 1960s?

☐ 1. Jack Schiff
☐ 2. Julius Schwartz
☐ 3. Joe Orlando
☐ 4. Mort Weisinger
☐ 5. Otto Binder

2 Who has his own spaceship?

☐ 1. Adam Strange
☐ 2. Swamp Thing
☐ 3. Rip Hunter
☐ 4. Hawkman
☐ 5. Cave Carson

3 Who is the "star" character in Alan Moore and Eddie Campbell's FROM HELL?

☐ 1. Satan
☐ 2. Gabriel
☐ 3. Ghost Rider
☐ 4. Jack the Ripper
☐ 5. Jason

4 Who is the superhero featured in Rick Veitch's MAXIMORTAL?

☐ 1. The New God
☐ 2. The Mink
☐ 3. Trueman
☐ 4. The Shield
☐ 5. Foreverman

5 Who lived on borrowed time?

☐ 1. Deadman
☐ 2. The Geek
☐ 3. Sergeant Rock
☐ 4. The Challengers of the Unknown
☐ 5. The Phantom Stranger

6 Who published the comic version of THE TIME MACHINE film?

☐ 1. AC
☐ 2. DC
☐ 3. Marvel
☐ 4. Gold Key
☐ 5. Dell

7 Who saved the Justice League from Kanjar Ro?

☐ 1. The Sea Devils
☐ 2. Metamorpho
☐ 3. The Red Tornado
☐ 4. Jay Garrick
☐ 5. Adam Strange

8 Who stole the Beyonder's energies in Marvel's SECRET WARS maxiseries?

☐ 1. Owen Reece
☐ 2. Doctor Doom
☐ 3. Galactus
☐ 4. Wolverine
☐ 5. Thanos

9 Who was Marvel's answer to Tarzan?

☐ 1. Wolverine
☐ 2. Ka-Zar
☐ 3. Sheena
☐ 4. Tigra
☐ 5. The Black Panther

10 Who was Superboy's best buddy back in Smallville?

☐ 1. Lex Luthor
☐ 2. Mon-El
☐ 3. Pete Ross
☐ 4. Pete Roberts
☐ 5. Professor Potter

11 Who was the artist who created Plastic Man and drew most of his early adventures?

☐ 1. Will Eisner
☐ 2. Jack Kirby
☐ 3. Mart Nodell
☐ 4. Joe Simon
☐ 5. Jack Cole

12 Who was the Star-Spangled Kid's sidekick?

☐ 1. Kid Eternity
☐ 2. Bucky
☐ 3. Stripesy
☐ 4. The Flagman
☐ 5. The Patriot

13 Who is Thor's half brother?

☐ 1. Samson
☐ 2. Loki
☐ 3. Fafner
☐ 4. Fenris
☐ 5. Odin

14 Who wrote THE UNCANNY X-MEN AND THE NEW TEEN TITANS crossover?

☐ 1. Marv Wolfman
☐ 2. Chris Claremont
☐ 3. Steve Gerber
☐ 4. Stan Lee
☐ 5. John Byrne

15 BARBARELLA was created for this magazine.

☐ 1. ESQUIRE
☐ 2. V. MAGAZINE
☐ 3. ETIENNE
☐ 4. LE MONDE
☐ 5. METAL HURLANT

16 COWBOY WESTERN changed its title in 1952 to this science-fiction one.

☐ 1. SPACE HERD
☐ 2. SPACE COWBOY
☐ 3. SPACE WESTERN
☐ 4. SPACE VIGILANTE
☐ 5. WEIRD COWBOY STORIES

17 Cynicism runs rampant in this comic.

☐ 1. WEIRD SCIENCE-FANTASY
☐ 2. SPACE ADVENTURES
☐ 3. WEIRD TALES
☐ 4. UFO
☐ 5. THE INVADERS

18 How many FLASH GORDON titles have there been?

☐ 1. One
☐ 2. Two
☐ 3. Three
☐ 4. Four
☐ 5. Five

19 In 1954, despite the anticomics crusaders, EC announced that they would be adding a fourth horror title. What was it to be called?

☐ 1. THE DEN OF INIQUITY
☐ 2. THE CHAMBER OF CHILLS
☐ 3. TALES OF TERROR
☐ 4. TALES FROM THE TOMB
☐ 5. THE CRYPT OF TERROR

20 In what program was Wolverine involved while working for Canada?

☐ 1. Canadian military
☐ 2. Weapon X
☐ 3. Alpha Flight
☐ 4. The Avengers
☐ 5. The Mounties

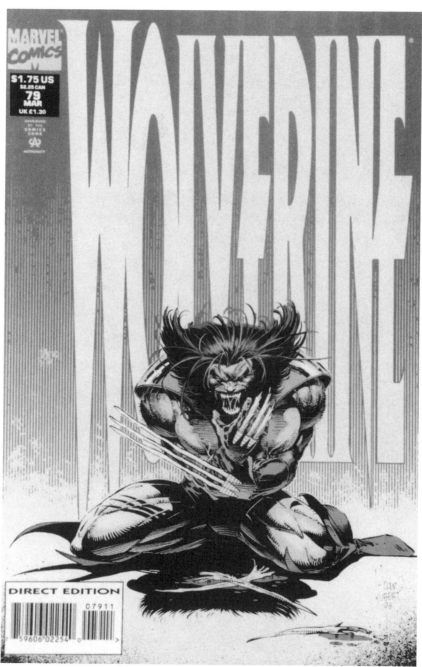

21 Spider-Man's nemesis, Venom, is partly an alien symbiote that Spidey once wore as a costume. In which Marvel Comics miniseries did Spider-Man acquire the symbiote/costume?

- ☐ 1. CONTEST OF CHAMPIONS
- ☐ 2. CRISIS ON INFINITE EARTHS
- ☐ 3. MARVEL SUPER HEROES SECRET WARS
- ☐ 4. SECRET WARS II
- ☐ 5. THE JUSTICE LEAGUE OF AMERICA vs. THE JUSTICE SOCIETY OF AMERICA

22 SUPERMAN was the second costumed adventurer created by Siegel and Shuster. Who was the first?

- ☐ 1. The Crimson Avenger
- ☐ 2. The Clock
- ☐ 3. Dr. Occult
- ☐ 4. Captain America
- ☐ 5. The Shadow

23 What 1950s comic wanted "factual reports" on flying saucers?

- ☐ 1. WEIRD SCIENCE-FANTASY
- ☐ 2. SPACE ADVENTURES
- ☐ 3. UFO
- ☐ 4. STRANGE WORLDS
- ☐ 5. IF

24 What alien race is responsible for the "x-factor" gene?

- ☐ 1. Kree
- ☐ 2. Skrulls
- ☐ 3. Galactus
- ☐ 4. The Celestials
- ☐ 5. Shi'ar

25 Which artist was hired by EC to imitate Wally Wood?

- ☐ 1. Joe Orlando
- ☐ 2. Gil Kane
- ☐ 3. Al Feldstein
- ☐ 4. Kelly Freas
- ☐ 5. Al Williamson

26 Which comic consulted with the University of Chicago for accuracy?

☐ 1. FLASH GORDON
☐ 2. BUCK ROGERS
☐ 3. SECRET AGENT X-1
☐ 4. DESTINATION MOON
☐ 5. 2001

27 What comic did Ziff-Davis launch in 1950?

☐ 1. AMAZING STORIES
☐ 2. AMAZING COMICS
☐ 3. PLANET COMICS
☐ 4. AMAZING ADVENTURES
☐ 5. ASTOUNDING SCIENCE-FICTION STORIES

28 What comic strip drew on Sigmund Freud's theories about dreams?

☐ 1. OUTLAND
☐ 2. LITTLE NEMO IN SLUMBERLAND
☐ 3. DREAMS OF A RAREBIT FIEND
☐ 4. THE FAR SIDE
☐ 5. BLOOM COUNTY

29 What comic used science-fiction authors to reach a new audience?

☐ 1. STRANGE ADVENTURES
☐ 2. WEIRD SCIENCE
☐ 3. THE MAD PLANET
☐ 4. MARVEL COMICS PRESENTS
☐ 5. TOM CORBETT, SPACE CADET

30 What science-fiction author referred legendary editor Julius Schwartz to DC to edit comics?

☐ 1. Harry Harrison
☐ 2. Ray Bradbury
☐ 3. Alfred Bester
☐ 4. Robert Bloch
☐ 5. Isaac Asimov

31 What was Adam Warlock originally known as?

☐ 1. Asterix
☐ 2. Them
☐ 3. Him
☐ 4. The One
☐ 5. Master

32 Which grand master of the field is generally credited with pioneering the genre of the romance comic, popular in the 1950s?

☐ 1. Jack Kirby
☐ 2. Will Eisner
☐ 3. Stan Lee
☐ 4. Julius Schwartz
☐ 5. John Romita, Sr.

33 Who created STRANGE ADVENTURES for DC?

☐ 1. H. L. Gold
☐ 2. Edmond Hamilton
☐ 3. Julius Schwartz
☐ 4. Alfred Bester
☐ 5. Stan Lee

34 Who saved Galactus' life?

☐ 1. Reed Richards
☐ 2. The Watcher
☐ 3. Silver Surfer
☐ 4. The Hulk
☐ 5. Captain Marvel

35 What was the name of the SPACE DETECTIVE?

☐ 1. Chief Inspector Lemming
☐ 2. Rod Hathaway
☐ 3. Lij Bailey
☐ 4. Kilgore Proud
☐ 5. Spurs Jackson

36 WEIRD SCIENCE and WEIRD FANTASY adapted many of his stories as comics.

☐ 1. Isaac Asimov
☐ 2. Ray Bradbury
☐ 3. Harlan Ellison
☐ 4. Harry Harrison
☐ 5. Robert A. Heinlein

37 Neal Adams got his start working in these, at first under his own name, then as a "ghost," before he began to work for DC in 1967.

☐ 1. Bubble gum inserts
☐ 2. Newspaper strips
☐ 3. Storyboards for movies
☐ 4. Advertising designs
☐ 5. Underground comics

38 This artist gave Spider-Man his distinctive look.

☐ 1. Todd MacFarlane
☐ 2. Steve Ditko
☐ 3. Jack Kirby
☐ 4. Don Heck
☐ 5. Joe Simon

39 This artist's work on THE AVENGERS in the 1960s and on WONDER WOMAN in the late 1970s is considered to be some of his best.

☐ 1. Steve Ditko
☐ 2. Don Heck
☐ 3. John Buscema
☐ 4. George Perez
☐ 5. Dick Giordano

40 Jack Kirby had a long career in his field. Where did he get his start drawing comics characters?

☐ 1. Walt Disney Studios
☐ 2. The Fleischer Bros. Studio
☐ 3. The Eisner-Iger Shop
☐ 4. Newspapers
☐ 5. U.S. Army

41 He was one of the earliest popular animators, and his work has been paid homage to in underground comics.

☐ 1. Walt Disney
☐ 2. Elliot Porter
☐ 3. Stan Brackage
☐ 4. Winsor McCay
☐ 5. None of these

42 People know him best known as "Moebius," but what's his real name?

☐ 1. Jean Giraud
☐ 2. Jean-Paul Basquiat
☐ 3. Jean-Marc L'Officier
☐ 4. Jacques Tardi
☐ 5. Paul Mitterand

43 This artist's early work includes TV animation and P.S. MAGAZINE. His work with Marvel's horror line was instrumental in its inception and continuation in the early 1970s.

☐ 1. Gil Kane
☐ 2. Jack Kirby
☐ 3. Mike Ploog
☐ 4. Tom Sutton
☐ 5. Esteban Maroto

44 This artist was one of the first to bring new materials and techniques to comics, including oils, charcoal, collage, and acrylics. His work on MOON KNIGHT brought him to fans' attention.

☐ 1. Jack Kirby
☐ 2. Frank Miller
☐ 3. Bill Sienkiewicz
☐ 4. James Fry
☐ 5. Stephen Platt

45 Joe Simon created this character, whose comic also featured the antics of Sub-Zero Man, the first supercold hero (beating Stan Lee's Jack Frost by more than a year).

☐ 1. BLUE BOLT
☐ 2. BLUE CIRCLE COMICS
☐ 3. ICE WORLD
☐ 4. BLACKHAWK
☐ 5. BIG SHOT COMICS

46　MARVEL COMICS was launched to be the comic equivalent of this science-fiction pulp of the same time period.

☐　1.　MARVEL MYSTERY STORIES
☐　2.　MARVEL SCIENCE STORIES
☐　3.　MARVEL STORIES
☐　4.　AMAZING MARVEL STORIES
☐　5.　None of these

47　This, the second Marvel comic book, drew its title from a pulp magazine in the same genre.

☐　1.　THRILLING WONDER COMICS
☐　2.　PLANET COMICS
☐　3.　DETECTIVE COMICS
☐　4.　DARING MYSTERY COMICS
☐　5.　WEIRD TALES

48　By the sixth issue of this Golden Age Marvel comic, this superwoman had discarded her skintight leopard costume, except on the cover.

☐　1.　Miss America
☐　2.　Miss Fury
☐　3.　Wonder Woman
☐　4.　Catwoman
☐　5.　She-Devil

49　This horror artist once assisted at autopsies, which may explain a lot.

☐　1.　Bernie Wrightson
☐　2.　L. B. Cole
☐　3.　Wally Wood
☐　4.　Jack Davis
☐　5.　Howard Nostrand

50　What's now DC Comics used to be National Periodical Publications. During World War II, they published comics under two different names. One was DC-Superman; what was the other?

☐　1.　All-Star Comics
☐　2.　Entertaining Comics
☐　3.　All-American Comics
☐　4.　Timely Comics
☐　5.　Flash Comics

50-POINT QUESTIONS

1 Hardboiled detective novelist Dashiell Hammett wrote what comic strip in the 1930s?

- ☐ 1. SMOKEY STOVER
- ☐ 2. LI'L ORPHAN ANNIE
- ☐ 3. SECRET AGENT CORRIGAN
- ☐ 4. SECRET AGENT X-9
- ☐ 5. BUCK ROGERS

2 Kei and Yuri are the main characters in what *manga* comic book?

- ☐ 1. AREA 88
- ☐ 2. BIO-BOOSTER GUYVER
- ☐ 3. DIRTY PAIR
- ☐ 4. LENSMAN
- ☐ 5. RANMA 1/2

3 A classic example of innovative use of panel structure and cinematic technique was the story "Master Race," in EC's IMPACT #1. Who was the artist who defied editorial instructions and created this masterpiece?

- ☐ 1. Wallace Wood
- ☐ 2. Bernie Krigstein
- ☐ 3. Jack Davis
- ☐ 4. Frank Frazetta
- ☐ 5. Al Williamson

4 In the first comic version of STAR TREK, the likenesses of the entire crew matched the TV show with one exception. Who was redone for the comic?

- ☐ 1. Kirk
- ☐ 2. Spock
- ☐ 3. McCoy
- ☐ 4. Uhura
- ☐ 5. Sulu

5 EC plagiarized two short stories by Ray Bradbury, "The Rocket Man" and "Kaleidoscope," and got caught by the author combining them into a single story with a different title. What was the title?

- ☐ 1. "Wish upon a Star"
- ☐ 2. "Home to Stay"
- ☐ 3. "The Flying Machine"
- ☐ 4. "Monkey See, Monkey Do"
- ☐ 5. "50 Girls 50"

6

In 1955, all comics publishers—except two—voluntarily submitted their stories to the Comics Code Authority and put the Code seal on their books. Which two publishers did not participate?

☐ 1. E.C. and Stanmor
☐ 2. E.C. and Ajax
☐ 3. Gilberton and Dell
☐ 4. ACG and Fawcett
☐ 5. Quality and Atlas

7

Richard F. Outcault was famous for creating which old-time comic book character?

☐ 1. The Yellow Kid
☐ 2. Buster Brown
☐ 3. Pogo
☐ 4. Dickie Dare
☐ 5. A and B

8

The 1994 WORLDS COLLIDE crossover involved characters from which two comic book companies meeting each other?

☐ 1. Marvel and DC
☐ 2. DC and Image
☐ 3. Marvel and Image
☐ 4. DC and Milestone Media
☐ 5. Image and Harris

9

What comic book company first published NEXUS?

☐ 1. First Comics
☐ 2. Warp Graphics
☐ 3. Capital Comics
☐ 4. Dark Horse Comics
☐ 5. Eclipse Comics

10

Beta Ray Bill was an alien with the powers of _____ .

☐ 1. Spider-Man
☐ 2. Thor
☐ 3. Mister Fantastic
☐ 4. The Thing
☐ 5. The Silver Surfer

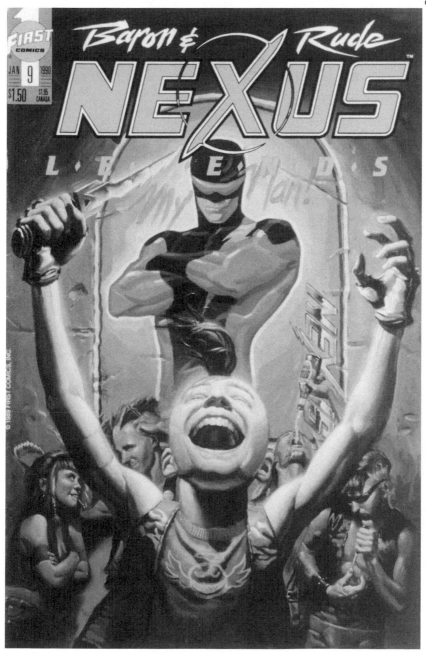

NEXUS LEGENDS © 1989 First Publishing, Inc.

11 BLAST-OFF ran unprinted stories from what canceled comic?

- ☐ 1. WEIRD SCIENCE
- ☐ 2. RACE FOR THE MOON
- ☐ 3. SPACE ADVENTURES
- ☐ 4. SPACE FAMILY ROBINSON
- ☐ 5. PLANET OF TERROR

12 For which comic did Harry Harrison do almost all the work himself?

- ☐ 1. WEIRD SCIENCE
- ☐ 2. CAPTAIN ROCKET
- ☐ 3. CELESTIAL MECHANICS
- ☐ 4. CAPTAIN VIDEO
- ☐ 5. STARWORLDS

13 How far away from Earth is the planet Rann?

- ☐ 1. Twenty-five trillion miles
- ☐ 2. Thirty-five trillion miles
- ☐ 3. Fifty trillion miles
- ☐ 4. 257 light-years
- ☐ 5. 257 light-years and two centuries into the future

14 How many publishers have put out a TWILIGHT ZONE comic?

- ☐ 1. One
- ☐ 2. Two
- ☐ 3. Three
- ☐ 4. Four
- ☐ 5. Five

15 In CRUSADER FROM MARS, name the couple sent to Earth.

- ☐ 1. Tarka and Zira
- ☐ 2. Tim and Tam
- ☐ 3. Kirk and Spock
- ☐ 4. Futura and Ormandy
- ☐ 5. Vor and Gor

16 In PLANET COMICS, what was Futura's real name?

☐ 1. Mary
☐ 2. Margaret
☐ 3. Mildred
☐ 4. Marcia
☐ 5. Maple

17 In what comic did J'Onn J'Onzz, Manhunter from Mars, first appear?

☐ 1. DETECTIVE COMICS
☐ 2. ACTION COMICS
☐ 3. PLANET COMICS
☐ 4. SPACE WESTERN
☐ 5. None of these

18 In what Silver Age comic did Zatanna the Magician first appear?

☐ 1. THE ATOM
☐ 2. THE FLASH
☐ 3. THE CHALLENGERS OF THE UNKNOWN
☐ 4. MY GREATEST ADVENTURE
☐ 5. HAWKMAN

19 After a six-year run in another comic, BUCK ROGERS finally got his own. Where did he start?

☐ 1. WEIRD TALES
☐ 2. FAMOUS FUNNIES
☐ 3. PLANET COMICS
☐ 4. ASTONISHING
☐ 5. WEEKLY STRIPPER

20 SPACE FUNNIES reprinted material from which comic book?

☐ 1. WEIRD SCIENCE
☐ 2. TARGET COMICS
☐ 3. SCOOP COMICS
☐ 4. PLANET COMICS
☐ 5. ROCKET COMICS

21 The comic STAR WARS IN 3-D featured an adventure on what planet?

- ☐ 1. Tatooine
- ☐ 2. Hoth
- ☐ 3. Datooine
- ☐ 4. Endor
- ☐ 5. Vega

22 The first newspaper strip reprints of FLASH GORDON appeared in which comic book?

- ☐ 1. WEEKLY STRIPPER
- ☐ 2. FAMOUS FUNNIES
- ☐ 3. KING COMICS
- ☐ 4. PLANET COMICS
- ☐ 5. WEIRD TALES

23 What comic reprinted Wally Wood's work of the 1950s in color?

- ☐ 1. WEIRD WORLDS
- ☐ 2. WORLDS OF WOOD
- ☐ 3. WORLDS OF FANTASY
- ☐ 4. WEIRD WONDER TALES
- ☐ 5. WALLY'S WORLDS

24 What comic was an adaptation of MAZA OF THE MOON?

- ☐ 1. RACE TO THE MOON
- ☐ 2. PHANTOM PLANET
- ☐ 3. ROCKET TO THE MOON
- ☐ 4. DESTINATION: MOON
- ☐ 5. RACE FOR THE MOON

25 What comic was subtitled "Weird Thrills of the Past and the Future"?

- ☐ 1. WEIRD SCIENCE-FANTASY
- ☐ 2. LOST WORLDS
- ☐ 3. PLANET COMICS
- ☐ 4. FORBIDDEN WORLDS
- ☐ 5. WEEKLY STRIPPER

26 When does MAGNUS, ROBOT FIGHTER take place?

- [ ] 1. A.D. 2500
- [ ] 2. A.D. 3000
- [ ] 3. A.D. 4000
- [ ] 4. A.D. 5000
- [ ] 5. A.D. 4500

27 Where is Captain Science's secret laboratory located?

- [ ] 1. The Moon
- [ ] 2. Mars
- [ ] 3. New Mexico
- [ ] 4. The Arctic
- [ ] 5. In orbit

28 Which of the following DC authors wrote science fiction?

- [ ] 1. Gardner Fox
- [ ] 2. Otto Binder
- [ ] 3. Edmond Hamilton
- [ ] 4. Alfred Bester
- [ ] 5. All the above

29 Who did the first cover for UNKNOWN WORLDS OF SCIENCE FICTION?

- [ ] 1. Wally Wood
- [ ] 2. Earl Norem
- [ ] 3. Frank Brunner
- [ ] 4. Frank Frazetta
- [ ] 5. Frank Kelly Freas

30 Who drew the comic MYTH ADVENTURES?

- [ ] 1. Douglas Niles
- [ ] 2. Phil Foglio
- [ ] 3. Joshua Quagmire
- [ ] 4. Don Martin
- [ ] 5. Kelly Freas

31 Who picked up publishing the comic TOM CORBETT, SPACE CADET after Dell quit?

☐ 1. Gold Key
☐ 2. DC
☐ 3. Marvel
☐ 4. EC
☐ 5. Prize

32 Who was the definitive SUPERMAN artist from the mid-1950s to the early 1960s?

☐ 1. Carmine Infantino
☐ 2. Wayne Boring
☐ 3. Jim Mooney
☐ 4. Kurt Schaeffenburger
☐ 5. Curt Swan

33 Who was the first science-fiction character, created specifically for the comic books, to have his own title?

☐ 1. Captain Video
☐ 2. Rex Dexter
☐ 3. Flash Gordon
☐ 4. Buck Rogers
☐ 5. Hunt Bowman

34 Who was The Space Ace?

☐ 1. Captain Rocket
☐ 2. Captian Video
☐ 3. Major Inapak
☐ 4. Buck Rogers
☐ 5. Flash Gordon

35 How did Captain America fix his broken shield at the end of the SECRET WARS?

☐ 1. Superglue
☐ 2. He didn't fix it.
☐ 3. Force of will
☐ 4. It wasn't broken.
☐ 5. None of these

36 The acknowledged TARZAN master, he also founded the School of Visual Arts, which taught most of the next generation of comic artists, including Wally Wood and SF author Harry Harrison.

☐ 1. Carl Barks
☐ 2. Hal Foster
☐ 3. Burne Hogarth
☐ 4. Lou Fine
☐ 5. Walt Disney

37 He created THE MAXX, and also drew an ALIENS miniseries.

☐ 1. Dale Keown
☐ 2. Dave Cockrum
☐ 3. Joe Simon
☐ 4. Sam Kieth
☐ 5. William Messner-Loebs

38 This longtime comic artist's highest points include ORION, EDGE OF CHAOS in HEAVY METAL, and the TARZAN and BUCK ROGERS newspaper strips.

☐ 1. Hal Foster
☐ 2. Wally Wood
☐ 3. Al Williamson
☐ 4. Gray Morrow
☐ 5. Lou Fine

39 His first work was in CHAMBER OF CHILLS (1972). He also adapted Rudyard Kipling stories into comics and drew WAR OF THE WORLDS.

☐ 1. Jack Kirby
☐ 2. Steve Ditko
☐ 3. P. Craig Russell
☐ 4. Sal Buscema
☐ 5. Frank Brunner

40 Hanna-Barbera's SPACE GHOST was his creation. He also worked on ZORRO for Gold Key in the 1950s.

☐ 1. Frank Thorne
☐ 2. Alex Toth
☐ 3. Hal Foster
☐ 4. Pat Boyette
☐ 5. Steve Ditko

41 He drew FLASH GORDON in the 1960s. In the 1950s, his work could be found in WEIRD FANTASY and WEIRD SCIENCE for EC.

☐ 1. Al McWilliams
☐ 2. Burne Hogarth
☐ 3. Jim Davis
☐ 4. Al Williamson
☐ 5. None of these

42 She spent three years as the lead feature in WOW COMICS before earning a title of her own.

☐ 1. Mary Marvel
☐ 2. Black Widow
☐ 3. Lady Luck
☐ 4. Madame Fatal
☐ 5. Betsy Boss

43 This character began in POLICE COMICS, then reappeared in her own title four years after POLICE COMICS came to an end.

☐ 1. Catwoman
☐ 2. Miss Fury
☐ 3. Phantom Lady
☐ 4. She-Devil
☐ 5. Lady Luck

44 Name the artist who drew the BATMAN/JUDGE DREDD crossover in 1991 and worked on the LOBO comic.

☐ 1. Simon Bisley
☐ 2. Arthur Adams
☐ 3. Val Semeiks
☐ 4. Neal Adams
☐ 5. Frank Miller

45 This artist began by drawing comics, but with Charlton's SPACE: 1999, he also began to write them.

☐ 1. William Rothman
☐ 2. Howard Pine
☐ 3. John Byrne
☐ 4. George Jefferson
☐ 5. Joe Staton

46 This artist designed the Silver Age Green Lantern and Atom, then redesigned the Captain Marvel costume for Marvel.

☐ 1. Bob Kane
☐ 2. Gil Kane
☐ 3. Lou Fine
☐ 4. Russ Manning
☐ 5. Robert Crumb

47 Jack Binder created the original DAREDEVIL for MLJ with him.

☐ 1. Jack Kirby
☐ 2. Neal Adams
☐ 3. Carl Barks
☐ 4. Don Rico
☐ 5. None of these

48 Name the artist who created the original Human Torch in 1939.

☐ 1. Carl Burgos
☐ 2. Carmine Infantino
☐ 3. Sergio Aragones
☐ 4. Alex Schomburg
☐ 5. Bill Everett

49 Joe Simon and Jack Kirby created this big-game hunter who turned to "hunting the beasts of civilization" for ADVENTURE COMICS.

☐ 1. Manhunter
☐ 2. The Shadow
☐ 3. The Punisher
☐ 4. Johnny Quest
☐ 5. The Guardian

50 This famous EC sci-fi artist began assisting Will Eisner on the SPIRIT strip in 1950. He trained at Hogarth's school with sci-fi writer (and former cartoonist) Harry Harrison.

☐ 1. Joe Orlando
☐ 2. Wally Wood
☐ 3. Hal Foster
☐ 4. Ray Bradbury
☐ 5. Jules Pfeiffer

SCIENCE FICTION

WORMHOLE

TRIVIA QUIZ

10-POINT QUESTIONS

1 In the 1938 radio broadcast THE WAR OF THE WORLDS, starring Orson Welles, where did the first Martians land?

- ☐ 1. Bedford Falls, NY
- ☐ 2. Grover's Corners, NH
- ☐ 3. Neptune, NJ
- ☐ 4. Grover's Mill, NJ
- ☐ 5. London, England

2 What famous science-fiction novel was originally written as a series of radio scripts?

- ☐ 1. 1984
- ☐ 2. BRAVE NEW WORLD
- ☐ 3. DUNE
- ☐ 4. STRANGER IN A STRANGE LAND
- ☐ 5. THE HITCHHIKER'S GUIDE TO THE GALAXY

3 The 1952 ABC radio program TOM CORBETT, SPACE CADET was based on the science-fiction novel SPACE CADET. Who wrote this novel?

- ☐ 1. Robert A. Heinlein
- ☐ 2. Lester del Rey
- ☐ 3. Paul Fairman
- ☐ 4. E. E. "Doc" Smith
- ☐ 5. Jack Williamson

4 Which award-winning science-fiction story by Harlan Ellison describes a radio that plays transmissions from the past but not from the present?

- ☐ 1. "Static"
- ☐ 2. "Laugh Track"
- ☐ 3. "Demon with a Glass Hand"
- ☐ 4. "Jeffty Is Five"
- ☐ 5. "Paladin of the Lost Hour"

5 What science-fiction character—who later appeared in films, TV shows, and novels—was originally intended as the hero of a radio series?

- ☐ 1. Doctor Who
- ☐ 2. Professor Quatermass
- ☐ 3. Captain Kirk
- ☐ 4. Perry Rhodan
- ☐ 5. Doc Savage

6

Name the July 19, 1959, episode of SUSPENSE starring Vincent Price in a radio dramatization of a story by Ambrose Bierce in which time is distorted and nothing is what it seems to be.

- ☐ 1. "Moxon's Master"
- ☐ 2. "An Occurrence at Owl Creek Bridge"
- ☐ 3. "The Middle Toe of the Right Foot"
- ☐ 4. "The Devil's Dictionary"
- ☐ 5. "The Damned Thing"

7

This man, who narrated many old-time radio broadcasts, was also Rod Serling's first choice as narrator of THE TWILIGHT ZONE.

- ☐ 1. Orson Welles
- ☐ 2. Brace Beemer
- ☐ 3. Clayton "Bud" Collyer
- ☐ 4. Fred Foy
- ☐ 5. Everett Sloane

8

What sound effect was heard at the beginning of each episode of the radio program INNER SANCTUM?

- ☐ 1. A creaking door
- ☐ 2. A Chinese gong
- ☐ 3. Sinister laughter
- ☐ 4. Echoing footsteps
- ☐ 5. Rattling chains

9

What science-fiction novelist also wrote radio scripts for the British Broadcasting Corporation at a desk in Room 101 of the BBC's Broadcasting House?

- ☐ 1. Olaf Stapledon
- ☐ 2. Roald Dahl
- ☐ 3. George Orwell
- ☐ 4. Arthur C. Clarke
- ☐ 5. Eric Frank Russell

10

What famous science-fiction movie was adapted into a weekly serial that ran on National Public Radio in 1981?

- ☐ 1. STAR WARS
- ☐ 2. STAR TREK: THE MOTION PICTURE
- ☐ 3. FORBIDDEN PLANET
- ☐ 4. THE DAY THE EARTH STOOD STILL
- ☐ 5. INVASION OF THE BODY SNATCHERS

11

The radio program THE SHADOW featured a mysterious crime fighter who had the power to turn invisible by clouding men's minds. What was the name of the Shadow's beautiful female assistant?

- ☐ 1. Silver St. Cloud
- ☐ 2. Lois Lane
- ☐ 3. Margo Lane
- ☐ 4. Pam North
- ☐ 5. Nora Charles

12

Gore Vidal's play VISIT TO A SMALL PLANET centered on a superpowered alien named Kreton. The 1960 movie version starred Jerry Lewis as a rather cretinous Kreton. Who played him onstage?

- ☐ 1. Jack Cassidy
- ☐ 2. Michael Redgrave
- ☐ 3. Claude Rains
- ☐ 4. Cyril Ritchard
- ☐ 5. Vincent Price

13

The science-fiction TV series QUANTUM LEAP contained a running tribute to this European playwright.

- ☐ 1. William Shakespeare
- ☐ 2. Eugene Ionesco
- ☐ 3. Samuel Beckett
- ☐ 4. Dylan Thomas
- ☐ 5. George Bernard Shaw

14

What 1987 Broadway musical took characters from several different fairy tales and switched them into one another's stories?

- ☐ 1. GRIMM FAIRY TALES
- ☐ 2. BEAUTY AND THE BEASTS
- ☐ 3. GOREY STORIES
- ☐ 4. INTO THE WOODS
- ☐ 5. ANYONE CAN WHISTLE

15

What 1961 science-fiction film became a 1982 off-Broadway musical, which in turn became a 1986 science-fiction musical?

- ☐ 1. THE INCREDIBLE SHRINKING MAN
- ☐ 2. LITTLE SHOP OF HORRORS
- ☐ 3. I WAS A TEENAGE FRANKENSTEIN
- ☐ 4. THE DAY THE EARTH STOOD STILL
- ☐ 5. WEREWOLVES ON WHEELS

16 What 1941 Broadway play starred Boris Karloff as a homicidal maniac who tried to kill everybody who told him he looked like Boris Karloff?

- ☐ 1. THE BLACK ROOM
- ☐ 2. THE DEVIL COMMANDS
- ☐ 3. ARSENIC AND OLD LACE
- ☐ 4. TEA AND SYMPATHY
- ☐ 5. YOU'LL FIND OUT

17 What very important science-fiction archetypes made their first appearance in the 1920 Czechoslovak play R.U.R.?

- ☐ 1. Martians
- ☐ 2. Telepaths
- ☐ 3. Time travelers
- ☐ 4. Clones
- ☐ 5. Robots

18 Two American stage musicals—one performed in 1902 and one performed in 1975—were based on this fantasy novel.

- ☐ 1. THE WONDERFUL WIZARD OF OZ
- ☐ 2. ALICE IN WONDERLAND
- ☐ 3. ALADDIN
- ☐ 4. THE SNOW QUEEN
- ☐ 5. DRACULA

19 Which STAR TREK episode's title is a quotation from Shakespeare's play HAMLET?

- ☐ 1. "Tomorrow Is Yesterday"
- ☐ 2. "A Taste of Armageddon"
- ☐ 3. "The Conscience of the King"
- ☐ 4. "Who Mourns for Adonais?"
- ☐ 5. "Whom Gods Destroy"

20 Which author, who is best known as a science-fiction novelist, also wrote a guide to Shakespeare's plays?

- ☐ 1. Robert Silverberg
- ☐ 2. Brian W. Aldiss
- ☐ 3. Isaac Asimov
- ☐ 4. Aldous Huxley
- ☐ 5. Olaf Stapledon

21 Which SF writer wrote many early detective stories under the name Ellis Hart?

☐ 1. Brett Easton Ellis
☐ 2. Harry Harrison
☐ 3. Gordon R. Dickson
☐ 4. Henry Slesar
☐ 5. Harlan Ellison

22 Which horror author has written mainstream novels under the name Anne Rampling?

☐ 1. Anne Rice
☐ 2. Kit Reed
☐ 3. Nancy Collins
☐ 4. V. C. Andrews
☐ 5. John Saul

23 Who wrote juvenile SF novels under the name Paul French?

☐ 1. Arthur C. Clarke
☐ 2. Robert A. Heinlein
☐ 3. Frederik Pohl
☐ 4. Gordon R. Dickson
☐ 5. Isaac Asimov

24 Harry Stubbs writes under what name?

☐ 1. Harry Harrison
☐ 2. Poul Anderson
☐ 3. Zenna Henderson
☐ 4. Hal Clement
☐ 5. James Gunn

25 Which author serialized his novel POLICE YOUR PLANET in SCIENCE FICTION ADVENTURES under the name Erik Van Lihn?

☐ 1. Philip K. Dick
☐ 2. Lester del Ray
☐ 3. Ray Bradbury
☐ 4. Clifford D. Simak
☐ 5. Jack Williamson

26 Who wrote the novelization of the film STAR WARS under the name "George Lucas"?

- ☐ 1. Matthew J. Costello
- ☐ 2. James Kahn
- ☐ 3. Alan Dean Foster
- ☐ 4. Brian Daley
- ☐ 5. L. Neil Smith

27 Who coined the term "sci-fi"?

- ☐ 1. Isaac Asimov
- ☐ 2. Harlan Ellison
- ☐ 3. Ray Bradbury
- ☐ 4. Forrest J Ackerman
- ☐ 5. Mark Adlard

28 Who founded AMAZING STORIES?

- ☐ 1. George Scithers
- ☐ 2. Hugo Gernsback
- ☐ 3. Kim Mohan
- ☐ 4. David Keller
- ☐ 5. Julius Schwartz

29 The February 15, 1959, episode of the show SUSPENSE dramatized the time-paradox story "The Signalman" about a train accident that is witnessed before it actually happens. Who wrote the original story?

- ☐ 1. H. P. Lovecraft
- ☐ 2. Guy de Maupassant
- ☐ 3. H. G. Wells
- ☐ 4. Charles Dickens
- ☐ 5. Rudyard Kipling

30 What was the original name of ANALOG magazine?

- ☐ 1. AMAZING STORIES
- ☐ 2. ASTOUNDING STORIES
- ☐ 3. TWO COMPLETE SCIENCE-ADVENTURE BOOKS
- ☐ 4. GALAXY
- ☐ 5. AIR WONDER STORIES

31

In fanspeak, what is a BEM?

☐ 1. Big-eared man
☐ 2. Bug-eyed monster
☐ 3. A type of waffle
☐ 4. A neo-fan
☐ 5. A professional writer

32

Although its name sounds like a potato, it was the first man-made satellite put into orbit.

☐ 1. *Spudnik*
☐ 2. *Sputnik*
☐ 3. *Potnik*
☐ 4. *Potatonik*
☐ 5. *Idaho*

33

Although he wasn't first to set foot on the moon, he did give NASA a buzz to say they'd landed.

☐ 1. Glenn
☐ 2. Aldrin
☐ 3. Miller
☐ 4. Ganglia
☐ 5. Jones

34

Name the first science-fiction magazine. (It began in 1925.)

☐ 1. ASTOUNDING STORIES
☐ 2. AMAZING STORIES
☐ 3. ASTONISHING STORIES
☐ 4. GALAXY
☐ 5. PLANET STORIES

35

What science-fiction pulp magazine spawned a comic book with a similar name?

☐ 1. WEIRD TALES
☐ 2. PLANET STORIES
☐ 3. ECLIPSE
☐ 4. AMAZING STORIES
☐ 5. ASTOUNDING SCIENCE FICTION

36 This is the only moon known to have volcanic activity (caused by tidal forces).

☐ 1. Titan
☐ 2. Io
☐ 3. Europa
☐ 4. Triton
☐ 5. Charon

37 This 1969 album by the Steve Miller Band pays tribute to an early SF novel.

☐ 1. STARSHIP
☐ 2. BRAVE NEW WORLD
☐ 3. STRANGER IN A STRANGE LAND
☐ 4. FUTURE GAMES
☐ 5. SAILOR ON THE SEAS OF FATE

38 Jefferson Airplane became this group, dominated by science-fictional themes.

☐ 1. Air Supply
☐ 2. Jefferson Starship
☐ 3. Starship
☐ 4. The Dark Star
☐ 5. Memories of Earth

39 What game company created and marketed the first role-playing game?

☐ 1. Tactical Simulations Research
☐ 2. Games Workshop
☐ 3. Wizards of the Coast
☐ 4. Arcadium
☐ 5. None of these

40 Until Walt Disney's THE LION KING, this science-fiction film was the most merchandised movie of all time.

☐ 1. E.T., THE EXTRATERRESTRIAL
☐ 2. STAR WARS
☐ 3. THE EMPIRE STRIKES BACK
☐ 4. RETURN OF THE JEDI
☐ 5. STAR TREK: THE MOTION PICTURE

41 Name the artist most known for his fantasy paintings featuring muscular, barely clad women.

- ☐ 1. Frank Kelly Freas
- ☐ 2. Vincent di Fate
- ☐ 3. Boris Vallejo
- ☐ 4. Alan M. Clark
- ☐ 5. Bob Eggleton

42 Name the artist who began by working on BUCK ROGERS and FLASH GORDON comic strips in the 1930s, then later on fantasy book covers.

- ☐ 1. Frank Kelly Freas
- ☐ 2. Don Maitz
- ☐ 3. Howard Waldrop
- ☐ 4. Frank Frazetta
- ☐ 5. Pat Morrissey

43 Name the artist who created MAD magazine's Alfred E. Neuman, and many other book and magazine covers.

- ☐ 1. Frank Kelly Freas
- ☐ 2. Don Martin
- ☐ 3. John Berkey
- ☐ 4. Richard Powers
- ☐ 5. Thomas Canty

44 Name the science-fiction cover artist whose nongenre work includes creating Captain Morgan for a series of rum ads.

- ☐ 1. Don Maitz
- ☐ 2. Michael Whelan
- ☐ 3. John Berkey
- ☐ 4. Boris Vallejo
- ☐ 5. Thomas Canty

45 What kind of farm did Luke Skywalker grow up on?

- ☐ 1. Metal farm
- ☐ 2. Moisture farm
- ☐ 3. Bantha farm
- ☐ 4. Silicatree farm
- ☐ 5. None of these

46 He was the Greek Titan chained to a rock for giving man fire.

☐ 1. Prometheus
☐ 2. Proteus
☐ 3. Pythagoras
☐ 4. Pluto
☐ 5. Charon

47 This god's serpent staff is able to open a magic door into the underworld.

☐ 1. Vulcan
☐ 2. Mercury
☐ 3. Saturn
☐ 4. Neptune
☐ 5. Athena

48 Averna was the entrance to which of the following?

☐ 1. The heavens
☐ 2. Abyss
☐ 3. Hades
☐ 4. Oceanus
☐ 5. All of these

49 Which of the following was a Gorgon?

☐ 1. Medusa
☐ 2. Stheno
☐ 3. Eurayle
☐ 4. All of these
☐ 5. None of these

50 This was the name for the ocean that surrounded the world.

☐ 1. Chaos
☐ 2. Oceanus
☐ 3. Continuum
☐ 4. Orbis
☐ 5. None of these

20-POINT QUESTIONS

1 Audiences who tuned in to the adventures of this radio superhero could send away for a secret decoder ring.

- ☐ 1. The Green Hornet
- ☐ 2. Flash Gordon
- ☐ 3. Buck Rogers
- ☐ 4. Chandu the Magician
- ☐ 5. Captain Midnight

2 STRANGEST OF ALL was a nonfiction radio program devoted to unusual and unexplained phenomena. The host was also credited with first making the public aware of flying saucers. Who was he?

- ☐ 1. Kenneth Arnold
- ☐ 2. Brad Steiger
- ☐ 3. Charles Fort
- ☐ 4. Timothy Green Beckley
- ☐ 5. Frank Edwards

3 A 1945-1946 series featured this crimefighter who had invented a capsule that made him invisible and a telepathic indicator that enabled him to read minds.

- ☐ 1. The Shadow
- ☐ 2. The Avenger
- ☐ 3. The Green Hornet
- ☐ 4. The Mysterious Traveler
- ☐ 5. The Whistler

4 What was the name of the ESCAPE episode (with a title similar to a later TV show) about a pilot who finds unknown terrors waiting when he flies higher than anyone had before?

- ☐ 1. "First Step Beyond"
- ☐ 2. "The Outer Limit"
- ☐ 3. "Sky Trek"
- ☐ 4. "Lost in Outer Space"
- ☐ 5. "Twilight Times"

5 From 1953 through 1957, Radio Luxembourg aired an English-language program about a rocket pilot whose adventures appeared in the British comic book THE EAGLE. The show had his name. Who was he?

- ☐ 1. DAN DARE
- ☐ 2. JET MORGAN
- ☐ 3. BUSTER CHARTERIS
- ☐ 4. CAPTAIN BIGGLES
- ☐ 5. SCOTT McCLOUD, SPACE ANGEL

6   The June 17, 1951, episode of DIMENSION X was a radio
dramatization of Isaac Asimov's first novel. What was the
title of this episode?

☐   1. "I, Robot"
☐   2. "Pebble in the Sky"
☐   3. "Foundation"
☐   4. "The Caves of Steel"
☐   5. "Marooned off Vesta"

7   On May 18 and May 25, 1944, the radio series
SUSPENSE broadcast a two-part adaptation of DONOVAN'S
BRAIN, about a scientist who falls under the control of a
dead man's brain. Who starred in it?

☐   1. Orson Welles
☐   2. Lew Ayres
☐   3. Basil Rathbone
☐   4. Claude Rains
☐   5. Peter Lorre

8   LUX RADIO THEATRE featured radio adaptations of films,
often using different actors than in the original. Which
actor played the alien Klaatu in their version of THE DAY
THE EARTH STOOD STILL?

☐   1. Claude Rains
☐   2. Michael Rennie
☐   3. James Mason
☐   4. Sir Cedric Hardwicke
☐   5. Dana Andrews

9   This actor, who starred in the radio series THE
ADVENTURES OF SUPERMAN, had to use two different
voices: one for Superman and one for Clark Kent.

☐   1. George Reeves
☐   2. Clayton "Bud" Collyer
☐   3. Kirk Alyn
☐   4. Alan Reed
☐   5. Tom Tyler

10   Cliff Richard starred in this musical about rock musicians
who are teleported to a distant planet. When it premiered
in London, it was the most expensive stage musical yet.

☐   1. TIME
☐   2. SPACE
☐   3. WARP
☐   4. QUANTUM
☐   5. SUMMER HOLOGRAM

11 Raul Julia was in this 1972 musical about an interplanetary garbageman 1,000 years in the future, on an asteroid called Ithaca.

- ☐ 1. QUARK
- ☐ 2. JUPITER'S JUNKMAN
- ☐ 3. THE THIEF OF GALAXIES
- ☐ 4. VIA GALACTICA
- ☐ 5. SAME TIME, NEXT LIGHT-YEAR

12 Both BELL, BOOK AND CANDLE and VISIT TO A SMALL PLANET were comedies. What else did these two Broadway productions have in common?

- ☐ 1. The same leading actor
- ☐ 2. The same leading actress
- ☐ 3. The same director
- ☐ 4. The same theater
- ☐ 5. The same cat

13 What 1942 Pulitzer Prize-winning comedy featured a dinosaur in the living room and 10 million years of history from the viewpoint of a suburban couple in New Jersey?

- ☐ 1. THE SKIN OF OUR TEETH
- ☐ 2. HEAVEN CAN WAIT
- ☐ 3. LEAVE HER TO HEAVEN
- ☐ 4. THE TIME OF OUR LIVES
- ☐ 5. HELLZAPOPPIN'

14 Who was the Broadway theater figure who began his career in the 1950s by writing scripts for TOPPER, the TV fantasy series about a couple of high-living ghosts?

- ☐ 1. Harold Prince
- ☐ 2. Bob Fosse
- ☐ 3. Stephen Sondheim
- ☐ 4. Joseph Papp
- ☐ 5. Andrew Lloyd Weber

15 The musical THE ROCKY HORROR PICTURE SHOW was originally performed in cabaret theaters, so that the audience could eat and drink during the stage performance. Who wrote and starred in it?

- ☐ 1. Graham Chapman
- ☐ 2. Jeffrey Bernard
- ☐ 3. John Mortimer
- ☐ 4. Brian O'Donoghue
- ☐ 5. Richard O'Brien

16 What well-known character in fantasy literature had a supporting role in a 1960 Broadway musical, and was the central character in another Broadway musical in 1983?

☐ 1. Alice (from ALICE IN WONDERLAND)
☐ 2. The Phantom of the Opera
☐ 3. King Arthur
☐ 4. Merlin the Magician
☐ 5. Tarzan of the Apes

17 In A NIGHT AT THE INN, an entity stalks and kills the men who stole its treasure. In THE GLITTERING GATE, two dead burglars pick the lock on Heaven's door. What Irish playwright wrote both plays?

☐ 1. William Butler Yeats
☐ 2. Oscar Wilde
☐ 3. George Bernard Shaw
☐ 4. Brendan Behan
☐ 5. Lord Dunsany

18 In what play by Spike Milligan and John Antrobus does a nuclear war destroy all life except for a few Englishmen, whom radiation is transforming into animals, furniture, and strange objects?

☐ 1. THE BED-SITTING ROOM
☐ 2. THE L-SHAPED ROOM
☐ 3. THE END OF LIFE AS WE KNOW IT
☐ 4. THE KILLING OF SISTER GEORGE
☐ 5. WHOOPS! APOCALYPSE!

19 WEIRD TALES magazine featured a sword-and-sorcery story titled "The Vengeance of Nitocris," by this author who later became one of America's greatest playwrights.

☐ 1. Arthur Miller
☐ 2. Thorton Wilder
☐ 3. Oscar Hammerstein II
☐ 4. Tennessee Williams
☐ 5. Eugene O'Neill

20 The British author F. Anstey wrote an 1885 fantasy novel about a statue that comes to life. This story inspired a 1943 Broadway musical starring Mary Martin. What was the musical's title?

☐ 1. PYGMALION
☐ 2. GALATEA
☐ 3. KIND SIR
☐ 4. ONE TOUCH OF VENUS
☐ 5. PLEASURES AND PALACES

21 Which actor, who performed in science-fiction and horror movies, got his start as a stagehand in a vaudeville theater in Colorado in the 1890s?

- ☐ 1. Boris Karloff
- ☐ 2. Lionel Atwill
- ☐ 3. Charles Middleton
- ☐ 4. Lon Chaney
- ☐ 5. Wallace Ford

22 The 1974 movie musical THE LITTLE PRINCE was about a boy from a distant asteroid. What Broadway stage director appeared in this movie, playing the role of a talking snake?

- ☐ 1. Harold Prince
- ☐ 2. Joseph Papp
- ☐ 3. Elia Kazan
- ☐ 4. Bob Fosse
- ☐ 5. Gower Champion

23 Which two SF writers collaborated on detective stories under the name "Sley Harson"?

- ☐ 1. Willey Ley and Harlan Ellison
- ☐ 2. Lester del Ray and Harry Harrison
- ☐ 3. Harlan Ellison and Henry Slesar
- ☐ 4. Charles L. Harness and Edmond Hamilton
- ☐ 5. Theodore Sturgeon and Robert Silverberg

24 Who wrote a novel as Kilgore Trout, as well as many DOC SAVAGE adventures as Kenneth Robeson?

- ☐ 1. Philip Jose Farmer
- ☐ 2. Kurt Vonnegut, Jr.
- ☐ 3. Ray Bradbury
- ☐ 4. R. L. Fanthorpe
- ☐ 5. Thomas M. Disch

25 Which fan, editor, and agent has written under the names Dr. Acula, Jacques DeForest Erman, Vespertina Torgosi, and Hubert George Wells?

- ☐ 1. Michael Resnick
- ☐ 2. Fritz Leiber
- ☐ 3. Forrest J Ackerman
- ☐ 4. Andy Hooper
- ☐ 5. Robert Bloch

26 Which author's name appeared in the credits of the television series THE STARLOST as Cordwainer Bird?

- ☐ 1. Ben Bova
- ☐ 2. Harlan Ellison
- ☐ 3. Philip K. Dick
- ☐ 4. Ray Bradbury
- ☐ 5. Rod Serling

27 Who edited AIR WONDER STORIES?

- ☐ 1. George Scithers
- ☐ 2. Hugo Gernsback
- ☐ 3. Damon Knight
- ☐ 4. David Keller
- ☐ 5. Julius Schwartz

28 Who was the artist most associated with Hugo Gernsback's AMAZING STORIES magazine?

- ☐ 1. Jack Gaughan
- ☐ 2. Frank Frazetta
- ☐ 3. Frank Kelly Freas
- ☐ 4. Frank R. Paul
- ☐ 5. Bob Eggleton

29 What was the original subtitle of AMAZING STORIES magazine?

- ☐ 1. THE MAGAZINE OF IMAGINATION
- ☐ 2. THE MAGAZINE OF SCIENTIFICTION
- ☐ 3. THE MAGAZINE OF FANTASY & SCIENCE FICTION
- ☐ 4. HOME OF THE SPACE LEAGUE
- ☐ 5. HOME OF SCIENCE FICTION ADVENTURE

30 NASA took over space exploration from this military agency.

- ☐ 1. The Army
- ☐ 2. The Navy
- ☐ 3. The Air Force
- ☐ 4. The Marines
- ☐ 5. The Coast Guard

31 Some astronomers think one of these lies at the center of our galaxy.

☐ 1. Quasar
☐ 2. Black hole
☐ 3. Neutron star
☐ 4. Cosmic string
☐ 5. Alien civilization

32 Bell Telephone discovered low-level radiation that is considered evidence for this celestial event.

☐ 1. Dark matter
☐ 2. Black holes
☐ 3. Cosmic strings
☐ 4. The Big Bang
☐ 5. Cold fusion

33 Name the gold record that went with the *Voyager* spacecraft.

☐ 1. THE BEST OF EARTH
☐ 2. SOUNDS OF EARTH
☐ 3. HUMANITY PLAYS
☐ 4. FROM EARTH TO THE STARS
☐ 5. COSMIC NOISES

34 This belt separates the inner solar system from the outer.

☐ 1. Van Allen Belt
☐ 2. Clark Belt
☐ 3. Black belt
☐ 4. Asteroid belt
☐ 5. Money belt

35 *Voyager 1* and *Voyager 2* were launched to take advantage of an unusual lineup of the planets in the early 1980s. Name it.

☐ 1. Syzygy
☐ 2. Great arc
☐ 3. Star line
☐ 4. Continum
☐ 5. Parallax

36 Name the space shuttle that exploded in 1987.

☐ 1. DISCOVERY
☐ 2. COLUMBIA
☐ 3. CHALLENGER
☐ 4. VOYAGER
☐ 5. ENTERPRISE

37 He wrote and sang about Ziggy Stardust.

☐ 1. Pink Floyd
☐ 2. David Bowie
☐ 3. Peter Hammill
☐ 4. Paul Kantner
☐ 5. Marty Balin

38 What was the DUNGEONS AND DRAGONS game before it became a role-playing game?

☐ 1. A war game
☐ 2. A fantasy novel
☐ 3. A board game
☐ 4. A card game
☐ 5. It was always a role-playing game

39 Name TSR's postapocalypse, science-fiction role-playing game.

☐ 1. FALLOUT
☐ 2. GAMMA WORLD
☐ 3. STAR WORLD
☐ 4. END TIMES
☐ 5. There was no SF game.

40 How many character classes did the DUNGEONS AND DRAGONS game originally have?

☐ 1. Four
☐ 2. Five
☐ 3. Six
☐ 4. Seven
☐ 5. Eight

41 The first run of STAR WARS trading cards appeared in this unlikely place.

- ☐ 1. On Coca-Cola cans and bottles
- ☐ 2. Inside bags containing Wonder Bread
- ☐ 3. Inside cereal boxes
- ☐ 4. Inside newspapers
- ☐ 5. With baseball cards

42 Who wrote the score for STAR WARS?

- ☐ 1. Michael Nyman
- ☐ 2. John Williams
- ☐ 3. Richard Strauss
- ☐ 4. Bernard Hermann
- ☐ 5. Joseph Cornell

43 This science-fiction cover artist also does the covers for THE CAT WHO . . . mystery series by Lilian Jackson Braun.

- ☐ 1. Alan M. Clark
- ☐ 2. Jill Bauman
- ☐ 3. George Barr
- ☐ 4. Jim Burns
- ☐ 5. Michael Whelan

44 Name the artist who is best known for his work on WEIRD TALES magazine in the 1930s, including designing its distinctive logo.

- ☐ 1. Hal Foster
- ☐ 2. Hannes Bok
- ☐ 3. Harry Harrison
- ☐ 4. Wally Wood
- ☐ 5. Joe Orlando

45 Name the artist who won the Hugo for Best Professional in 1979 and now works for NASA.

- ☐ 1. Thomas Canty
- ☐ 2. Vincent Di Fate
- ☐ 3. Harry O. Morris
- ☐ 4. J. K. Potter
- ☐ 5. H. R. Geiger

46 Name the early science-fiction and fantasy artist who often cast movie stars in his story illustrations, and whose work excelled in the glamorous and the macabre.

- ☐ 1. Hannes Bok
- ☐ 2. Virgil Finlay
- ☐ 3. Steven Fabian
- ☐ 4. Thomas Canty
- ☐ 5. George Barr

47 Name the U.K. illustrator whose work with the presses DRAGON'S DREAM and PAPER TIGER have been quite influential.

- ☐ 1. Roger Eklund
- ☐ 2. Roger Dean
- ☐ 3. Alan M. Clark
- ☐ 4. Don Maitz
- ☐ 5. Thomas Canty

48 The first Death Star was destroyed by these STAR TREK weapons.

- ☐ 1. Phasers
- ☐ 2. Photon torpedos
- ☐ 3. Disintegrators
- ☐ 4. Blasters
- ☐ 5. None of these

49 According to the Greeks, this Titan created humanity.

- ☐ 1. Zeus
- ☐ 2. Proteus
- ☐ 3. Prometheus
- ☐ 4. Pluto
- ☐ 5. Charon

50 Athena burst out of whose head, fully grown?

- ☐ 1. Apollo
- ☐ 2. Zeus
- ☐ 3. Diana
- ☐ 4. Aphrodite
- ☐ 5. None of these

30-POINT QUESTIONS

1 He wrote the theme music for THE ADDAMS FAMILY TV series.

- ☐ 1. Bernard Hermann
- ☐ 2. Charles Ives
- ☐ 3. Les Mizzy
- ☐ 4. The Beatles
- ☐ 5. John Denver

2 One of Rod Serling's mentors was this man, who wrote science-fiction scripts and horror stories for radio shows in the 1940s.

- ☐ 1. Henry Kuttner
- ☐ 2. Henry Corwin
- ☐ 3. Norman Corwin
- ☐ 4. Irwin Corey
- ☐ 5. Roger Corman

3 From 1951 to 1953, the British Broadcasting Company aired a radio serial based on this then-recent series of linked novels.

- ☐ 1. Isaac Asimov's FOUNDATION trilogy
- ☐ 2. C. S. Lewis' PERELANDRA trilogy
- ☐ 3. C. S. Lewis' THE CHRONICLES OF NARNIA
- ☐ 4. Edgar Rice Burroughs' JOHN CARTER novels
- ☐ 5. J. R. R. Tolkien's THE HOBBIT and THE LORD OF THE RINGS

4 Singing cowboy Gene Autry hosted a popular country-western radio show. What was the name of that radio program, which received several plugs in his 1935 movie THE PHANTOM EMPIRE?

- ☐ 1. RIDERS OF THE PURPLE SAGE
- ☐ 2. HAPPY TRAILS
- ☐ 3. SONS OF THE PIONEERS
- ☐ 4. GHOST RIDERS IN THE SKY
- ☐ 5. GENE AUTRY'S MELODY RANCH

5 SUSPENSE starred Henry Hull in one of Edgar Allan Poe's short stories, and used that same story again later, with Jose Ferrer. What was the title of the story?

- ☐ 1. "The Black Cat"
- ☐ 2. "The Tell-Tale Heart"
- ☐ 3. "The Pit and the Pendulum"
- ☐ 4. "The Cask of Amontillado"
- ☐ 5. "William Wilson"

6

The April 22, 1950, episode of DIMENSION X was "Report on the Barnhouse Effect," about a man who could mentally control objects. Who wrote the story that provided the basis for the radio show?

☐ 1. John W. Campbell, Jr.
☐ 2. Kurt Vonnegut, Jr.
☐ 3. Robert A. Heinlein
☐ 4. Frederik Pohl
☐ 5. Fletcher Pratt

7

Whom did Jason Robards, Sr., play in the radio series, which ran from 1932 through 1936, about a man with supernatural powers? (The film version of this series starred Bela Lugosi as the same character.)

☐ 1. Chandu the Magician
☐ 2. Mandrake the Magician
☐ 3. Mister Wong
☐ 4. The Voodoo Man
☐ 5. Black Dragon

8

Which actor, who later starred in Ray Harryhausen's version of MYSTERIOUS ISLAND, played Batman on several episodes of the radio program THE ADVENTURES OF SUPERMAN?

☐ 1. Lewis Wilson
☐ 2. J. Carroll Naish
☐ 3. Michael Anderson
☐ 4. Gary Merrill
☐ 5. Glenn Anders

9

TARZAN OF THE APES was a syndicated radio program broadcast from 1932 through 1935. What actor, who played Tarzan on film, supplied the radio voice of Tarzan?

☐ 1. Johnny Weismuller
☐ 2. Buster Crabbe
☐ 3. James Pierce
☐ 4. Lex Barker
☐ 5. Herman Brix

10

The June 24, 1950, episode of DIMENSION X featured a radio version of material that also became a science-fiction movie produced by George Pal. What was the title of this episode?

☐ 1. "Destination: Moon"
☐ 2. "The Time Machine"
☐ 3. "The War of the Worlds"
☐ 4. "First Men in the Moon"
☐ 5. "The Seven Faces of Doctor Lao"

11

What episode of the anthology series SUSPENSE featured Ronald Colman in a radio adaptation of a story, by H. P. Lovecraft, about a monstrous creature that menaces a town in New England?

- ☐ 1. "The Colour out of Space"
- ☐ 2. "The Case of Charles Dexter Ward"
- ☐ 3. "The Outsider"
- ☐ 4. "The Dunwich Horror"
- ☐ 5. "Pickman's Model"

12

Orson Welles was the creative force behind the MERCURY THEATRE ON THE AIR. In 1938, for its very first program, it aired a dramatization of which famous novel?

- ☐ 1. THE STRANGE CASE OF DOCTOR JEKYLL AND MISTER HYDE
- ☐ 2. THE WAR OF THE WORLDS
- ☐ 3. DRACULA
- ☐ 4. FRANKENSTEIN, OR THE MODERN PROMETHEUS
- ☐ 5. THE INVISIBLE MAN

13

Before actor Al Hodge played the spaceman hero of CAPTAIN VIDEO, he played the title role in a radio serial that featured science-fiction plotlines. What character did Hodge portray?

- ☐ 1. Captain Midnight
- ☐ 2. Jack Armstrong
- ☐ 3. Buck Rogers
- ☐ 4. The Shadow
- ☐ 5. The Green Hornet

14

What scriptwriter for the radio series DIMENSION X made the transition to TV by writing several teleplays for THE TWILIGHT ZONE, and is now best known for his television writing?

- ☐ 1. Earl Hamner, Jr.
- ☐ 2. Buck Houghton
- ☐ 3. Richard Matheson
- ☐ 4. Montgomery Pittman
- ☐ 5. George Clayton Johnson

15

In Woody Allen's play DEATH KNOCKS, the specter of Death gambles with a Jewish businessman for the possession of his immortal soul. What game does Death play with his victim?

- ☐ 1. Chess
- ☐ 2. Checkers
- ☐ 3. Gin rummy
- ☐ 4. Scrabble
- ☐ 5. Monopoly

16 This British comedy revue, which had long stage runs in Edinburgh, London, and New York, featured a scene titled "The Heat-death of the Universe."

- ☐ 1. CAMBRIDGE CIRCUS
- ☐ 2. GOOD EVENING
- ☐ 3. MONTY PYTHON LIVE!
- ☐ 4. BEYOND THE FRINGE
- ☐ 5. AND NOW FOR SOMETHING COMPLETELY DIFFERENT

17 Zero Mostel and Gene Wilder starred in the film version of what stage play about men who gradually turn into animals?

- ☐ 1. THE PRODUCERS
- ☐ 2. THE HIPPOPOTAMUS
- ☐ 3. RHINOCEROS
- ☐ 4. THE ELEPHANT MAN
- ☐ 5. THE BED-SITTING ROOM

18 Which of the actors in the film version of CARRIE also appeared in the Broadway musical CARRIE, but in a different role?

- ☐ 1. Sissy Spacek
- ☐ 2. William Katt
- ☐ 3. Amy Irving
- ☐ 4. Priscilla Pointer
- ☐ 5. Betty Buckley

19 In 1977, STAR TREK's Leonard Nimoy starred in which play that probes the borders between sanity and madness?

- ☐ 1. THESPIS
- ☐ 2. EQUUS
- ☐ 3. THANATOS
- ☐ 4. FIVE-FINGER EXERCISE
- ☐ 5. THE THIN BLUE LINE

20 Which actor, who appeared in several science-fiction films, starred on Broadway in 1981 as a hideously deformed man in the play THE ELEPHANT MAN?

- ☐ 1. Harrison Ford
- ☐ 2. Tim Curry
- ☐ 3. Arnold Schwarzenegger
- ☐ 4. Mark Hamill
- ☐ 5. Richard Kiel

21 In WAITING FOR GODOT, two men named Estragon and Vladimir find themselves unable to escape from their waiting. Whom do the characters Estragon and Vladimir symbolize?

☐ 1. Life and Death
☐ 2. Burns and Allen
☐ 3. Sanity and Madness
☐ 4. Abbott and Costello
☐ 5. Laurel and Hardy

22 THE PRISONER was filmed in Portmeirion. Almost thirty years earlier, what play with a fantasy theme was written in this village by an author who spent many summers there?

☐ 1. OUTWARD BOUND
☐ 2. BLITHE SPIRIT
☐ 3. BERKELEY SQUARE
☐ 4. AN INSPECTOR CALLS
☐ 5. MACHINAL

23 In 1948, Boris Karloff starred on Broadway in THE LINDEN TREE. Which actress, who played the housekeeper in this play, also performed with Karloff in the film THE BRIDE OF FRANKENSTEIN?

☐ 1. Una O'Connor
☐ 2. Elsa Lanchester
☐ 3. Valerie Hobson
☐ 4. Marilyn Harris
☐ 5. Heather Angel

24 Enid Bagnold's comedy A MATTER OF GRAVITY is about an elderly woman who frequently becomes weightless and rises into the air. The 1976 Broadway production of this play featured what actress?

☐ 1. Helen Hayes
☐ 2. Mary Martin
☐ 3. Frances Sternhagen
☐ 4. Katherine Hepburn
☐ 5. Maureen Stapleton

25 Isaac Asimov's science-fiction story "The Up-to-Date Sorcerer" borrows part of its plot from a nineteenth-century fantasy play titled THE SORCERER. Who wrote it?

☐ 1. Gilbert and Sullivan
☐ 2. Oscar Wilde
☐ 3. Dion Boucicault
☐ 4. Florence Farr
☐ 5. George Bernard Shaw

26 What horror author writes funny fantasy under the name Lionel Fenn?

☐ 1. Charles L. Grant
☐ 2. Dean Koontz
☐ 3. Harlan Ellison
☐ 4. John Farris
☐ 5. Michael McDowell

27 What husband-and-wife team combined to write a television tie-in under the name Sandy Schofield?

☐ 1. A. E. Van Vogt and E. Mayne Hull
☐ 2. Ben and Barbara Bova
☐ 3. Kristine Katherine Rusch and Dean Wesley Smith
☐ 4. Henry Kuttner and C. L. Moore
☐ 5. Frederik Pohl and Judith Merril

28 British author Eric Arthur Blair wrote under what pseudonym?

☐ 1. Aldous Huxley
☐ 2. Brian W. Aldiss
☐ 3. Harry Harrison
☐ 4. George Orwell
☐ 5. Michael Moorcock

29 What action-adventure novelist wrote several soft-core porn novels as Dan Britain?

☐ 1. Nick Carter
☐ 2. Robert Silverberg
☐ 3. Don Pendleton
☐ 4. Warren Murphy
☐ 5. Richard Sapir

30 Who founded the publishing company Ace Books?

☐ 1. A. A. Wyn
☐ 2. Ian Ballantine
☐ 3. Donald A. Wollheim
☐ 4. Tom Doherty
☐ 5. Bill Fawcett

31 Who was the first editor of ISAAC ASIMOV'S SCIENCE FICTION MAGAZINE?

- ☐ 1. George Scithers
- ☐ 2. Isaac Asimov
- ☐ 3. Shawna McCarthy
- ☐ 4. Hugh B. Cave
- ☐ 5. Patrick Price

32 The OXFORD ENGLISH DICTIONARY credits this writer with the first modern use of "android."

- ☐ 1. Isaac Asimov
- ☐ 2. Clifford D. Simak
- ☐ 3. Ray Bradbury
- ☐ 4. Poul Anderson
- ☐ 5. Henry Kuttner

33 He coined the term "inner space."

- ☐ 1. Isaac Asimov
- ☐ 2. Anton Chekhov
- ☐ 3. J. G. Ballard
- ☐ 4. Brian Aldiss
- ☐ 5. Harlan Ellison

34 He is the most famous translator of THE ARABIAN NIGHTS into English.

- ☐ 1. H. G. Wells
- ☐ 2. Sir Richard Burton
- ☐ 3. Lawrence of Arabia
- ☐ 4. Saki
- ☐ 5. Sabu

35 This cloud is believed to be where comets come from.

- ☐ 1. Oort
- ☐ 2. Comet
- ☐ 3. Haley
- ☐ 4. Wort
- ☐ 5. Van Allen

36 In the 1950s this planet was believed to be like the moon, revolving at the same speed it rotates, thus always keeping the same face to the sun.

- ☐ 1. Mercury
- ☐ 2. Jupiter
- ☐ 3. Saturn
- ☐ 4. Neptune
- ☐ 5. Pluto

37 What was the name of the first living creature to orbit Earth?

- ☐ 1. Yuri
- ☐ 2. Scott
- ☐ 3. Laika
- ☐ 4. Bongo
- ☐ 5. Joe

38 How many planets (aside from Earth) did the ancient Greeks know about?

- ☐ 1. Four
- ☐ 2. Five
- ☐ 3. Six
- ☐ 4. Seven
- ☐ 5. Ten

39 Halley's Comet reappears every how many years?

- ☐ 1. 67
- ☐ 2. 76
- ☐ 3. 56
- ☐ 4. 65
- ☐ 5. 86

40 How many planets have been discovered to have rings?

- ☐ 1. One
- ☐ 2. Two
- ☐ 3. Three
- ☐ 4. Four
- ☐ 5. Five

41

Who was the first astronomer to use a telescope?

- ☐ 1. Copernicus
- ☐ 2. Kepler
- ☐ 3. Newton
- ☐ 4. Galileo
- ☐ 5. Herschel

42

Gustav Holst wrote this suite, named for the members of the solar system.

- ☐ 1. HOME SYSTEM
- ☐ 2. THE PLANETS
- ☐ 3. EARTH, SUN AND MOON
- ☐ 4. MUSIC OF THE SPHERES
- ☐ 5. THE WANDERING STARS

43

Name the Philip Glass opera, produced in 1988, featuring an alien abduction and time travel.

- ☐ 1. VALIS
- ☐ 2. 1,000 AIRPLANES ON THE ROOF
- ☐ 3. THE MARRIAGE BETWEEN ZONES
- ☐ 4. KOYANISQUATSI
- ☐ 5. EINSTEIN ON THE BEACH

44

What fast-food restaurant sold STAR TREK II: THE WRATH OF KHAN glasses?

- ☐ 1. McDonald's
- ☐ 2. Burger King
- ☐ 3. Arby's
- ☐ 4. Roy Rogers
- ☐ 5. Wendy's

45

Name the well-known artist who won the 1953 Hugo for Best Cover, shortly before becoming a full-time astrologer.

- ☐ 1. Virgil Finlay
- ☐ 2. Hannes Bok
- ☐ 3. Hal Foster
- ☐ 4. Jack Gaughan
- ☐ 5. Paul Lehr

46 He won the Best Artist Hugo every year between 1954 and 1960.

☐ 1. Ed Emshwiller
☐ 2. Hannes Bok
☐ 3. Frank Kelly Freas
☐ 4. Jack Gaughan
☐ 5. Jim Burns

47 This artist painted covers for Arthur C. Clarke's VENUS PRIME series and for Robert Silverberg and Karen Haber's MUTANT series. He won a Hugo in 1987.

☐ 1. Don Maitz
☐ 2. Jim Burns
☐ 3. Frank Kelly Freas
☐ 4. Rick Sternbach
☐ 5. Alan M. Clark

48 Paris judged a beauty contest among goddesses and received this woman as a bride.

☐ 1. Athena
☐ 2. Venus
☐ 3. Aphrodite
☐ 4. Diana
☐ 5. Helen

49 Whose three-headed dog did Orpheus sing to sleep?

☐ 1. Pluto
☐ 2. Charon
☐ 3. Zeus
☐ 4. Mercury
☐ 5. Saturn

50 Name the boatman of the River Styx.

☐ 1. Pluto
☐ 2. Cerberus
☐ 3. Charon
☐ 4. Persephone
☐ 5. None of these

40-POINT QUESTIONS

1 Who played the title role on the radio program FLASH GORDON?

- ☐ 1. Buster Crabbe
- ☐ 2. Ezra Stone
- ☐ 3. Gale Gordon
- ☐ 4. Clayton "Bud" Collyer
- ☐ 5. Charles Middleton

2 In 1990, the British Broadcasting Corporation aired a radio play based on this novel by H. G. Wells. The actors supplied the voices of men and animals; no women's voices were used.

- ☐ 1. THE FOOD OF THE GODS
- ☐ 2. TONO-BUNGAY
- ☐ 3. THE FIRST MEN IN THE MOON
- ☐ 4. STAR-BEGOTTEN
- ☐ 5. THE ISLAND OF DOCTOR MOREAU

3 Which character in the SUPERMAN comic books originated as a character on the radio show THE ADVENTURES OF SUPERMAN?

- ☐ 1. Perry White
- ☐ 2. Lana Lang
- ☐ 3. Martha Kent
- ☐ 4. Lex Luthor
- ☐ 5. Jimmy Olsen

4 What weekly radio show was notorious for offering the ghastliest sound effects? In a typical episode, audiences heard the sound of a man being turned inside out by a sinister fog.

- ☐ 1. X MINUS ONE
- ☐ 2. LIGHTS OUT
- ☐ 3. THE MYSTERIOUS STRANGER
- ☐ 4. INNER SANCTUM
- ☐ 5. DIMENSION X

5 The radio program THE SAINT often featured mad scientists and doomsday inventions, although the TV and book versions did not. Who played the Saint on CBS in 1947, on Mutual in 1949, and on NBC in 1950?

- ☐ 1. George Sanders
- ☐ 2. Vincent Price
- ☐ 3. Charles Laughton
- ☐ 4. Douglas Dumbrille
- ☐ 5. Cyril Ritchard

6   The science-fiction radio series LATITUDE ZERO ran from 1943 through 1948. What was the main setting for the adventures in LATITUDE ZERO?

☐   1. A submarine
☐   2. A secret air base
☐   3. The South Pole
☐   4. A colony on Mars
☐   5. A lost city in equatorial Africa

7   SPACE PATROL ran on the ABC radio network from 1950 through 1955. The patrol's headquarters were located in a place called Terra. What was Terra?

☐   1. A colony on Mars
☐   2. A hidden city on Earth
☐   3. An orbiting space station
☐   4. A man-made planet
☐   5. A fancy name for Earth

8   What radio series featured a ghoulish host who journeyed by train to the scene of each week's episode—and just when the hero was about to be eaten by monsters, rode off into the night?

☐   1. MIDNIGHT EXPRESS
☐   2. THE MYSTERIOUS TRAVELER
☐   3. THE AWFUL DOCTOR WEIRD
☐   4. THE DARK STRANGER
☐   5. THE END OF THE LINE

9   The October 12, 1954, broadcast of THE WAR OF THE WORLDS on the program LUX RADIO THEATRE cast Pat Crowley in Anne Robinson's role from the film. Who played the starring role of the scientist?

☐   1. Orson Welles
☐   2. Gene Barry
☐   3. Dana Andrews
☐   4. Kevin McCarthy
☐   5. Joseph Cotten

10   On the September 13, 1943, broadcast of THE PHANTOM OF THE OPERA on LUX RADIO THEATRE, which movie star gave voice to the Phantom?

☐   1. Basil Rathbone
☐   2. Boris Karloff
☐   3. Lon Chaney, Jr.
☐   4. Herbert Lom
☐   5. Claude Rains, reprising his film performance

11 One radio superhero had a sidekick named Ichabod Mudd, played by actor Hugh Studebaker. Which radio series featured Ichabod Mudd?

- [ ] 1. BUCK ROGERS IN THE TWENTY-FIFTH CENTURY
- [ ] 2. THE ADVENTURES OF SUPERMAN
- [ ] 3. THE GREEN HORNET
- [ ] 4. TOM CORBETT, SPACE CADET
- [ ] 5. THE ADVENTURES OF CAPTAIN MIDNIGHT

12 Robert A. Heinlein's classic story "The Green Hills of Earth," about a blind spaceman, was adapted into an episode of this radio program.

- [ ] 1. X MINUS ONE
- [ ] 2. DIMENSION X
- [ ] 3. BEYOND TOMORROW
- [ ] 4. HALL OF FANTASY
- [ ] 5. TOM CORBETT, SPACE CADET

13 Many classic radio shows are lost because they were broadcast live, with no transcripts. But, from 1973 to 1975, surviving transcripts of what series were broadcast once a month on NBC radio?

- [ ] 1. LIGHTS OUT
- [ ] 2. DIMENSION X
- [ ] 3. FLASH GORDON
- [ ] 4. X MINUS ONE
- [ ] 5. BUCK ROGERS IN THE TWENTY-FIFTH CENTURY

14 Actor Maurice Tarplin played the mad scientist who lived near a cemetery and narrated this radio series that emphasized ghoulish horror rather than adventure. What was the show's name?

- [ ] 1. THE STRANGE DOCTOR WEIRD
- [ ] 2. THE WEIRD DOCTOR STRANGE
- [ ] 3. LIGHTS OUT
- [ ] 4. INNER SANCTUM
- [ ] 5. THE SECRETS OF DOCTOR GRAVES

15 In 1956, CBS RADIO WORKSHOP broadcast a two-part adaptation of a major science-fiction novel. The author of the original novel served as its narrator. Who was the author, and what was his novel?

- [ ] 1. Ray Bradbury, THE MARTIAN CHRONICLES
- [ ] 2. Isaac Asimov, THE CAVES OF STEEL
- [ ] 3. Robert A. Heinlein, STARSHIP TROOPERS
- [ ] 4. Hal Clement, A MISSION OF GRAVITY
- [ ] 5. Aldous Huxley, BRAVE NEW WORLD

16

During the 1930s and 1940s, who wrote and produced more than 500 radio scripts dealing with SF, fantasy, and horror themes? (He also wrote and directed two SF movies: FIVE and THE TWONKY.)

☐ 1. Henry Kuttner
☐ 2. Arch Oboler
☐ 3. Norman Corwin
☐ 4. Lewis Padgett
☐ 5. Edmond Hamilton

17

One of EVERYMAN'S THEATRE's best episodes was "Two," the story of the last man and woman left on Earth after a nuclear war. The man was played by Raymond Edward Johnson. Who played the last woman?

☐ 1. Joan Crawford
☐ 2. Bette Davis
☐ 3. Carole Lombard
☐ 4. Barbara Stanwyck
☐ 5. Agnes Moorehead

18

What stage play is about a meek bank clerk who is teleported to a distant planet and becomes a superhero whose brain waves cause instant death? (The scenery and poster were by comics artist Neal Adams.)

☐ 1. PARADOX
☐ 2. SPACE
☐ 3. TOMORROW
☐ 4. FOREVER
☐ 5. WARP

19

What play by Crane Wilbur became a 1925 silent film, starring Lon Chaney, about a couple who can't start their car in a rainstorm and so become prisoners of a mad scientist who turns men into women?

☐ 1. THE ROCKY HORROR SHOW
☐ 2. THE MONSTER
☐ 3. THE MIRACLE MAN
☐ 4. LONDON AFTER MIDNIGHT
☐ 5. A BLIND BARGAIN

20

In the 1966 musical IT'S A BIRD, IT'S A PLANE, IT'S SUPERMAN, what was the name of the evil scientist who vowed to destroy Superman?

☐ 1. Lex Luthor
☐ 2. Rex Ruthor
☐ 3. Abner Sedgwick
☐ 4. Abner Yokum
☐ 5. Lena Thorul

21 The guest star in the STAR TREK episode "Elaan of Troyius" was European-born actress France Nuyen. She and STAR TREK's William Shatner had appeared together in what 1958 Broadway play?

☐ 1. THE WORLD OF SUZIE WONG
☐ 2. THE WORLD OF HENRY ORIENT
☐ 3. A SHOT IN THE DARK
☐ 4. TEAHOUSE OF THE AUGUST MOON
☐ 5. THE REMARKABLE MR. MARKESAN

22 This was the very first American musical—a sword-and-sorcery melodrama featuring wizards. First produced in New York City in 1866, it ran for 475 performances. What was its title?

☐ 1. THE BLACK CROOK
☐ 2. THE BLACK GOBLIN
☐ 3. THE PINK FAIRY
☐ 4. THE PRINCESS AND THE GOBLINS
☐ 5. THE MOON MAIDEN

23 RED PLANET, a 1932 play about a married couple who try to contact Mars with a new kind of radio, featured this male lead, who also appeared in THE MUMMY and SVENGALI.

☐ 1. David Manners
☐ 2. Bramwell Fletcher
☐ 3. Henry Victor
☐ 4. Noble Johnson
☐ 5. Edward Van Sloan

24 What 1914 fantasy novel written by L. Frank Baum was based on his musical comedy that was performed in Los Angeles in 1913?

☐ 1. THE SCARECROW OF OZ
☐ 2. THE LAND OF OZ
☐ 3. TIK-TOK OF OZ
☐ 4. QUEEN ZIXI OF IX
☐ 5. THE MASTER KEY

25 If some crucial event in the past had occurred differently, the present and future would be radically altered. What was the title of a 1932 Broadway play by Arthur Goodman exploring this theme?

☐ 1. IF THE KAISER HAD WON
☐ 2. IF BOOTH HAD MISSED
☐ 3. LEE'S VICTORY AT GETTYSBURG
☐ 4. THE MURDER OF GEORGE WASHINGTON
☐ 5. IF CHRIST HAD NOT DIED

26 H. P. Lovecraft's favorite movie was the film version of what Balderston play about a twentieth-century man who travels back in time to the mind and body of his 18th-century ancestor?

☐ 1. BID TIME RETURN
☐ 2. I'LL NEVER FORGET YOU
☐ 3. HANGOVER SQUARE
☐ 4. BERKELEY SQUARE
☐ 5. PICCADILLY INCIDENT

27 What operetta by Gilbert and Sullivan features a spooky Gothic castle, an ancient curse, and a chorus line of musical ghosts?

☐ 1. THE SORCERER
☐ 2. RUDDIGORE
☐ 3. IOLANTHE
☐ 4. UTOPIA, LIMITED
☐ 5. PRINCESS IDA

28 HOW I WONDER was a play about an astronomy professor who tries to prevent an atomic war that will destroy all life. He was played by _____, who had already seen the end of humanity in a film.

☐ 1. Ralph Richardson
☐ 2. John Gielgud
☐ 3. Ernest Thesiger
☐ 4. Raymond Massey
☐ 5. Leclic Banks

29 "Papa" John Phillips, the leader of the pop group the Mamas and the Papas, also wrote the script and songs for MAN ON THE MOON. Who was the impresario who financed this fiasco?

☐ 1. Andrew Lloyd Weber
☐ 2. Andy Warhol
☐ 3. Harold Prince
☐ 4. Gower Champion
☐ 5. Lord Delfont

30 Who wrote the 1968 detective story "The Hippie Slayer" under the name Jay Solo?

☐ 1. Harlan Ellison
☐ 2. Ray Bradbury
☐ 3. Frederik Pohl
☐ 4. Judith Merril
☐ 5. Andre Norton

31 Under what name did Dean Koontz write the science-fiction novel INVASION (published by Laser Books)?

- ☐ 1. Brian Coffey
- ☐ 2. Owen West
- ☐ 3. David Axton
- ☐ 4. Aaron Wolfe
- ☐ 5. Leigh Nichols

32 Which horror writer did three film novelizations under the name Jack Martin?

- ☐ 1. Matthew J. Costello
- ☐ 2. William Peter Blatty
- ☐ 3. Richard Matheson
- ☐ 4. Dennis Etchison
- ☐ 5. Clive Barker

33 C. M. Kornbluth collaborated with what female writer to produce two novels by Cyril Judd?

- ☐ 1. Marion Zimmer Bradley
- ☐ 2. C. L. Moore
- ☐ 3. Judith Merril
- ☐ 4. Zenna Henderson
- ☐ 5. James Tiptree, Jr.

34 What Golden Age SF writer wrote a historical novel under the name Frederick R. Ewing, and a detective novel under the name Ellery Queen?

- ☐ 1. Robert A. Heinlein
- ☐ 2. Theodore Sturgeon
- ☐ 3. Fritz Leiber
- ☐ 4. Robert Bloch
- ☐ 5. Harlan Ellison

35 What horror and suspense writer wrote under the name Tarleton Fiske, as well as house names such as Will Folke, Wilson Kane, and John Seldon?

- ☐ 1. Robert Bloch
- ☐ 2. Richard Matheson
- ☐ 3. Ray Bradbury
- ☐ 4. Charles Beaumont
- ☐ 5. George Clayton Johnson

36 He established the Fantasy Foundation.

☐ 1. Isaac Asimov
☐ 2. Damon Knight
☐ 3. Forrest J Ackerman
☐ 4. Ronald Anthony Quinn
☐ 5. Jack Kirby

37 ALGOL, a prominent fanzine, was edited by whom?

☐ 1. Dick Lynch
☐ 2. Andrew Porter
☐ 3. Charles N. Brown
☐ 4. Darrell Schweitzer
☐ 5. Harry Houdini

38 A satellite continuously orbiting above the same spot on Earth is in this.

☐ 1. A static orbit
☐ 2. A geosynchronous orbit
☐ 3. An Earth-inclined orbit
☐ 4. A permanent orbit
☐ 5. None of these

39 What are meteors called after they enter Earth's atmosphere?

☐ 1. Asteroids
☐ 2. Hemorrhoids
☐ 3. Meteorites
☐ 4. Flying rocks
☐ 5. Meteors

40 Who first saw the red spot on Jupiter, whose four main moons are named for him?

☐ 1. Copernicus
☐ 2. Kepler
☐ 3. Hegel
☐ 4. Galileo
☐ 5. Euclid

41

Although only one division in them is visible from Earth, *Voyager* showed that they actually are very finely divided. What are they?

☐ 1. Comets
☐ 2. Moons
☐ 3. Sunspots
☐ 4. Saturn's rings
☐ 5. Colored bands

42

What does the SETI program search for?

☐ 1. Terrestrial intelligent life
☐ 2. Extraterrestrial intelligent life
☐ 3. Other solar systems with planets
☐ 4. Black holes
☐ 5. Extraterrestrial life forms

43

What is the only planet not to be examined by an unmanned probe?

☐ 1. Earth
☐ 2. Mars
☐ 3. Saturn
☐ 4. Neptune
☐ 5. Pluto

44

The name of this moon of Pluto was associated with Pluto in mythology, too.

☐ 1. Persephone
☐ 2. Ceres
☐ 3. Cerberus
☐ 4. Charon
☐ 5. Mercury

45

H. P. Lovecraft's fungal invaders come from this planet, discovered in the 1930s.

☐ 1. Yuggoth
☐ 2. Charon
☐ 3. Pluto
☐ 4. Neptune
☐ 5. Uranus

46 Name the American space station that fell into the Indian Ocean in the 1970s.

☐ 1. *Sky Station*
☐ 2. *Sky Lab*
☐ 3. *Mir*
☐ 4. *Space Station Freedom*
☐ 5. *Space Station X-1*

47 This science-fiction opera, Philip Glass's first, ends on a spaceship.

☐ 1. 1,000 AIRPLANES ON THE ROOF
☐ 2. CHRISTOPHER COLUMBUS
☐ 3. EINSTEIN ON THE BEACH
☐ 4. THE MARRIAGE BETWEEN ZONES THREE, FOUR AND FIVE
☐ 5. THE MAKING OF REPRESENTATIVE FOR PLANET 8

48 Name the artist whose realistic paintings and illustrations earned him many Hugo Awards in the 1980s.

☐ 1. Michael Whelan
☐ 2. Jim Burns
☐ 3. Don Maitz
☐ 4. Alan M. Clark
☐ 5. Jack Gaughan

49 Name the artist whose sharply defined paintings of spaceships with a palette knife are his trademark.

☐ 1. Rick Sternbach
☐ 2. George Barr
☐ 3. John Berkey
☐ 4. Alan M. Clark
☐ 5. Boris Vallejo

50 Name the artist who launched Frank Frazetta's career in science fiction by recommending him to work on Edgar Rice Burroughs' books.

☐ 1. Rick Sternbach
☐ 2. Jack Gaughan
☐ 3. Steven Fabian
☐ 4. Roy Krenkel
☐ 5. Frank Kelly Freas

50-POINT QUESTIONS

1 What 1913 novel by Sir Arthur Conan Doyle did the BBC plan to broadcast as a serial during World War II but later cancel, due to fears that the audience might mistake the radio broadcast for actual news events?

☐ 1. WHEN THE EARTH SCREAMED
☐ 2. THE VALLEY OF FEAR
☐ 3. THE LOST WORLD
☐ 4. THE POISON BELT
☐ 5. THE HORROR OF THE HEIGHTS

2 The March 1, 1955, episode of SUSPENSE featured an adaptation of a Ray Bradbury story. Two later TV versions of this story featured Olivia de Havilland and Drew Barrymore. What was the story?

☐ 1. "I Sing the Body Electric"
☐ 2. "The Veldt"
☐ 3. "All Summer in a Day"
☐ 4. "The Million-Year Picnic"
☐ 5. "The Screaming Woman"

3 On October 3, 1957, the radio series X MINUS ONE dramatized the story "A Wind Is Rising," about scientists from Earth who cannot survive the harsh weather on Venus. Who wrote the original story?

☐ 1. Robert Silverberg
☐ 2. Frederik Pohl
☐ 3. Henry Kuttner
☐ 4. Robert Sheckley
☐ 5. Ray Bradbury

4 THE LAND OF THE LOST was a children's program that took place in a mysterious undersea world where people could breathe underwater. Who played the talking fish, Red Lantern?

☐ 1. Jackie Cooper
☐ 2. Jackie Coogan
☐ 3. Jack E. Leonard
☐ 4. Jackie Gleason
☐ 5. Art Carney

5 OG, SON OF FIRE was a 1934 radio show that took place in the Stone Age. The characters were cavemen who fought prehistoric monsters and a savage environment. The hero was Og. Who was the villain?

☐ 1. Black Hands
☐ 2. Crooked Foot
☐ 3. Evil Heart
☐ 4. Big Tooth
☐ 5. Long Spear

6

What weekly science-fiction radio anthology ran on Mutual in 1950 and 1951? (The program's ongoing premise was that each week's story took place in the future, after the year 2000.)

- ☐ 1. TWO THOUSAND AND ONE
- ☐ 2. TWO THOUSAND PLUS
- ☐ 3. BEYOND TWO THOUSAND
- ☐ 4. THE TWENTY-FIRST CENTURY
- ☐ 5. "F" IS FOR FUTURE

7

One of Bill Cosby's routines is about a chicken heart that is subjected to growth hormones and grows until it takes over Earth. This was inspired by an episode of what radio show?

- ☐ 1. LIGHTS OUT
- ☐ 2. X MINUS ONE
- ☐ 3. INNER SANCTUM
- ☐ 4. I LOVE A MYSTERY
- ☐ 5. DIMENSION X

8

In 1991, Britain's Radio 4 broadcast the SF-comedy serial SPACEACHE, a parody of science-fiction space operas. The author of SPACEACHE had a fairly unusual name. Who was it?

- ☐ 1. Spider Robinson
- ☐ 2. Snoo Wilson
- ☐ 3. Tanith Lee
- ☐ 4. Roald Dahl
- ☐ 5. Delos W. Lovelace

9

In 1936, what weekly radio series on CBS dramatized horror and science-fiction stories by many authors, including Lord Dunsany and Ambrose Bierce? (Most episodes were written by Norman Corwin.)

- ☐ 1. NORMAN CORWIN PRESENTS
- ☐ 2. PLAYHOUSE 90
- ☐ 3. COLUMBIA THEATRE
- ☐ 4. COLUMBIA PLAYHOUSE
- ☐ 5. THE COLUMBIA WORKSHOP

10

The Canadian Broadcasting Corporation ran a series of adaptations of classic horror stories; among them were "The Monkey's Paw," "The Yellow Wallpaper," and "The Screaming Skull." Name this show.

- ☐ 1. THEATRE 10:30
- ☐ 2. ARE YOU ALONE?
- ☐ 3. ALONE IN THE DARK
- ☐ 4. WE KNOW YOU'RE OUT THERE
- ☐ 5. SPOOKY, EH?

11 Phonograph recordings of several of Arch Oboler's LIGHTS OUT episodes were rebroadcast in 1970, but for legal reasons were aired under a new title. What was it?

☐ 1. ARCH OBOLER THEATER
☐ 2. THE DEVIL AND MISTER O
☐ 3. MIDNIGHT THEATRE
☐ 4. ALONE IN THE DARK
☐ 5. SCIENCE FICTION THEATER

12 A radio actor with a versatile voice could play many characters. What actor provided the radio voices for three famous characters: the spaceman Buck Rogers, crimefighter Dick Tracy, and Batman?

☐ 1. Olan Soule
☐ 2. Willis Bouchey
☐ 3. Matt Crowley
☐ 4. Westbrook Van Voorhees
☐ 5. Philip Ober

13 The SUSPENSE adaptation of FRANKENSTEIN starred Herbert Marshall as Victor Frankenstein. What actor played the monster and appeared in the 1951 movie THE THING FROM ANOTHER WORLD?

☐ 1. James Arness
☐ 2. George Fenneman
☐ 3. Kenneth Tobey
☐ 4. Paul Frees
☐ 5. Robert Cornthwaithe

14 In 1953 and 1954, the ABC radio network broadcast a serial about an intrepid spaceman who had an appropriate name. What was the title of this program?

☐ 1. STARR OF SPACE
☐ 2. LUCKY STARR
☐ 3. CAPTAIN FUTURE
☐ 4. CAPTAIN COMET
☐ 5. CAPTAIN ROCKETT

15 What was Arch Oboler's 1956 play about the first expedition to the moon called? (The five crewmen have enough oxygen for only two men to get back to Earth, and an atomic war is about to happen.)

☐ 1. THE DAWN OF THE DODO
☐ 2. THE FLIGHT OF THE PENGUIN
☐ 3. THE NIGHT OF THE AUK
☐ 4. THE YEAR OF THE DRAGON
☐ 5. THE DAY OF THE DOVE

16 MERLIN featured a unicorn, an evil sorceress, and a musical score by composer Elmer Bernstein. Years earlier, Bernstein had composed the music for one of the worst SF movies ever made. What was it?

☐ 1. PLAN NINE FROM OUTER SPACE
☐ 2. GLEN OR GLENDA?
☐ 3. ROBOT MONSTER
☐ 4. LITTLE SHOP OF HORRORS
☐ 5. INVASION OF THE PUPPET PEOPLE

17 What actor, who later made guest appearances on STAR TREK and THE WILD, WILD WEST, was cast in HOW TO MAKE A MAN as a robot named Adam?

☐ 1. Michael Dunn
☐ 2. Michael Forrest
☐ 3. Logan Ramsey
☐ 4. John Abbott
☐ 5. John Colicos

18 In E=MC SQUARED, Einstein's theory of relativity is shown in the form of a burlesque show. What narrator and stage manager of this travesty would later explain scientific concepts to TV audiences?

☐ 1. Don Herbert
☐ 2. Bob Keeshan
☐ 3. E. G. Marshall
☐ 4. Hugh Brannum
☐ 5. Shepherd Menken

19 H. G. Wells's THE WAR OF THE WORLDS takes place in the real-life English town of Woking. In 1955, the New Victoria Theatre in Woking presented the premiere of an opera inspired by which movie?

☐ 1. THE WAR OF THE WORLDS
☐ 2. KING KONG
☐ 3. THE INVISIBLE MAN
☐ 4. DOCTOR CYCLOPS
☐ 5. THE BRIDE OF FRANKENSTEIN

20 In what 1927 play do two aviators—one male, one female—return after the first interplanetary flight to find a scientist has invented a pill that makes men turn female and women turn male?

☐ 1. ADAM AND EVE
☐ 2. MALE AND FEMALE
☐ 3. VENUS
☐ 4. MARS
☐ 5. THE CHANGELING

21   In 1962, he adapted C. S. Lewis's PERELANDRA into an opera, and in 1967, he worked with J. R. R. Tolkien on THE ROAD GOES EVER ON. Yet he is best remembered as half of a British comedy team. Name him.

- [ ] 1. Dudley Moore
- [ ] 2. Ernie Wise
- [ ] 3. Alfie Bass
- [ ] 4. Ronnie Corbett
- [ ] 5. Donald Swann

22   VENUS-SHOT was a 1966 comedy about a rocket engineer named Fletcher Pratt who spends his honeymoon building a spaceship. The actor who starred also appeared in STAR TREK: THE NEXT GENERATION and DEEP SPACE 9. Who was he?

- [ ] 1. Colm Meany
- [ ] 2. Mark Lenard
- [ ] 3. Marc Alaimo
- [ ] 4. Avery Brooks
- [ ] 5. Patrick Stewart

23   What SF writer has written several historical romances under the name Rosemary Edghill?

- [ ] 1. Marion Zimmer Bradley
- [ ] 2. Tanya Huff
- [ ] 3. eluki bes shahar
- [ ] 4. Andre Norton
- [ ] 5. Anne McAffery

24   What horror writer has written under the names Nick Carter, Clayton Moore, and Lee Davis Willoughby?

- [ ] 1. Dean Koontz
- [ ] 2. Ramsay Campbell
- [ ] 3. Richard Laymon
- [ ] 4. Joe R. Lansdale
- [ ] 5. Gary Brandner

25   What name did Henry George Weiss use for his contributions to AMAZING in the early years of the pulps?

- [ ] 1. Edgar Rice Burroughs
- [ ] 2. Francis Flagg
- [ ] 3. Murray Leinster
- [ ] 4. E. E. Smith
- [ ] 5. John Taine

26 Mathematician Eric Temple Bell wrote SF under what name?

☐ 1. John Taine
☐ 2. William Tenn
☐ 3. Walter M. Miller, Jr.
☐ 4. Kurt Vonnegut, Jr.
☐ 5. Thomas M. Disch

27 What writer is also referred to as Mrs. A. E. van Vogt?

☐ 1. Zenna Henderson
☐ 2. E. Mayne Hull
☐ 3. Marion Zimmer Bradley
☐ 4. Leigh Brackett
☐ 5. Margaret St. Clair

28 What American science-fiction writer wrote under the psuedonym William Tenn?

☐ 1. Philip Klass
☐ 2. E. E. Smith
☐ 3. Raymond A. Palmer
☐ 4. Olaf Stapledon
☐ 5. Theodore Sturgeon

29 What horror writer published stories in THE TWILIGHT ZONE magazine under the name Oliver Lowenbruck?

☐ 1. Joe R. Lansdale
☐ 2. Robert McCammon
☐ 3. Dean Koontz
☐ 4. Skipp and Spector
☐ 5. David J. Schow

30 What U.S. writer has written under the names Victor Appleton, Jack Arnett, Laura Lee Hope, and Carolyn Keene?

☐ 1. Michael Stackpole
☐ 2. Brad Strickland
☐ 3. Michael Avallone
☐ 4. Mike McQuay
☐ 5. Mike Resnick

31 This was the first exploratory satellite launched by the United States.

☐ 1. *Pioneer*
☐ 2. *Pilgrim*
☐ 3. *Investigator*
☐ 4. *Explorer*
☐ 5. *Mariner*

32 What did *Voyager* see casting shadows on the planet Neptune?

☐ 1. Moons
☐ 2. Clouds
☐ 3. Rings
☐ 4. Asteroids
☐ 5. *Voyager* itself

33 Name the largest volcano yet found in the solar system.

☐ 1. Groucho Mons
☐ 2. Chico Mons
☐ 3. Harpo Mons
☐ 4. Olympus Mons
☐ 5. Heriod Mons

34 In 1979, what probe almost hit a moon that it had just discovered in orbit around Saturn?

☐ 1. *Voyager 1*
☐ 2. *Voyager 2*
☐ 3. *Voyager 3*
☐ 4. *Pioneer II*
☐ 5. *Explorer 2*

35 This planet was found mathematically, by calculating the orbital disturbance it caused to its known neighbor.

☐ 1. Uranus
☐ 2. Saturn
☐ 3. Neptune
☐ 4. Mars
☐ 5. Mercury

36 David Bedford wrote an opera based on this 1971 Roger Zelazny novel.

- ☐ 1. NINE PRINCES IN AMBER
- ☐ 2. JACK OF SHADOWS
- ☐ 3. THE DOORS OF HIS FACE, THE LAMPS OF HIS MOUTH
- ☐ 4. THE EINSTEIN INTERSECTION
- ☐ 5. FLOW MY TEARS, THE POLICEMAN SAID

37 Name the artist who began as an illustrator, and later wrote THE SCARLET PIMPERNEL.

- ☐ 1. Emma Orczy
- ☐ 2. Rod Ruth
- ☐ 3. H. G. Wells
- ☐ 4. Vernor Vinge
- ☐ 5. Jack Dann

38 Name the artist who is best known for his illustrations of Frank Herbert's classic novel DUNE, done for its serialization in ANALOG magazine.

- ☐ 1. Ed Emschwiller
- ☐ 2. Allen Koszowski
- ☐ 3. Rod Ruth
- ☐ 4. John Schoenherr
- ☐ 5. Boris Vallejo

39 Name the artist who won the British SF Award for both Best Short Story and Best Artist in 1987.

- ☐ 1. Jim Burns
- ☐ 2. Bruce Pennington
- ☐ 3. Michael Whelan
- ☐ 4. Keith Roberts
- ☐ 5. Alan Lee

40 This musician went into the underworld to recover his love, Eurydice.

- ☐ 1. Othello
- ☐ 2. Orpheus
- ☐ 3. Agamemnon
- ☐ 4. Laocoon
- ☐ 5. Daphne

41

What was the more common name of Pallas?

- ☐ 1. Zeus
- ☐ 2. Athena
- ☐ 3. Apollo
- ☐ 4. Hermes
- ☐ 5. Pluto

42

In the 1950s, this short-lived magazine set the style for sci-fi movie mags.

- ☐ 1. FAMOUS MONSTERS OF FILMLAND
- ☐ 2. STARLOG
- ☐ 3. CINEFANTASTIQUE
- ☐ 4. OMNI
- ☐ 5. SPACEMAN

43

This artist's pulp illustration of BUCK ROGERS IN THE 25TH CENTURY is one of the most famous covers in science fiction.

- ☐ 1. Frank R. Paul
- ☐ 2. Virgil Finlay
- ☐ 3. Ed Emschwiller
- ☐ 4. Hannes Bok
- ☐ 5. John Berkey

44

The subtitle "The Modern Prometheus" appears on which of these seminal works of science fiction?

- ☐ 1. DRACULA
- ☐ 2. FRANKENSTEIN
- ☐ 3. MAN AND SUPERMAN
- ☐ 4. SLAN
- ☐ 5. I, ROBOT

45

Although Isaac Asimov codified the "Three Laws of Robotics," Eando Binder helped popularize them in his stories about this character.

- ☐ 1. Adam Link
- ☐ 2. The Vision
- ☐ 3. Robo-Man
- ☐ 4. The Doom Patrol
- ☐ 5. Metal Men

46

What song by the performance-rock band the Tubes was taken from a sci-fi movie?

- ☐ 1. WHITE PUNKS ON DOPE
- ☐ 2. DESTINATION UNKNOWN
- ☐ 3. ATTACK OF THE FIFTY-FOOT WOMAN
- ☐ 4. SOYLENT GREEN
- ☐ 5. SILENT RUNNING

47

A former PLAYBOY Playmate, this actress was chosen by Hammer Films to star alongside Peter Cushing in the studio's proposed VAMPIRELLA film.

- ☐ 1. Pamela Anderson
- ☐ 2. Barbi Benton
- ☐ 3. Barbara Leigh
- ☐ 4. Dorothy Stratton
- ☐ 5. Brandi Brandt

48

One of the comics industry's master artists, in the early 1960s he designed many of the MARS ATTACKS trading cards.

- ☐ 1. Jack Kirby
- ☐ 2. Wally Wood
- ☐ 3. Jack Davis
- ☐ 4. Gil Kane
- ☐ 5. Graham Engels

49

A close friend of Forrest J. Ackerman, this artist was the designer of Vampirella's scant costume.

- ☐ 1. Trina Robbins
- ☐ 2. Wendy Pini
- ☐ 3. Frank Frazetta
- ☐ 4. Mercy Van Vlack
- ☐ 5. Ramona Fradon

50

During the 1970s, RED SONJA artist Frank Thorne attended comics conventions as the Wizard in the WIZARD AND RED SONJA SHOW; with him traveled five women as different versions of Sonja. What female comic artist played one of the Sonjas?

- ☐ 1. Dale Messick
- ☐ 2. Fauve
- ☐ 3. Trina Robbins
- ☐ 4. Wendy Pini
- ☐ 5. Julie Bell

SCIENCE FICTION

MOVIES

ANSWERS

10-POINT ANSWERS

1

Correct Answer: 1

Molly Ringwald appeared with Peter Strauss in SPACEHUNTER: ADVENTURES IN THE FORBIDDEN ZONE.

2

Correct Answer: 3

Both of these films received "X" ratings at their initial release. Many critics panned the films, rating them "B" for boring.

3

Correct Answer: 1

Several classic film monsters make an appearance, including the voice of Vincent Price as the Invisible Man.

4

Correct Answer: 5

Whoopi Goldberg also played a popular recurring role in television's STAR TREK: THE NEXT GENERATION.

5

Correct Answer: 5

Murray is a television weatherman assigned to cover the events on Groundhog Day.

6

Correct Answer: 2

And it's all based on sworn testimony!

7

Correct Answer: 3

Dan O'Herlihy, not Danny De Vito, starred in THE LAST STARFIGHTER.

8

Correct Answer: 3

James Whale directed some of the early sound era's most stylish classics, including the 1936 version of SHOW BOAT.

9

Correct Answer: 2

Ira Levin wrote ROSEMARY'S BABY. He also wrote the dystopian 1970 novel THIS PERFECT DAY, which presaged the cyberpunk era of science fiction.

10

Correct Answer: 2

In THE LAND THAT TIME FORGOT, a World War I submarine discovers a strange land area near the South Pole, complete with dinosaurs and other creatures.

11 Correct Answer: 2

The results are temporary, and Charly loses his newfound mental powers.

12 Correct Answer: 5

Several Washington, DC, landmarks are shown in the film.

13 Correct Answer: 4

Michael Rennie gained wide popularity as the hero of the television series THE THIRD MAN.

14 Correct Answer: 3

Mako plays the wizard who accompanies Conan in each film.

15 Correct Answer: 3

Stanley, Dorian, and Milo the dog wear the mask.

16 Correct Answer: 3

DAUGHTER OF DARKNESS is set in Romania.

17 Correct Answer: 5

Elvis Presley was fond of "Thus Spake Zarathustra" and often used it as entrance music at his concerts.

18 Correct Answer: 1

STARGATE was a surprise hit at the box office.

19 Correct Answer: 4

Marvin Berry calls his cousin Chuck so that he can hear McFly play over the phone.

20 Correct Answer: 3

William F. Claxton directed the 1972 film NIGHT OF THE LEPUS.

21 Correct Answer: 2

Colin Clive plays the title role. Boris Karloff plays the monster.

22 Correct Answer: 2

Bill Murray plays the Jack Nicholson scene in the 1986 musical remake.

MOVIES   10-POINT ANSWERS

23
Correct Answer: 2

MARY POPPINS lost the 1964 Best Picture Oscar to MY FAIR LADY.

24
Correct Answer: 4

Eugene Levy and Heather McComb also star in STAY TUNED.

25
Correct Answer: 4

Jon Lovitz's films include A LEAGUE OF THEIR OWN and BIG.

26
Correct Answer: 2

The cast of KING KONG LIVES includes Brian Kerwin, John Ashton, Frank Maraden, and Linda Hamilton.

27
Correct Answer: 5

Stuart Walker directed the 1935 film WEREWOLF OF LONDON.

28
Correct Answer: 2

Edgar Rice Burroughs pioneered the science-fantasy adventure novel.

29
Correct Answer: 3

The cast of PREDATOR includes Carl Weathers, Elpidia Carrillo, and Bill Duke.

30
Correct Answer: 1

Arthur Conan Doyle also created Sherlock Holmes.

31
Correct Answer: 3

Donald Sutherland, Brooke Adams, Jeff Goldblum, and Veronica Cartwright also star in the 1978 version of INVASION OF THE BODY SNATCHERS.

32
Correct Answer: 3

John Hurt was an Oscar nominee for his work in MIDNIGHT EXPRESS and in THE ELEPHANT MAN.

33
Correct Answer: 3

Bela Lugosi was born in Lugos, Hungary, in 1882.

34
Correct Answer: 3

Geoff Murphy directed the futuristic action film FREEJACK.

35

Correct Answer: 4

Mary Lambert directed both the 1989 film PET SEMATARY and the 1992 sequel, PET SEMATARY II.

36

Correct Answer: 4

Melinda Dillon also earned an Oscar nomination for Best Supporting Actress for the 1981 film ABSENCE OF MALICE.

37

Correct Answer: 2

William Shatner plays a veterinarian trying to stop tarantulas in Arizona.

38

Correct Answer: 3

Snake Plissken is sent into New York to rescue the President.

39

Correct Answer: 5

Cary Grant played the Mock Turtle and Gary Cooper, the White Knight.

40

Correct Answer: 3

The rebels are forced to flee from Hoth when attacked by troops from the Empire.

41

Correct Answer: 3

The screenplay for THE ANDROMEDA STRAIN was adapted by Nelson Gidding.

42

Correct Answer: 2

The plague is a result of biological warfare between China and Russia.

43

Correct Answer: 5

Like many intellectually challenging films, ZARDOZ generated considerable controversy and is not to all tastes.

44

Correct Answer: 2

The super-low-budget DARK STAR has been called the best film ever made for $60,000.

45

Correct Answer: 2

The character is named Frankenstein because of the scars from his auto-racing accidents.

46

Correct Answer: 4

Tim Curry delivers the line to Susan Sarandon and Barry Bostwick.

47

Correct Answer: 2

DEMOLITION MAN was directed by Marco Brambilla.

48

Correct Answer: 2

Roger Zelazny's novel is much better regarded than is the film.

49

Correct Answer: 5

Lee Frost directed the comic horror film THE THING WITH TWO HEADS.

50

Correct Answer: 5

An aircraft hangar in Alabama was used as a sound stage for the Wyoming landing scenes in CLOSE ENCOUNTERS OF THE THIRD KIND.

20-POINT ANSWERS

1

Correct Answer: 2

George Lucas is reported to have nine episodes of the STAR WARS saga planned.

2

Correct Answer: 2

John Landis wrote the script for AN AMERICAN WEREWOLF IN LONDON and also directed it.

3

Correct Answer: 2

Martians send monsters to drive off the first human explorers to reach Mars in this 1959 film.

4

Correct Answer: 2

Karloff played the monster in the 1931 version of FRANKENSTEIN and the Frankenstein scientist character in the 1958 film FRANKENSTEIN—1970.

5

Correct Answer: 4

PROJECT MOONBASE was the theatrical release of an unsold pilot for a television series.

6

Correct Answer: 5

Sissy Spacek won an Oscar for her performance as Loretta Lynn in COAL MINER'S DAUGHTER.

7

Correct Answer: 1

Balaban's career also includes memorable supporting roles in MIDNIGHT COWBOY and 2010.

8

Correct Answer: 1

William Shakespeare's fantasy/comedy was a 1935 Oscar nominee, losing to MUTINY ON THE BOUNTY. All four of the other films listed predate 1935, but none were nominees for Best Picture.

9

Correct Answer: 2

Wells battles Jack the Ripper.

10

Correct Answer: 3

Pierce also created the makeup for the 1943 version of PHANTOM OF THE OPERA.

11
Correct Answer: 3
Kalidor aids Red Sonja in her quest for revenge.

12
Correct Answer: 5
The film 2010 is based on the novel by Arthur C. Clarke.

13
Correct Answer: 4
THE BEAST MUST DIE is also known as BLACK WEREWOLF.

14
Correct Answer: 2
As in many of his screen appearances, Tor Johnson has no dialogue.

15
Correct Answer: 2
There are two Australian directors named George Miller. The one who directed the Mad Max films was a practicing physician before turning to films.

16
Correct Answer: 2
Leo McKern, Eleanor Bron, and Victor Spinetti costar with the Beatles.

17
Correct Answer: 1
The blood gives him the oxygen he needs.

18
Correct Answer: 2
Bela Lugosi's career was at its peak in the 1930s.

19
Correct Answer: 2
ED WOOD won Oscars for Best Makeup and Best Supporting Actor. Only Best Picture winner FORREST GUMP won more Oscars at the 1995 ceremonies.

20
Correct Answer: 3
Michael Ironside also played the evil sea park owner in FREE WILLY.

21
Correct Answer: 4
Michael Biehn's films include NAVY SEALS and TOMBSTONE.

22
Correct Answer: 2
NIGHTFALL was directed by Paul Mayersberg.

23

Correct Answer: 5

Lionel Atwill's films include DOCTOR X, MYSTERY OF THE WAX MUSEUM, and the 1939 version of THE HOUND OF THE BASKERVILLES.

24

Correct Answer: 3

John McTiernan's films include NOMADS, DIE HARD, and THE HUNT FOR RED OCTOBER.

25

Correct Answer: 3

Nicol Williamson's films include ROBIN AND MARIAN, RETURN TO OZ, and THE EXORCIST III.

26

Correct Answer: 2

Carolyn Jones received a 1957 Best Supporting Actress Oscar nomination for THE BACHELOR PARTY, and played Morticia Addams in the popular television sitcom THE ADDAMS FAMILY.

27

Correct Answer: 5

Richard Dawson hosted television's FAMILY FEUD.

28

Correct Answer: 4

Emilio Estevez's films include WISDOM, YOUNG GUNS, and THE MIGHTY DUCKS.

29

Correct Answer: 2

Don Johnson starred in the popular television series MIAMI VICE.

30

Correct Answer: 3

The cast for the 1987 television remake included Wil Wheaton of STAR TREK: THE NEXT GENERATION.

31

Correct Answer: 1

The 1982 film CONAN THE BARBARIAN was produced by Buzz Feitshans and Raffaella de Laurentiis.

32

Correct Answer: 3

Jackie Cooper, who was born in 1921, was a 1930 Best Actor nominee for the classic child-and-his-dog movie SKIPPY. Cooper's uncle, Norman Taurog, won an Oscar for directing the film.

33

Correct Answer: 5

Robert A. Heinlein's THE PUPPET MASTERS was published in 1951.

34

Correct Answer: 5

Wildfire has an atomic bomb for a self-destruct mechanism.

35

Correct Answer: 5

The Eternals supply weapons to the Exterminators to keep the population of the Brutals under control.

36

Correct Answer: 1

Student John Carpenter also made the 1970 Oscar-winning live-action short subject THE RESURRECTION OF BRONCO BILLY, although the film's producer, and not Carpenter, got the Oscar.

37

Correct Answer: 1

Boris Karloff plays the monster and O. P. Heggie the hermit, in the landmark 1935 film BRIDE OF FRANKENSTEIN.

38

Correct Answer: 5

Sylvester Stallone became a star in the 1976 Oscar-winning Best Picture ROCKY.

39

Correct Answer: 4

Logan is a Sandman assigned to infiltrate the resistance forces.

40

Correct Answer: 4

THE PAGEMASTER combines live action and animation.

41

Correct Answer: 1

It was a dark and stormy night.

42

Correct Answer: 2

A master criminal from the year 1996 is awakened from a forty-year cryonic sleep and sent to kill an underground resistance leader.

43

Correct Answer: 2

NAKED LUNCH stars Peter Weller as William Lee, a fictional characterization of author William S. Burroughs.

44

Correct Answer: 5

"Are we not men?" (Both films deal with animals that are changed into humans.)

45

Correct Answer: 4

Jon Pertwee and Nyree Dawn Porter also star.

46

Correct Answer: 2

Drew Barrymore is the daughter of actor John Barrymore, Jr.

47

Correct Answer: 4

Richard Marquand's films include BIRTH OF THE BEATLES and JAGGED EDGE.

48

Correct Answer: 5

Val Kilmer's films include TOP GUN, THE DOORS, and BATMAN FOREVER.

49

Correct Answer: 4

Tina Turner was the subject of the 1993 biofilm WHAT'S LOVE GOT TO DO WITH IT.

50

Correct Answer: 2

The plot concerns an attempt to clone a new race of Nazis.

30-POINT ANSWERS

1
Correct Answer: 2

Jeffrey Coombs and director Stuart Gordon also made FROM BEYOND.

2
Correct Answer: 1

ALWAYS is about a ghost who returns to help his girlfriend go on with her life.

3
Correct Answer: 1

Brion James played the slow-witted replicant Leon in BLADE RUNNER.

4
Correct Answer: 5

Goldman's other films include BUTCH CASSIDY AND THE SUNDANCE KID and MAVERICK.

5
Correct Answer: 5

Although in many ways similar to, and from the same era as, the early Quatermass films, this 1956 British film is not a part of the Quatermass series.

6
Correct Answer: 3

Cocteau's masterpiece was highly influential on later film versions of this story.

7
Correct Answer: 2

Much of the story is told in flashbacks via the framing device of the interview.

8
Correct Answer: 2

Ralph Nelson directed this motion picture, a 1968 release.

9
Correct Answer: 5

Lansing costars with Lee Meriwether and Patty Duke.

10
Correct Answer: 1

Although she terms both films "atrocious," on the advice of her agent, Andre Norton had her credit restored for the sequel.

11
Correct Answer: 1

Peggy is a reporter who betrays Stanley to the criminal night club owner, Dorian.

12

Correct Answer: 5

When doctors remove silver bullets from the metalbeast, it comes back to life.

13

Correct Answer: 2

Douglas Rain also starred in the 1957 version of OEDIPUS REX.

14

Correct Answer: 3

The Mano de Dios amber mine is said to be in the Dominican Republic.

15

Correct Answer: 3

The film was reissued in 1982 with the advertising copy "The Film That J. R. Shot!"

16

Correct Answer: 3

The cast of this 1944 movie includes Martha O'Driscoll, Leo Carillo, Andy Devine, and Lon Chaney, Jr.

17

Correct Answer: 1

THEM! is one of the best-regarded science-fiction films of the 1950s.

18

Correct Answer: 2

The time-traveling Marty McFly pretends to be Darth Vader from the planet Vulcan in order to motivate his future father to ask his future mother for a date.

19

Correct Answer: 1

THE BLACK CAT with Boris Karloff and Bela Lugosi was made in 1934. In 1941, Lugosi appeared in an unrelated film of the same name.

20

Correct Answer: 3

HAPPILY EVER AFTER was produced by Filmation Studios.

21

Correct Answer: 3

Michael Ironside's films include TOTAL RECALL and HIGHLANDER II: THE QUICKENING.

22

Correct Answer: 5

Hy Averback directed the 1966 film CHAMBER OF HORRORS. (There is an unrelated 1940 film with the same title.)

23

Correct Answer: 5

TALES FROM THE CRYPT was later a successful television series.

24

Correct Answer: 4

Mostly filmed in 1923, this silent classic underwent two years of postproduction changes before being released.

25

Correct Answer: 5

Nastassja Kinski and Malcolm McDowell star in the 1982 version of CAT PEOPLE.

26

Correct Answer: 3

Martine Beswick's films include THUNDRBALL, MELVIN AND HOWARD, and ONE MILLION YEARS B.C.

27

Correct Answer: 2

Paul Reubens plays Amilyn, the vampire.

28

Correct Answer: 4

Sidney Blackmer's film career spans seven decades.

29

Correct Answer: 3

George Sanders' family moved to England during the Russian revolution. In 1951, he won a Best Supporting Actor Oscar for his memorable performance as a mean-spirited drama critic in ALL ABOUT EVE.

30

Correct Answer: 1

The script for THE BRAIN EATERS is credited to Gordon Urquhart.

31

Correct Answer: 2

Michael Nesmith was one of the pioneers in the production of music videos.

32

Correct Answer: 1

John de Lancie played the enigmatic Q on STAR TREK: THE NEXT GENERATION.

33

Correct Answer: 5

Lenny Bruce and Jack Henley received cowriting credit for THE ROCKET MAN.

34

Correct Answer: 1

One of CARRIE's supporting cast members is Amy Irving's mother, Priscilla Pointer.

35

Correct Answer: 4

Kirk and crew go back to the 20th century to bring humpback whales into their future, where whales are extinct.

36

Correct Answer: 5

Darryl Hannah debuted in THE FURY, Brian DePalma's 1978 film about psychic twins who meet by telepathy.

37

Correct Answer: 3

The atomic explosion from the self-destruct might have mutated it differently.

38

Correct Answer: 5

SILENT RUNNING was partially filmed on board the retired aircraft carrier *Valley Forge*.

39

Correct Answer: 3

IT'S ALIVE did only marginal box office in the United States, but was very popular in Europe. The film has gained considerable critical respect over the years.

40

Correct Answer: 4

Claire Bloom and Christie Matchett costar in THE ILLUSTRATED MAN.

41

Correct Answer: 2

The Monster becomes alarmed and bolts from the stage.

42

Correct Answer: 2

The victims are told they have a chance Carousel will renew them, though this is not true.

43

Correct Answer: 4

All of the restaurants in this totalitarian future are Taco Bells.

44

Correct Answer: 5

Virginia Madsen plays Princess Irulian.

45

Correct Answer: 1

DUNE was a 1984 Oscar nominee for achievement in sound recording.

46

Correct Answer: 3

John Hough directed the 1978 film RETURN FROM WITCH MOUNTAIN.

47

Correct Answer: 4

TREMORS was directed by Ron Underwood.

48

Correct Answer: 1

Alastair Sim's films include SCHOOL FOR SCOUNDRELS and THE RULING CLASS.

49

Correct Answer: 3

In the 1954 movie GOG, Gog is a nonhuman robot.

50

Correct Answer: 1

Dennis Quaid, Meg Ryan, and Martin Short star in INNERSPACE.

40-POINT ANSWERS

1

Correct Answer: 3

Released in 1932, the Fredric March version of DR. JEKYLL AND MR. HYDE was directed by Rouben Mamoulian.

2

Correct Answer: 5

All of the above starred in the 1988 film ALIEN NATION, which later became a FOX television series.

3

Correct Answer: 2

Andy Warhol is rumored never to have watched the completed version of ANDY WARHOL'S FRANKENSTEIN.

4

Correct Answer: 3

Bela Lugosi's career was already in decline. Ava Gardner would become one of the major stars of the 1950s.

5

Correct Answer: 1

BRIDE OF THE GORILLA was directed by Curt Siodmak.

6

Correct Answer: 5

SON OF SINBAD also featured Dale Robertson and Lili St. Cyr.

7

Correct Answer: 2

PHANTASM was written, directed, photographed, and produced by Don Coscarelli.

8

Correct Answer: 4

The visitor takes a room at a boardinghouse to better understand the people of Earth.

9

Correct Answer: 1

"Songs for Drella," by Lou Reed and John Cale, is a tribute to Andy Warhol.

10

Correct Answer: 4

John Carpenter also directed the film and cowrote the screenplay.

11

Correct Answer: 1

Amy Irving's films include YENTL and CROSSING DELANCEY.

12

Correct Answer: 4

They are excavating raptor remains in Montana's Badlands.

13

Correct Answer: 1

Chuck Russell also directed A NIGHTMARE ON ELM STREET 3: DREAM WARRIORS.

14

Correct Answer: 4

Nimoy's first film appearances were in QUEEN FOR A DAY and RHUBARB, in 1951.

15

Correct Answer: 4

James Blish also wrote SPOCK MUST DIE, the first STAR TREK novel.

16

Correct Answer: 4

Robby the Robot first appeared in FORBIDDEN PLANET.

17

Correct Answer: 5

Victor Halperin also directed Carole Lombard and Randolph Scott in the 1933 film SUPERNATURAL.

18

Correct Answer: 4

Robert Stevenson was an Oscar nominee for Best Director in 1964, for MARY POPPINS.

19

Correct Answer: 3

John Farrow directed his daughter Mia Farrow in her screen debut in the 1959 film JOHN PAUL JONES.

20

Correct Answer: 3

Lamont Johnson has directed such well-regarded made-for-TV movies as THE EXECUTION OF PRIVATE SLOVIK, FEAR ON TRIAL, and OFF THE MINNESOTA STRIP.

21

Correct Answer: 4

Peter Ustinov won two Best Supporting Actor Oscars for SPARTACUS and TOPKAPI. In 1968 he was nominated for his screenplay for HOT MILLIONS.

22

Correct Answer: 2

Eddie Romero codirected MAD DOCTOR OF BLOOD ISLAND and directed BEAST OF THE DEAD.

23

Correct Answer: 5

While UCLA has a good many alumni in the film industry, Mark Damon may be the only one whose areas of study there were literature and business administration.

24

Correct Answer: 2

Clint Eastwood plays a lab assistant in the 1955 film REVENGE OF THE CREATURE.

25

Correct Answer: 5

The 1992 film SLEEPWALKERS was directed by Mick Garris.

26

Correct Answer: 3

Jack Nance (sometimes billed as John Nance) has also appeared in BARFLY, GHOULIES, and THE HOT SPOT.

27

Correct Answer: 4

The time machine bears a nameplate that says "Manufactured by H. George Wells."

28

Correct Answer: 1

Rosemary believes her baby to be dead, but discovers him among coven members.

29

Correct Answer: 4

SOLAR CRISIS also stars Annabel Schofield, Corin Nemec, and Brenda Bakke.

30

Correct Answer: 4

John Voight received a 1978 Best Actor Oscar for COMING HOME.

31

Correct Answer: 2

IT! THE TERROR FROM BEYOND SPACE was written by Jerome Bixby. While there is a general acknowledgment that this film influenced the writing of ALIEN, the story is not a direct copy.

32

Correct Answer: 2

Lloyd Bridges is the father of actors Jeff Bridges and Beau Bridges.

33

Correct Answer: 5

LeVar Burton, Maxwell Caulfield, Talia Balsam, and Bobby DiCicco star in THE SUPERNATURALS.

34

Correct Answer: 1

The longer version was prepared for television and video.

35

Correct Answer: 3

TOTAL RECALL deals with the question of what is reality and what is cyber-induced perception.

36

Correct Answer: 3

In the twist ending, it is the robot who is the master.

37

Correct Answer: 4

After the 1950s, Hugh Marlowe appeared frequently on television, including the lead in the daytime soap opera ANOTHER WORLD.

38

Correct Answer: 3

The story "The Puppet Masters" was serialized in the September, October, and November 1951 issues.

39

Correct Answer: 4

James Bridges wrote the screenplay for COLOSSUS: THE FORBIN PROJECT, adapting D. F. Jones's novel.

40

Correct Answer: 5

The earlier version follows the novel more closely than THE OMEGA MAN but lacks good production values.

41

Correct Answer: 2

Sadly, Edward G. Robinson did not live to receive the special Oscar awarded him in 1973, shortly after his death.

42

Correct Answer: 4

The plot involves messages that may or may not be coming from Mars.

43

Correct Answer: 5

The underground society is a totalitarian replica of a Middle American farming town.

44

Correct Answer: 4

The full title of the film is DR. STRANGELOVE: OR, HOW I LEARNED TO STOP WORRYING AND LOVE THE BOMB.

45 Correct Answer: 4

Several versions of SOLARIS exist with running times that greatly vary.

46 Correct Answer: 4

Robert Vaughn provides the voice of Proteus.

47 Correct Answer: 4

DEMON SEED was directed by Donald Cammell. Julie Christie and Fritz Weaver play the lead roles.

48 Correct Answer: 1

In 1986, Michael Crawford originated the title role in the stage musical version of THE PHANTOM OF THE OPERA.

49 Correct Answer: 4

Angelo Rossitto plays Master, and Paul Larsson plays Blaster.

50 Correct Answer: 1

Floyd Crosby won an Oscar in 1931 for his work on the semi-documentary TABU. He is the father of David Crosby, of Crosby, Stills and Nash.

50-POINT ANSWERS

1

Correct Answer: 2

While boating, he passed through a mysterious glowing fog. Shortly thereafter, he began to shrink.

2

Correct Answer: 3

Warhol's Dracula needs the blood of virgin women to rejuvenate himself.

3

Correct Answer: 3

Tim Burton's films include BATMAN, EDWARD SCISSORHANDS, and ED WOOD.

4

Correct Answer: 1

ISLAND OF LOST SOULS was directed by Erle C. Kenton.

5

Correct Answer: 2

SON OF FRANKENSTEIN followed BRIDE OF FRANKENSTEIN.

6

Correct Answer: 4

Although primarily known as an actor, Hopper has directed several well-regarded films, including the 1969 landmark EASY RIDER.

7

Correct Answer: 4

John Mollo also won a Best Costuming Oscar for GANDHI.

8

Correct Answer: 5

The visitor arrives in a flying saucer.

9

Correct Answer: 4

Films directed by John "Bud" Cardos include KINGDOM OF THE SPIDERS and NIGHT SHADOWS.

10

Correct Answer: 5

Rip Torn's early career was noted for his performances on stage and in film in such Tennessee Williams works as BABY DOLL and SWEET BIRD OF YOUTH.

11

Correct Answer: 4

Sylvia Sidney's film career began in 1927, and includes Lewis Milestone's 1952 production of LES MISERABLES.

12

Correct Answer: 3

Huntz Hall is one of several people to have costarred with both Bela Lugosi and Martin Landau. The others include Gregory Walcott and Josephine Hutchinson.

13

Correct Answer: 4

STAR WARS lost the Best Picture Oscar to ANNIE HALL.

14

Correct Answer: 5

The robot on the poster looks like it was lifted from FORBIDDEN PLANET.

15

Correct Answer: 4

The 1982 film version of this story is titled THE THING.

16

Correct Answer: 2

The time-traveling Marty McFly has trouble convincing people that in his future, Ronald Reagan becomes President.

17

Correct Answer: 1

Dean Jagger won the 1949 Best Supporting Actor Oscar for TWELVE O'CLOCK HIGH.

18

Correct Answer: 2

Eric Stoltz was thought to be too intense in the role, so he was replaced by Michael J. Fox.

19

Correct Answer: 4

John Kinsella (Dwyer Brown) is the father of Ray Kinsella (Kevin Costner).

20

Correct Answer: 3

Cliff Edwards introduced the song "Singing in the Rain" in THE HOLLYWOOD REVIEW OF 1929, and later was a regular on television's THE MICKEY MOUSE CLUB SHOW.

21

Correct Answer: 5

In additon to a fine body of film work, Sir Ralph Richardson was also a noted Shakespearean stage actor.

22

Correct Answer: 3

Ernie Hudson's films include WEEDS and THE HAND THAT ROCKS THE CRADLE.

23

Correct Answer: 4

Though his early career was spent in England working in film, Robert Day later came to California, where he also worked in television.

24

Correct Answer: 3

John Ashley was one of the producers of the hit television series THE A-TEAM.

25

Correct Answer: 1

Dean Jones's career includes such diverse films as JAILHOUSE ROCK, BEETHOVEN, and TORPEDO RUN.

26

Correct Answer: 1

Ernest Laszlo's films include SHIP OF FOOLS (for which he won an Oscar), ON THE BEACH, and JUDGMENT AT NUREMBERG.

27

Correct Answer: 2

Eugene Lourie worked with Abel Gance on NAPOLEON, and with Jean Renoir on GRAND ILLUSION and RULES OF THE GAME. He was an Oscar nominee in 1969 for the special effects in KRAKATOA—EAST OF JAVA.

28

Correct Answer: 5

Clint Eastwood directed and starred in UNFORGIVEN.

29

Correct Answer: 5

Wyott Ordung directed and starred in the 1954 film THE MONSTER FROM THE OCEAN FLOOR.

30

Correct Answer: 1

Byron Haskin also directed CONQUEST OF SPACE and ROBINSON CRUSOE ON MARS.

31

Correct Answer: 3

Maurice Evans's films include THE WAR LORD, TERROR IN THE WAX MUSEUM, and SCROOGE.

32

Correct Answer: 5

The capsules lose their power after 27 days.

33

Correct Answer: 4

John Hurt is probably most frequently remembered for having the alien burst out of his chest in ALIEN.

34

Correct Answer: 5

Inoshiro Honda created most of the pantheon of Japanese movie monsters while collaborating with his friend Akira Kurosawa on some of Japan's best-regarded "art" films.

35

Correct Answer: 3

James Clavell's novels include SHOGUN, NOBLE HOUSE, and TAI-PAN. He also wrote the screenplay for the popular 1963 hit THE GREAT ESCAPE.

36

Correct Answer: 4

NO PLACE LIKE HOMICIDE stars Kenneth Connor, Shirley Eaton, Donald Pleasence, and Michael Gough.

37

Correct Answer: 4

Vampira (actress Maila Nurmi) began her movie hosting career in 1954, on KABC-TV in Los Angeles.

38

Correct Answer: 5

During her distinguished career, Bette Davis received ten Oscar nominations for Best Actress, winning in 1935 for DANGEROUS and in 1938 for JEZEBEL.

39

Correct Answer: 2

Many of the story elements from STAR WARS can be found in THE HIDDEN FORTRESS.

40

Correct Answer: 2

David Wayne's films include PORTRAIT OF JENNIE, HOW TO MARRY A MILLIONARE, and the 1974 version of THE FRONT PAGE.

41

Correct Answer: 3

Walon Green produced and directed. The narrator, Nils Hellstrom, was played by Lawrence Pressman.

42

Correct Answer: 5

Vincent Price plays Francois Delambre in both films. He did not appear in the 1965 sequel, CURSE OF THE FLY, or in the 1986 remake of the original film.

43

Correct Answer: 2

Ray Russell adapted the screenplay for MR. SARDONICUS and wrote the novel on which it is based.

44

Correct Answer: 4

The title refers to the high-speed air currents that dominate the planet.

45

Correct Answer: 4

Alain Robbe-Grillet's screenplay for LAST YEAR AT MARIENBAD received a 1961 Oscar nomination, losing to the screenplay for DIVORCE, ITALIAN STYLE.

46

Correct Answer: 4

John Fowles adapted his highly regarded novel for cinematographer-turned-director Guy Green, but the result was not popular with either critics or audiences.

47

Correct Answer: 3

Ed Begley is the father of actor Ed Begley, Jr., and Talia Coppola (later billed as Talia Shire) is the sister of director Francis Ford Coppola.

48

Correct Answer: 3

YOUNG DR. JEKYLL MEETS FRANKENSTEIN doesn't exist in real life. For the film ENSIGN PULVER, stock footage from THE WALKING DEAD was used.

49

Correct Answer: 4

The film later became a long-running joke on Jack Benny's television program.

50

Correct Answer: 3

Producer Roger Corman also makes a cameo appearance.

TELEVISION

ANSWERS

10-POINT ANSWERS

1

Correct Answer: 5

As a psychologist, Mulder abhors drug treatments for patients and prefers hypnotic regression therapy.

2

Correct Answer: 3

Her original assignment was intended to be used to close down the X-Files, but she soon came to Mulder's defense and defended the X-Files with verifiable scientific proof.

3

Correct Answer: 5

The *Seaview* was built by the Nelson Institute to explore the ocean depths.

4

Correct Answer: 2

Thrush was the evil opposite of U.N.C.L.E.

5

Correct Answer: 2

Steven Spielberg, through his company Amblin Entertainment, produced AMAZING STORIES.

6

Correct Answer: 3

Sinclair was removed from his position as commander and reassigned as an Earth ambassador to the Minbari home world.

7

Correct Answer: 2

At the height of his popularity, Alf was the star of a sitcom, a Saturday morning cartoon series, and a Marvel comic book.

8

Correct Answer: 1

The Draconians tried to use Buck as a spy.

9

Correct Answer: 2

THE AVENGERS is the show dealing with "extraordinary crimes against the people and the State."

10

Correct Answer: 3

MAX HEADROOM began in the UK.

11

Correct Answer: 3

Max advertised for Coke.

12

Correct Answer: 2

They called it "Breaking out."

13

Correct Answer: 3

Mr. Bean was a particularly idiotic alien.

14

Correct Answer: 2

This SUPERBOY pilot, produced by ADVENTURES OF SUPERMAN producer Whitney Ellsworth in 1961, was never aired.

15

Correct Answer: 1

Eric Pierpoint went on to become a regular on USA's SILK STALKINGS.

16

Correct Answer: 4

Evigan played Cardigan. Shatner, who created the series, had a supporting role.

17

Correct Answer: 4

Ironside was also a regular on the V series.

18

Correct Answer: 5

Dozier produced and narrated the 1960s BATMAN and GREEN HORNET series. (He also developed a WONDER WOMAN series, but it never went anywhere.)

19

Correct Answer: 3

While at Princeton, Cain apparently dated Brooke Shields.

20

Correct Answer: 4

Mumy plays the Minbari named Lennier; Lockhart was a guest star on the episode "The Quality of Mercy."

21

Correct Answer: 2

Jeff Bridges played the alien who cloned the form of a dead photojournalist and took on his identity.

22

Correct Answer: 3

Straker was a commander. Bizarrely, his second in command was a colonel.

23

Correct Answer: 3

The Andersons created UFO, with Gerry serving as executive producer and Sylvia credited with providing "Century 21 Fashions." They cowrote the first episode, "Identified."

24

Correct Answer: 4

Seymour has also played an alien scientist on THE NEXT GENERATION, a character in a holo-novel on STAR TREK: VOYAGER, and Tina McGee's mother on THE FLASH.

25

Correct Answer: 2

The bombing of New York's World Trade Center prevented WWOR, Channel 9, from broadcasting on the night that BABYLON 5's pilot was to air.

26

Correct Answer: 5

Shatner starred in "Cold Hands . . ." as an astronaut infected with a Venusian virus. Nimoy costarred in "I, Robot," the story of a robot on trial for the murder of its creator.

27

Correct Answer: 2

Only the first two seasons were in black and white.

28

Correct Answer: 4

Lambert reprised his role as Connor MacLeod, cousin to Paul's Duncan MacLeod, for the HIGHLANDER pilot.

29

Correct Answer: 3

Reid played Sergeant Bennett in three first-season episodes.

30

Correct Answer: 4

Hunt was the commander on SPACE RANGERS.

31

Correct Answer: 2

Darian's device was shaped like a car-alarm activator; his AI adviser, SELMA, was disguised as a credit card.

32

Correct Answer: 1

Bennett also produced several of the STAR TREK films.

33

Correct Answer: 3

When BUCK ROGERS ended its run, Gray moved on to the short-lived comedy series SILVER SPOONS.

34 Correct Answer: 1

Although unrecognizable under all his makeup, Kevin Peter Hall was both the alien Predator and the Bigfoot called Harry.

35 Correct Answer: 2

After MANIMAL was mauled by poor ratings, Anderson went on to a career in made-for-TV movies.

36 Correct Answer: 1

Hall starred in the "ElectraWoman and Dyna-Girl" segment of THE KROFFT SUPER SHOW.

37 Correct Answer: 1

Andy Griffith constructed his rocket from used parts purchased from NASA.

38 Correct Answer: 2

Although they may have appeared to be normal when they drank tea. . . .

39 Correct Answer: 3

Lee starred in POOR DEVIL as Satan.

40 Correct Answer: 1

Oh, the pain, the pain. . . .

41 Correct Answer: 2

Mary Ellen Stuart starred as Holley Hathaway, a schoolteacher picked by Ralph to take his costume and continue his work with FBI agent Bill Maxwell.

42 Correct Answer: 4

Mark Hamill is also the voice of the Hobgoblin in the recent SPIDER-MAN animated series.

43 Correct Answer: 2

"In the end, there can be only one."

44 Correct Answer: 4

This was the only televised appearance of Adam West and Burt Ward as Batman and Robin since the BATMAN series.

45

Correct Answer: 4

Haiduk has also appeared on the soap opera ANOTHER WORLD.

46

Correct Answer: 3

Daredevil was played by Rex Smith. The Kingpin was played by John Rhys-Davies, known for his role as Sallah in two INDIANA JONES movies.

47

Correct Answer: 2

Toth also designed BIRDMAN AND THE GALAXY TRIO.

48

Correct Answer: 3

Hatcher frequently guest-starred on MACGYVER as the accident-prone Penny.

49

Correct Answer: 4

KILLDOZER was based on the Theodore Sturgeon science-fiction story of the same name.

50

Correct Answer: 1

TARDIS is an acronym standing for Time And Relative Dimensions In Space.

20-POINT ANSWERS

1

Correct Answer: 5

Robert Bloch did not write for THE TWILIGHT ZONE.

2

Correct Answer: 2

THE TWILIGHT ZONE first aired in 1959.

3

Correct Answer: 2

Anne Francis was the department store mannequin who came to life in "The After Hours."

4

Correct Answer: 4

Data's daughter—an android created by Data—is named Lal.

5

Correct Answer: 2

Data builds his daughter in "The Offspring."

6

Correct Answer: 4

Starbuck reappears in the final GALACTICA 1980 episode, in which we last see him marooned on a desert planet.

7

Correct Answer: 2

Mitch Pileggi plays Assistant Director Skinner on THE X-FILES.

8

Correct Answer: 2

Earthmen are "The Invaders." They arrived on the alien planet in the same flying saucer model used in the film FORBIDDEN PLANET.

9

Correct Answer: 2

In this classic Cold War era episode, a nuclear attack has been announced.

10

Correct Answer: 2

When he hears the chimes, Number 6 realizes that he hasn't escaped from the village.

11

Correct Answer: 2

The Fox Network film DARK HORIZON was aired several years after the show's cancellation.

12

Correct Answer: 5

Rees took the role of Dr. John Breakstone.

13

Correct Answer: 4

Bowman is now a coproducer on THE X-FILES.

14

Correct Answer: 2

Shimerman played Pascal in BEAUTY AND THE BEAST.

15

Correct Answer: 2

Peter and Michael DeLuise signed on as Dagwood and Piccolo on the *seaQuest*.

16

Correct Answer: 5

Between the fifth and sixth seasons, Red Dwarf was stolen, and so Holly—who was male in the first two seasons, female in the next three—did not appear in the sixth season's episodes.

17

Correct Answer: 3

Crosby, Tasha Yar in THE NEXT GENERATION's first season, played Dr. Gretchen Kelley in LOIS AND CLARK's second year.

18

Correct Answer: 2

This episode featured the actual Robby the Robot model used in several MGM films; Robby also showed up in "The Condemned of Space."

19

Correct Answer: 5

Landau was a regular on MISSION: IMPOSSIBLE and the star of SPACE: 1999. He was in THE OUTER LIMITS episode "The Man Who Was Never Born."

20

Correct Answer: 3

West starred in this story of several expeditions to Mars that are all wiped out by a strange monster.

21

Correct Answer: 2

McShane, who plays the title role in LOVEJOY, played the man who feeds off energy in this episode.

22

Correct Answer: 5

Beacham played Sarah Bonsanquet, the secretary to the admiral in charge of a top-secret Navy project that Straker is investigating.

23

Correct Answer: 4

Piller was a coproducer of this Parker Stevenson vehicle.

24

Correct Answer: 1

Asimov cocreated the series with former HILL STREET BLUES story editor Wagner.

25

Correct Answer: 1

Thomerson played this character who switched gender periodically.

26

Correct Answer: 2

The movie also featured Stuart Whitman and Robert Wagner.

27

Correct Answer: 1

The show would run until 1955.

28

Correct Answer: 3

Weinstein's first sale was that STAR TREK animated episode. He would go on to write DEEP DOMAIN, THE COVENANT, AND THE CROWN, and many more novels, as well as becoming the writer of DC's monthly TREK comic.

29

Correct Answer: 2

SPACE PATROL was a 1950s live-action series on ABC, produced by Mike Moser.

30

Correct Answer: 1

Carmel, probably best known for playing Harry Mudd on STAR TREK, was the villain in the Batman–Green Hornet team-up.

31

Correct Answer: 2

They were called, prosaically, THE INCREDIBLE HULK and THE RETURN OF THE HULK.

32

Correct Answer: 2

Patrick Macnee went on to portray the dashing John Steed in THE AVENGERS.

33

Correct Answer: 2

Although killed by Cylons in the GALACTICA pilot, Springfield went on to have a short but successful career as a pop singer in the early 1980s.

34

Correct Answer: 4

Richard Anderson portrayed the immortal Dr. Richard Malcolm/Dr. Malcolm Richards in THE NIGHT STRANGLER.

35

Correct Answer: 5

Victor Buono was King Tut in BATMAN and Dr. Schubert in THE MAN FROM ATLANTIS.

36

Correct Answer: 4

Her career undamaged by her appearances on WONDER WOMAN, Winger went on to star in such films as TERMS OF ENDEARMENT and AN OFFICER AND A GENTLEMAN.

37

Correct Answer: 4

Sarah Douglas also costarred in the film THE PEOPLE THAT TIME FORGOT.

38

Correct Answer: 5

Silvers was the star of the 1950s comedy series SGT. BILKO.

39

Correct Answer: 2

Lenard played the villainous Urko.

40

Correct Answer: 4

Matheson himself adapted "Amelia," about a woman's nightmarish experience with an evil fetish doll come to life.

41

Correct Answer: 4

The pilot was remade the following year as PLANET EARTH.

42

Correct Answer: 3

Boggs's shortcomings were balanced by the greater intellect of his traveling companion, a junior history buff played by Meeno Peluce.

43

Correct Answer: 4

Jones played the title character in the 1980 film FLASH GORDON.

44

Correct Answer: 5

IT'S ABOUT TIME costarred comedienne Imogene Coca of the 1950s comedy series YOUR SHOW OF SHOWS.

45

Correct Answer: 5

Before playing Maya, Catherine Schell guest-starred in the episode "Guardian of Piri."

46

Correct Answer: 2

At no time in the film do we see the truck driver . . . only his boots.

47

Correct Answer: 1

Custer's last stand was featured in the TIME TUNNEL episode "Massacre" and THE TWILIGHT ZONE episode "The 7th Is Made up of Phantoms."

48

Correct Answer: 1

Elfman, the lead singer and writer for the music group Oingo Boingo, also wrote the theme for the film (and later TV series) WEIRD SCIENCE.

49

Correct Answer: 3

Sorbo finished second to Dean Cain for the role of Superman on LOIS AND CLARK: THE NEW ADVENTURES OF SUPERMAN.

50

Correct Answer: 2

The title was inspired by David Bowie's song "Golden Years," which was used as the series's theme.

30-POINT ANSWERS

1

Correct Answer: 2

The Borg first appeared in the episode "Q Who."

2

Correct Answer: 3

Peter Tuddenham provided the voice of Orac.

3

Correct Answer: 3

The alien invasion fleet came from Andromeda.

4

Correct Answer: 3

Tooms needed to eat the liver to keep alive.

5

Correct Answer: 1

An alien parasite is discovered in an ice core thousands of years old.

6

Correct Answer: 2

"The Doomsday Machine," with a teleplay written by science-fiction author Norman Spinrad, won the 1967 Hugo.

7

Correct Answer: 4

The astronauts disappear, because they should not have lived to return.

8

Correct Answer: 2

Dana Elcar, who played Sheriff Patterson in DARK SHADOWS, later became a MACGYVER cast member.

9

Correct Answer: 4

Erwin Schrodinger (1887–1961) developed the theory of quantum mechanics, part of which posits the existence of unlimited alternate worlds. Quinn named his cat after him.

10

Correct Answer: 3

Johnson, who had been a story editor for THE SIX MILLION DOLLAR MAN, created the Jamie Sommers character and developed THE BIONIC WOMAN. Later, he developed the other three series, though he had nothing to do with V: THE FINAL BATTLE or the V series.

11

Correct Answer: 1

Brown played Rawhide on BUCKAROO BANZAI, then went on to play John Danziger on EARTH 2.

12

Correct Answer: 2

Warner played Jor-El in the LOIS AND CLARK episode "Foundling," a Grail seeker in the BABYLON 5 episode "Grail," and an interrogator in the STAR TREK: THE NEXT GENERATION episode "Chain of Command."

13

Correct Answer: 1

Lucas programmed the voder in the pilot episode.

14

Correct Answer: 4

Shipp played the Flash, Hamill played the Trickster, and Nader played Pike. Danny Elfman wrote the show's theme music.

15

Correct Answer: 3

Hooten even had the trademark Fu Manchu mustache of the comic book character.

16

Correct Answer: 2

Scott, who played Joachim, Khan's right-hand man in STAR TREK II, played the Phoenix, an "ancient astronaut" come to Earth.

17

Correct Answer: 4

Dotrice played Father on the show.

18

Correct Answer: 1

He was credited in the episode as "Dan Travanty."

19

Correct Answer: 4

This story of a group of Vietnam vets, all of them shot with bullets made of an odd substance, was first aired on November 21 and 28, 1964.

20

Correct Answer: 3

Snodgrass wrote the teleplay based on Martin's novella.

21

Correct Answer: 1

Lee played the captain of an alien ship bound for Earth.

22

Correct Answer: 3

Barwick was the series' script editor.

23

Correct Answer: 5

Janis played Quark's supervisor and Mindy's father.

24

Correct Answer: 3

Gerrold, best known for writing the popular STAR TREK episode "The Trouble with Tribbles," was the story editor for this Sid and Marty Kroft production.

25

Correct Answer: 5

RED DWARF's third season ended in December 1989; the fourth season didn't debut until February 1991.

26

Correct Answer: 4

Mobley was committed to CUSTER, and thus couldn't take on the role of Batgirl.

27

Correct Answer: 2

Ross, who wrote all but one of the Catwoman scripts on BATMAN, wrote the pilot.

28

Correct Answer: 4

O'Connor played an alien emissary sent to judge Earth in this THE DAY THE EARTH STOOD STILL pastiche.

29

Correct Answer: 3

Lister figured it was the easiest way to become an officer, and therefore outrank Rimmer. However, he failed it.

30

Correct Answer: 1

Donald Pleasence appeared in the Carpenter-directed HALLOWEEN and ESCAPE FROM NEW YORK.

31

Correct Answer: 5

To distance himself from the show, Ellison had the show's creation credited to his pen name, "Cordwainer Bird."

32

Correct Answer: 3

Julie Newmar starred as Rhoda the robot.

33

Correct Answer: 3

"Cool Air" was the story of a doctor who used a special refrigeration unit to keep himself alive.

34

Correct Answer: 5

INTERRUPTED JOURNEY is the title of the book on which THE UFO INCIDENT was based.

35

Correct Answer: 3

In 1977, the series title was changed to SECRETS OF ISIS.

36

Correct Answer: 3

"Return of the Sorcerer" costarred MY FAVORITE MARTIAN and future INCREDIBLE HULK star Bill Bixby.

37

Correct Answer: 4

At the time, the oversized seaweed monster was on loan to LOST IN SPACE.

38

Correct Answer: 1

CYBERFORCE was directed by Russell Mulcahy, who also helmed the first HIGHLANDER film.

39

Correct Answer: 5

The "I" in I-MAN stood for Indestructible.

40

Correct Answer: 3

Boba Fett appeared in a cartoon segment of the special, two years before his live-action appearance in THE EMPIRE STRIKES BACK.

41

Correct Answer: 1

Conried was also the voice of Snidely Whiplash in the DUDLEY DORIGHT cartoons.

42

Correct Answer: 4

Bloch himself adapted his story "Yours Truly, Jack the Ripper" for this episode.

43

Correct Answer: 5

In addition to hosting the series, Newland directed all of its episodes.

44

Correct Answer: 3

The giant robot has soared again in recent years, in THE NEW ADVENTURES OF GIGANTOR.

45

Correct Answer: 4

The superimposing process was known as Syncro-Vox.

46

Correct Answer: 4

Lorenzo Semple, Jr., was also the scripter of NEVER SAY NEVER AGAIN, the final appearance of Sean Connery as James Bond.

47

Correct Answer: 2

Frank has been studying the martial arts since he was four years old.

48

Correct Answer: 4

Skerritt played Robert Palmer, a fast-rising politician who transformed into a "hound from Hell" to kill his political opponents.

49

Correct Answer: 2

NBC execs were afraid that children might want to emulate the Torch's flaming abilities.

50

Correct Answer: 3

Bernsen is best known for his role as lawyer Arnie Becker on the drama series L.A. LAW.

40-POINT ANSWERS

1

Correct Answer: 2

Commodore Pike led the trial board.

2

Correct Answer: 3

Alien DNA was in "The Erlenmeyer Flask."

3

Correct Answer: 2

Nomad combined with Tan Ru.

4

Correct Answer: 2

Yonada was the spaceship world.

5

Correct Answer: 2

Believe it or not, POLICE SURGEON became THE AVENGERS.

6

Correct Answer: 1

Ed Asner played the role in his usual gruff Lou Grant manner.

7

Correct Answer: 1

Ensign Ro was originally supposed to be a regular.

8

Correct Answer: 4

Uhura takes control.

9

Correct Answer: 3

Both halves of Lazarus and both universes would be destroyed.

10

Correct Answer: 5

This subplot spelled the beginning of the last days for DARK SHADOWS, as ratings began to wane.

11

Correct Answer: 1

Nicholas Blair was played by Humbert Allen Astredo.

12

Correct Answer: 5

A shadow demon pursues Hawkes until he falls to his death from Widows' Hill.

13

Correct Answer: 4

If they miss the wormhole, the next one will open in 30 years. This is a danger, especially if they get caught in a world like the Nuclear Winter or the melted Polar Ice Caps Earth.

14

Correct Answer: 3

He played Dennis/Denise on TWIN PEAKS.

15

Correct Answer: 3

CLIFF HANGERS lasted three months in early 1979.

16

Correct Answer: 3

TV veteran Fields wrote the teleplay for "The Inner Light," which won the Hugo Award for Best Dramatic Presentation at the 51st Annual World Science Fiction Convention.

17

Correct Answer: 3

Bikel also played Worf's foster father in the STAR TREK: THE NEXT GENERATION episode "Family."

18

Correct Answer: 5

David Ross played him in the episode "Kryten," then, when the character became a regular, Llewellyn took over the role.

19

Correct Answer: 4

They were named after Lister's hero, the zero-G football star Jim Bexley Speed.

20

Correct Answer: 2

Zevon has written several songs with science-fiction themes, so he was definitely an appropriate choice.

21

Correct Answer: 4

By the middle of the third season, the crew used Starbug exclusively.

22

Correct Answer: 3

Besides this corporate association, Captain Midnight was known for sending secret messages that you needed a special decoder to understand. (Who says marketing is a new concept?)

23

Correct Answer: 2

Clemenson, who played Socrates Poole on BRISCO COUNTY, had a recurring role as Rollie Vale.

24 Correct Answer: 3

Kolbe directed both "All Good Things . . . ," the NEXT GENERATION finale, and "The Caretaker," the premiere of VOYAGER.

25 Correct Answer: 1

Scott played the doctor who operated on an ape to grant her intelligence.

26 Correct Answer: 2

This episode was also a cautionary tale about an Immortal who develops a deadly drug.

27 Correct Answer: 2

Gordon and Gansa wrote many episodes of both shows.

28 Correct Answer: 3

A very unfamous young Spielberg directed this gaze into an ecologically disastrous future.

29 Correct Answer: 2

Although the series was based on Heinlein's novel SPACE CADET, Heinlein never wrote any episodes. Bester, author of THE DEMOLISHED MAN, did.

30 Correct Answer: 4

George Reeves directed many episodes of the show in its later years.

31 Correct Answer: 3

Sterling Halloway was the voice of Winnie-the-Pooh.

32 Correct Answer: 3

Buck's base was secreted behind a waterfall in Niagara Falls, NY.

33 Correct Answer: 2

The opticon scillometer was an invention of Captain Video's.

34 Correct Answer: 5

TOM CORBETT, SPACE CADET was set in the year 2335.

35 Correct Answer: 1

And Spielberg has been making up for it ever since by putting nice, sweet children in his later films.

36

Correct Answer: 5

Bakshi also supervised the animation of the late 1980s series THE NEW ADVENTURES OF MIGHTY MOUSE.

37

Correct Answer: 5

At the time, the giant Portuguese man-of-war was on loan to LAND OF THE GIANTS.

38

Correct Answer: 4

Newton was replaced by Gerard Christopher.

39

Correct Answer: 5

Carradine played such notable horror characters as Dracula.

40

Correct Answer: 2

Norliss was a reporter who battled an ancient demon spirit.

41

Correct Answer: 5

Auberjonois plays Odo on STAR TREK: DEEP SPACE NINE.

42

Correct Answer: 3

In 1980, the trio teamed again in the animated series THE DRAK PACK.

43

Correct Answer: 5

Springfield was replaced by Geraint Wyn Davies in the role of vampire police detective Nicholas Knight.

44

Correct Answer: 1

The change was made to avoid copyright infringement with Mighty Atom, a mouse in TICK TOCK TALES comics in the 1940s and 1950s.

45

Correct Answer: 5

Kasem was also the voice of Shaggy in the SCOOBY-DOO cartoons.

46

Correct Answer: 3

A pre-DALLAS Patrick Duffy starred as Mark Harris, THE MAN FROM ATLANTIS.

47

Correct Answer: 1

Frank Gorshin played the villainous Riddler on BATMAN.

48

Correct Answer: 5

"Wild Journey" guest-starred Bruce Dern and Yvonne (Batgirl) Craig.

49

Correct Answer: 2

"The Stranger Within" starred Barbara Eden, better known for I
DREAM OF JEANNIE.

50

Correct Answer: 1

Carolyn Jones—Morticia of THE ADDAMS FAMILY—guest-starred as
the college registrar in the episode "Demon in Lace."

50-POINT ANSWERS

1
Correct Answer: 4

Halloway was captain in "Tapestry."

2
Correct Answer: 3

The ruins are on Tagus III.

3
Correct Answer: 4

It is mentioned in "Up the Long Ladder."

4
Correct Answer: 3

"Warrior's Gate" features the final appearance of Romana and K-9, two of the fourth Doctor's traveling companions.

5
Correct Answer: 4

"The Dalek Masterplan" was the longest, running 12 episodes.

6
Correct Answer: 1

Dick Smith is one of Hollywood's most respected creators of "gross faces."

7
Correct Answer: 2

Neil Simon came to watch the production, and the actors had a field day hamming it up for him during the last taping session.

8
Correct Answer: 5

Quinn stated that he didn't think time travel was even possible.

9
Correct Answer: 4

Not only is it his birthday; the 11:21 that repeatedly appears on digital clocks on the show is a reference to his wife's birthday.

10
Correct Answer: 4

We see Mulder type this in on an episode.

11
Correct Answer: 4

Conway played the heroic pilot.

12
Correct Answer: 4

Patrick Newell played Steed's boss, "Mother."

13

Correct Answer: 2

However, they stand for "Bronze Swimming Certificate" and "Silver Swimming Certificate."

14

Correct Answer: 2

Debbie Ash played a fantasy version of Marilyn in "Better Than Life," and Pauline Bailey played a waxdroid version in "Meltdown."

15

Correct Answer: 5

Davison made his television debut in that episode as a bumbling alien named Elmer.

16

Correct Answer: 3

Singer directed the episode "The Derelict," where he was credited as "Alex Singer."

17

Correct Answer: 1

Gough played a crotchety scientist in the episode.

18

Correct Answer: 3

Mansfield's Vena was one of the first sex symbols on genre television.

19

Correct Answer: 2

Played by Al Hodge, the Video Ranger helped Captain Video on his adventures from 1949 to 1953.

20

Correct Answer: 5

FLASH GORDON starred Steve Holland, Joe Nash, and Irene Champion in this short-lived version of the oft-retold story.

21

Correct Answer: 1

Thomas costarred with Pierre Brice and Judy Geeson in this 1977 TV film.

22

Correct Answer: 1

The Immortal Kuyler drank absinthe for centuries and, since Immortals can't die, it drove him mad.

23

Correct Answer: 2

When bidding farewell to Sinclair in the episode, Bester saluted with an "okee-dokee" sign and said, "Be seeing you," à la THE PRISONER.

24

Correct Answer: 5

Weston played the improbably named Wilbur Wormsley, one of Rod Brown's fellow rangers.

25

Correct Answer: 4

This Jonathan Harris vehicle aired on Saturday mornings on CBS.

26

Correct Answer: 5

This space travel series starring William Lundigan premiered in 1959 and ran for one season.

27

Correct Answer: 4

Lucas, the producer of TREK's third season, wrote this failed pilot.

28

Correct Answer: 1

This group arrested Murphy's wife for supporting a prominent opponent of OCP's welfare system.

29

Correct Answer: 5

Van Ark was part of the group led by Boone's Masten Thrust into a prehistoric land buried in the polar wastes.

30

Correct Answer: 1

Abrams worked on both series.

31

Correct Answer: 2

Boretz used very little of the story from AMAZING FANTASY #15 in his screenplay.

32

Correct Answer: 1

Thompson played the role of the six-inch-tall man who worked as a spy.

33

Correct Answer: 3

Ben Welden also appeared with SUPERMAN star George Reeves in the 1940 film TEAR GAS SQUAD.

34

Correct Answer: 5

Time travelers Tony Newman and Doug Phillips meet Rudyard Kipling in "The Night of the Long Knives."

35

Correct Answer: 3

JET JACKSON was one of TV's earliest SF shows.

36

Correct Answer: 2

The show never lasted to its second *single* year.

37

Correct Answer: 5

Rocky flew off into oblivion by the end of 1954.

38

Correct Answer: 4

Knight played bumbling newscaster Ted Baxter on THE MARY TYLER MOORE SHOW.

39

Correct Answer: 4

"Cry of Silence" starred Eddie Albert of GREEN ACRES fame.

40

Correct Answer: 2

The screenplay for DRACULA was written by Richard Matheson.

41

Correct Answer: 4

"The Forms of Things Unknown" also served as the pilot for the unsold series THE UNKNOWN.

42

Correct Answer: 4

"The Fatal Impulse" starred a little-known actress named Mary Tyler Moore.

43

Correct Answer: 5

Suzanne Pleshette went on to costar as Emily on THE BOB NEWHART SHOW.

44

Correct Answer: 2

THE MIGHTY HEROES were Diaper Man, Cuckoo Man, Rope Man, Strong Man, and Tornado Man.

45

Correct Answer: 3

Dicks is the author of a number of novelizations of DOCTOR WHO episodes.

46

Correct Answer: 4

Carlin went on to appear in such film gems as CAR WASH.

47

Correct Answer: 2

"Bears" was Stefano's term for the horrifying denizens of THE OUTER LIMITS.

48

Correct Answer: 4

THE TIME TRAVELERS was coproduced by Rod Serling and Irwin Allen.

49

Correct Answer: 5

Oakland appeared in a variety of TV shows, among them THE TWILIGHT ZONE.

50

Correct Answer: 5

Use of the mushroom would improve a person's ESP abilities.

HOW CAN HE MOVE SO FAST?

AARROHH

STOP HIM! HE'S ONLY ONE MAN

SCIENCE FICTION

Comics

ANSWERS

10-POINT ANSWERS

1

Correct Answer: 1

The Eradicator had deluded itself into thinking it was Superman for a brief period.

2

Correct Answer: 1

Dick was the youngest member of the Flying Graysons, a world-famous family of trapeze artists.

3

Correct Answer: 2

Wonder Woman appeared in every one of the first 106 issues of SENSATION COMICS.

4

Correct Answer: 4

According to a recent origin story, Cloak and Dagger are actually mutants whose powers were activated by experimental drugs.

5

Correct Answer: 2

Stark's alcoholism has long been a running theme in the IRON MAN comic.

6

Correct Answer: 1

E.C. settled for the obvious, but eventually had to change WEIRD SCIENCE-FANTASY to INCREDIBLE SCIENCE FICTION to avoid the Comics Code ban on use of the word "Weird" in comic book titles.

7

Correct Answer: 2

Thorne's work on the RED SONJA series was a springboard for a career portraying voluptuous women, including his own creation, Ghita.

8

Correct Answer: 4

SEDUCTION OF THE INNOCENT was sloppily researched and poorly written, but it had millions of parents up in arms, denouncing comic books as lurid trash.

9

Correct Answer: 5

William Gaines's E.C. Publications published titles such as TALES FROM THE CRYPT as "Entertaining Comics," and PICTURE STORIES FROM THE BIBLE under the "Educational Comics" name.

10

Correct Answer: 1

A "rube" is foolish, as were many of Goldberg's machines.

11 Correct Answer: 4

It had four parts.

12 Correct Answer: 3

The name Marvelman was changed to Miracleman in the U.S. to avoid legal problems with Marvel Comics.

13 Correct Answer: 5

The only published issue of FANTASY QUARTERLY featured the first appearance of ELFQUEST.

14 Correct Answer: 2

Jim Lee's WILDC.A.T.S. is now a television cartoon.

15 Correct Answer: 5

Witch Hazel and Little Itch were constantly harassing a poor little girl who happened to look just like Lulu, and who always beat them in the end—often unintentionally.

16 Correct Answer: 2

Carol Danvers—the former Ms. Marvel—is now Binary, a member of the spacefaring pirates, the Starjammers.

17 Correct Answer: 2

Ditko would continue to provide the art, and many of the plots, for the first 38 issues of THE AMAZING SPIDER-MAN.

18 Correct Answer: 3

Kirby created the first Spider-Man rough.

19 Correct Answer: 5

Tundra was formed by Eastman to publish the work of other comics creators. It was bought out by Kitchen Sink Press in 1993.

20 Correct Answer: 4

The original GREEN LANTERN had scripts by many SF novelists.

21 Correct Answer: 2

MAD has used that slogan since the 1950s.

22

Correct Answer: 3

It's generally assumed to have been the voice of God that spoke to the late Jim Corrigan.

23

Correct Answer: 1

Conan began as a novel by Robert E. Howard.

24

Correct Answer: 4

Traveling to Vietnam as a consultant to the U.S. Army, Stark was wounded when a booby trap exploded, lodging shrapnel in his heart.

25

Correct Answer: 2

THE DARK KNIGHT RETURNS introduced a fourteen-year-old girl who became Robin after saving Batman's life.

26

Correct Answer: 2

The original concept for Cerebus was a purely satirical parody of Conan the Barbarian.

27

Correct Answer: 5

Green Lantern would be fun, but probably requires too many special effects.

28

Correct Answer: 5

Not only does Lord Julius look and act like Groucho Marx, but he speaks and thinks like him as well.

29

Correct Answer: 1

During the closing days of World War II, Bucky was killed in the explosion that placed Captain America in suspended animation for 20 years.

30

Correct Answer: 4

J'onn J'onzz is the Manhunter from Mars, and one of the members of the Justice League of America and the Justice League Task Force.

31

Correct Answer: 5

The "black light" plunged evildoers into darkness and confusion, giving her the advantage she needed.

32

Correct Answer: 4

"Excelsior" means "higher" or "upward."

33

Correct Answer: 5

Queen Hippolyte, ruler of the Amazons of Paradise Island, sculpted a daughter—named Diana—out of clay. Diana was then brought to life by the goddess Aphrodite and grew up to become Wonder Woman.

34

Correct Answer: 5

DC still publishes STAR TREK and STAR TREK: THE NEXT GENERATION comics. Marvel published a 17-issue STAR TREK series in 1979, GOLD KEY published a STAR TREK comic in the early 1970s, and MALIBU currently publishes a STAR TREK: DEEP SPACE NINE comic.

35

Correct Answer: 3

Sue Dibny has helped her husband, Ralph—the Elongated Man—on a number of his adventures.

36

Correct Answer: 1

After being "killed," former investigator Denny Colt lived under Wildwood Cemetery, and ventured out to fight crime as The Spirit in Will Eisner's classic series.

37

Correct Answer: 5

The amazing Amazon was deliberately created by William Moulton Marston to fill the perceived lack of a comic book star with whom girls could identify.

38

Correct Answer: 4

Exiled to Earth by his father, Odin, to learn humility, Thor became one of the founding members of the superhero group The Avengers.

39

Correct Answer: 4

McCay's LITTLE NEMO remains one of the most beloved classic strips.

40

Correct Answer: 2

Vance Astro (real name Astrovik) is a hero from an alternate Marvel Universe future, and one of the founding members of the Guardians of the Galaxy.

41

Correct Answer: 2

Since his creation, the Green Hornet—and his faithful chauffeur, Kato—has appeared in comic books, a short-lived TV show, and even the 1960s BATMAN TV series.

42

Correct Answer: 4

MAD. The name says it all.

43

Correct Answer: 1

Carl Barks is known for his innovative and exciting Scrooge McDuck stories.

44

Correct Answer: 1

Robert Crumb, of course.

45

Correct Answer: 1

William Elder worked for E.C., doing most of their war comics.

46

Correct Answer: 1

Hal Foster drew TARZAN, and created the strip PRINCE VALIANT.

47

Correct Answer: 2

Paul Gustavson worked on several comics at the same time in the early 1930s.

48

Correct Answer: 1

Samuel "Jerry" Iger and Will Eisner ran a studio that located and hired new talent, as well as refined what they already had. Albert Feldstein, Lou Fine, and Reed Crandall were among the many studio artists.

49

Correct Answer: 2

Rob Liefeld also created the first Image comic, YOUNGBLOOD.

50

Correct Answer: 2

Moebius was also a cocreator of the Western hero Lt. Blueberry.

20-POINT ANSWERS

1

Correct Answer: 3

The Heap first clambered out of that marsh in AIR FIGHTERS COMICS #3.

2

Correct Answer: 5

After THE SANDMAN #18 ("A Midsummer Night's Dream") won this award in 1992, the rules were changed so comic books were no longer eligible.

3

Correct Answer: 1

Blastaar, like Annihilus, another FF villain, was from the Negative Zone.

4

Correct Answer: 2

Burden has produced issues of FLAMING CARROT COMICS on an irregular schedule for over ten years.

5

Correct Answer: 4

Mr. Mind looked utterly harmless—but he was one mean worm!

6

Correct Answer: 5

What ELSE would you call a ghost horse?

7

Correct Answer: 5

How did they miss FUTURE LOVE? The closest they came was "Invasion of the Love Robots!" in an issue of Ziff-Davis' AMAZING ADVENTURES.

8

Correct Answer: 5

The extremely controversial XXX comic BLACK KISS was created by Howard Chaykin for Vortex Comics.

9

Correct Answer: 5

The reformation of Eel O'Brien and the origin of Plastic Man occurred in POLICE COMICS #1.

10

Correct Answer: 1

"True crime" comics were successful for about a decade before the censorship movement of the 1950s drove them from the comics racks of America.

11

Correct Answer: 2

Asterix is a Gaul.

12

Correct Answer: 4

He was going through a bout of multiple personalities and feared he would become a menace.

13

Correct Answer: 4

Superman and the Flash did, but it wasn't clear who won.

14

Correct Answer: 4

JIMMY OLSEN became one of the comics that made up Kirby's "Fourth World."

15

Correct Answer: 4

COMICO PRIMER #2 featured the first appearance of Grendel.

16

Correct Answer: 3

Jack "Cadillac" Tenrec is the one of the few Old Blood Mechanics living in the known world.

17

Correct Answer: 3

LOVE AND ROCKETS is still the dominant comic in the "slice of life" genre.

18

Correct Answer: 5

The Sub-Mariner first appeared in a minimally circulated comic, MOTION PICTURE FUNNIES WEEKLY, then debuted in color in MARVEL COMICS #1. Both stories were written and drawn by Everett.

19

Correct Answer: 3

ZOT derives much from the quick, descriptive style of Japanese *manga*.

20

Correct Answer: 5

Todd was introduced after the first Robin, Dick Grayson, became Nightwing. Todd was later killed by the Joker.

21

Correct Answer: 4

The first single-genre titles were DETECTIVE PICTURE STORIES and DETECTIVE COMICS, both premiering in 1936.

22 Correct Answer: 1

The Hulk was an Avenger for only two issues, but he did help found the team.

23 Correct Answer: 1

The Vision at one time was married to Wanda Maximoff, the Scarlet Witch, who was a member of three superpowered groups: the Brotherhood of Evil Mutants, the Avengers, and Force Works.

24 Correct Answer: 1

Richard Corben often signed his name as "Gore," as a tribute to E.C. artist Graham Ingels, who used to sign much of his horror work "Ghastly."

25 Correct Answer: 1

The three-issue series STEED AND MRS. PEEL was written by Grant Morrison and drawn by Ian Gibson.

26 Correct Answer: 1

Sim's early art was heavily derivative of Barry Smith's early work on Marvel's CONAN THE BARBARIAN comic.

27 Correct Answer: 2

While most villains were content with just wrecking Avengers Mansion, the Masters of Evil actually destroyed it.

28 Correct Answer: 4

Ronald Lithgow was a senator's speechwriter before being transformed into Concrete.

29 Correct Answer: 4

Arnus and Freeman are aliases of Icon; Metcalfe is Hardware; Kent is Superman.

30 Correct Answer: 2

Wanting a unique battle cry, the Tick chose the first thing that came to mind: "Spoon!"

31 Correct Answer: 5

The main weapon of the first several Grendels was a fighting fork, the length of a spear with two electrified prongs on the end.

32

Correct Answer: 5

Logan is Wolverine's real name, although it's unknown whether it's his first name or last name.

33

Correct Answer: 4

Ray Palmer gained his size-changing powers from a portion of white star matter.

34

Correct Answer: 2

An updated version of the Brotherhood of Evil caused no end of trouble for the New Teen Titans/New Titans.

35

Correct Answer: 5

Due to an impurity in the ring's material, the Green Lantern's weapon is powerless against yellow.

36

Correct Answer: 4

Lead was killing him, so Superboy projected him into the Phantom Zone.

37

Correct Answer: 4

Long before Indiana Jones, there was Adam Strange, Archaeologist.

38

Correct Answer: 2

The Beyonder made his return to the Marvel Universe in SECRET WARS II.

39

Correct Answer: 2

Based on the novella ARMAGEDDON 2419, BUCK ROGERS was the first SF comic strip.

40

Correct Answer: 5

With such members as Duo Damsel, Bouncing Boy, and Matter-Eater Lad, the Legion of Superheroes is the largest supergroup.

41

Correct Answer: 1

"Pieface" was the first Eskimo in comicdom.

42

Correct Answer: 3

MARVEL CLASSIC adapted novels into comic form.

43 Correct Answer: 4

Turok first appeared in Dell's FOUR-COLOR COMICS #596, in 1954.

44 Correct Answer: 4

After being sickly and weak since 1962, May Parker finally "bought it" in this 1995 comic.

45 Correct Answer: 4

Writer Alan Moore and artist Dave Gibbons's maxiseries WATCHMEN won a special Hugo in 1986.

46 Correct Answer: 1

One wonders why no one ever tried science-fiction romance; perhaps publishers didn't think girls liked science fiction.

47 Correct Answer: 5

"Crime" and "horror" are still gone. "Weird" came back in 1971; "terror," in 1992; and "suspense" never left.

48 Correct Answer: 1

Jack Kirby adapted the film 2001 as a MARVEL TREASURY EDITION before writing and penciling the 2001 comic book series.

49 Correct Answer: 3

Crumb, the creator of ZAP, was the most prominent member of the underground comix movement of the 1960s.

50 Correct Answer: 2

Gene Colan has worked on DAREDEVIL, IRON MAN, THE SUB-MARINER, and NIGHT FORCE. He is best known for his collaboration with writer Marv Wolfman on the TOMB OF DRACULA series.

30-POINT ANSWERS

1

Correct Answer: 2

TABOO discontinued publication in 1993, and FROM HELL was thenceforth released directly in trade paperback form.

2

Correct Answer: 5

Having been issued by three different publishers, NINJA HIGH SCHOOL is among the most popular U.S. *manga*-style comics.

3

Correct Answer: 3

DESTINATION MOON appeared in the first issue of STRANGE ADVENTURES.

4

Correct Answer: 3

Ellison made his first sale to WEIRD SCIENCE-FANTASY.

5

Correct Answer: 4

Four different comic book series have come out of the TV show.

6

Correct Answer: 2

A story arc dealing with Peter Parker's roommate, Harry Osborn, being a drug user ran without the CCA seal.

7

Correct Answer: 3

As B. B. Flemm, Jon Sable was a best-selling children's book writer.

8

Correct Answer: 4

Like most Fiction House titles, PLANET COMICS featured plenty of heroines—not out of feminism, but because Fiction House loved pinup art!

9

Correct Answer: 1

The first five issues of THE CROW were published by Caliber Press. O'Barr then took the story to Tundra, where it was finished.

10

Correct Answer: 2

Especially notable were some of the BUCK ROGERS covers drawn by Frank Frazetta near the end of FAMOUS FUNNIES' long run.

11

Correct Answer: 5

Once a member of the Hellfire Club, Emma Frost is now one of the instructors for GENERATION X.

12 Correct Answer: 4

Two SPACE: 1999 comics were released at the same time by the same company, Charlton Comics.

13 Correct Answer: 4

It became INCREDIBLE SCIENCE FICTION.

14 Correct Answer: 3

Every issue of THE TWILIGHT ZONE had Rod Serling somewhere on the cover.

15 Correct Answer: 2

And what a nap *that* was. . . .

16 Correct Answer: 2

In the film BUCKAROO BANZAI: ADVENTURES IN THE 8TH DIMENSION, a comic book series that followed the exploits of the Doc Savage-like Banzai was mentioned. In the real world, Marvel Comics published only a three-issue adaptation of the film.

17 Correct Answer: 3

The magic potion brewed by their Druid Getafix made them invincible.

18 Correct Answer: 3

Alfred Bester wrote comics while he was learning his craft.

19 Correct Answer: 3

Harry Harrison drew comics for E.C., among others.

20 Correct Answer: 1

STRANGE ADVENTURES was DC Comics' premier SF comic.

21 Correct Answer: 2

Sex was the first topic to be dealt with bluntly and clearly.

22 Correct Answer: 3

PLANET COMICS (from the publisher of PLANET STORIES, a pulp fiction magazine) was first.

23 Correct Answer: 1

The Phoenix Force was an alien entity.

24

Correct Answer: 1

Norrin Radd, a native of the planet Zenn-La, offered himself to Galactus in exchange for the world devourer's pledge to not destroy Zenn-La. In return, Galactus imbued Radd with cosmic powers and made him his herald, the Silver Surfer.

25

Correct Answer: 2

Unlike the TV show LOST IN SPACE, the children were Tim and Tam.

26

Correct Answer: 1

The "Zeta-Beam" was Strange's method of travel between Earth and Alpha Centauri.

27

Correct Answer: 4

Koenig wrote an issue of the STAR TREK comic; Takei cowrote a STAR TREK ANNUAL; DeLancie cowrote a STAR TREK: THE NEXT GENERATION ANNUAL.

28

Correct Answer: 4

SPACE PATROL began as an ABC radio show.

29

Correct Answer: 2

Gaiman's book was published in the 1980s, long before he came to prominence in the comic book field.

30

Correct Answer: 5

In addition to NEXT MEN, Byrne created BABE and DANGER UNLIMITED. He is widely known for working on the adventures of such mainstream characters as Superman, Wonder Woman, and the X-Men.

31

Correct Answer: 5

Gold Key published the first STAR TREK comic book.

32

Correct Answer: 1

Through a bizarre accident, criminal Eel O'Brien gained stretching abilities and decided to fight crime as Plastic Man.

33

Correct Answer: 3

During the maxiseries CRISIS ON INFINITE EARTHS, Barry Allen sacrificed his life to try and save the Earth-One from the Anti-Monitor, who was wiping out the multiple parallel dimensions.

34

Correct Answer: 4

Harvey Kurtzman edited MAD from #1, in 1952, through #28, in 1956, five issues after the transformation to magazine form. Al Feldstein subsequently edited it for more than 30 years.

35

Correct Answer: 4

Thunderbird was the first X-Man to die, killed by Count Nefaria in UNCANNY X-MEN #94.

36

Correct Answer: 3

Moon Girl's adventures changed their approach several times in a mere eight issues before E.C. gave up and replaced her with a romance title: A MOON, A GIRL . . . ROMANCE!

37

Correct Answer: 2

He is the leader of L.E.G.I.O.N.

38

Correct Answer: 2

Asimov's most recent comic book work can be found in the pages of Tekno Comics' LEONARD NIMOY'S PRIMORTALS and ISAAC ASIMOV'S I-BOTS.

39

Correct Answer: 2

The adaptation was presented in a unique text-next-to-art format, later used by Kyle Baker in his graphic novel WHY I HATE SATURN.

40

Correct Answer: 3

George Evans worked on ACES HIGH for 12 years without a byline.

41

Correct Answer: 3

During his long career, Don Heck worked on such titles as THE AVENGERS and THE DEFENDERS for Marvel, and STEEL and WONDER WOMAN for DC.

42

Correct Answer: 4

"Ghastly" Graham Ingels' work on CRYPT OF TERROR, VAULT OF TERROR, and HAUNT OF HORROR for EC helped establish him as the premier horror comic artist.

43

Correct Answer: 3

David Lapham currently writes and draws his self-published comic book, the crime-fiction series STRAY BULLETS.

44

Correct Answer: 3

Frank Miller is widely recognized for his Batman miniseries THE DARK KNIGHT RETURNS, as well as for his work on DAREDEVIL, ELEKTRA: ASSASSIN, and the MARTHA WASHINGTON series, cocreated with artist Dave Gibbons.

45

Correct Answer: 1

Alex Raymond's main work was in the newspaper strips.

46

Correct Answer: 2

Walt Simonson also revamped THOR and THE FANTASTIC FOUR for Marvel.

47

Correct Answer: 1

Dave Stevens' THE ROCKETEER has become known less for re-creating the feeling of a Saturday morning movie serial than for restarting the career of 1950s pinup queen Bettie Page.

48

Correct Answer: 2

Bernie Wrightson began his career in 1969. It was in HOUSE OF SECRETS that Swamp Thing first lumbered into sight.

49

Correct Answer: 2

Mort Meskin was the artist responsible for the Vigilante's cowboy look, unique in a world of flashy superheroes.

50

Correct Answer: 4

Captain Marvel got his start in WHIZ COMICS.

40-POINT ANSWERS

1

Correct Answer: 4

Mort Weisinger was the Silver Age editor of the "Superman family" comics.

2

Correct Answer: 4

Natives of the planet Thanagar, Katar Hol—Hawkman—and his wife, Shayera—Hawkgirl—were interplanetary police officers who traveled between worlds in a spaceship.

3

Correct Answer: 4

FROM HELL is an analytical comic about the time and events surrounding the Jack the Ripper killings.

4

Correct Answer: 3

Trueman's origins as both a superhero and a fictional comic book character were the subject of MAXIMORTAL.

5

Correct Answer: 4

When four men survived a plane crash, they believed that they were living on borrowed time. To make better use of their second chance at life, they formed the Challengers of the Unknown.

6

Correct Answer: 5

DELL published the comic book adaptation of George Pal's film THE TIME MACHINE.

7

Correct Answer: 5

Adam Strange did.

8

Correct Answer: 2

In his quest for absolute power, Doctor Doom stole the Beyonder's godlike power in SECRET WARS.

9

Correct Answer: 2

The Lord of the Savage Land, Ka-Zar—whose real name is Lord Kevin Plunder—is married to the Chicago-born jungle queen, Shanna the She-Devil.

10

Correct Answer: 3

In the 1980s, Pete married Lana Lang.

11

Correct Answer: 5

Jack Cole's wildly inventive art was much of the fun of reading Plastic Man's adventures.

12

Correct Answer: 3

In a reversal of the usual roles, the Star-Spangled Kid had an adult sidekick, a bruiser known as Stripesy.

13

Correct Answer: 2

The adopted son of Odin, Loki is Thor's half brother and the god of mischief.

14

Correct Answer: 2

Though it was written by UNCANNY X-MEN writer Claremont, THE NEW TEEN TITANS writer and cocreator, Marv Wolfman, was consulted on the plot.

15

Correct Answer: 2

BARBARELLA was created for V. MAGAZINE in 1962. However, the character is more widely known from the movie of the same name, which starred Jane Fonda as the spacefaring adventuress.

16

Correct Answer: 3

SPACE WESTERN began in 1952.

17

Correct Answer: 1

WEIRD SCIENCE-FANTASY presented a cynical view of humanity.

18

Correct Answer: 5

There have been five.

19

Correct Answer: 5

Alas, the collapse of the horror market killed the idea, and what would have been CRYPT OF TERROR #1 was instead published as TALES FROM THE CRYPT #46.

20

Correct Answer: 2

Although his code name was Wolverine, Logan's designation was "Weapon X."

21

Correct Answer: 3

Spidey's new costume was one of many changes in various Marvel characters made in the SECRET WARS miniseries.

22 Correct Answer: 3

Dr. Occult first appeared in NEW FUN COMICS #6, in 1935.

23 Correct Answer: 1

WEIRD SCIENCE-FANTASY ran "factual" reports on UFOs.

24 Correct Answer: 4

The Celestials are responsible for the "x-factor" gene, which triggers mutant abilities in humans.

25 Correct Answer: 1

Joe Orlando was hired to be "another Wally Wood."

26 Correct Answer: 2

The results in BUCK ROGERS were space suits and domed cities, among others developments.

27 Correct Answer: 4

They launched AMAZING ADVENTURES.

28 Correct Answer: 2

LITTLE NEMO, by Winsor McCay, did.

29 Correct Answer: 1

STRANGE ADVENTURES hired SF authors as original story writers.

30 Correct Answer: 3

Alfred Bester told Schwartz, his agent, about the opening.

31 Correct Answer: 3

In his original appearance in an issue of THE FANTASTIC FOUR, Warlock was known only as "Him."

32 Correct Answer: 1

Jack Kirby, in collaboration with his longtime partner, Joe Simon, pioneered this field.

33 Correct Answer: 3

SF agent Julius Schwartz became a comics editor with STRANGE ADVENTURES.

34

Correct Answer: 1

In the FANTASTIC FOUR story line "The Death of Galactus," Reed Richards saved the world devourer's life. Reed was later put on trial by a court of extraterrestrials for this crime against the universe.

35

Correct Answer: 2

Rod Hathaway was the Space Detective.

36

Correct Answer: 2

Both comics printed many adaptations of Ray Bradbury stories.

37

Correct Answer: 2

Neal Adams began working in the newspapers on the BEN CASEY comic strip.

38

Correct Answer: 2

In addition to Spider-Man, Steve Ditko is known for his unique approach to Doctor Strange, Master of the Mystic Arts. In later years, he has worked on such titles as ROM: SPACEKNIGHT, THE FURTHER ADVENTURES OF INDIANA JONES, and PHANTOM 2040 for Marvel. He also created SHADE, THE CHANGING MAN for DC.

39

Correct Answer: 2

Don Heck worked on both series, as well as THE X-MEN, IRON MAN, and TALES OF SUSPENSE.

40

Correct Answer: 4

Kirby got his start in newspapers, then worked as an "in-betweener" on Popeye cartoons for the Fleischer Brothers animation studio, then joined the Eisner-Iger shop in the 1930s.

41

Correct Answer: 4

Winsor McCays's first cartoons appeared in 1897, but his more famous LITTLE NEMO IN SLUMBERLAND began in 1911.

42

Correct Answer: 1

As Moebius, Giraud is best known for his work on such projects as ARZACH, THE AIRTIGHT GARAGE, and LT. BLUEBERRY.

43

Correct Answer: 3

Mike Ploog worked on such Marvel horror titles as WEREWOLF BY NIGHT and GHOST RIDER.

44

Correct Answer: 3

Bill Sienkiewicz worked with Frank Miller on the graphic novel DAREDEVIL: LOVE AND WAR and the miniseries ELEKTRA: ASSASSIN, and with Chris Claremont on THE NEW MUTANTS.

45

Correct Answer: 1

BLUE BOLT was a cowboy, but his stories were backed up by some chilling stuff.

46

Correct Answer: 2

MARVEL SCIENCE STORIES was the SF pulp that lent its adjective to comic publishing, founding what would become one of comics' all-time success stories.

47

Correct Answer: 4

DARING MYSTERY COMICS was the second comic launched by Marvel.

48

Correct Answer: 2

Miss Fury quickly changed into more mundane attire.

49

Correct Answer: 2

Cole has produced thousands of pieces of art, not only for comics but also for book and magazine covers.

50

Correct Answer: 3

The All-American line included the original versions of the Flash, Green Lantern, the Atom, and other classic superheroes.

50-POINT ANSWERS

1

Correct Answer: 4

Hammett had been hired to write SECRET AGENT X-9, a strip in the tradition of his novels and short stories; however, he lasted only a year as writer.

2

Correct Answer: 3

Kei and Yuri are the destructive women code-named THE DIRTY PAIR.

3

Correct Answer: 2

Bernie Krigstein removed panel borders Al Feldstein had drawn, reworking several sequences.

4

Correct Answer: 4

In the Gold Key comic version, Uhura was white.

5

Correct Answer: 2

Bradbury read "Home to Stay" and politely reminded E.C. to pay $50 for the rights—which they did.

6

Correct Answer: 3

Gilberton's line of CLASSICS ILLUSTRATED and Dell's various titles were considered too "clean" to need the seal.

7

Correct Answer: 5

The Yellow Kid appeared in the HOGAN'S ALLEY strip in 1895, considered the first American comic strip. It was later renamed THE YELLOW KID. BUSTER BROWN debuted in 1902.

8

Correct Answer: 4

The crossover had Superman, Steel, and Superboy meeting Static, Icon, Rocket, the Blood Syndicate, and Hardware.

9

Correct Answer: 3

Capital Comics published NEXUS from issue #1 through #6, at which point First Comics began to publish it.

10

Correct Answer: 2

Created by Walt Simonson during his tenure as writer and artist of THE MIGHTY THOR, Bill had the same powers as Thor, right down to his own version of Thor's hammer, Mjolnir.

11 Correct Answer: 2

Unprinted RACE FOR THE MOON stories were reprinted in BLAST-OFF.

12 Correct Answer: 2

CAPTAIN ROCKET was Harry Harrison's cartoon.

13 Correct Answer: 1

Twenty-five trillion miles, but Adam Strange got there instantaneously via Zeta Beam.

14 Correct Answer: 4

There have been four publishers—three for the first series, and one for the newest.

15 Correct Answer: 1

Tarka and Zira were sent to Earth to fight evil.

16 Correct Answer: 4

Marcia Reynolds was Futura.

17 Correct Answer: 1

This happened on the cusp of the Silver Age—November 1955—with DETECTIVE COMICS #225.

18 Correct Answer: 5

Zatanna—daughter of Zatara the magician—made her first appearance in HAWKMAN #4. Like her father, Zatanna worked her magic by speaking the words of her spells backward.

19 Correct Answer: 2

FAMOUS FUNNIES ran Buck for six years before moving him into a comic of his own.

20 Correct Answer: 2

SPACE FUNNIES reprinted material from TARGET COMICS.

21 Correct Answer: 2

STAR WARS IN 3-D featured an adventure on Hoth, the ice planet seen in the film THE EMPIRE STRIKES BACK.

22

Correct Answer: 3

KING COMICS was where FLASH GORDON first appeared in comic book form.

23

Correct Answer: 2

WORLDS OF WOOD—published by Eclipse Comics—was not about lumber; it was a miniseries reprinting some of Wally Wood's early work.

24

Correct Answer: 3

ROCKET TO THE MOON was an adaptation of MAZA OF THE MOON, by Otis A. Kline.

25

Correct Answer: 2

LOST WORLDS ran "Weird Thrills of the Past and the Future" as its subtitle.

26

Correct Answer: 3

MAGNUS, ROBOT FIGHTER—created by Russ Manning—takes place in 4000 A.D.

27

Correct Answer: 3

Captain Science, like the late stage of the Manhattan Project, hid in New Mexico.

28

Correct Answer: 5

Yes, even Gardner Fox wrote a couple of science fiction novels.

29

Correct Answer: 5

Kelly Freas, a long-time SF magazine artist, drew this comic cover.

30

Correct Answer: 2

Phil Foglio originally drew the MYTH ADVENTURES comic, which was a series adapting the Robert Asprin novels. He was followed by Jim Valentino (later a founding father of Image Comics) and Ken Mitchroney.

31

Correct Answer: 5

Prize published TOM CORBETT after Dell stopped.

32

Correct Answer: 2

Wayne Boring's Superman had a very distinctive but subtle look. His ears were slightly pointy, his chin was big and a tad dimpled.

33 Correct Answer: 2

Rex Dexter was the first SF character to get his own book, REX DEXTER OF MARS.

34 Correct Answer: 3

Major Inapak was the Space Ace.

35 Correct Answer: 3

Captain America fixed his shield by force of will.

36 Correct Answer: 3

Burne Hogarth founded this important school.

37 Correct Answer: 4

Sam Kieth also did the EPIRICUS THE SAGE graphic novels for Dark Horse, and was the first artist on Neil Gaiman's SANDMAN series for DC.

38 Correct Answer: 4

Gray Morrow also ghosted RIP KIRBY. He is known as well for his work on the ZATANNA backup series for DC Comics.

39 Correct Answer: 3

Craig Russell also plotted and illustrated DOCTOR STRANGE ANNUAL #1, and adapted the short story "The Golden Apples of the Sun" for Topps's RAY BRADBURY COMICS.

40 Correct Answer: 2

Alex Toth also drew HOT WHEELS comics.

41 Correct Answer: 4

Al Williamson also drew the comic adaptation of THE EMPIRE STRIKES BACK, and drew STAR WARS until it folded.

42 Correct Answer: 1

MARY MARVEL COMICS was her title, a counterpart to CAPTAIN MARVEL COMICS.

43 Correct Answer: 3

Phantom Lady was revived because of her sex appeal, especially under the guidance of artist Matt Baker.

44

Correct Answer: 1

Simon Bisley drew that combination.

45

Correct Answer: 3

John Byrne—whose first professional artwork was on Charlton's WHEELIE AND THE CHOPPER BUNCH—began writing with SPACE: 1999.

46

Correct Answer: 2

Gil Kane worked with Kirby and Simon on their comics in the 1940s, and is one of the leading action artists in the comics field.

47

Correct Answer: 4

Jack Binder and Don Rico created the original DAREDEVIL, who wore a half-red/half-blue costume.

48

Correct Answer: 1

Carl Burgos created the original Human Torch in 1939. The Torch—an android with the ability to burst into flame—made his debut in MARVEL COMICS #1.

49

Correct Answer: 1

Manhunter hunted men in the pages of ADVENTURE COMICS.

50

Correct Answer: 2

Wally Wood began his career working in the newspapers.

SCIENCE FICTION

WORMHOLE

ANSWERS

10-POINT ANSWERS

1

Correct Answer: 4

In the Mercury Theatre's radio adaptation of THE WAR OF THE WORLDS, the Martians landed at Grover's Mill, NJ.

2

Correct Answer: 5

Douglas Adams originally wrote THE HITCHHIKER'S GUIDE TO THE GALAXY as two radio serials (broadcast in 1978 and 1980) before adapting them into a novel.

3

Correct Answer: 1

Robert A. Heinlein was the author of SPACE CADET.

4

Correct Answer: 4

"Jeffty Is Five" contains references to old radio shows and other cultural artifacts.

5

Correct Answer: 2

Author Nigel Kneale originally wrote THE QUATERMASS EXPERIMENT as a radio serial, although it ultimately became a television drama.

6

Correct Answer: 2

"An Occurrence at Owl Creek Bridge" is about a man who falsely believes that he has escaped the hangman's noose, and who lives through many hours of time in the last instant before his death.

7

Correct Answer: 1

Although Orson Welles agreed to narrate THE TWILIGHT ZONE, he wanted so much money that Rod Serling decided to narrate the show himself.

8

Correct Answer: 1

When they heard a creaky door slowly opening, audiences knew that they were entering the INNER SANCTUM.

9

Correct Answer: 3

George Orwell worked in Room 101, which was also the name of the torture chamber in his novel 1984.

10

Correct Answer: 1

The National Public Radio version of STAR WARS featured Mark Hamill and other actors from the original film.

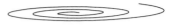

11
Correct Answer: 3

Margo was just one of the many "agents" working with the Shadow in his neverending fight against crime.

12
Correct Answer: 4

Sir Cyril Ritchard was the star (and director!) of Gore Vidal's science-fiction play on Broadway.

13
Correct Answer: 3

The hero of QUANTUM LEAP was named Samuel Beckett, in honor of the author of WAITING FOR GODOT.

14
Correct Answer: 4

Sleeping Beauty, Rapunzel, Snow White, and Little Red Ridinghood got their plotlines mixed up while going INTO THE WOODS.

15
Correct Answer: 2

LITTLE SHOP OF HORRORS was a stage musical about a man-eating plant. The London critics called it "blooming lovely!"

16
Correct Answer: 3

Boris Karloff played Jonathan Brewster, the psychotic killer who looked like Boris Karloff, in ARSENIC AND OLD LACE.

17
Correct Answer: 5

The title of Karel Capek's play R.U.R. stood for ROSSUM'S UNIVERSAL ROBOTS. (By the way, *rossum* is the Czech word for "brain," and *robot* is from the Czech word for "slave.")

18
Correct Answer: 1

THE WIZARD OF OZ and THE WIZ were two stage adaptations of L. Frank Baum's novel THE WONDERFUL WIZARD OF OZ.

19
Correct Answer: 3

HAMLET, act II, scene 2: "The play's the thing wherein I'll catch the conscience of the king."

20
Correct Answer: 3

ASIMOV'S GUIDE TO SHAKESPEARE (Doubleday, 1970) examines each of Shakespeare's plays in its historical context.

21

Correct Answer: 5

Several of Ellison's "Ellis Hart" stories appeared in the 1950s in such publications as GUILTY DETECTIVE STORY MAGAZINE and SUREFIRE DETECTIVE MAGAZINE.

22

Correct Answer: 1

Rice's mildly erotic Rampling books include EXIT TO EDEN and BELINDA.

23

Correct Answer: 5

Isaac Asimov wrote the LUCKY STARR series, which began with DAVID STARR, SPACE RANGER in 1952 and concluded with LUCKY STARR AND THE RINGS OF SATURN in 1958.

24

Correct Answer: 4

Hal Clement is the author of several well-regarded SF novels, including NEEDLE and MISSION OF GRAVITY.

25

Correct Answer: 2

Lester del Rey was the editor of SCIENCE FICTION ADVENTURES at the time.

26

Correct Answer: 3

Alan Dean Foster is widely credited with writing the novelization of STAR WARS under the name George Lucas.

27

Correct Answer: 4

Ackerman coined "sci-fi," a takeoff on "hi-fi."

28

Correct Answer: 2

Hugo Gernsback founded AMAZING STORIES, the first science-fiction magazine.

29

Correct Answer: 4

Charles Dickens was a passenger during a Victorian Era railway disaster.

30

Correct Answer: 2

ASTOUNDING was retitled ANALOG by editor John W. Campbell, Jr.

31

Correct Answer: 2

BEMs are bug-eyed monsters.

32

Correct Answer: 2

Sputnik was the first man-made satellite.

33

Correct Answer: 2

Buzz Aldrin was the pilot of the lunar lander, and first man to speak from the lunar surface, saying, "Contact light."

34

Correct Answer: 2

AMAZING STORIES was first, calling itself a magazine of "scientifiction."

35

Correct Answer: 2

PLANET STORIES spawned PLANET COMICS.

36

Correct Answer: 2

Io is pushed and pulled by tides between Jupiter and the other, outer moons.

37

Correct Answer: 2

BRAVE NEW WORLD (the novel) was written by Aldous Huxley in the 1930s.

38

Correct Answer: 2

Jefferson Airplane became Jefferson Starship.

39

Correct Answer: 1

TSR created the first role-playing game with DUNGEONS AND DRAGONS.

40

Correct Answer: 2

STAR WARS was the most merchandised movie of all time, until Disney's LION KING came out.

41

Correct Answer: 3

Boris Vallejo is best known for such paintings.

42

Correct Answer: 4

Frank Frazetta is best known for the early SF comics he drew.

43

Correct Answer: 1

Frank Kelly Freas created Alfred E. Neuman, among other things.

44
Correct Answer: 1
Don Maitz created Captain Morgan.

45
Correct Answer: 2
Luke grew up on a moisture farm.

46
Correct Answer: 1
Prometheus was punished by Zeus for giving man fire.

47
Correct Answer: 2
Mercury's staff can do many such things.

48
Correct Answer: 3
Averna was the entrance to Hades.

49
Correct Answer: 4
They were all Gorgons.

50
Correct Answer: 2
Oceanus was the ocean that surrounded the world.

20-POINT ANSWERS

1

Correct Answer: 5

If you can find a CAPTAIN MIDNIGHT secret decoder ring after all these years, it's worth a lot of money.

2

Correct Answer: 5

Frank Edwards, author of FLYING SAUCERS—SERIOUS BUSINESS, was also the host of the radio show STRANGEST OF ALL.

3

Correct Answer: 2

Scientist Jim Brandon fought crime as the Avenger.

4

Correct Answer: 2

"The Outer Limit"—no relation to the later TV show—was the radio episode.

5

Correct Answer: 1

DAN DARE, Britain's answer to BUCK ROGERS, was the hero of Radio Luxembourg's serial.

6

Correct Answer: 2

"Pebble in the Sky" was based on Isaac Asimov's science-fiction novel of the same name.

7

Correct Answer: 1

DONOVAN'S BRAIN rhymes with CITIZEN KANE. The radio actor who fled from the brain was Orson Welles.

8

Correct Answer: 2

Michael Rennie, who starred as Klaatu in the film THE DAY THE EARTH STOOD STILL, reprised his role in the radio version.

9

Correct Answer: 2

Clayton Collyer dropped his voice a full octave whenever Clark Kent turned into Superman.

10

Correct Answer: 1

In addition to Lord Olivier's holographic head, and a bunch of lasers, TIME featured a script and songs by Dave Clark of the Dave Clark Five.

11

Correct Answer: 4

VIA GALACTICA is still remembered as one of the worst flops in Broadway history.

12

Correct Answer: 5

The well-trained Siamese cat who played Pyewacket, the witch's cat in the original Broadway cast of BELL, BOOK AND CANDLE, was also in VISIT TO A SMALL PLANET.

13

Correct Answer: 1

It was Thornton Wilder's bizarre comedy THE SKIN OF OUR TEETH.

14

Correct Answer: 3

Stephen Sondheim's very first professional job was as a scriptwriter for the TV fantasy show TOPPER.

15

Correct Answer: 5

Richard O'Brien wrote THE ROCKY HORROR SHOW and also played the role of Riffraff the butler.

16

Correct Answer: 4

The sorcerer, who had a minor role in the musical CAMELOT, later became the star of his own show, MERLIN.

17

Correct Answer: 5

Edward Plunkett, Lord Dunsany, was the author of more than 50 macabre stage plays.

18

Correct Answer: 1

One of the characters in THE BED-SITTING ROOM actually mutates into a bedroom, complete with four-poster bed.

19

Correct Answer: 4

Thomas Lanier "Tennessee" Williams—who was actually from Louisiana—wrote "The Vengeance of Nitocris."

20

Correct Answer: 4

Mary Martin played the goddess Venus, brought to life in ONE TOUCH OF VENUS.

21

Correct Answer: 4

Lon Chaney was a stagehand and an actor in his older brother John's Colorado theater.

22

Correct Answer: 4

Bob Fosse gave a snake-hipped performance as the serpent in THE LITTLE PRINCE.

23

Correct Answer: 3

Ellison and Slesar collaborated on several stories in the 1950s that appeared in such magazines as GUILTY DETECTIVE STORY MAGAZINE.

24

Correct Answer: 1

Philip Jose Farmer wrote the 1974 Trout novel, many Doc Savage adventures, and a history of the pulp-era hero.

25

Correct Answer: 3

Among his many accomplishments, Forrest J Ackerman was also editor of FAMOUS MONSTERS OF FILMLAND.

26

Correct Answer: 2

Harlan Ellison used the Bird name after extensive changes in his original concept for the show.

27

Correct Answer: 2

Hugo Gernsback edited AIR WONDER STORIES.

28

Correct Answer: 4

Frank R. Paul's splendid paintings helped give AMAZING STORIES a distinctive look.

29

Correct Answer: 2

Hugo Gernsback coined the term "scientifiction" and used it as much as possible.

30

Correct Answer: 3

The Air Force was originally in charge of space exploration.

31

Correct Answer: 2

Some believe that a black hole is at the center of our galaxy.

32

Correct Answer: 4

Bell Telephone's microwave radiation is considered the best evidence for the Big Bang theory yet.

33

Correct Answer: 2

SOUNDS OF EARTH was on the *Voyager* probes.

34

Correct Answer: 4

The asteroid belt separates the inner solar system from the outer.

35

Correct Answer: 1

Syzygy is the term for the lineup of planets that happens every 176 years.

36

Correct Answer: 3

CHALLENGER exploded 73 seconds into its launch, killing the entire crew.

37

Correct Answer: 2

David Bowie wrote and sang about Ziggy Stardust.

38

Correct Answer: 1

DUNGEONS AND DRAGONS began as a miniatures war game.

39

Correct Answer: 2

GAMMA WORLD was TSR's SF game.

40

Correct Answer: 1

It had four classes: Magic-User, Cleric, Fighter, Thief.

41

Correct Answer: 2

The first run of STAR WARS cards appeared inside bags of Wonder Bread.

42

Correct Answer: 2

John Williams wrote the score for STAR WARS.

43

Correct Answer: 2

Jill Bauman has made a specialty of cats in her paintings.

44

Correct Answer: 2

Hannes Bok did many illustrations for WEIRD TALES during its original run.

45

Correct Answer: 2

Vincent diFate also writes about SF illustration and lectures on art.

46 Correct Answer: 2

Virgil Finlay has had a strong influence on many artists who have come after him.

47 Correct Answer: 2

Roger Dean and his brother, Martyn, run both presses.

48 Correct Answer: 2

Photon torpedos were used to destroy the first Death Star.

49 Correct Answer: 3

The Greeks said that Prometheus created man on a whim.

50 Correct Answer: 2

Athena burst fully grown from Zeus's head.

30-POINT ANSWERS

1

Correct Answer: 3

Les Mizzy wrote the theme.

2

Correct Answer: 3

Norman Corwin, one of the most prolific scriptwriters during the Golden Age of radio, encouraged Rod Serling to become a writer.

3

Correct Answer: 1

Isaac Asimov's novels FOUNDATION, FOUNDATION AND EMPIRE, and SECOND FOUNDATION became the BBC serial FOUNDATION.

4

Correct Answer: 5

Not even death rays and underground slugfests could delay the next broadcast from GENE AUTRY'S MELODY RANCH.

5

Correct Answer: 3

"The Pit and the Pendulum"—based on Poe's classic horror story—was the basis of the scripts for both of these broadcasts.

6

Correct Answer: 2

Kurt Vonnegut, Jr., was the author of "Report on the Barnhouse Effect."

7

Correct Answer: 1

Jason Robards, Sr., starred on the radio as Chandu the Magician.

8

Correct Answer: 4

Gary Merrill was one of several actors who played the costumed crime fighter Batman.

9

Correct Answer: 3

James Pierce, who starred in the 1927 movie serial TARZAN AND THE GOLDEN LION, also played Tarzan on the radio.

10

Correct Answer: 1

Robert A. Heinlein's script provided the basis for the radio play "Destination: Moon" and for the movie of the same name.

11

Correct Answer: 4

The radio play "The Dunwich Horror" was based on Lovecraft's story of the same name.

12

Correct Answer: 3

On July 11, 1938, Orson Welles cast himself in the title role of Dracula. The Martians didn't arrive until October.

13

Correct Answer: 5

In 1936, Al Hodge became the first of several radio actors to play the Green Hornet.

14

Correct Answer: 1

Earl Hamner, Jr., wrote scripts for DIMENSION X and TWILIGHT ZONE before creating his TV series THE WALTONS.

15

Correct Answer: 3

The title DEATH KNOCKS is a pun: a "knock" is a six-card hand in Gin rummy.

16

Correct Answer: 4

Jonathan Miller wrote and performed "The Heat-death of the Universe" as part of the chaos in BEYOND THE FRINGE.

17

Correct Answer: 3

Zero Mostel was the man who became a rhinoceros in Eugene Ionesco's play RHINOCEROS.

18

Correct Answer: 5

Betty Buckley, who played the schoolteacher in the movie CARRIE, was Carrie's mother in the stage version.

19

Correct Answer: 2

EQUUS was written by Peter Shaffer, the twin brother of writer Anthony Shaffer.

20

Correct Answer: 4

Mark Hamill of STAR WARS fame appeared onstage as the Elephant Man.

21

Correct Answer: 5

Estragon and Vladimir are based on the film characters played by Stan Laurel and Oliver Hardy.

22

Correct Answer: 2

BLITHE SPIRIT, a comedy about a beautiful ghost who returns from the dead to break up her husband's second marriage, was written by Noel Coward in the Watch House at Portmeirion.

23

Correct Answer: 1

Irish actress Una O'Connor was the woman who saw the monster climb out of the burning windmill in THE BRIDE OF FRANKENSTEIN. She also played the landlady in THE INVISIBLE MAN.

24

Correct Answer: 4

Katherine Hepburn (with some hidden wires) became weightless during every performance of A MATTER OF GRAVITY.

25

Correct Answer: 1

THE SORCERER is a comic opera by Gilbert and Sullivan.

26

Correct Answer: 1

Charlie Grant's most recent Fenn adventures feature failed actor Kent Montana.

27

Correct Answer: 3

The husband-and-wife team of Kristine Katherine Rusch and Dean Wesley Smith penned a STAR TREK: DEEP SPACE 9 novel under the name Sandy Schofield.

28

Correct Answer: 4

Blair, as George Orwell, penned the SF classics 1984 and ANIMAL FARM.

29

Correct Answer: 3

Don Pendleton wrote THE GODMAKERS and REVOLT! as Britain.

30

Correct Answer: 1

A. A. Wyn founded Ace Books in 1953; Don Wollheim was his science-fiction editor.

31

Correct Answer: 1

George Scithers won two Hugo Awards for his start-up work on ISAAC ASIMOV'S SCIENCE FICTION MAGAZINE.

32

Correct Answer: 2

Simak gets credit—but an earlier occurrence is in a Jack Williamson story.

33

Correct Answer: 3

Ballard coined the term "inner space" in 1962.

34

Correct Answer: 2

Sir Richard Burton spent years translating THE ARABIAN NIGHTS into English.

35

Correct Answer: 1

The Oort cloud is the presumed source of all comets.

36

Correct Answer: 1

Mercury rotates away from the sun very slowly, almost as slowly as it orbits the sun, but not quite.

37

Correct Answer: 3

Laika, a Russian dog, was first to orbit Earth in 1957, inside *Sputnik 2*.

38

Correct Answer: 2

They knew of five: Mercury, Venus, Mars, Jupiter, and Saturn. Uranus and the more distant ones require a telescope to see them.

39

Correct Answer: 2

Halley's Comet reappears every 76 years.

40

Correct Answer: 4

Four planets have definite rings: Saturn, Uranus, Neptune, and Jupiter!

41

Correct Answer: 4

Galileo was forced to deny his astronomical observations, or be excommunicated from the Catholic Church.

42

Correct Answer: 2

THE PLANETS is Holst's musical portrait of the solar system.

43

Correct Answer: 2

1,000 AIRPLANES ON THE ROOF is the opera.

44

Correct Answer: 2

Burger King sold the STAR TREK II glasses.

45

Correct Answer: 2

Hannes Bok won the Hugo in 1953 with Ed Emshwiller.

46

Correct Answer: 3

Frank Kelly Freas won the Hugo many times because of his evocative illustrations.

47

Correct Answer: 2

Jim Burns won the Hugo for Best Professional Artist in 1987.

48

Correct Answer: 5

Paris received Helen as his prize for choosing Aphrodite as most beautiful, thus causing the Trojan War.

49

Correct Answer: 1

Pluto's dog was sung to sleep.

50

Correct Answer: 3

Charon is the boatman of the River Styx.

40-POINT ANSWERS

1

Correct Answer: 3

Actor Gale Gordon, best known for his television appearances with Lucille Ball, played spaceman Flash Gordon on the radio.

2

Correct Answer: 5

Although several actresses were in the radio version of THE ISLAND OF DOCTOR MOREAU, they provided the voices of male animals who had been transformed into humanoid creatures.

3

Correct Answer: 1

Perry White, the editor of THE DAILY PLANET, was originally a character on the SUPERMAN radio show before he appeared in comic books.

4

Correct Answer: 2

The sound-effects man turned a wet rubber glove inside out very slowly while crushing a wooden basket to create the sound of a man being turned inside out for LIGHTS OUT.

5

Correct Answer: 2

Between his movie roles, Vincent Price was kept busy playing Simon Templar on three radio networks.

6

Correct Answer: 1

Despite its misleading title, LATITUDE ZERO was about the crew of an experimental submarine.

7

Correct Answer: 4

In the radio show SPACE PATROL, Terra was a man-made planet slightly larger than Earth.

8

Correct Answer: 2

THE MYSTERIOUS TRAVELER was the cackling commuter.

9

Correct Answer: 3

Dana Andrews starred in the LUX RADIO THEATRE production of THE WAR OF THE WORLDS.

10

Correct Answer: 1

Basil Rathbone was the radio Phantom. A studio technician provided the sound of the deadly chandelier.

11

Correct Answer: 5

"Icky" Mudd was the loyal mechanic who installed the various supergadgets in Captain Midnight's airplane.

12

Correct Answer: 2

"The Green Hills of Earth" became the December 14, 1950, episode of DIMENSION X.

13

Correct Answer: 4

Episodes of X MINUS ONE, originally recorded and broadcast in the 1950s, were resurrected in the 1970s.

14

Correct Answer: 1

Despite its laughable title, THE STRANGE DOCTOR WEIRD tried to frighten its listeners.

15

Correct Answer: 5

Aldous Huxley narrated the radio adaptation of his novel BRAVE NEW WORLD.

16

Correct Answer: 2

Arch Oboler was the head writer for LIGHTS OUT and several other major radio series, as well as doing FIVE and THE TWONKY.

17

Correct Answer: 1

Joan Crawford was the last woman on Earth in Arch Oboler's "Two."

18

Correct Answer: 5

If you can find a copy of the Neal Adams poster for WARP, it is a valuable collector's item today.

19

Correct Answer: 2

THE MONSTER starred Wilton Lackaye as the mad scientist. Lon Chaney took the part in the film version.

20

Correct Answer: 3

Abner Sedgwick was the villian because the producers of this Broadway show didn't want to pay National Periodical Publications for the rights to use Superman's cartoon nemesis, Lex Luthor.

21

Correct Answer: 1

France Nuyen portrayed Suzie Wong, and William Shatner played the painter who captured her image.

22

Correct Answer: 1

THE BLACK CROOK was the first musical written for the American stage.

23

Correct Answer: 2

Bramwell Fletcher—who was featured in the film THE MUMMY as the archaeologist who went insane when he saw it come to life—starred in the stage play RED PLANET.

24

Correct Answer: 3

L. Frank Baum's stage musical THE TIK-TOK MAN OF OZ became his book TIK-TOK OF OZ.

25

Correct Answer: 2

IF BOOTH HAD MISSED, President Lincoln would escape death in 1865 and deal with a national crisis in 1866.

26

Correct Answer: 4

In BERKELEY SQUARE, a man traveled back in time and didn't find it as he expected.

27

Correct Answer: 2

Gilbert and Sullivan wrote RUDDIGORE as a parody of Gothic stage melodramas.

28

Correct Answer: 4

Canadian actor Raymond Massey, who survived a global war in the H. G. Wells film THINGS TO COME, was the astronomer who tried to save Earth in HOW I WONDER.

29

Correct Answer: 2

One of the low points of artist Andy Warhol's career was this atrocious science-fiction musical.

30

Correct Answer: 1

The Ellison tale appeared in THE ADAM BEDSIDE READER.

31

Correct Answer: 4

INVASION, by Aaron Wolfe, was the ninth release in the short-lived SF line published in Canada.

32

Correct Answer: 4

After writing THE FOG under his own name, Dennis Etchison wrote
HALLOWEEN 2, HALLOWEEN 3, and VIDEODROME as Martin.

33

Correct Answer: 3

Kornbluth and Judith Merril wrote GUNNER CADE and OUTPOST
MARS, both in 1952.

34

Correct Answer: 2

Theodore Sturgeon wrote the Queen novel THE PLAYER ON THE
OTHER SIDE.

35

Correct Answer: 1

Robert Bloch sometimes used the Fiske name for stories published
during the run of his syndicated radio show, STAY TUNED FOR
HORROR.

36

Correct Answer: 3

Ackerman established the Fantasy Foundation to preserve all kinds of
SF materials for posterity.

37

Correct Answer: 2

Andrew Porter edited ALGOL.

38

Correct Answer: 2

A geosynchronous orbit is one that stays above the same spot on the
Earth.

39

Correct Answer: 1

Meteors are called asteroids before they crash.

40

Correct Answer: 4

Galileo first saw the red spot on Jupiter more than 400 years ago.

41

Correct Answer: 4

Saturn's rings are divided into many smaller rings, but only the largest
division can be seen from Earth.

42

Correct Answer: 2

SETI is the Search for Extra-Terrestrial Intelligence.

43

Correct Answer: 5

Pluto is the only planet not examined by a probe in the 20th century.

44

Correct Answer: 4

Charon, boatman of the River Styx, is the name of Pluto's moon.

45

Correct Answer: 3

Pluto was the planet Lovecraft's Fungi from Yuggoth came from.

46

Correct Answer: 2

Sky Lab fell into the Indian Ocean when its orbit decayed.

47

Correct Answer: 3

EINSTEIN ON THE BEACH is this early opera.

48

Correct Answer: 1

Michael Whelan won most of the Hugos in the 1980s.

49

Correct Answer: 3

John Berkey is best known for his spaceship paintings that appeared on paperback book covers in the 1970s.

50

Correct Answer: 4

Roy Krenkel was discovered by Donald Wollheim.

50-POINT ANSWERS

1

Correct Answer: 4

In Doyle's novel THE POISON BELT, Earth passes through a belt of interstellar gas that poisons the planet's atmosphere.

2

Correct Answer: 5

"The Screaming Woman" was Ray Bradbury's original source for this radio script.

3

Correct Answer: 4

"A Wind Is Rising" was adapted from a magazine story by Robert Sheckley.

4

Correct Answer: 5

Years before Ed Norton went down into the sewers, Art Carney was already underwater in THE LAND OF THE LOST.

5

Correct Answer: 4

The caveman who wanted to steal all the fire and keep it for himself was Big Tooth.

6

Correct Answer: 2

Each week, TWO THOUSAND PLUS took its radio audience beyond the year 2000.

7

Correct Answer: 1

"Chicken Heart," written by Arch Oboler, was an episode of the classic radio program LIGHTS OUT.

8

Correct Answer: 2

SPACEACHE, by Snoo Wilson, was originally a novel published in 1984.

9

Correct Answer: 5

Some of the finest radio scripts produced by the Columbia Broadcasting System were written for THE COLUMBIA WORKSHOP.

10

Correct Answer: 1

THEATRE 10:30 was Canada's late-night horror show.

11

Correct Answer: 2

The "O" in THE DEVIL AND MISTER O stood for Oboler.

12

Correct Answer: 3

Buck Rogers, Batman, and Dick Tracy were played by several different actors, but Matt Crowley was the only radio actor who played all three.

13

Correct Answer: 4

Actor Paul Frees—who later supplied the voice of Boris Badenov in the "Bullwinkle" cartoons—did the grunts and snarls of the monster in this radio adaptation of FRANKENSTEIN.

14

Correct Answer: 1

Captain Starr was the hero of STARR OF SPACE.

15

Correct Answer: 3

Arch Oboler's script contains no mention of auks and no explanation of its title, THE NIGHT OF THE AUK.

16

Correct Answer: 3

ROBOT MONSTER featured Elmer Bernstein's music, plus a guy wearing a diver's helmet and a gorilla suit.

17

Correct Answer: 1

Michael Dunn, a talented dwarf who played the evil scientist Doctor Loveless on THE WILD, WILD WEST, played Clifford Simak's robot on Broadway.

18

Correct Answer: 3

E. G. Marshall, who hosted TV's NATIONAL GEOGRAPHIC specials and appeared in Stephen King and George Romero's 1982 film CREEPSHOW, was the nuclear-powered narrator.

19

Correct Answer: 2

THE SECOND MRS. KONG, an opera composed by Harrison Birtwistle, puts King Kong onstage alongside the Egyptian god Anubis and a woman from a seventeenth-century Vermeer painting.

20

Correct Answer: 3

At the final curtain, the Venusians invite the aviators back to VENUS, the planet named for the goddess of Love, which they had visited.

21

Correct Answer: 5

Donald Swann, the musical half of the comedy team Flanders and Swann, composed the science-fiction opera PERELANDRA.

22

Correct Answer: 3

Before portraying the Cardassian leaders Gul Macet and Gul Dukat, Marc Alaimo starred in VENUS-SHOT as the fictional Fletcher Pratt . . . which was also the name of a real-life SF author.

23

Correct Answer: 3

eluki bes shahar has written books under the Edghill name in three genres, including such titles as TURKISH DELIGHT, SPEAK DAGGERS TO HER, and THE SWORD OF MAIDEN'S TEARS.

24

Correct Answer: 5

Gary Brandner wrote THE DEATH'S HEAD CONSPIRACY as Carter and the Westerns WESLEY SHERIDAN as Clayton Moore, and THE EXPRESS RIDERS as Lee Davis Willoughby.

25

Correct Answer: 2

As Flagg, Weiss first contributed to AMAZING in 1927. Other short pieces appeared in WEIRD TALES. His novel THE NIGHT PEOPLE was published in 1947.

26

Correct Answer: 1

John Taine was the author of many stories and the novel THE TIME STREAM, originally serialized in THRILLING WONDER.

27

Correct Answer: 2

E. Mayne Hull made her greatest impact with the Arthur Blord series of stories, which were assembled into the novel PLANET FOR SALE in 1954.

28

Correct Answer: 1

Philip Klass penned the novels OF MEN AND MONSTERS and A LAMP FOR MEDUSA under the Tenn name.

29

Correct Answer: 5

David J. Schow published "Coming Soon to a Theater Near You" and "Lonesome Coyote Blues" under the Lowenbruck name in ROD SERLING'S THE TWILIGHT ZONE MAGAZINE.

30

Correct Answer: 4

Mike McQuay wrote two Tom Swift novels under the Appleton name and a Bobbsey Twins and Nancy Drew novel under the Hope and Keene names, respectively. As Arnett, he penned the BOOK OF JUSTICE series.

31

Correct Answer: 4

Explorer was the first American satellite.

32

Correct Answer: 2

Neptune was the only planet whose clouds were observed casting shadows.

33

Correct Answer: 4

Mars' Olympus Mons is the largest volcano on any planet in the solar system.

34

Correct Answer: 4

Pioneer 11 almost hit the moon it had discovered; that moon is now named Pioneer Rock because of this near miss.

35

Correct Answer: 3

Neptune was discovered in the 19th century through mathematics.

36

Correct Answer: 2

JACK OF SHADOWS is also the name of the opera.

37

Correct Answer: 1

Emma Orczy began her career as an illustrator before becoming a writer.

38

Correct Answer: 4

John Schoenherr's illustrations for DUNE have been collected into THE ILLUSTRATED DUNE.

39

Correct Answer: 4

Keith Roberts is best known as a writer, but his art is also very good.

40

Correct Answer: 2

Orpheus went after his love, only to lose her.

41

Correct Answer: 2

Pallas Athena was this goddess's full name.

42

Correct Answer: 5

Forry Ackerman's SPACEMAN lasted less than a year, but it made an impact on impressionable minds.

43

Correct Answer: 1

Frank R. Paul's cover for AMAZING STORIES featured Buck Rogers.

44

Correct Answer: 2

Mary Shelley's subtitle to FRANKENSTEIN was quite revealing to those who knew the Prometheus mythos.

45

Correct Answer: 1

Adam Link appeared in short stories, comics adaptations, and even in one episode of the original TWILIGHT ZONE series.

46

Correct Answer: 3

The Tubes were smitten by ATTACK OF THE FIFTY-FOOT WOMAN.

47

Correct Answer: 3

When Hammer Films closed before the film started production, Leigh became the official Vampirella model for Warren Comics, appearing on a number of the magazine's covers.

48

Correct Answer: 2

Wally Wood is best known for his work for E.C. Comics' science-fiction comics, Marvel's DAREDEVIL, and the "Outer Space Spirit" continuity of THE SPIRIT comic strip.

49

Correct Answer: 1

As the story goes, Trina Robbins described the outfit over the telephone to Frank Frazetta so that he could work on the cover painting for VAMPIRELLA #1.

50

Correct Answer: 4

Wendy Pini, along with her husband Richard, went on to create the long-running comic book fantasy series ELFQUEST.

MAROONED OFF VESTA

THE SURVEY

We asked every member of the Science Fiction and Fantasy Writers Association (SFFWA) some questions about science fiction, fantasy, and horror books and films. Over 75 writers responded.

The following authors took part in the survey: Janet Asimov, John Gregory Betancourt, Waldo T. Boyd, Bruce Boston, Kent Brewster, Mike Byers, Richard Lee Byers, Grant Carrington, Jack L. Chalker, Brian C. Coad, Melissa Crandall, Marianne J. Dyson, Charles D. Eckert, Ru Emerson (Roberta Cray), Nancy Etchemendy, Rutledge E. Etheridge, Mark Fewell, John L. Flynn, Charles L. Fontenay, Jonathan Frater, Jerry Goodz, Larry Hammer, David M. Harris, Marilyn J. Holt, Wayne Hooks, Brian A. Hopkins, D. A. Houdek, Dean Ing, Phyllis Ann Karr, Jeffery D. Kooistra, Aimee Kratts, Jean Lamb, Kathryn Lance, Marie A. Landis, Alice Laurence, Katherine Lawrence, Tom Ligon, Sydney Long, Steve Martindale, Holly Wade Matter, Charles G. McGraw, Dean McLaughlin, John Morressy, Yvonne Navarro, Gerald David Nordley, Lisanne Norman, Patrick O'Leary, Joe Patrouch, John Peel, Lawrence Person, Tamora Pierce, Steven Piziks, Tom Purdom, John W. Randal, Alis Rasmussen, Mike Resnick, Warren G. Rochelle, Chuck Rothman, Richard Rowand, D. F. Sanders, Ron Sarti, A. L. Sirois, Sarah Smith, Ralph A. Sperry, Brenda Gates Spielman, Del Stone, Jr., Ian Randal Strock, Kiel Stuart, Cecilia Tan, Jane Toombs, Edo van Belkom, Gene van Troyer, Cynthia Ward, Don Webb, Catherine Wells, Leslie What, Kathleen Woodbury, and Paul Edwin Zimmer.

Some of the responses were surprising, and some of them weren't. Here they are—the answers to what science fiction writers read, watch, and enjoy.

MAROONED OFF VESTA

The SFFWA members were given a simple scenario: If you were "Marooned off Vesta" in a small spaceship with only ten science fiction, fantasy, or horror books to read until you are rescued (which could take years—luckily you have enough food, water, and air on board), what ten science fiction, fantasy, or horror books would you want to have to help pass the time?

THE FAVORITES—BY THE NUMBERS

Over 425 books (or series of books) were mentioned in all, from ancient times to brand new, from mythology to high fantasy to space opera to cutting-edge cyberpunk. Many books were mentioned only once—either people's personal favorites or forgotten classics. But many books came up over and over again. Sixty-two books were mentioned three times or more, topped by J. R. R. Tolkein's *The Lord of the Rings* trilogy, which received nearly 50 percent more votes than its closest runner-up, Frank Herbert's *Dune*. Seven books tied with six responses and six books tied with five responses; all the rest had fewer. Here, then, by the numbers, are the writers' choices of the best books to have with you if you're ever marooned:

1.	*The Lord of the Rings*	J. R. R. Tolkein	23
2.	*Dune*	Frank Herbert	16
3.	*Stranger in a Strange Land*	Robert A. Heinlein	10
4.	*The Moon Is a Harsh Mistress*	Robert A. Heinlein	10
5.	The Foundation Trilogy (all or some)	Isaac Asimov	9
6.	*Neuromancer*	William Gibson	8
7.	*The Stars My Destination*	Alfred Bester	8
8.	*Dhalgren*	Samuel R. Delany	7
9.	*Hyperion Cantos*	Dan Simmons	7
10.	*The Martian Chronicles*	Ray Bradbury	7
11.	*The Stand*	Stephen King	7
12.	*Alice in Wonderland/Through the Looking Glass*	Lewis Carroll	6
13.	*The Book of the New Sun*	Gene Wolfe	6
14.	*A Canticle for Liebowitz*	Walter M. Miller, Jr.	6
15.	*Doomsday Book*	Connie Willis	6
16.	*Dracula*	Bram Stoker	6
17.	*Gravity's Rainbow*	Thomas Pynchon	6
18.	*Last and First Men*	Olaf Stapledon	6
19.	*The Dispossessed*	Ursula K. LeGuin	5
20.	*Dragonriders of Pern* (some or all)	Anne McCaffrey	5
21.	The Gormenghast Trilogy	Mervyn Peake	5
22.	*Lucifer's Hammer*	Larry Niven and Jerry Pournelle	5

23. *The Past Through Tomorrow*   Robert A. Heinlein   5
24. *The Time Machine*   H. G. Wells   5

TOP BOOKS—WEIGHTED

When the list of favorites is weighted (so that first-place entries are worth more than second-place entries, and so on), the results of the survey change. The same books are still at the top, but a lot of other favorites come closer. Here are the top 20 (21, actually, since there is a tie at #20 between *The Past Through Tomorrow* and *Dracula*). The balance had a weighted value of below 40.

 1. *The Lord of the Rings*   J. R. R. Tolkein   212
     (some or all)
 2. *Dune*   Frank Herbert   146
 3. *The Moon Is a Harsh Mistress* Robert A. Heinlein   96
 4. *Stranger in a Strange Land*   Robert A. Heinlein   89
 5. *The Stars My Destination*   Alfred Bester   74
 6. The Foundation Trilogy   Isaac Asimov   59
     (some or all)
 7. *A Canticle for Liebowitz*   Walter M. Miller, Jr.   58
 8. *The Dispossessed*   Ursula K. LeGuin   54
 9. *Gravity's Rainbow*   Thomas Pynchon   54
10. *Last and First Men*   Olaf Stapledon   53
11. *Dhalgren*   Samuel R. Delany   51
12. *Neuromancer*   William Gibson   49
13. *The Time Machine*   H. G. Wells   47
14. *The Martian Chronicles*   Ray Bradbury   47
15. *Hyperion Cantos*   Dan Simmons   46
16. *The Science Fiction Hall of Fame* various editors   45
17. *The Book of the New Sun*   Gene Wolfe   45
18. *The Stand*   Stephen King   45
19. The Gormenghast Trilogy (some   Mervyn Peake   43
     or all)
20. *The Past Through Tomorrow*   Robert A. Heinlein   41
21. *Dracula*   Bram Stoker   41

MOST POPULAR WRITERS

Fourteen writers had four or more books named in the survey. Robert A. Heinlein led all novelists with an astonishing *17* books listed, including two in the top five overall. Sixteen authors had four or more books mentioned.

ROBERT A. HEINLEIN [17 BOOKS]

The Door into Summer
Double Star
The Rolling Stones
Friday
Citizen of the Galaxy
Starship Troopers
The Past Through Tomorrow
Expanded Universe
The Moon Is a Harsh Mistress
Between Planets
To Sail Beyond the Sunset
Stranger in a Strange Land
Glory Road
Time for the Stars
Time Enough for Love
Starman Jones
Tunnel in the Sky

ISAAC ASIMOV [8 BOOKS]

The Asimov Chronicles
The Gods Themselves
The Hugo Winners (editor)
Isaac Asimov's Encyclopedia of the Bible
The Caves of Steel
Before the Golden Age
I, Robot
The Foundation Trilogy

ARTHUR C. CLARKE [8 BOOKS]

Rendezvous with Rama
The Nine Billion Names of God
Childhood's End
The Other Side of the Sky
Across the Sea of Stars
2001: A Space Odyssey
Against the Fall of Night
The City and the Stars

RAY BRADBURY [7 BOOKS]

Collected Stories of Ray Bradbury
Dandelion Wine
The Martian Chronicles
Something Wicked This Way Comes
The Illustrated Man
The October Country
Fahrenheit 451

LARRY NIVEN [7 BOOKS]

Lucifer's Hammer (with Jerry Pournelle)
Ringworld
Footfall (with Jerry Pournelle)
Dreampark (with Steven Barnes)
Oath of Fealty (with Jerry Pournelle)
The Mote in God's Eye (with Jerry Pournelle)
Protector

POUL ANDERSON [6 BOOKS]

Fire Time
Midsummer Tempest
Tau Zero
The High Crusade
The King of Ys
Satan's World

STEPHEN KING [6 BOOKS]

It
The Shining
Needful Things
Salem's Lot
The Stand
The Dark Half

URSULA K. LEGUIN [6 BOOKS]

Always Coming Home
The Lathe of Heaven
The Earthsea Trilogy (some or all)
The Left Hand of Darkness
The Dispossessed
Malafrena

HARLAN ELLISON [5 BOOKS]

Dangerous Visions (editor)
The Essential Ellison
Strange Wine
Shatterday
Again, Dangerous Visions (editor)

Andre Norton [5 Books]

Witch World
Year of the Unicorn
The Elvenbane (with Mercedes Lackey)
Starman's Son
Star K'aat

Edgar Rice Burroughs [4 Books]

Tarzan of the Apes
The Gods of Mars
Warlord of Mars
A Princess of Mars

Philip K. Dick [4 Books]

Martian Time Slip
Do Androids Dream of Electric Sheep?
The Complete Short Fiction of Philip K. Dick
The Three Stigmata of Palmer Eldritch

Barbara Hambly [4 Books]

The Dark Hand of Magic
Those Who Hunt the Night
The Ladies of Mandrigyn
The Dark Hand of Magic

TANITH LEE [4 BOOKS]

Personal Darkness
Silver Metal Lover
Kill the Dead
The Birthgrave

FRITZ LEIBER [4 BOOKS]

Conjure Wife
The Swords of Lankhmar
The Wanderer
The Leiber Chronicles

ROBERT SILVERBERG [4 BOOKS]

Across a Billion Years
Dying Inside
Lord Valentine's Castle
The Book of Skulls

ANTHOLOGIES

Thirteen anthologies were listed by survey respondees, in addition to the 400-plus novels. The favorite was the multivolume *Science Fiction Hall of Fame*. Harlan Ellison's classic *Dangerous Visions* followed closely behind.

The Science Fiction Hall of Fame	various editors
Dangerous Visions	Harlan Ellison, editor
The Best of Science Fiction	Groff Conklin, editor
The Hugo Winners	Isaac Asimov, editor
Again, Dangerous Visions	Harlan Ellison, editor
The Astounding Science Fiction Anthology	John W. Campbell, Jr., editor

The Ascent of Wonder	David Hartwell and Kramer, editors
Before the Golden Age	Isaac Asimov, editor
Dark Destiny #1	Edward Kramer, editor
Famous Science Fiction Stories	Healy and McComas, editors
Great Tales of Terror and the Supernatural	Wise and Frasier, editors
Modern Science Fiction	Norman Spinrad, editor
POLY: New Speculative Writing	Lee Ballantine, editor

TRILOGIES AND SERIES—CHEATING ON THE SPACESHIP LIBRARY

Many people couldn't bear to limit themselves to ten books and found a way out by naming their favorite series. J. R. R. Tolkien's *The Lord of the Rings* outpolled everything else on the survey. Runner-up Frank Herbert's *Dune* has numerous sequels, although many writers specified that they meant only the first book. In all, nearly 30 series were mentioned. Three authors—Edgar Rice Burroughs, C. S. Lewis, and Julian May—had two series listed on the survey.

The Lord of the Rings (some or all)	J. R. R. Tolkein	23
Dune	Frank Herbert	16
The Foundation Trilogy	Isaac Asimov	9
Hyperion Cantos	Dan Simmons	7
The Book of the New Sun	Gene Wolfe	6
Alice in Wonderland/Through the Looking Glass	Lewis Carroll	6
Dragonriders of Pern	Anne McCaffrey	5
The Past Through Tomorrow	Robert A. Heinlein	5
The Gormenghast Trilogy	Mervyn Peake	5
Startide Rising (and its sequels)	David Brin	4
The Chronicles of Narnia	C. S. Lewis	3
The Earthsea Trilogy (actually 4 books now)	Ursula K. LeGuin	3
Perelandra (and its sequels)	C. S. Lewis	3
The Last Herald Mage	Mercedes Lackey	2
A Princess of Mars (and its sequels)	Edgar Rice Burroughs	2
The Saga of the Pliocene Exile	Julian May	2
Sandman (#1–75; comic book)	Neil Gaiman et al.	2
Tarzan of the Apes	Edgar Rice Burroughs	2

The Worm Ouroborous (and its sequels)	E. R. R. Eddison	2
Camber of Culdi (and its sequels)	Katherine Kurtz	1
Cities in Flight	James Blish	1
Deverry Cycle	Katherine Kerr	1
The Fuzzy Papers (*Little Fuzzy, Fuzzy Sapiens, Fuzzies and Other People*)	H. Beam Piper	1
The Galachi Milieu Trilogy	Julian May	1
The Lensman Series	E. E. "Doc" Smith	1
Memory, Sorrow, and Thorn Trilogy	Tad Williams	1
The Prydain Chronicles	Lloyd Alexander	1
The Riddlemaster Trilogy	Patricia McKillip	1

THE BIGGEST OPTIMISTS AND PESSIMISTS

Some writers were sure that it would take a long time to rescue them from being "Marooned off Vesta," so they padded their libraries with trilogies and other long series of books. One of the most popular single titles chosen was Samuel Delany's *Dhalgren*, 879 pages of small type. The three books in Tad Williams' Memory, Sorrow, and Thorn trilogy (*The Dragonbone Chair*, *The Stone of Farewell*, and *To Green Angel Tower*) total more than 2,500 pages.

On the other hand, Edwin Abbot's *Flatland* is only 156 pages, and R. A. MacAvoy's *Tea with the Black Dragon* is only 166 pages. Some people don't expect to wait long on that spaceship. . . .

THE MARS FIXATION

There were eight different books listed with "Mars" in the title. Clearly, our fascination with the red planet hasn't died down yet, since several of the books are recent.

1.	*The Gods of Mars*	Edgar Rice Burroughs
2.	*Green Mars*	Kim Stanley Robinson
3.	*Mars*	Ben Bova
4.	*Moving Mars*	Greg Bear

5. *A Princess of Mars*   Edgar Rice Burroughs
6. *Red Mars*   Kim Stanley Robinson
7. *Shadow over Mars* (aka *The* Leigh Brackett
   Nemesis from Terra)
8. *Warlord of Mars*   Edgar Rice Burroughs

THE MOST IMPORTANT SF BOOKS OF THE LAST 50 YEARS

Writers were also asked the following: What are the five must-read science fiction books of the post-World War II era?

THE FAVORITES—BY THE NUMBERS

Over 150 books (or series of books) were mentioned in all. They varied from the immediate postwar era to the recent past, such as the 1994 Hugo winner, Connie Willis' *Doomsday Book*. As with all the lists, many books were mentioned only once. Almost half the books cited had more than one person listing them, however. Three books ran far ahead of the pack—Frank Herbert's *Dune*, Robert A. Heinlein's *Stranger in a Strange Land*, and William Gibson's cyberpunk classic *Neuromancer*. The top ten filled out with classic works from Isaac Asimov, Alfred Bester, Ray Bradbury, Arthur C. Clarke, Ursula K. LeGuin, and two other novels by the remarkably popular Heinlein. Here are the top 20 (no other books received more than 4 votes apiece):

1.	*Dune*	Frank Herbert	24
2.	*Stranger in a Strange Land*	Robert A. Heinlein	20
3.	*Neuromancer*	William Gibson	17
4.	*The Left Hand of Darkness*	Ursula K. LeGuin	11
5.	*The Moon Is a Harsh Mistress*	Robert A. Heinlein	11
6.	*The Stars My Destination*	Alfred Bester	11
7.	The Foundation Trilogy	Isaac Asimov	10
8.	*The Martian Chronicles*	Ray Bradbury	9
9.	*Childhood's End*	Arthur C. Clarke	8
10.	*The Man Who Sold the Moon*	Robert A. Heinlein	8
11.	*Ender's Game*	Orson Scott Card	7
12.	*The Book of the New Sun*	Gene Wolfe	6
13.	*A Canticle for Liebowitz*	Walter M. Miller, Jr.	6
14.	*The Dispossessed*	Ursula K. LeGuin	6
15.	*2001: A Space Odyssey*	Arthur C. Clarke	5
16.	*Hyperion Cantos*	Dan Simmons	5
17.	*The Man in the High Castle*	Philip K. Dick	5
18.	*Ringworld*	Larry Niven	5

| 19. | *Starship Troopers* | Robert A. Heinlein | 5 |
| 20. | *1984* | George Orwell | 5 |

TOP POST—WORLD WAR II SCIENCE FICTION BOOKS—WEIGHTED

When the list of favorites is weighted (so that first-place entries are worth more than second-place entries, and so on), the results of the survey don't change much. Interestingly, many of the books that are favorites to be marooned will fall much lower on the must-read lists. Just because these are the most important books doesn't mean people want to be locked up with them and nothing else to read forever. Here are the top 24 (with a six-way tie at 19):

1.	*Dune*	Frank Herbert	91
2.	*Stranger in a Strange Land*	Robert A. Heinlein	71
3.	*Neuromancer*	William Gibson	62
4.	*The Stars My Destination*	Alfred Bester	38
5.	*The Moon Is a Harsh Mistress*	Robert A. Heinlein	35
6.	*The Left Hand of Darkness*	Ursula K. LeGuin	35
7.	The Foundation Trilogy (some or all)	Isaac Asimov	31
8.	*The Martian Chronicles*	Ray Bradbury	31
9.	*Ender's Game*	Orson Scott Card	27
10.	*Childhood's End*	Arthur C. Clarke	25
11.	*The Dispossessed*	Ursula K. LeGuin	21
12.	*The Book of the New Sun*	Gene Wolfe	20
13.	*A Canticle for Liebowitz*	Walter M. Miller, Jr.	19
14.	*Way Station*	Clifford D. Simak	18
15.	*Perelandra* (some or all of trilogy)	C. S. Lewis	17
16.	*Starship Troopers*	Robert A. Heinlein	16
17.	*Ringworld*	Larry Niven	15
18.	*1984*	George Orwell	14
19.	*The Demolished Man*	Alfred Bester	13
20.	*Fahrenheit 451*	Ray Bradbury	13
21.	*I, Robot*	Isaac Asimov	13
22.	*Parable of the Sower*	Octavia Butler	13
23.	*Rendezvous with Rama*	Arthur C. Clarke	13
24.	*Stand on Zanzibar*	John Brunner	13

THE MOST IMPORTANT FANTASY BOOKS OF THE LAST 50 YEARS

SFFWA members were then asked: What are the five must-read fantasy books of the post–World War II era?

THE FAVORITES—BY THE NUMBERS

Over 125 fantasy books (or series of books) were mentioned in all, but only 34 books were listed more than once. J. R. R. Tolkien's *The Lord of the Rings* gained over twice as many votes as its nearest competitor, Ursula K. LeGuin's The Earthsea Trilogy, and more than three times as many as Tolkein's *The Hobbit*, which placed third. Anne McCaffrey's *The Dragonriders of Pern*, nominally science-fiction with strong fantasy elements, placed fourth. Here are the top 12:

1.	*The Lord of the Rings*	J. R. R. Tolkein	37
2.	The Earthsea Trilogy	Ursula K. LeGuin	15
3.	*The Hobbit*	J. R. R. Tolkein	11
4.	*Dragonriders of Pern* (series)	Anne McCaffrey	8
5.	*The Chronicles of Narnia*	C. S. Lewis	7
6.	*Watership Down*	Richard Adams	7
7.	*The Once and Future King*	T. H. White	5
8.	*The Last Unicorn*	Peter S. Beagle	5
9.	*The Anubis Gate*	Tim Powers	4
10.	*The Chronicles of Amber* (series)	Roger Zelazny	4
11.	*The Fionavar Tapestry (series)*	Guy Gavriel Kay	4
12.	*The Mists of Avalon*	Marion Zimmer Bradley	4

TOP FANTASY BOOKS—WEIGHTED

When the list of favorites is weighted (so that first-place entries are worth more than second-place entries, and so on), J. R. R. Tolkein takes over the top two spots, with *The Hobbit* moving into second place behind *The Lord of the Rings*. Otherwise, the numbers remain similar. Here are the top 15:

1.	*The Lord of the Rings*	J. R. R. Tolkein	171
2.	*The Hobbit*	J. R. R. Tolkein	51
3.	The Earthsea Trilogy	Ursula K. LeGuin	48
4.	*Dragonriders of Pern*	Anne McCaffrey	30
5.	*The Chronicles of Narnia*	C. S. Lewis	25
6.	*Watership Down*	Richard Adams	22
7.	*The Once and Future King*	T. H. White	19
8.	*The Last Unicorn*	Peter S. Beagle	16
9.	*The Fionavar Tapestry*	Guy Gavriel Kay	15
10.	*The Anubis Gate*	Tim Powers	14
11.	*The Mists of Avalon*	Marion Zimmer Bradley	13
12.	*Little, Big*	John Crowley	12
13.	*Glory Road*	Robert A. Heinlein	11
14.	*The Xanth Series*	Piers Anthony	11
15.	*The Chronicles of Amber*	Roger Zelazny	10

THE MOST IMPORTANT HORROR BOOKS OF THE LAST 50 YEARS

Writers were asked: What are the five must-read horror books of the post–World War II era?

THE FAVORITES—BY THE NUMBERS

Over 85 horror books (or series of books) were mentioned in all, but fewer than 30 books were listed more than once. Not surprisingly, Stephen King dominated the list, with five of the top ten books, led by *The Stand* and *The Shining*. Not far behind those two, Anne Rice's series of vampire novels placed third overall. Here are the top 15:

1.	*The Stand*	Stephen King	15
2.	*The Shining*	Stephen King	13
3.	*Interview with the Vampire* (or its sequels)	Anne Rice	10
4.	*The Haunting of Hill House*	Shirley Jackson	7
5.	*Salem's Lot*	Stephen King	7
6.	*Something Wicked This Way Comes*	Ray Bradbury	7
7.	*Boys' Life*	Robert McCammon	6
8.	*Firestarter*	Stephen King	6
9.	*It*	Stephen King	6
10.	*Ghost Story*	Peter Straub	6
11.	*The Books of Blood*	Clive Barker	5
12.	*Carrie*	Stephen King	5
13.	*The Exorcist*	William Peter Blatty	5
14.	*I Am Legend*	Richard Matheson	5
15.	*The Silence of the Lambs*	Thomas Harris	5

TOP HORROR BOOKS—WEIGHTED

When the list of favorites is weighted (so that first-place entries are worth more than second-place entries, and so on), Stephen King's hold on the hearts of horror readers becomes even stronger. King's *The Stand* and

The Shining remain far ahead of all competitors, and his *Salem's Lot* moves into third place. Three other Stephen King books place within the top ten. Shirley Jackson's novel *The Haunting of Hill House* remains in fourth place, with Anne Rice's *Interview with the Vampire* (and its sequels) moving down to 15.

1.	*The Stand*	Stephen King	64
2.	*The Shining*	Stephen King	48
3.	*Salem's Lot*	Stephen King	28
4.	*The Haunting of Hill House*	Shirley Jackson	27
5.	*Interview with the Vampire* (or its sequels)	Anne Rice	25
6.	*The Exorcist*	William Peter Blatty	23
7.	*Ghost Story*	Peter Straub	23
8.	*It*	Stephen King	20
9.	*Carrie*	Stephen King	19
10.	*Firestarter*	Stephen King	19
11.	*I Am Legend*	Richard Matheson	19
12.	*Something Wicked This Way Comes*	Ray Bradbury	19
13.	*The Books of Blood*	Clive Barker	16
14.	*The Silence of the Lambs*	Thomas Harris	13
15.	*Conjure Wife*	Fritz Leiber	10

MASTERS OF HORROR

More than any of the other genre, the horror survey was dominated by a few writers. Four people had three or more books listed (not counting books within a series, like Anne Rice's *Interview with the Vampire* and its sequels). Stephen King led the list with an astonishing *13* books listed—one out of every seven horror titles on the survey. Perennial best-sellers Dean R. Koontz and Robert McCammon each placed five titles on the list, and four of Peter Straub's books appeared.

STEPHEN KING

Salem's Lot
It
Firestarter
The Stand

The Shining
Christine
The Dead Zone
Misery
Carrie
Pet Sematary
Night Shift
The Dark Half
The Long Walk

DEAN R. KOONTZ

Watchers
The Servants of Twilight
Cold Fire
Strangers
Hideaway

ROBERT R McCAMMON

They Thirst
Mystery Walk
Swan Song
Boys' Life
Mine

PETER STRAUB

Ghost Story
Floating Dragon
Koko
Shadow Land

THE WRITERS' WRITERS

Then we asked: Name the five science-fiction, fantasy, and horror writers who most influenced your work.

THE WRITERS' REPLIES

Nearly 200 writers were listed as influences by SFFWA members. By far the greatest source acknowledged was Robert A. Heinlein, who dominated all other authors on the list. Another grand master, Ray Bradbury, came in second, almost doubling the vote of third-place Isaac Asimov and doubling fourth-place Stephen King. Here are the top 28:

1.	Robert A. Heinlein	31
2.	Ray Bradbury	18
3.	Isaac Asimov	10
4.	Stephen King	9
5.	Ursula K. LeGuin	9
6.	J. R. R. Tolkien	8
7.	Andre Norton	7
8.	Edgar Rice Burroughs	6
9.	Theodore Sturgeon	6
10.	Alfred Bester	5
11.	Arthur C. Clarke	5
12.	Samuel R. Delany	5
13.	Philip K. Dick	5
14.	Edgar Allan Poe	5
15.	Poul Anderson	4
16.	Lois McMaster Bujold	4
17.	Orson Scott Card	4
18.	Harlan Ellison	4
19.	William Gibson	4
20.	Robert E. Howard	4
21.	H. P. Lovecraft	4
22.	Anne McCaffrey	4
23.	Frederick Pohl	4
24.	Robert Silverberg	4
25.	Clifford D. Simak	4
26.	H. G. Wells	4

27. Kate Wilhelm   4
28. Connie Willis   4

(Note: Eleven authors tied at 3 votes each: Marion Zimmer Bradley, John Brunner, L. Sprague de Camp, Thomas Disch, Frank Herbert, Joe R. Lansdale, C. S. Lewis, Larry Niven, Robert Sheckley, Jules Verne, and Roger Zelazny.)

MEDIA FANTASIES

Writers were asked: What are your five favorite science-fiction, fantasy, or horror movies and TV shows?

MOVIES TO WRITE BY

Over 150 movies were listed, more than half of them receiving only one mention. The clear winner was George Lucas' three film *Star Wars* saga. *Star Wars* was the runaway first-place winner, with nearly double the votes of the two second-place finishers—one of which was Lucas' sequel, *The Empire Strikes Back. The Return of the Jedi*, the third film in the trilogy, also finished in the top ten. Other series of films also did well. All six *Star Trek* movies placed on the list, led by *Star Trek IV: The Voyage Home*. Both *Terminator* films gathered strong support, as did *Alien* and its sequel *Aliens* (but not *Alien³*, the third film in the series, which received no votes). Classic fantasy and science-fiction films did well, including *Forbidden Planet, The Day the Earth Stood Still*, and *The Wizard of Oz*. Several films had two different versions on the list, most notably *The Thing* and *Beauty and the Beast*. The top responses were:

1.	*Star Wars*	32
2.	*The Empire Strikes Back*	17
3.	*2001: A Space Odyssey*	17
4.	*Alien*	14
5.	*Blade Runner*	14
6.	*Forbidden Planet*	12
7.	*Star Trek IV: The Voyage Home*	10
8.	*E. T.*	9
9.	*The Return of the Jedi*	9
10.	*The Terminator*	9
11.	*Aliens*	7
12.	*The Day the Earth Stood Still*	7
13.	*Jurassic Park*	6
14.	*Star Trek II: The Wrath of Khan*	5
15.	*The Thing from Another World* (1951)	5

16.	*The Wizard of Oz* (1939)	5
17.	*Brazil*	4
18.	*Field of Dreams*	4
19.	*Highlander*	4
20.	*Raiders of the Lost Ark*	4
21.	*Starman*	4
22.	*Terminator 2: Judgment Day*	4
23.	*The Abyss*	3
24.	*Close Encounters of the Third Kind*	3
25.	*The Dark Crystal*	3
26.	*Dune*	3
27.	*Frankenstein* (1931, Boris Karloff)	3
28.	*Groundhog Day*	3
29.	*The Haunting*	3
30.	*The Nightmare Before Christmas*	3
31.	*The Princess Bride*	3
32.	*Star Trek: The Motion Picture*	3
33.	*Star Trek III: The Search for Spock*	3
34.	*Star Trek VI: The Final Frontier*	3

JANET ASIMOV'S FAVORITE MOVIES

Star Trek IV: The Voyage Home
The *Star Wars* trilogy
Snow White (Disney)
Mary Poppins
The Jungle Book (Disney)

JACK CHALKER'S FAVORITE MOVIES

Forbidden Planet
The Uninvited
This Island Earth
The Empire Strikes Back
The Invisible Boy

MIKE RESNICK'S FAVORITE MOVIES

They Might Be Giants
Field of Dreams
All That Jazz
Forbidden Planet
Dr. Strangelove

CLASSIC TELEVISION

Over 75 movies were listed, only about half as many as the movies mentioned. The clear favorites were the four *Star Trek* series, all of which placed in the top ten. Surprisingly, classic *Star Trek* remained ahead of its younger kindred in popularity, although *Star Trek: The Next Generation* is only a hair behind. Although it had aired for only one season, *Star Trek: Voyager* was in a tie for fourth. Other classic TV shows commanded tremendous interest. *The Twilight Zone* and *The Outer Limits* in particular remain enormously popular. The top 22 choices (no other shows received more than 3 votes) are:

1.	*Star Trek*	33
2.	*Star Trek: The Next Generation*	32
3.	*The Twilight Zone*	20
4.	*The X-Files*	20
5.	*The Outer Limits*	19
6.	*Star Trek: Voyager*	19
7.	*Star Trek: Deep Space 9*	17
8.	*Babylon 5*	15
9.	*Doctor Who*	8
10.	*The Prisoner*	7
11.	*Highlander: The Series*	6
12.	*Alien Nation*	5
13.	*Twin Peaks*	5
14.	*Quantum Leap*	4
15.	*Red Dwarf*	4
16.	*Sliders*	4
17.	*Battlestar Galactica*	3

BRUCE BOSTON'S FAVORITE TV SHOWS

The Twilight Zone
Star Trek
The Outer Limits (original)
Space: 1999
Dr. Who

JACK CHALKER'S FAVORITE TV SHOWS

The Outer Limits (original)
Thriller
Science Fiction Theatre (holds up)
Babylon 5 (so far)
The Avengers

A GLIMPSE INTO THE FUTURE

The next question was: If only five books from the twentieth century could survive 20,000 years into the future, what should those five books be (any genre)?

TIME CAPSULES

Those writers who felt qualified to speculate, chose a . . . quirky mix of titles. Based on the top five books mentioned, archaeologists from 20,000 years in the future would see human society reflected in a fantastic mirror indeed, led by J. R. R. Tolkein's *The Lord of the Rings*, the Bible (which is hardly a 20th-century work but was heavily favored anyway), Anne Frank's *Diary of a Young Girl*, James Joyce's *Ulysses*, and *Catch-22* by Joseph Heller. Opinions diverged widely on this question; although more than 250 books were listed overall, fewer than 40 titles were mentioned by more than one respondent. The top 15 are:

1.	*The Lord of the Rings*	J.R.R. Tolkien	10
2.	The Bible (various editions)		6
3.	*Diary of a Young Girl*	Anne Frank	5
4.	*Catch-22*	Joseph Heller	4
5.	*Dune*	Frank Herbert	4
6.	*The Old Man and the Sea*	Ernest Hemingway	4
7.	*Oxford English Dictionary*		4
8.	*Ulysses*	James Joyce	4
9.	*A Canticle for Liebowitz*	Walter M. Miller, Jr.	3
10.	*Collected Poems*	T. S. Eliot	3
11.	*Gone with the Wind*	Margaret Mitchell	3
12.	*The Moon Is a Harsh Mistress*	Robert Heinlein	3
13.	*1984*	George Orwell	3
14.	*The Rise and Fall of the Third Reich*	William L. Shirer	3
15.	*Stranger in a Strange Land*	Robert Heinlein	3

BEGGING TO DIFFER

A number of respondents didn't think the question could be answered. "I couldn't begin to answer this," said Jack L. Chalker. Mike Resnick commented, "They'd *all* be incomprehensible." Other writers questioned whether fiction or non-fiction works should be given more importance.

GENRE WARS

The top ten books cited were divided fairly evenly among non-fiction, science fiction/fantasy, and fiction (the Bible getting votes in both historical and religious categories). Frank Herbert's *Dune* was the second most popular science-fiction work, in fifth place in frequency of citations; Walter M. Miller, Jr.'s, *A Canticle for Liebowitz* was in ninth place. The *Oxford English Dictionary* and *The Rise and Fall of the Third Reich* rounded out the non-fiction category. Ernest Hemingway's *The Old Man and the Sea* shared fictional quarters with *Ulysses* and *Catch-22*. Other notable science-fiction/fantasy mentions included Robert Heinlein's *The Moon Is a Harsh Mistress* and *Stranger in a Strange Land*, Olaf Stapledon's *Last and First Men*, and Austin Tappan Wright's *Islandia*.

WRITERS FOR ETERNITY

Eight writers were mentioned three or more times on the list, led by Isaac Asimov.

ISAAC ASIMOV

The Asimov Chronicles
Asimov's Biographical Encyclopedia of Science and Technology
Asimov's Chronology of Science and Discovery
The Foundation Trilogy

RAY BRADBURY

Fahrenheit 451
The October Country
The Martian Chronicles

WILLIAM FAULKNER

Absalom, Absalom!
As I Lay Dying
Intruder in the Dust
Light in August

HERMANN HESSE

Demian
Steppenwolf
Siddhartha

JAMES JOYCE

Ulysses
Finnegans Wake
Dubliners

STEPHEN KING

It
The Stand
Carrie

JOHN STEINBECK

Of Mice and Men
East of Eden
The Grapes of Wrath

MARK TWAIN

Huckleberry Finn
Tom Sawyer
Short Works of Mark Twain